Residual Effect

Residual Effect

Sydney Porter

Residual Effect

Cover Image: Copyright © Johan Swanepoel, johanswanepoel.com
Book Cover Design: Lance Buckley
Book Formatting: Erik Gevers

To my father
George
a voracious reader

Acknowledgments

This was a journey I did not take alone. A few words of gratitude is no measure of the appreciation I have for those who helped me. Kris Long and Jamie Taylor who I unmercifully badgered to immediately read every chapter or paragraph I wanted them to give me feedback on. I'm surprised either one of you still talk to me.

Cynthia Kloss, my sister, Marca Lamore and Talle Hasis were a great help in my editing process. Thank you for catching what I overlooked or didn't make coherent.

To a fellow author, Bob Guise. Sharing your knowledge with a novice is in a word, selfless. Thank you for your generosity.

Most recently, Jenna Craft, and her eagle eyes gave me a much needed hand in the re-edit. I value your help and insight. Thank you.

Lastly to Erik Gevers, who did a Herculean job formatting my book. Thank you.

Prologue

Wednesday, October 24, 2001

It was near dusk. Remnants of the earlier rain were drooling down the brick of the French Quarter buildings. The humidity hung heavy. They filed out of Arnaud's dressed in their perfectly tailored dark suits. The three princes of Bourbon Street, followed by their families and close friends. It had been a long week. All that was left was handshakes, kisses, and hugs. Frank DiLeo was laid to rest.

Dominic, Frank's son and his two cousins, Joe and Christos were huddled together cross-checking their mental notes, making sure all the i's were dotted and t's crossed.

Joe loosened his tie and unfastened the first button of his shirt. "Jesus Christ, it's still hot. You'd think the rain would have cooled it off a little," he muttered. "What are we going to do with all those fucking flowers?"

Dominic chuckled, "I told the priest to keep what he wanted and send the rest to the Catholic Nursing Home."

Chris closed his eyes and gave a slight disapproving shake of his head. "You're sending funeral flowers to a nursing home?"

"For fuck's sake Chris, they aren't going to know where they came from," Joe said with a slight smirk. "I'm sure they'll take the 'Rest In Peace' ribbons off before delivering them."

At that point, Joe and Dominic were laughing. Chris wanted to reprimand them for their irreverence, but it was the first smile he had seen on either of his cousin's faces in a week. "Did you take care of the priest?" Chris's eyes were going from one to the other for acknowledgment.

"Yes," Joe and Dominic answered in unison. All three of them were laughing now.

"The prick double-dipped," Dominic snickered.

"Fucking priest," Joe said under his breath.

The women were standing far enough away to give the men privacy but close enough to be under their watchful eyes. Joe's laughter quieted when he met her gaze.

"How are you doing?" Dominic asked.

Never taking his eyes off her, Joe's lips thinned into a forced smile.

Dominic gave him an openhanded tap on the cheek, his way of showing support. "Ma wants us to come to the house for a little bit," Dominic said, trying to redirect Joe's focus.

A few minutes later, they were coupled off. Joe took her hand, and they all walked the half block down Bienville to Bourbon Street. "We're parked on Conti," Joe said as they headed down Bourbon still holding her hand. His cousins walked in the opposite direction with their wives.

Bourbon Street was already closed to traffic. Tourists were in the middle of the street with drinks in hand sporting tacky T-shirts. Music flowed out of the opened doors of clubs. The usual tap dancers, hawkers, and hustlers mingled with the crowd, attempting to lure money out of their pockets. The cacophony of Bourbon Street was in full swing.

When she felt she was out of the family's eyes, she gave her hand a slight twist, trying to free herself. Joe tightened his grip. The doors to the DiLeo's strip clubs were closed.

"When are you opening back up?" she asked.

"We're opening all the bars at 9:00 tonight," Joe replied, checking his watch.

As they walked down Bourbon, a few people approached Joe to pay their condolences. Nearing the end of the block, she could see the bar on the corner of Conti. She could feel her pulse quickening with thoughts of Sandy. Sandy's hands in her hair. Sandy's breath on her neck. Sandy's lips on her body.

"Are you okay?" Joe asked.

"Yes, why?"

"You look flushed."

"It's just the heat."

Joe steered her towards the car. "Thank you," he said as he

opened the car door for her.

"For what?"

"Being here."

She could hear the regret in his voice. "Not this time," she thought. "You won't smooth talk me back in again."

The DiLeos

Frank DiLeo was born on March 9, 1923. That made him a Pisces. A water sign. Nothing could be more fitting for a man born in the middle of the Atlantic Ocean.

His parents were on a ship on its way to New Orleans from Palermo, Sicily when Valentina gave birth. That was the first and last time Frank went third class.

Adjusting to life in New Orleans was not as difficult as Salvatore and Valentina thought it might be. New Orleans was home to such a sizable Sicilian community, that the French Quarter was at that time referred to as Little Palermo. Italian was spoken throughout the quarter.

They were able to rent a small house that once served as a slave quarter. Salvatore's ability to fix practically anything kept food on the table and his carpentry skills soon became sought after.

Frank's little brother Vincent was born two months before his third birthday. On Frank's 10th birthday he was given a bicycle. It was Frank's pride and joy, as well as his freedom. Now when he ran errands for his mother or father, he wouldn't have to have his little brother in tow. Before long Frank had built a small business running errands on his bike throughout the French Quarter. Tony Frazzano was part of Frank's customer base. Tony had a couple of bars which fronted for his numbers racket. He was also connected with illegal activities on the docks. Rumor had it that Tony ran black whores for a well-heeled white clientele. Of course, Salvatore gave his son a stern warning about Tony and his kind. Frank was able to reassure his parents that his only interaction with Tony was the occasional delivery of a muffuletta. (A Sicilian sandwich created in New Orleans made on a round loaf of bread.) Though true when Frank said it, it wouldn't be long before his duties with Tony would expand.

Much to Frank's chagrin, on Vincent's 10th birthday he also received a bicycle. By then, Frank was heavily involved with the numbers. He would zigzag through the streets on his bike picking up brown paper bags filled with money and betting slips, dropping them off to Tony. His little brother following him around like a puppy dog wouldn't be good for business. So reluctantly Frank gave Vincent a few of his customers. Mostly older women whose husbands were busy or deceased. In retrospect, it turned out to be a good move. Frank was able to rid himself of high maintenance, slow pay customers as well as his little brother in one shot.

Frank was 15 when much to everyone's surprise, his baby sister Nina was born. He adored her and never missed a chance to help care for her. By the time Frank turned 21, he was an intricate part of Tony's organization. There was no man Tony counted on more. Frank was wise beyond his years. He kept his eyes open, and his mouth shut. Any job given him was handled decisively. Vincent got into Tony's organization as a favor to Frank. Tony wasn't keen on the idea, but Frank assured Tony that he could keep his little brother in line. In years to come, that became a full-time job. Vincent had two skills, he could fight, and he could fuck. One of Tony's by then three brothels, catered to extreme eccentricities. Vincent started as muscle and bagman for that one. After a couple of years, Tony gave some of the dock action to Vincent. He spoke the same language as those guys. Unbeknownst to Tony, Frank had to clean up a few of his brother's screw-ups. Had Tony become aware of this, Vincent would have been out. Tony couldn't take to Vincent and would never have direct contact with him. Vincent was too flashy, mouthy and full of himself for Tony's liking.

Both of the DiLeo boys lived at home, and as good Italian boys, they gave money to their parents. Frank weekly and Vincent when Frank threatened to kick his ass. You could say Vincent spent his money like a drunken sailor, but that would be an insult to drunken sailors. He was a clothes horse. Godchaux's on Canal Street was an upscale department store. That was Vincent's house of worship. The girls loved Vincent, what's not to love. He was a good looking guy who dressed well and spent money on them.

Frank was the polar opposite of his brother in many ways. He had plans for his life, and throwing his hard-earned money around wasn't part of them. He was going to have a nice home and family, take care of his parents, and was going to make sure his baby sister had a good education so she wouldn't have to depend on any man. Yes, Frank had plans.

On Frank's 26th birthday, he felt he had enough stashed away to put his plans into action. He would tell Tony of his growing feelings for his daughter Carmela. She would soon be 18. Frank could provide her a life of comfort. He would love and protect her for the rest of his life. That's what he would tell Tony when he asked for Carmela's hand. It would be months later before he could have that talk.

Tony held court daily at his office located in the back end of one of his bars. In the past week he was manic, double-checking details he usually left to Frank. What was going on with Tony, Frank wondered? It made him nervous.

It was 9:30 in the morning when Frank unlocked the door to the bar. Much to his surprise, Tony was already there, standing behind the bar. Angelo LaLicata was half sitting on a barstool. Frank's heart sank. Angelo was a strong arm for Tony, handling collections and occasionally things that needed a more resolute outcome.

"Lock the door behind you," Tony said.

Frank did and walked up to the bar, pulled out a stool, and sat down. On the bar were two glasses, a bottle of grappa, a large glass ashtray and Tony's ever-present Chesterfield cigarettes and Zippo lighter. Tony grabbed a glass from the back bar and put it in front of Frank. "Catch-up," Tony said as he poured grappa into Frank's glass. Frank was not a big drinker and never in the day but thought better of refusing. There was only one cigarette butt in the ashtray so they couldn't have been there long.

They talked business for ten minutes and bullshit for five. Frank was a little more at ease by the time Angelo left, but something was up. Frank could feel it. When he got back to his seat at the bar after letting Angelo out, Tony had poured two more shots of grappa. Frank gave an eye roll.

"Last one," Tony laughed.

They toasted and drank. Tony then threw his glass so hard, that it shattered into small pieces when it hit the brick wall. Frank froze. This was out of character for Tony.

"I'm having lung surgery the day after tomorrow," Tony said as he picked up a cigarette and lit it. "Too late now," he said, talking to the cigarette and then took a long drag. "We have a lot to go over." The two men sat there until 3:30 going over every possible scenario.

Frank walked home, crestfallen. Could he live up to Tony's expectations? Frank was with Tony's wife and daughter at the hospital when the doctor came out of surgery. The doctor had a positive tone, but noted recovery would be long. Tony's wife took the doctors hands and kissed them, tears of joy rolling down her face.

Frank's temporary transition to the throne was relatively smooth. Angelo efficiently handled the few hiccups. The first one being his brother. Frank was out of patience with Vincent's whoring around. On more than one occasion Frank had to deal with the husband of some woman Vincent had taken up with.

It would be several months before Tony returned to the office. Tony's home being off-limits with few exceptions, the men were taken aback when they first saw the diminished man sitting behind the desk two months after his surgery. Surprising to no one, Tony took on a figurehead position in his organization. There would be a lot more added to Frank's plate before he turned 27.

Just after Nina DiLeo's birth, Salvatore bought a large house in the lower quarter. It was a once beautiful home that was converted into apartments by a slumlord. The property had deteriorated through the years. The landlord put as little money as possible into upkeep. When he died, the bank was thrilled that Salvatore made an offer. It took Salvatore every free minute in the next three years to restore it to its original beauty. His workshop was on the first floor. Staircases hugged both sides of the doorway going to the second-floor porch and main entrance. The third floor had four bedrooms. The slave quarters was turned into a three-car garage which was accessed through the large courtyard in the back of the house. Salvatore brought that property from eyesore to envy.

At noon Monday through Saturday, Valentina would bring Salvatore's lunch down to his workshop. It was four months shy of Frank's 27th birthday when Valentina found her husband dead in his workshop. Salvatore DiLeo suffered a massive coronary at 54 years old. Frank took on the responsibility of his mother and sister. He had hard decisions to make. First, he straightened out his brother. He was done twisting his brother's arm for household money. He told Vincent in no uncertain terms that he handed their mother money weekly or he could pack his shit up and move in with one of his whores.

After the dust had settled and Frank's new responsibilities were set in motion, it was time to address his relationship with Carmela. Once Tony was on the mend, Frank and Carmela told him of their intentions, but after his father's death, Frank could no longer give Carmela the life he had promised. So Frank laid his cards on the table. If they married, their life together would include Valentina and Nina.

"I've loved you since I can remember," Carmela said. "You taking care of your family only makes me love you more."

Five months after his father's death, they had a small private wedding. Tony wanted to give his daughter a wedding they would talk about for years, but that would have meant waiting at least a year after Salvatore's death, out of respect. Valentina insisted Frank and Carmela take the large bedroom. Truth be known, she was no longer comfortable in that space without her beloved Salvatore.

The next few years brought more sadness as Carmela suffered two miscarriages.

Frank became the proud owner of two strip clubs when the owner split owing him money. He put his brother in charge of both. After all, who else would be more comfortable around women taking their clothes off than Vincent.

Salvatore's workshop became Vincent's apartment. Frank had a kitchenette put in but Vincent still ate all his meals upstairs.

Carmela gave birth to a healthy baby boy when Frank was 34. She would have one more pregnancy, which ended in yet another miscarriage. Dominic, Frank, and Carmela's boy brought back life to the DiLeo family. He was the happiest baby anyone had ever seen. Everything and everybody made him smile.

On the first weekend in June, Vincent was in Godchaux's looking at a Father's Day display of ties. It was a long time since he thought of his father. Just then, a smile came to his face. He spotted a tie that in his mind's eye, was the ugliest tie he had ever seen.

A sales clerk offered assistance. Vincent asked for a gift box and card. She scurried off.

An attractive young woman was watching Vincent. As she got closer to the table Vincent picked up the tie and snickered. He would get that tie for his brother Frank for Father's Day as a gift from his newborn son, Dominic.

She came closer to the table, saying, "your father must have a good sense of humor."

"My father passed away seven years ago," Vincent replied.

"I'm sooo sorry," she said mortified.

Her look made Vincent smile. "I'm getting a tie for my brother. He just had a baby boy. It will be his first Father's Day gift to his dad."

"That's so thoughtful."

Hearing that prompted Vincent to put down the gaudy tie and pick up a beautiful conservative tie he knew his brother would like. It made him feel good. He held it up for her approval.

She smiled, "your nephew has good taste."

"Yes, he does," his smile broadened putting out his hand, "Vince DiLeo."

"Leigh Fontenot," she said extending her hand.

They had coffee. The next day they had lunch. In the following weeks, they went to movies, jazz clubs, and dinners. Vincent couldn't get enough of Leigh. He did all he could to sweep her off her feet, and it worked. Leigh was everything the other women he had known were not. She was poised, elegant, and stylish. After only two weeks of dating, Vincent brought her home for dinner. A first for him.

Leigh was tall. She was eye to eye with Vincent when wearing two-inch heels. Thin with porcelain skin and hair so dark brown, it appeared black to some. She had impeccable manners. She gave Valentina a beautifully wrapped gift when introduced. She was so obviously from a different world, Frank wondered what she was doing with Vincent.

Valentina pointed out to Carmela what a handsome couple they made in Italian.

"English Ma," Vincent admonished her.

The large dining table was set for seven plus a high chair. Valentina, Frank, Carmela, Leigh, Vincent, Nina, and her friend Diana sat down at the table full of food. Vincent explained the different dishes as they were passed to Leigh. The food was delicious, and the never-ending conversation was cheerful. Vincent and Frank were taking little jabs at each other like teenagers. Little Dominic was laughing in his high chair. Nina and Diana monopolized Leigh with questions about Loyola. Leigh had just graduated and was happy to mentor the soon to be sophomores. Leigh envied Vincent's family, coming from her austere upbringing.

Nina watched through the window as Vincent and Leigh left. After a few minutes, she surmised, "I think they went into Vincent's apartment."

"Fatti gli affari tuoi," (mind your own business) Frank said.

Vincent was not the first man she had been with. Leigh had a boyfriend in college. It was, however, the first time she had a climax, and the second and the third. She would be leaving in a week on a three week trip to Europe with her parents. She didn't know how she was going to survive without Vincent for that long. Leigh sang the praises of Vincent DiLeo to her parents throughout Europe. The week they got back, Leigh insisted her parents have Vincent for dinner. It was an uneasy evening for all. The Fontenot's took his self-confidence as arrogance and found his olive complexion unnerving. The dinner was painfully awkward for everyone. Leigh was furious with her parents. After she walked Vincent out, she was ready to confront them.

Before she was able to get a word out, her father said in calm even tone, "you bring a man into my home that is one ancestor away from a nigger?" Leigh was pinned to her spot in shock. "He is common and crass. You will not see him again."

Leigh married Vincent two months later. Leigh and her parents never spoke again. There was a title fight in Miami Vincent wanted to see, so he took Leigh there for their honeymoon. They stayed in Vincent's apartment when they got back until they closed on their Creole cottage, which was just around the corner from the DiLeo home. Frank took care of the down payment as a wedding gift from the family.

Valentina insisted they take the furniture from the downstairs apartment. Leigh wanted her little home to be a showcase and soon replaced everything with furniture from the best stores. Her spending habits mirrored that of her husbands. Leigh would quickly find out that having money and coming from money were two distinctly different things. It would not be long before they were behind on the mortgage. With money problems, came arguments, and before long, other women. Leigh tried to reconcile with her parents, but they wouldn't return her calls or letters. Leigh was recoiling into darkness.

Leigh and Vincent would have dinner with the family a couple of times a week. Vincent joked about her lack of culinary skills, so when Valentina made her famous sauce, she would send a big dish to their house. Frank walked into the kitchen one afternoon, and Valentina asked him to take the bag on the kitchen table to Vincent's cottage. He grabbed the spare set of keys to their home and walked over. He knocked on the front door. When he got no answer, he went around to the back and let himself in. The minute he opened the door, he smelled the gas. Leigh was lying on the kitchen floor. Frank turned off the gas, picked up Leigh and carried her to his house.

Everything happened at an accelerated pace. The doctor was on his way. Frank sent Nina back to the cottage with a note for Vincent. The door was wide open when Nina got there. There was still a faint smell of gas. She opened all the windows first. Put the sauce in the refrigerator and left the note on the kitchen table. There was a large bowl on the table with papers in it. She used it to anchor the note. The word foreclosure popped out at Nina from the bowl.

Later that evening, the family sat at the kitchen table, waiting for Vincent to show up. Frank had made a dozen calls in an attempt to find his brother.

"He's your brother," Valentina pleaded. "You can't let Leigh and him lose their home."

"Ma, I've been helping him his whole life. It seems like all I do is bail Vincent out of one mess after another. Money goes through his hands like water. Do you have any idea of how much your son makes?" Frank was struggling to keep his voice calm. "They'll have to live here until they can get back on their feet." He noticed his mother's eyes becoming glassy as she fought back tears. He got up and went to his office. He wanted to kill his brother.

Just after midnight, Vincent walked into his house. He thought it odd that all the windows were open. As he was closing them, he called Leigh's name several times. Vincent checked the bedroom then went to the kitchen, grabbed a beer out of the refrigerator, and sat down at the table. He saw the note, picked it up, and read it out loud. "Your wife is at my house. Get your ass over here." He crumpled the note and threw it. "His house. It's his fucking house now." He finished his beer and walked over.

Frank heard him come in, "Vince?"

"Yes."

Frank got up from his desk and went into the kitchen.

"You summoned me?" Vincent said snidely. Frank handed him the foreclosure notice.

Furious Vincent shrieked, "that fucking cunt brought this to you?"

Frank hit his brother so hard and so fast that Vincent landed flat on the floor. Nina came rushing downstairs after hearing the commotion. She got to the kitchen in time to see Vincent scrambling to get to his feet with Frank standing over him. Nina ran to Vincent to help him up.

"Your wife tried to commit suicide today, you worthless piece of shit," Frank said, then took a deep breath to regain his composure. "Gas! She's okay. She's upstairs sleeping."

"I want to see her."

"You smell like sex and liquor. Go home, Vince, clean yourself up. Get some rest. There's nothing you can do tonight. She's going to need you at 100%."

Vincent was at Leigh's side when she woke the next morning.

As he headed downstairs, Vincent could smell the coffee and bacon coming from the kitchen. The whole family was getting ready for their day.

"How is she?" Valentina asked Vincent as he walked into the kitchen. He didn't answer. He walked over to the counter and poured himself a cup of coffee.

"Doctor Dentici called. He will be over this morning to check on Leigh," Carmela said.

Frank made a gesture to silence his wife. Vincent turned around with coffee cup in hand, his back to the counter. He said nothing. He just watched baby Dominic in his high chair, eating scrambled eggs with his hands. So happy, eggs and fist going in his mouth at once.

Vincent's face contorted from blank to misery. He made his way outside as the tears began. Frank waited until Vincent was cried out before joining him.

"She's pregnant Frank. She not only tried to kill herself; she wanted to kill my baby."

Vincent's tears started again. Frank hugged his brother until they stopped.

Vincent and Leigh settled into the downstairs apartment. Her depression worsened.

The women of the house cared for her. Joseph Anthony DiLeo was born healthy, with a full head of black hair. Leigh showed little interest in Joe. Valentina, Carmela, and Nina took turns checking in on Leigh and baby Joe. The ladies would change, bathe, and feed the baby. Vincent finally agreed to send his wife to a sanitarium. Little Joe's crib was moved up to Dominic's room.

The Fontenot's consented to see Frank. He believed they deserved to know what was happening with their daughter. Frank was surprised to see they were so much older than his mother. They invited him in, offered a cold drink, and gave him their full attention. Frank was unvarnished in his details of their daughter's existence since she left their home. They thanked Frank for coming and asked that he not contact them again. Frank told no one of the meeting. His empathy for Leigh grew. He would make sure her little boy was raised with the love she never had or could give.

Nina and her friend Diana were Christmas season employees at D.H. Holmes department store on Canal Street. It was the third year they held these positions. Diana was in cosmetics this year, and Nina was in hosiery. Nina wasn't wild about this years placement, but it was better than sitting around the house during Christmas break with the ongoing Vincent/Leigh drama.

The girls were fast friends since their freshman year at Loyola. Both were first-generation Americans, Diana's parents were from Greece. The two girls were headed down Canal for lunch when Diana grabbed Nina's forearm to stop her. They had just passed two young men speaking Greek to each other, confused about the money the street vendor wanted for his goods. The vendor was trying to take advantage of them. Diana put a stop to it; she told them in Greek what was the street vendors intent. The men put their money back in their pockets and started walking with the girls down Canal. Nina was clueless as to what was happening since the three were speaking Greek. Finally, Nina asked.

"Diana, what's going on?"

"They're buying us lunch," Diana replied casually.

"What!" Nina said louder than intended.

"Please, we are —" he looked to Diana for a word.

"Grateful," she said.

"Yes, grateful for your help."

Nina had always found Greek men to be better looking than Sicilians. Their classic features more appealing, but this man, this boy speaking to her in his broken English was an Adonis.

During lunch, the boys, Nick and his friend Theo, both 19, spoke about the ship and their first voyage to New Orleans. They were told about Decatur Street and the Greek clubs and restaurants that catered to sailors from their country. Nina told them everything they needed to know about Bourbon Street having first-hand knowledge since her brother owned four bars, two of which were strip clubs.

The boys walked them back to the store after lunch. They said their goodbyes and the girls disappeared into the employee entrance. Four and one-half hours later, they exited the same door done for the day.

Nick Sarris was waiting there by himself. He and Diana had a short conversation in Greek. Then in English, he asked, "may I walk you home?" to Nina.

She looked at Diana, who smiled and nodded, giving her blessing. They talked about their dreams. They spoke of their realities: his travels, her family. Nick seemed quite impressed with her family home. She awkwardly explained that her sister-in-law just got back from a long illness, so she was unable to invite him in. It didn't seem to faze him. He asked if she would have dinner with him the following night.

She could not wait to tell Diana. This beautiful creature wanted to have dinner with her.

The next day dragged like she was doing time. Nick was once again, waiting for her at the employee entrance. This time he took both her hands and kissed her on the cheek. He and Diana spoke a few words in Greek, and they were on their way.

"Do you like Greek food?" he asked.

"Love and I mean love Greek food," Nina replied.

He took her to a small Greek restaurant on Decatur. The food was excellent, and he was amazed at her knowledge of the cuisine. They talked about Diana and the many meals she had at her home. They went to a Greek club after dinner. They danced and drank ouzo. He told her his ship would leave early the next morning. She jotted down her address on a cocktail napkin and asked him to write. He walked her home and kissed her goodbye.

The amount of mail delivered to the DiLeo home over the holidays was mind-boggling. Nina was sure everyone in New Orleans sent them a Christmas card. Valentina was at the table going through them and cross-checking her list to make sure she had reciprocated.

"This one is for you sweetheart," Valentina said as she handed the letter to Nina. It was postmarked from Greece, no return address. "Who do you know in Greece?" Valentina asked.

"A cousin of Diana's that visited last summer." Why am I lying Nina thought as she opened the envelope?

No salutations, just I'll see you on January 19th. Nina chalked up the curtness to the language barrier. Nick was coming back. That's all that mattered to her.

As the date grew near, Nina grew anxious. He didn't have her phone number, and she was no longer working at Holmes. She had classes that day. The 19th came and went, no Nick. She was upset with herself for being so affected by him.

The following night when Frank got home, he walked through the house to the living room and looked out the window. He came back into the kitchen and picked up the phone, calling downstairs.

"Leigh, is Vince home?" .... "There's a guy across the street staring at the house." ... "I don't know; I just got home."

Nina ran to the window, then ran downstairs and across the street into the man's arms.

To say her two brothers were stunned would be soft-selling it. Nick stayed for dinner with her less than enthusiastic brothers. Leigh was eager to point out that they were acting equally as bad as her parents did towards Vincent. That turned them around a little. The women were fawning over Nick.

He would only be in town four days this trip. Nina and Nick spent every free moment together. She even cut a few classes to be with him. His last night in New Orleans Nick rented a room. When he saw evidence of her virginity on the sheets, he begged her forgiveness. He wrongfully assumed because of her age and family business that she was experienced. Nina did her best to reassure Nick that it was something she wanted also. They had the same plans as before. He would contact her with a date of his return. He also had her phone number this time. She got his address but no phone number.

She missed him immediately and so sent a letter the very next day after his departure. She wanted it to be waiting for him when he got home. It was almost three weeks before she heard anything from Greece. It was her letter returned to her. It had postal markings in Greek. She called Diana to get the translation. It broke Diana's heart to tell her best friend the address did not exist. Nina was devastated. She couldn't eat or sleep. Nobody knew what to do for her. It was a couple of weeks since she got the returned letter and she wasn't doing much better. Diana was visiting. Nina's best friend was the only one that knew the whole story. Diana had more experience when it came to sex. She lost her virginity like every other red-blooded American girl, on her senior prom night.

Nina asked her counsel. She hadn't had a period since her night with Nick. Nina was under the impression that she couldn't get pregnant the first time. Diana was astonished by her friend's naiveté. Diana convinced Nina that she needed Frank's help. So the two girls sat down in Frank's office and told him what her worst fear was. Diana held Nina's hand the whole time. Frank knew his sister needed her friend to get through this and so reserved his objection to an outsider being privy to the family business.

Frank was gentle and understanding with his little sister. He wanted her to be confident in whatever decision she made. He laid out all her options and offered his full support.

"I'm sorry I hurt you," Nina said to Frank sobbing.

He came around his desk and squatted down in front of his sister, "I love you, and you will always be my little girl. Now let's find out if there is something to worry about. We'll have Doctor Dentici check you out. You've been so upset lately, your system might be out of wack. Everything stays in this room until we know for sure what we're dealing with."

It was four days before the test came back. Nina didn't want an abortion. She didn't know how she would handle the pregnancy, but she knew abortion was out. Nina would probably have to go away to have the baby. She would not be graduating with her class. She would be too far along to hide it. Frank told the rest of the family. Vincent, of course, wanted to hunt Nick down and castrate him.

Nina was much calmer now that it was out. She looked at the hard realities of those times. Should she give her baby up for adoption? Should she give it to her brother Frank and his wife Carmela to raise as their own? How can any woman make that decision?

Frank was in his office at the back of the bar. He was sitting behind the desk once occupied by Tony Frazzano. He answered the phone. It was his sister. No hello, she just went right into it.

"I got a letter from Nick. From Greece."

The hope in his sister's voice was heart-wrenching. "What did it say?"

"He will be here in three days," she said.

"Okay, listen to me baby girl. If he calls, say nothing to him on the phone," He got no response. "Do you understand me?"

"Yes," she said softly. "What should I say?"

"Invite him to the house. Understand?"

"Yes," her voice barely audible.

That night after dinner, Frank told Nina to get the letter and come to his office. When she got there, Frank was behind the desk, and Vincent was sitting in a chair in front of the desk. Nina sat next to Vincent.

Frank reached his arm out. "Let me see the letter." Nina reluctantly passed it to him. Frank opened it, looked at it. Looking at the back of the page he asked, "is this it?"

Nina wordlessly nodded.

"What?" Vincent asked, putting his arm out to reach for the letter, "let me see it." Frank tossed it over. "What the fuck!" Vincent yelled and jumped out of the chair.

"Vince, please," Frank said.

"No Frank, fuck this," Vincent said, waving the letter. "This is how you call a whore."

Nina was now in tears. Frank got up and went to her. "Stop it, Vince. Now!" Frank said as he hugged his sister. The letter was the same as the last, just the date of his return.

Three days later, Nick sat in Frank's office, shocked, confused, and scared. He barely knew this girl, and now he was expected to marry her. Her brothers handled everything. The entire thing was an out of body experience for Nick. His ship left without him. They were married in the church rectory with enough witnesses to vouch for its legitimacy. He would be given a job with the family. His very young life was all laid out for him. Nina was sweet, but his feelings for her waned given the circumstances. Nina woke early one morning to see her already dressed husband's back walking quietly out of the bedroom. Nina DiLeo Sarris never saw him again. Four months later Nina gave birth to the most beautiful baby anyone had laid their eyes on, Christos DiLeo Sarris.

Soon after his birth, Frank and Carmela gave up the large bedroom to accommodate the three boys. Dominic, Joe, and Chris grew up together in that room. The closest of brothers couldn't match the love these three shared for each other.

For years to come the last thing Frank would do before he went to bed is open the door to the boy's bedroom and say, "Buonanotte i miei tre piccoli principi." (goodnight my three little princes)

Chivas On The Rocks

Wednesday, October 13, 1993

"I'll have another Chivas on the rocks," Joe said to the bartender leaning between two barstools. "You want another?" he asked his friend standing behind him.

"Absolute and soda with a lime and Palmer wants one of his pink drinks," Bob chuckled.

"And two Absolute's, one with soda and one with cranberry, lime in both please." Joe handed the drinks back to his friends as the bartender made them. The crowd was thinning out as people went to their tables for dinner. The three sat down at the bar, waiting for their perpetually late friend. The door at the end of the bar opened. A woman walked in and sat at the first stool, which cornered the bar giving her a clear view of everyone. Joe waved, and she waved back. He flagged the bartender, "Get Felice a drink on us please."

"Who's that?" Palmer asked.

"Felice Sax, her family owns Sax Music on Carondelet," Joe said.

"Really," Palmer replied. "I took accordion lessons there when I was a kid."

"Accordion?" Bob laughed.

Felice raised her glass and mouthed thank you to Joe.

"She's gotta be six feet if she's an inch," Bob said.

"She's a little shorter than me. I'm six even," Joe replied.

"She's gorgeous. She looks like a young Ava Gardner," Palmer remarked.

"Yeah, if Ava Gardner gained fifty pounds," Bob chuckled.

"You're a dick," Joe sounded pissed.

At that same moment, Joe saw her through the back bar mirror. She came in the restaurant entrance. He turned and watched her walk through the dining room toward the bar. She owned the room. Her mahogany hair was in a haphazard updo. She had classic features with a long elegant neck. A faint shadow of her tight body was visible through her skirt and linen blouse. He felt himself getting hard. She sat next to Felice.

Without a hello, she started talking. "Well, I had a shit day. I had so many returns, I'm going to have to write Lambert's a check this week," she said sarcastically. "I hope yours was better."

"Considerably," Felice smiled. "I sold the purple Italian leather sectional that's in the window. $3,200."

"Wow, good for you," she replied. "You're buying." They both laughed.

"Did you see your boss down there?" Felice asked.

"You're going to have to narrow that down. I have several," she joked.

"Joe."

"Joe DiLeo?" she sounded surprised. "Which one is he?" Her body shifted on the barstool to catch a glimpse.

"Which one is he?" Felice asked. "You've never met Joe?"

"No."

"You've worked there what, seven or eight months now?" Felice asked in disbelief.

She shrugged her shoulders. "I'm only there three nights a week. Maybe he doesn't frequent those types of establishments," she snickered. "So which one?"

"The bartender's talking to him now. Dark hair, good looking," Felice said.

She turned a little more in the stool to get a better look. "You think he's good looking?"

"Yes, you don't?"

"The Brioni suit helps."

"How do you know it's a Brioni suit?"

"The same way you know a Henredon sofa."

The bartender placed a cocktail napkin in front of her. "The gentlemen," he nodded toward the three, "would like to get you a drink."

"Chivas on the rocks, please. Oh and a glass of water."

Trey walked in through the bar door, broad smile, dripping southern charm. He walked up to Felice the minute he spotted her. "Hey girl, how are you doing?"

"Good Trey, what are you up too?"

"Having dinner with those three stiffs," Trey joked, waving down the bar to his friends. "I'm glad I ran into you. I think our piano needs tuning. Does your father have someone he can send to the house?"

"Yes, a really good guy my father's been using for years," Felice said, reaching for her purse. She handed him a card from her fathers business. "Just call my dad, and he can schedule it for you."

Trey took the card. "I'll have my wife give him a call. Thank you."

The bartender had returned with her drink. He placed the scotch in front of her and the water behind. When she looked up to thank him, she caught a glimpse of Joe standing next to her.

It amused Joe to see her hair was held up wrapped around a pen. He visualized himself running his tongue up her long delicate neck. As if reading his mind, she turned, slowly looked up at him and her lips parted. His dick was getting hard again.

Felice broke the spell. "Trey, Joe, this is my friend Sam. Trey and Joe are attorneys."

"The four of us graduated Tulane together," Trey explained, head nodding towards his other two friends. "I went on to have a prestigious career." They all laughed.

"Sam works at Lambert's," Felice continued.

"That's a designer clothing store on Canal," Joe said to Trey, "in case you want to update your wardrobe." They all laughed again. Sam thanked Joe for the drink. "You're most welcome. Is Sam short for Samantha?"

"No, it's just Sam." She had this same conversation every day of her life. There was a time she thought of going by her middle name.

"Your father named you Sam?" Joe smirked.

"My mother did," her answer was clipped.

Joe was surprised by her curt demeanor.

"Ladies, would you like to join us for dinner?" Trey asked. "You would be saving me from the mundane conversation those three have to offer."

"Yes, please," Joe interjected. "It will give you a chance to have a nice meal."

The three of them looked at Joe, trying to register what they just heard.

"No thank you," Sam replied so quickly, it seemed like a run-on to Joe's sentence.

They said their goodbyes and the two men joined their friends.

"What was that?" Trey asked. Joe didn't answer. "Wait until you hear this one," Trey said to the other two men, then he held up one finger to stop the conversation while he gave the bartender his drink order.

Joe took a sip from his drink and noticed another one in front of him. "What's this?" Joe asked the bartender.

"Your drink," the bartender replied.

Joe raised the glass in his hand, "I have my drink."

"That's the girl's drink that you were talking to," the bartender explained.

Joe looked back down the bar. "She has her drink."

"That's water."

Joe closed his eyes and shook his head in disbelief. "Fuuuuck!"

Trey was laughing so hard they could barely understand what he was saying. "First you insult her and then you take her drink."

"The drink you bought her?" Palmer asked.

Now Trey was doubled up with laughter; people were staring. "Oh god, oh god," Trey repeated, trying to catch his breath. "And you're the cocksman of the group," Trey started howling again.

Before Joe had a chance to correct it, the girls had gone.

"What an asshole," Sam said loud enough for passersby on Royal Street to hear. "Does that prick think we're homeless? I'm surprised he didn't drop his pocket change in my drink. Oh, that's right, he couldn't, he took the drink away from me."

"Would you please calm down. People are looking."

"You're not incensed?"

"No, I'm not. He didn't take my drink," Felice laughed. "I still can't believe you've worked there that long and never met him."

"I haven't."

"He's a really good guy," Felice continued. "Maybe he was a little drunk."

"I know drunk. He wasn't drunk," Sam replied.

Felice stopped her in front of Mencher and Son Fine Home Furnishings. "There it is," Felice said as they looked in the window.

It was a room vignette, featuring the purple leather sectional.

"It's really beautiful. I didn't expect that when you said purple leather."

"Speaking of leather," Felice said, "your chair has shipped. It will be here tomorrow. You still have a balance on it. Are you going to be able to swing it this week?"

"I thought you said it would be here in eight weeks?" Sam asked.

"I said six to eight weeks. It's been six weeks. I can put off the delivery for a couple of weeks if that helps. I'll say you're out of town."

"That'll work. Thanks, you're the best."

"I know," Felice laughed. "One of the guys is leaving. His partner got transferred. They're moving at the end of next month. Why don't you give me a copy of your resumé and I'll pass it along," Felice suggested.

"Thank's, but I know nothing about furniture," Sam replied.

"You know how to sell. The rest I can teach you. The worst salesman on the floor is making more then you are at two jobs."

"I appreciate it. I really do, but if I leave Lambert's it won't be for another sales job," Sam said.

"Sam, I love you, and I know you have a dream, but you have to eat while you're waiting for your dream to come true. Promise me you will consider it?"

Sam said she would to placate Felice. "So what's his story?"

"Who?"

"Joe," Sam replied.

"The man you can't stand?"

"Yeah, that one."

"Well as you know, he's an attorney. He runs the family businesses, that's pretty much it."

"Is he married?" Sam asked.

"He was years back. I don't think it lasted very long. Do yourself a favor and forget whatever stupid idea you have. I can't think of a faster way to lose a job then to sleep with the boss."

"I'm not going to fuck him, I'm going to fuck with him," Sam giggled. Felice gave Sam a wearied look. "Oh, don't give me that look. I'm screwing with you. The man doesn't come in the bar. I'll probably never see him again."

"I'll bet you dollars to donuts he shows up at Lambert's within a week," Felice said.

"You think?"

"Yes, and if he does, you need to tell him that you are one of his employees."

"Promise Mom," Sam joked. "You want to have dinner tomorrow? I'll cook."

"That goes without saying," Felice smiled, "but I can't. I have a date."

"Tell me."

"There's nothing to tell; it's a first date."

Felice lived vicariously through her best friend Sam when it came to men. Although one of the most stunning women you will ever see, her size and insecurities held her back. Her weight was her deepest secret. She wouldn't even tell Sam and she told Sam everything. Most of her first dates were also last dates. When Sam got back to New Orleans, she made a concerted effort to get Felice out of the tents she called dresses and into more form-fitting clothes. The work what you got theory.

They were at the corner of Royal and Toulouse, they kissed cheeks and parted ways each to their respective homes. Sam was only halfway through her day. A quick dinner and a lot more makeup. Then off to Joe DiLeo's strip club.

Azure

There was nothing spectacular about Claude Thibodeau. An average guy with one attribute few people possess, the ability to listen. When you spoke to him, he made you feel like the only person in the room. You felt heard, counted, unique. Most people that knew him considered him a friend. Claude had a penchant for uptown married ladies searching for attention, who didn't mind subsidizing his lifestyle. He also had a taste for younger men who enjoyed the feel of leather on their bodies.

Claude's father, Maurice worked for Frank DiLeo many years before retiring back to Houma. Claude was working at Azure Gentleman's Club as the doorman/bouncer/hawker and pseudo manager for six years now. It was nearing 1:00 in the morning when Joe walked in, still in a suit minus the tie.

"You're up past your bedtime," Claude joked.

"Hey Claude," Joe said, giving Claude a friendly slap on the shoulder. "How's your dad?"

"Real good, thanks," Claude replied.

"Is Dominic around?"

"He's upstairs in the office."

"Alone?"

"I'm not sure. I think so," Claude grinned.

Joe didn't want to bust in on anything. "Do me a favor Claude, call up there and let him know I'm at the bar."

"Sure."

"Who's that?" Joe asked looking at the bar.

"Crystal."

Joe thanked Claude and went to the bar. She was at the register with her back to the customers. Because her uniform was little more than a bikini, he could see her Venus dimples. Joe called her name to get her attention. She didn't turn. He called again, this time louder to match the volume of the music. She put a napkin in front of him. Her eyes appeared huge with the heavy makeup. Her long auburn hair had that just fucked look.

"Hot little thing," Joe thought. "Hi Crystal, I'm Joe, Dominic's cousin."

She pointed with one finger to the girl on the stage next to the bar. "Crystal," she said. "What can I get for you, Joe?"

"Club soda with a piece of lime please."

She walked away before he could get another word in. "This fucking guy has no idea who I am," Sam thought. "He just met me a few hours ago. WOW!"

He looked up at the stage watching the girl hanging upside down on the stripper pole. Rock hard oversized boobs and bleach blonde hair. "How could Claude think I was asking about her?" Joe thought.

She returned with his drink. "So what's your name?" Joe asked.

"Really!" she replied sarcastically.

"Cagna arrogante," (arrogant bitch) Joe said out loud, then picked up his drink and took a sip. She gave him a blank look and walked away. "All I did was call her by the wrong name. She's too thin-skinned to work Bourbon Street," Joe thought.

Dominic pulled out the stool next to him. "Why didn't you come upstairs?"

"Because I wasn't sure if I'd be walking in on something," Joe joked.

"That shit is over with Cuz."

"Sure Dom, whatever you say," Joe laughed.

"No Joe, I'm serious. I came close to losing my family this time," Dominic said in a rare serious moment.

"Can I get you something, Dom?" she asked.

"No sweetheart, I'm good," Dominic replied.

"That one has an attitude," Joe said when she walked away.

"Sam?" Dominic chuckled. "She can get a little feisty."

"Did you say, Sam?" Joe closed his eyes and took a deep breath. "This can't be happening," he thought. "What a chameleon."

"Sam," Dominic called her over.

She could see the resemblance with them sitting next to each other. They both had, what some called bedroom eyes. Joe's hair was slightly darker, his complexion, slightly lighter and features a more refined version of Dominic's.

"Sam, have you met my cousin Joe?" Dominic smirked.

She glared at Joe then said to Dominic, "tuo ugino e' uno stronzo." (your cousin is an asshole)

"Most women don't say that until after they've slept with him," Dominic chuckled. "I didn't know you spoke Italian." Then he said to Joe, "she looks Irish."

With no hole available to crawl into, Joe retreated to the office with Dominic trailing behind. Before they got down to business, Joe reluctantly told Dominic about his inauspicious introduction to Sam.

"That's hysterical."

"Yes Dom, fucking hysterical."

"You must have shit when she started to speak Italian. What did you call her?"

"An arrogant bitch. What do we know about her?"

Dominic handed Joe a folder out of the file cabinet. It contained a short employment application, a W4, and a copy of her social security card.

"Her name actually is Sam. Mancuso that explains the Italian. She does look Irish; you're right about that. Only 23. Boyfriend?"

Dominic laughed, "you're a piece of work. She was a package deal. Her and a stripper."

"Lesbian, I can work with that," Joe joked.

"Guy, good looking kid. He worked next door at Blush up until a few weeks ago."

"Her emergency contact is Giacomo Mancuso. That's Jack, right?"

"Yes," Dominic confirmed.

They got down to business after that. Before they knew it, Claude called up to let them know he was on his way out in five minutes.

"We can wrap it up," Joe said to Dominic.

"You wanna hang back for a few minutes? Make sure your girlfriend is gone," Dominic grinned.

"I'm good," Joe smiled.

The room was practically dark. Claude was at the front door with his keys in hand. Joe felt a twinge of disappointment that he missed Sam.

"You didn't have to wait," Dominic said to Claude.

"I'm waiting for Sam. She's in the ladies room." They could hear the door open at the back of the room. "Come on Sam," Claude yelled.

"I'm coming; I'm coming, I'm coming." They heard a chair topple over. "Shit."

"Sam, are you okay?" Claude called out.

"I'm okay."

Then he saw her. She had tight jeans on and the blouse she wore earlier. You could see the black bikini top through the blouse. Her hair was piled on top of her head with strands falling down the back and sides. Joe didn't realize how petite she was. She had heels on earlier.

The three men stood back to allow her to exit first. Joe smiled when he saw her hair twisted around a pen.

"Buonanotte Sam," Joe said.

"Goodnight Joe," Sam replied, her eyes smiling. At least Joe thought they were.

The four parted, the DiLeo's going up Bourbon, Sam and Claude walking down Bourbon.

"I see you and Joe had a little thing," Claude smirked.

"No," Sam laughed and then proceeded to tell the brief history of her and Joe.

"You had him off his game."

"Let's hope so or the guy will never get laid," Sam joked. "Do you think he's hot? Felice does but I don't see it."

"You don't see it! He's Stanley fucking Kowalski in a suit," Claude laughed and bumped shoulders with Sam. "Joe's a fun ride," then Claude's tone shifted, "but that's all he is."

"You know this first hand?" Sam chuckled.

"I wish. Joe suffers from madonna-whore complex, and you work in their strip joint. So Sha," (cajun slang for the french cher) "don't expect to be invited to Sunday supper anytime soon."

"That's okay, my sauce is probably better, which I am making tomorrow. I'll bring you some Saturday."

"And the meatballs. I'll make myself a po' boy."(traditional New Orleans sandwich on a french baguette)

"I'm gonna fix you up; I'll bring some nice fresh bread too."

Claude walked Sam to her door then stopped at his favorite leather bar on the way home.

Sam took a shower, made herself a drink, and went out to her balcony. The air smelled of night-blooming jasmine. She replayed her encounter with Joe as if it were on a loop. She picked herbs from the pots hanging on the wrought iron railing, went inside, poured herself another scotch and proceeded to make meatballs.

Charity

Felice found the perfect apartment for her best friend Sam and her very hot boyfriend Andrew. She ushered them up the stairs talking up the attributes of the lower end of the quarter and the street, Chartres itself. Felice could tell by the looks on their faces, that they didn't share her enthusiasm about the apartment. While on the balcony, Sam watched two men across the street loading boxes into a truck. It was a beautiful building, well maintained. Andrew went over to talk to them. They moved in two days later. Sam always credits Felice with finding her great apartment.

Brick walls, hardwood floors, and a high ceiling. Nice size bedroom with a walk-in closet. Large dining/living room. The gallery (large balcony) went the length of those two rooms. Small bathroom next to the recently updated kitchen with a loft above. The loft had a wrought iron rail with floor to ceiling windows opposite. It was perfect for Sam's studio.

Sam had her art supplies and cameras. She also had anything you would ever need in a kitchen. A beautiful beige and eggshell herringbone silk and linen sofa and a 19-inch portable tv. Plus a top of the line queen size mattress and box spring, thanks to a previous boyfriend. He said her old mattress was too soft for him, so he sprang for a new one. Andrew brought with him a chest of draws, a 42-inch tv with a stand, a Weber grill still in the box and a Lazy-boy recliner, which Sam hated.

Andrew had a job waiting for him at Blush Ladies Lounge, a male strip club on Bourbon Street. Sam had two interviews lined up. Lambert's Fine Clothier and Azure Gentlemen's Club. Azure was a strip club next to Blush. Both of which were owned by the DiLeo's. She got both jobs. At Lambert's, she would work four days a week.

Tuesday, Wednesday, Friday and Saturday. That would be enough hours to get health insurance through the store. Azure three nights a week tending bar. Wednesday, Saturday and Sunday.

Sam and Andrew dated briefly in high school. He was her prom date. They started dating again shortly before he took the job in New Orleans. They were both recovering from bad breakups and found relocating appealing. They were two people in need of a crutch. In September, Andrew got the job offer in Las Vegas. He asked Sam to come along, knowing what her answer would be. Their split was melancholy, but it was time. Neither one of them needed a crutch anymore.

Thursday, October 14, 1993

Now that Andrew was gone she enjoyed her sparsely furnished apartment even more. It was Thursday, and she was off from both jobs. After her morning run, she made her sauce, added sausage, and her already prepared meatballs. She cleaned, did laundry, all the things most people found tedious, she found relaxing. Her mind would wander. She went up to her studio and laid out the pictures she had taken at the boxing gym in Bywater. She started her next piece. That night she watched Mad About You, Wings and Seinfeld. Halfway through Frazier, the phone rang. Poor Felice had another shitty date.

"There is an ass for every seat," Sam said, "and you will find yours."

"Am I the ass or the seat?" Felice laughed.

She told Felice about the bumbling Joe DiLeo. Felice was cracking up. Sam always had great delivery when it came to conveying a story. She would put her satirical spin on it. Felice once again reiterated that this was a very off night for the usually self-assured man. Felice coerced Sam into going to her parents for Shabbat dinner on Friday. Sam didn't have the heart to say no after Felice's lousy date.

Saturday, October 16, 1993

Saturday was a double shift. She had a good day at the store. Went home, had dinner, and changed. She packed up sauce, meatballs and bread for Claude. The night was busy, which she liked. It made the time go faster. She never really liked working there, the way men leered at her, staring at her body instead of her eyes when speaking to her. It made her skin crawl.

She wished she would have applied to a few other places. Now with Andrew gone and all the household bills her responsibility, she felt trapped. Plus the thought of what would happen if Lambert's found out she worked at a strip club made her nervous. She would love to get a job at Christos', a jazz club also owned by the DiLeo's. Those bartenders made the best money on Bourbon Street. Once Chris was by himself waiting for Dominic, and she asked if an opening came available, would he consider her. It was the most polite rejection she ever got. He told her it was not their habit to move employees from one establishment to another. Claude cautioned her against pursuing it any further. He explained to her that if they think she's looking for another job, they will let her go.

On Saturday Sam worked the bar with another girl. Tanya was Azure's full-time bartender. Sam worked her nights off, and they worked together on Saturday's. Tanya was a dancer at the club until she got a botched boob job in Mexico. You get what you pay for. She had an extremely high pitched voice. She sounded like a cartoon mouse. She told Sam it was because her vocal cords were underdeveloped and so stretched as she grew, which resulted in a mouse voice. Speaking of rodents, she would rat out anyone and everyone to Dominic. Claude would say, she's in Dominic's ear and on his dick. She played dumb, but there was nothing stupid about her.

On Saturdays, Sam worked the end of the bar furthest from the door. Tanya was supposed to work the majority of the bar since Sam took care of the waitresses drinks and washed the glasses. But Tanya would get into conversations with guys and Sam had to pick up her slack. It was almost midnight. Dominic was at the door, talking to Claude when Joe and Chris walked in. They talked for a minute; then Joe started walking to the end of the bar. Tanya followed from behind the bar. He stopped when he was across from Sam. Sam put a napkin in front of Joe.

"Hi Joe, what can I get you?" Sam asked.

"I got it," Tanya interrupted, "I think one of the girls needs drinks."

"Sam's got it," Joe intervened, then looked at the service bar. "Can you take care of that Tanya?"

"Of course Joe," she replied and hurried to the service bar.

Sam looked at him, waiting for him to speak. "How are you doing tonight?" Joe asked.

"Good, you?"

"She's not making this easy," Joe thought. "I'm good," he replied and ordered his drinks. "Did you work at Lambert's today?"

"Yes."

"I got this at Lambert's," he said, giving one sleeve a small tug.

"It came in a wine color also," she pointed out.

Tanya made her way back to hearing range and started washing glasses.

"Do you think I should have gotten the wine color?" he asked.

"I think it would be a good color for you."

A man at the other end of the bar had his glass held up calling Tanya's name. She rushed down the bar.

Sam put the drinks down. Joe thanked her and handed her a twenty-dollar bill. "Put that in your cup."

"Thank you," she smiled at him.

"I'll let you get back to work."

"Don't rush," she grinned. "It's the first time Tanya washed a glass since I've been here." They both laughed.

"What a beautiful smile," Joe thought.

"Thanks Joe," she said, moving on to another customer.

He picked up the drinks, and Tanya was once again in front of him. "Are your drinks okay Joe?"

"Everything's fine, Tanya. Thank you."

He joined his cousins and Claude. "Why isn't she on stage?" Joe asked Dominic.

"Believe me; I've more than once pointed out the money she could be making."

"And?"

"She said she didn't want to be objectified."

"She's going to have to stay home to avoid that," Joe laughed.

Seconds later, a man jumped up, knocking over his barstool, which got their attention. Sam was cupping her left hand with her right hand, blood flowing down her arm. All the color gone from her panicked face. Joe hurdled the bar. He could see the bone between

Sam's thumb and index finger. He told Tanya to get him a towel. She handed Joe one off the bar. He tossed it aside. "Clean," he snapped. "Sam, look at me." She kept staring at her hand. "Sam, guardami negli occhi." (look into my eyes) She looked up at him. "We are just going to take a quick trip to Charity. You're going to be fine."

Joe led Sam out of the bar and around the corner to his car. In any other city in America, a woman in a black bikini with a blood-soaked towel wrapped around her hand would draw attention. Not in New Orleans on Bourbon Street. Fortunately, there were no major traumas when they got to Charity Hospital. They got Sam into a room and started to attend to her. The nurse handed Joe admission papers and asked him to fill them out. He in return, asked the nurse for a hospital gown for Sam.

A man came in looking too young to be a doctor. "Hi, I'm Doctor Gardot," he said as he picked up Sam's hand.

"Sam Mancuso," she said meekly.

"Samantha?"

"No," Joe replied, "just Sam." The doctor turned and looked up at Joe. "Joe DiLeo, my family owns the club where Miss Mancuso was injured."

The doctor looked back at her hand. "So tell me how you did this."

"I was washing a glass, and it broke. It's so white," Sam said, looking at her hand. The doctor gave her a puzzled look. "My bone."

The doctor snickered.

"It was an electric glass washer with rotating brushes," Joe interjected.

A nurse walked in with a silver pan.

"Sam we'll be getting you stitched up in a minute, but first we need to soak your hand in this solution. It's a disinfectant, and it will numb your hand. I'll be back in a few and show you my great sewing skills," he gave Sam a big smile and exited the room.

"This asshole is hitting on her," Joe thought.

"Are you finished with that?" The nurse asked, looking at Joe with the clipboard.

"Not quite yet."

"Okay honey," the nurse said to Sam, "you're going to put your hand in here. It's going to sting for a minute."

Joe moved closer to Sam. When he was 16, he got a fishing hook stuck in his hand. He remembered going through something similar and the pain. She put her hand into the solution and the pain registered. She grabbed Joe's forearm and gripped it tightly. He watched her silently process the pain, holding her breath at first, then slow deep breaths with her mouth open. As her breathing normalized, her eyes came up and she quickly released her grip on his arm.

"I'm sorry."

"Don't be."

Before the nurse left, she sternly directed Joe to finish the paperwork.

"Okay, let's get this done," Joe said.

They went through the name, address, and then place of birth.

"New Orleans," Sam said.

"No born, where were you born?"

"New Orleans, right here Charity Hospital."

"Really?"

"Yes, really," Sam replied.

"Emergency contact?"

"Giacomo Mancuso."

Before Sam could give Joe the phone number, he asked, "Jack?"

"Yes," Sam replied.

"My mother always said they honeymooned in Miami Beach so my dad could go to the Jack Mancuso heavyweight title fight," Joe grinned.

"Light heavy. My uncle fought at light heavyweight," Sam said.

"Really, that was your uncle?"

"Again, really," she smiled.

Joe laughed, and they finished the paperwork.

While the doctor was stitching Sam up, Joe found a payphone and checked in with Dominic. When he got back, Sam and the doctor were cajoling away. "What the fuck," Joe thought.

"Am I going to be able to run? I usually run three miles a day," Sam asked.

"I would give that a couple of weeks," the doctor replied.

"A couple of weeks?" Sam asked surprised.

"Running can be a bit jarring, plus on these streets you could always stumble or fall. Two weeks," he ordered.

"What about work?" Sam asked.

"Anytime, as long as you aren't using that hand, it shouldn't be an issue."

"Should she see an orthopedic specialist?" Joe asked.

"I don't think that's necessary," the doctor replied as he got up. "I'll leave a prescription for pain pills in case you feel some discomfort. The nurse is going to give you a tetanus shot and then you will be good to go. Nice meeting you Sam."

"Thank you, Doctor Gardot," Sam smiled.

"The doctor looked at Joe, "Mr. DiLeo."

"Doctor."

They stopped at the bar to collect Sam's things. He took her home and insisted on getting her up to her apartment. He looked around, trying to assess what was her deal. It was a beautiful apartment, meticulously clean but hardly any furniture.

An elegant sofa, with two framed boxing posters above. One of her uncle's title fight in Miami, the other of her cousin's golden gloves matches. A small tv on the opposite wall. It was sitting on a makeshift bookshelf, made out of milk crates and plywood. Books and a small radio on the lower shelves. A large potted fig tree in one corner. A folding card table with two folding chairs.

"Would you like a drink?" Sam asked, walking out of the bedroom. She was struggling with the belt to her robe.

"Yes please," Joe said, walking over to Sam. "May I?" he asked in reference to the tie belt she was wrestling.

She held her hands up in defeat. "Please." He tied the belt. She felt uncomfortably close. "So, a drink," Sam said as she stepped back.

Joe followed her into the kitchen. She took out two glasses from the upper cabinet next to the refrigerator and a 1.75 liter of Chivas from the cabinet below.

"Large economy size," Joe laughed.

She got an ice cube tray from the freezer. Joe took it from her hand, "let me do that." After icing the glasses, he refilled the tray and placed it back in the freezer. The freezer was close to full with plastic containers of sauce. One was marked, Felice. Sam sat at the card table, and Joe walked back to the poster.

"Uncanny," Sam said.

"Just what I was thinking. The poster from the fight we talked about." Joe gave his body a little shake to imply a shiver. He looked at the other poster.

"Those are my cousins. They fought on the same card that night."

"Did either one fight pro?" Joe asked.

"No, just golden gloves."

"How long have you lived here?" Joe asked as he walked over to the windows looking at the balcony.

"About eight months," Sam answered.

"Nice grill, Joe said, and what do you have going out here?"

"The table?" Sam asked.

Joe nodded.

"I'm stripping it. Then I'm going to stain and wax it. Felice said it was well constructed. I found it on Royal, just sitting on the curb. Felice thought it would make a cool tv stand."

"You and Felice are pretty friendly."

"She's my best friend. She's like a sister to me."

"I've always liked Felice," Joe inputted. "Can I ask you a question without ruffling your feathers?"

"That would depend on the question," Sam replied.

"Why are you so set against dancing? Do you have any idea how much money you would make?"

"While I'm up there on exhibit taking my clothes off. Yes, I know what I could make. I'm not comfortable with that."

"But you're comfortable with your boyfriend stripping?"

"His body, his choice."

Joe let it go. He could see she was becoming agitated. "How's the hand?"

"It's starting to throb."

"Did they give you anything for pain?"

"No, just the prescription. If I need it tomorrow, I'll get it filled. I don't have to take a pill every time I get a scratch."

"Sam, nine stitches is hardly a scratch. I want you to see an orthopedist. Dominic will give you a call with a name and number of the doctor."

"I'll just get the name from him tonight," Sam replied.

"Sam, you're not working until a doctor gives the okay."

"A doctor did give the okay," Sam's voice was elevating.

Joe smiled and walked over to Sam. "Dominic will call you." Then he put his glass on the table and pulled his money clip out of his pocket peeling off two, one hundred dollar bills. Joe put them on the table while saying, "to help cover your lost time."

"Pick up your money." She gave him a hard look. Joe didn't move. She repeated herself and added, "and leave, please. I'm tired."

He picked up the money and replaced it with his business card. "If you need anything, call me." He let himself out.

She was able to get back to work the following Wednesday. When she told Felice what happened, she got a lecture much to her surprise.

"His first responsibility is to his business as an owner and an attorney. As far as him trying to give you money, that's a nice thing, Sam. Very few bosses would do that. And lastly, you work in a strip club. Him asking you about dancing is not an unusual question. How you still have a job is beyond me. I mean, you called the man an asshole. Who does that?"

Sam was taken aback. Her friend always understood her side of things. Felice suggested she be proactive. Send him a note, thanking him for his help that night and apologizing for her behavior. Sam couldn't see how that would have an impact, but it did. Joe appreciated the gesture.

Amaretto

Sunday, October 17, 1993

It was almost 5 A.M. when Joe left Sam's apartment. It had been a long time since he'd been in the quarter that late. He stopped at Verti Marte on Royal and got a shrimp po' boy to go, then drove up Royal out of the French Quarter to his home on Prytania. He went in through the side entrance, which led directly into the kitchen. He got a beer out of the refrigerator, then ate his po' boy and drank his beer standing at the kitchen counter listening to his phone messages. Staring out onto the courtyard, his mind raced. How eerie was that Jack Mancuso fight poster? "You can't come up with odds on that," he thought. "What is it with that girl? She's hot but crazy. The hot ones always are. God, she's hot." He felt himself getting hard. The sun was breaking. He gathered the sandwich wrappings and beer bottle and threw them in the trash. "Jesus Christ, I'm drinking beer for breakfast. What am I, 19?"

He went upstairs and jumped in the shower. He lathered up with his favorite bath gel. It was a clean scent. Joe wasn't one of those guys who primped. A shave and a comb through his wet hair were it, but he liked the scent of this expensive bath gel. The gel let his hand slide back and forth on his cock easily. He rested his forehead on his arm against the cool tile and visualized her. His hands gripping her hair while his cock is sliding down her throat. He groaned her name out loud when he came, then started laughing. "Sam, Sam, Sam." It sounded so strange to him. "Who the fuck names their daughter Sam?"

He got dressed, a pair of jeans and a polo shirt. He grabbed the first shirt from the stack in the drawer. Put it back, shuffled through the pile and pulled a wine-colored shirt out. He went back down to the kitchen and made a pot of coffee. Sleep eluded him. He got his newspaper off the front porch and paged through it drinking his coffee, standing at the kitchen counter. He poured his second cup and took it into his office and got into paperwork. Real estate taxes, license renewal for the four bars, bank statements, and insurance. It was 11:30 when he called his uncle's house. When he didn't get an answer, he called Chris, the same thing. Then it hit him, Sunday, church. He called Dominic and left a message to get a bartender for tonight and an orthopedic doctor for Sam to see. He was done, ready to crash. His last thoughts were of Sam, the poster, and his parents.

Leigh had to have Vincent. She didn't realize the impact of her decision until it was too late. The life she had planned for herself was gone. The garden district home was replaced by a creole cottage and then a one-bedroom apartment. Instead of running a house, she was cleaning one. Instead of dinner parties, there were spaghetti suppers with the in-laws. Before long, the telltale signs of other women were on Vincent's clothes. The only way out of this prison was her parent's forgiveness. She never got that. Her sentence for going against their wishes was life. Her lifelong friends had little time for her. She led a lonely existence. The DiLeo women tried to bring her into the fold, but she chose to stay in her own purgatory. She forever regretted her suicide attempt. Her guilt distanced her from her son. Vincent spent more time on the street then home. Once little Joey was old enough to go to the bathroom by himself, Vincent would take him along during the day. By the time Joe was in fifth grade, he had seen the inside of whore houses, strip joints, and poker parlors, always sworn to father/son secrecy.

As loved as Joe was by his uncle and aunts, he longed for the relationship with his parents that his cousins had with theirs.

Vincent was found floating face down in the Mississippi when Joe was eleven. It surprised no one that knew him. It was a large funeral, but very few sincerely mourned, his wife included.

Leigh got a job at Godchaux's where she once shopped on her

father's account. She met a wealthy widower and was remarried within 18 months of Vincent's death. She moved into her new husband's uptown home with her son. Joe started to act out. In fear of jeopardizing her marriage, she asked Frank if Joe could move back into the DiLeo home. Joe was happy to be back in the cramped bedroom with his cousins.

Joe woke up a little after 4:30 P.M., took a quick shower and put on the jeans and polo shirt he wore earlier. He went into his office and gathered the paperwork he would be needing. Then into the kitchen to check his messages. He had two.

"Got your message. Took care of the bartender. Ma wants to know if you're coming for dinner? Call the house." Joe erased it.

"Heeeey, it's Jennifer. I'm back from Europe. Just thought I'd give you a call. Call me so we can catch up. Kisses."

"Hell no," Joe said out loud as he erased the message. He called the house, and Dominic answered. "I'm on my way," Joe said.

"How long?"

"I'm leaving my house now. Do the math."

Joe got there in 25 minutes. He took a short detour to pass by Sam's apartment.

"Hi Aunt Carmela," Joe said just before he kissed her on the cheek.

"You got a special dispensation from the pope? You don't have to go to mass anymore?" she asked.

Joe didn't want to go into the details of last night, so he just apologized. He went to the refrigerator, opened the door, and stared. Closed it, got a glass out of the cabinet and filled it with water from the faucet.

"That color looks good on you, Joey."

"Thanks, are they in the den?"

"Yes, are you okay?"

"I'm good Auntie Carm, just a little tired."

The den had a pool table, tv, a sectional sofa and a small bar with three stools. This room use to be Frank's office until he moved it into the apartment downstairs after Leigh moved out. Dominic was behind the bar. Chris and Frank were sitting on the sectional. The tv was on; no one was watching it. Joe put his briefcase on the large square cocktail table and opened it up.

"You want a drink, Joe?" Dominic asked.

"No thanks Dom, I've been hitting it pretty hard. I think I'll coast," Joe said as he started pulling papers out of his briefcase.

"That can wait until after dinner," Frank said, "Dominic and Chris were telling me about the girl you took to the hospital last night. Is she going to be alright?"

"Nine stitches, we're sending her to a specialist before she comes back to work. We don't want anything to come back and bite us in the ass later."

"Good."

"Want to hear something weird?" Joe said to all three. "Remember the story about my dad choosing Miami for a honeymoon so he could go to a title fight?" All three acknowledged, having heard the story many times. "Sam's uncle was the boxer dad wanted to see, and it gets better. I took her home, and she has the poster from that fight, framed, hanging on her wall."

"Your grandmother would be making the sign of the cross right now," Frank laughed.

Nina stuck her head in the door to announce dinner. After dinner, they went down to the office.

Joe started, "let's get those glass washers out of all the bars."

"You know we lease those. We have a contract with the company," Dominic pointed out.

"I can break that," Joe said.

"So can I. You're not the only one in the family that went to law school," Dominic snapped.

"I didn't mean anything by that Dom," Joe apologized.

Dominic waved his hand to let Joe know he was okay, "I'll call the rep tomorrow."

Joe went on, "we've got to make some decisions on the Blue Room. It's hemorrhaging money."

"You think we should sell it?" Chris asked.

"No, but we can't take a bath much longer. We need to come up with a new format," Joe said.

"I honestly thought a comedy club would be a winner," Chris

explained.

"Chris, we all thought it was a good idea. Now we know why nobody did it before." Frank said, and they all laughed. "Joe, did you have something in mind?"

"I think we should try to clone Christos'," Joe looked around for reaction.

"How much is that going to cost us?" Chris asked.

"$25,000. if we half-ass it, double that to do it right. I can get Charlie to give us some prices," Joe said.

"I'd like to see a bigger bar in the room," Dominic added.

"Joe, give Charlie a call and see if he can sit down with us next week," Frank said.

"Now I want to throw this out there. I've been thinking about this for a while. Does everyone know what a check-cashing store is?" Joe was waiting for confirmation.

"It's self-explanatory," Dominic snickered.

"Well, they do more than cash checks. They do a lot of bank services and take utility payments. They also do payday and car loans with pretty impressive interest," Joe explained.

"Devil's advocate," Dominic said. "Say a waitress or bartender doesn't have a checking account. Why wouldn't they go to the bank where their employer banks?"

"The bank is going to charge them for cashing the check, or it's after regular banking hours," Joe answered.

"You mean our bank charges our employees to cash our checks," Chris was astonished.

"Yep," Joe's said.

"So you want to open one?" Frank asked.

"No, I want to open three or four in Orleans and Jefferson parishes. This could be our retirement program."

The men all looked at one another in silence. Finally, Frank spoke up. "Put some numbers together."

They wrapped up their business. On the way out, Frank put his hand on Dominic's shoulder to hold him back. Chris and Joe waited outside. "Are you having a problem with your cousin."

"No, Dad, I overreacted. I'm a little on edge lately." Dominic paused, "I've had to talk Sarah off the ledge again. She's been threatening divorce."

"Are you still fooling around with that stripper?"

47

"Bartender."

"Okay bartender, what difference does that make?"

"Did Joe tell you about that?" Dominic asked.

"He didn't have to; your business is all over Bourbon Street."

"It's over Dad."

"I'll talk to your wife. You keep your business off the street. Okay?" Frank rubbed Dominic's shoulder.

"So did you give Joe the same lecture when he had his thing with Tanya?" Dominic laughed.

"Your cousin's single. He can fuck as many whores as he wants. You have something to lose."

Dominic kissed his father on the cheek, "I know Dad."

"This girl that got hurt, does your cousin have something going with her?"

"He wishes," Dominic snickered and told his father the story of how Joe and Sam met.

Frank chuckled, "she's Italian?"

"Yes, and Dad, her meatballs are as good as grandmas were. She brought Claude some last night. And the sauce," Dominic rolled his eyes back.

"Make sure you stay away from that one," Frank joked.

"I think Joe would have my balls if I got near her." They were laughing as they walked out.

Joe's ride home was full of reflection. Joe had it figured out. He was going to head to New York right out of law school. Securities law was going to be his ticket to wealth and freedom from the DiLeo business. He loved his family, and he had no disrespect for the men his uncle did business with. Joe just wanted more. Five weeks prior to his graduation, Joe was contacted by an estate attorney regarding his maternal grandmother's will. Joe was surprised to find out his mother wasn't aware of this.

Joe inherited his maternal grandparents home in the garden district. Plus close to $200,000 in stocks, bonds, and cash. He had never laid eyes on either one of them. Leigh was shocked, if not jealous of her son's windfall. This, after all, was the house she grew up in. It was her parent's final slap across the face. Joe moved into the house and took his uncles advice. His uncle suggested he take six months and then weigh his options. Six months became twelve, and he still was unsure if he wanted to remain in New Orleans.

The federal government decided for him. His uncle and Dominic were indicted for racketeering. They both eventually ended up in federal prison only after their attorney's fees almost financially ruined them. Joe had no choice. He had to take over in his uncle's absence.

Frank and Dominic's convictions were eventually overturned except for one little beef on Dominic. He was out with time served and parole; one of the last paroles before they abolished them in the federal system. The real consequence being; his license to practice law was now gone forever. The feds had no intention of letting the DiLeo's go unscathed.

The year and a half his cousin and uncle were in prison, Joe managed to clean up the family business. He distanced the family from illegal activities. That cut the profits, but Joe figured spending the earnings on attorney fees didn't make much sense either.

He bought a French Quarter building at auction for a song and with Charlie's help turned the building into 16 small but beautiful condominiums. They all sold within four months of completion. Joe also bought out a guy with a fledgling valet business. He had contracts in two good size hotels. Joe got four more hotels and a casino in Biloxi.

Joe was also putting together a nice stock portfolio for the family. Chris was on board with everything his cousin did. He wasn't born with the wise guy gene.

When Frank and Dominic got out, Joe laid out his plans for the future of the family. Frank down deep knew he was a dying breed. His main concern was making sure the family was financially set. Dominic was resistant but came around when Joe reminded him of the day the FBI showed up with a warrant and ransacked his home in front of his wife and kids.

It was only 9:30 when Joe got home. He checked his messages. None, good, no messages no problems. He put his briefcase in the office. Sat at his desk with the intent to do some work to no avail. He picked up the phone and dialed a number by memory.

"Hi, any chance you could come over tonight?"

An hour later, she was at the door. A little friendly small talk and they headed upstairs.

She walked into the guest room, and put her large satchel on a chair in the corner, went to the nightstand and asked, "is this for me?"

"Yes."

She picked up the two one hundred dollar bills; the very same ones that sat on Sam's table early that morning. "How do you want me?" she asked.

"Naked."

She laughed, "that part, I know."

"On your stomach," Joe said, looking down at the satchel. "May I?"

"Take what you need."

He took out wrist and ankle cuffs. He put another pillow under her to prop her ass up higher. At the right head corner of the bed, he pulled a strap from between the box spring and mattress with a D ring at the end. He cuffed her wrist and attached it to the D ring. He repeated the process at the other three corners. He opened one of the nightstand drawers and pulled out a ball gag wrapped in cellophane.

"I don't need that," she grinned.

"You will tonight," Joe smiled back.

He put the gag on her, pulled off his shirt, and retrieved a riding crop from her bag. He gently dragged the tip of the crop from the nape of her neck down her back to her tail bone. Then he pulled it back and struck.

He sat in his master suite, giving her privacy. Joe's master suite could have easily been in Southern Homes. It was originally two bedrooms connected through the bathroom. Now the two rooms were joined by a beautifully carved archway. He had a bar built into the wall. The upper half showcased the crystal glassware. The bottom half had a sink built into the counter. Cherry finished cabinets housed an ice maker, small refrigerator and shelves for liquor. A silk sofa and two occasional chairs faced a large tv. The room was both elegant and masculine. The decor followed through to the bedroom. The bathroom was state of the art, with a jacuzzi tub and separate oversized shower.

"Joe, I'm leaving," she said from the hallway.

"Can you come in here for a minute?"

She walked in. Joe thought she was better looking now that half her makeup was on the sheets in the guest room.

"Can I get you a drink?" Joe waved his hand in a motion to sit down.

"I'll stand," she walked up next to him at the bar. "Do you have Tia Maria?"

"No, but I have amaretto. That's sweet."

"I like amaretto."

He handed her the drink. "Are you okay?" remembering the welts he left on her ass and thighs.

"I'll be fine," she smiled. She was proud to point out that the gag wasn't necessary.

"You were right. Do you enjoy it?" Joe asked. "I mean would you do this if money wasn't involved?"

"Yes," she smiled. "I enjoy it. The money is the icing on the cake." She walked over to a chair, put her drink on the coffee table, and eased herself down, gripping the arms of the chair.

Joe chuckled, "so how did you get involved in this lifestyle?"

"You mean what horrible childhood trauma happened to make me this way?"

"I'm sorry. I didn't mean to imply that. You can tell me to mind my own fucking business."

Her smile eased his embarrassment. "Joe, I'm not a victim of circumstances. I had a happy and healthy childhood in Kettering, Ohio. Loving parents who never laid a hand on me. I was in a relationship with my high school sweetheart. Engaged! We came here for Mardi Gras. Not the last one. The one before that. He got into a fight in a bar and got himself arrested. So I went out for a few drinks by myself. I met a woman. She bought me a drink. We talked. I had never been with a woman before. After we made love, she asked if she could spank me. It felt so natural to me. Like I found something I didn't know I was missing.

"I went home with my boyfriend, but we kept in touch. Her letters excited me. She invited me to stay with her for a week visit, under the conditions, I understood what our relationship would be. She explained in great detail what she was and what she expected of me. I couldn't wait. I came, and I never left."

"Thank you," Joe said.

"Now let me ask you a question. Were you asking out of curiosity, or are you trying to work something out?"

"I'm not sure," Joe replied walking her to the door. "Do you still see her?"

"She's my dominatrix," the girl smiled and she stepped out of the door.

Cinderella

Wednesday, October 20, 1993

Claude had been walking Sam home since Andrew left, in spite of the fact he lived less than two blocks from the club. It was a good excuse to stop and have a drink at his favorite leather bar.

"Was it busy Sunday?" Sam asked as they walked down Bourbon.

"For a couple of hours. I don't think you missed that much."

"Do you know what that bitch Tanya left for me from Saturday's tips? $39. The bar was full when I got hurt. I know I put at least $50 in the cup myself. Joe left me twenty."

"Say something to Dominic," Claude suggested.

"Sure, hey Dominic, your girlfriend is screwing me on the split. How do you think that will fly?" Sam said, sarcastically.

"Ex-girlfriend," Claude grinned.

"Really? Since when?" Sam asked.

"It's been a couple of weeks now. I thought I told you."

"No Claude, you didn't. Why is she still there? She's a shitty bartender."

"A couple of years ago a dancer got busted for soliciting. That would have violated Dominic's parole. Tanya stepped up and said she was the manager. They charged her with pandering. It was a bullshit deal. The whole thing got thrown out on entrapment. The DiLeo's never forget a favor. Tanya is there as long as she wants to be."

"She was all over Joe the other night."

"Girl, that's old news. Joe was doing her before Dominic."

"WHAT!"

"Yep, That was your boyfriend's piece for a while," Claude laughed.

"Knock off that boyfriend shit. Well, I guess Chris will be next."

"I'd bet my leather wardrobe that would never happen," Claude grinned.

"Glad to hear he has higher standards than his cousins," Sam joked.

"Sha, that man would never cheat on his wife. I've seen him turn down women most men would crawl over broken glass to get."

"That's sweet. Hard to believe a guy that good looking is like that. I guess his cousins are picking up his slack," they both laughed.

"How's your hand?"

"It's okay," she said, wiggling her thumb.

"Aren't you right-handed?" Claude asked.

"Yeah, why?"

"I just thought it odd that you were washing glasses with your left hand."

"It wasn't glasses; it was one glass, detective Thibodeau. I had money in my right hand and the dirty glass in my left. I was in front of the glass washer, so I just flipped the switch and washed it," her voice elevating.

"Don't get pissy. I was just asking. As long as your right hand is okay, you can start that picture of me you've been promising."

"I've been giving that some thought. I want to do a hardcore leather picture," Sam said, almost excited.

"I knew if you were here long enough you'd come over to the dark side."

"Don't break out the whips and chains just yet. You don't have a convert. I just want to do something edgy."

"Fess up, that gorgeous Andrew had to be a little kinky," Claude probed.

"Andrew was a lot of things, but kinky was not one of them."

"You're breaking my heart," Claude laughed. "Have you heard from him?"

"I talked to him last week. He likes it there."

"Do you miss him?"

"Would it sound cold if I said no?"

"It sounds honest. So who's next," Claude joked.

"I'm just going to stick to sport fucking for a while," they laughed.

Thursday, October 21, 1993

"Felice Sax, line one, Felice Sax, line one," went over the store speakers.

She picked up the nearest phone, "this is Felice."

"Hey, are you with a customer?" Sam asked.

"No, what's up?"

"I've gotta go to the post office, and I thought I'd stop by."

"That sounds good. I'm taking my dinner break around 4:30. Mr. B's?"

"Do you have a punch card from that place you're trying to fill?" Sam chuckled.

"It's close to the store, and I think they have the best gumbo in town," Felice said, "and the best shrimp and grits."

"You made your point," Sam laughed. "Should I meet you there or come to the store?"

"Don't come to the store. I told my boss I couldn't deliver your chair because you were out of town. Remember?"

"Sorry. Are you in trouble for that?" Sam was concerned.

"Nooo, I just don't want him to think I lied."

"You did lie," they laughed.

They ate at the bar, and never ran out of conversation. Felice was kidding Sam about her upcoming blind date. Unlike Felice who had many of them, this was a first for Sam.

"So tell me again how you got roped into this," Felice asked.

"Well, he has just relocated from New York and his aunt who I work with thought we would have a lot in common because we're both from the east coast."

"That makes absolutely no sense," Felice laughed.

"Believe me, being from South Florida and being from New York is practically the same thing."

"What if he's a complete jerk?" Felice pointed out.

"I made it clear that I didn't want any backlash if it didn't work out."

"Wouldn't it be funny if he turned out to be the man of your dreams."

"Yes Cinderella it would," Sam chuckled.

Friday, October 22, 1993

Fifteen minutes before Lambert's closed he showed up. Ruth left out a few details about her nephew. Ruth's nephew was 6'5"and big. You would be hard-pressed to figure out which one had less interest in the other. Their conversation at dinner was strained. He made a few comments about her petite size. She made mention of how surprising his height was to her. He didn't have that New York edge about him. He was more reserved. Sam liked her men a little more aggressive. Had she not had to face Ruth in the morning, she would have disappeared on a trip to the ladies room.

They hadn't even ordered dinner yet, so she had at least another hour of his company to look forward to. "Not exactly the match made in heaven your aunt was hoping for," she blurted out. He looked at Sam in disbelief. "There wasn't a good way of saying that, but down deep, you're thinking the same thing."

He didn't know what the hell to do. He had never been in such an awkward position before.

Sam reached over the table and put her hand over his and said, "I'm well aware of how insane I must sound to you, but hear me out, please. I promise you this ends well."

"I'm listening," he replied with an air of caution.

"I have the perfect girl for you."

"That's what my Aunt Ruth said about you," he chuckled.

Sam went into her wallet and showed him two pictures she had of her and Felice. One was taken on Fort Lauderdale beach two years prior. He could clearly see her size.

The other picture was taken five years ago. It was of both their families together. She took the pictures out of the jacket and handed them to him.

"She's beautiful," he said as if speaking to himself. "How tall is she?" he asked, not looking up from the pictures.

"She's 5'10"," Sam answered.

"She's Jewish?" he asked.

"What made you ask that?" Sam wondered.

He turned the family picture around, "she's wearing a Star of David."

"Is that a deal-breaker?" Sam asked.

"Sam, I'm Jewish."

"Daniel Sullivan is Jewish?" Sam laughed.

"My mother and Ruth are sisters. Didn't Ruth tell you that?"

Sam smiled, "this is perfect." They spent the next half hour talking about Felice. Daniel could tell how much Sam cared for Felice.

"I want to meet her, but there is a small glitch. I'm leaving town Sunday morning. I've got a meeting in your old neck of the woods, Fort Lauderdale. Then I go back to New York to arrange shipping my things."

"Call me crazy," Sam said.

"Since I've met you," Daniel joked.

"I'm calling Felice. I'll see if she can meet us for a drink. She can stop on her way home from her parents."

"She's at Shabbat?" Daniel asked.

"Yeah, but they're not religious. I think the last time they were at temple was Felice's Bat Mitzvah. It's tradition like Italians have spaghetti dinners on Sunday," Sam flippantly said as she flagged down a waiter. She got change and the directions to the payphone.

"Let me get this straight. You want to pawn your date off on me?" Felice whispers so her parents couldn't hear.

"You have to trust me on this. He's the perfect guy for you. Who cares how you met him. Please just meet us for a drink."

"What's wrong with him? Why is he not perfect for you?"

"Have you not been listening? He's 6'5", I'm 5'3", we look like a fucking carnival act. Plus no chemistry."

"So what makes you think we will have chemistry?"

"Oh my god, stop overthinking this. Just meet us for a drink. If it doesn't work, it doesn't work. Felice, he's a nice guy."

Felice got there as they were ordering their coffee and dessert. Daniel's eyes lit up when he saw Felice. He never took them off of her. This was a different man than the one Sam had dinner with. Daniel was Prince Charming to Felice's Cinderella. Sam couldn't be happier taking a back seat. As they walked out of Bayona's, Felice asked about the dinner.

"It was fantastic," Sam said.

"I've never eaten here," Felice pointed out.

"I can fix that. Have dinner with me when I get back?" Daniel asked.

"That sounds wonderful," Felice smiled.

"I know both of you work tomorrow, but it's early. Maybe we

could go listen to some jazz," Daniel suggested.

"I'm going to bow out, but you two go ahead. Christos is just one block down Conti. They have great jazz," Sam said.

Daniel insisted on taking Sam home and so not to belabor her exit she agreed to a cab. Daniel gave the driver $10.00 for a $3.00 cab ride. Daniel had class.

Saturday, October 23, 1993

Sam couldn't wait to talk to Felice the next day. Unfortunately, Felice had an early morning sales meeting on Saturday's, so she would have to wait for the juicy details. Most mornings Sam took the riverfront streetcar up to Canal. Since her accident she walked to work, trying to make up a little for her missed morning run. She turned heads walking up Chartres in her off white suit. Her hair was pulled back into a loose low ponytail. As she walked past Mena's she spotted Joe getting up from a table. She picked up her pace. Just as she thought she made a clean getaway, she heard Joe call her name. She turned and stood still. Joe did a short jog to her.

"How's the thumb?" he grinned.

She put her hand up level with his face and wiggled her thumb, "it's good, thanks."

"I got your card," Joe said as Chris and another man joined him.

"Hi Chris," Sam smiled.

"Sam, you look lovely this morning," Chris responded.

"Thank you."

Chris went on, "Sam, this is our friend and contractor Charlie." Sam put her hand out, and Charlie cupped her hand with both of his and shook it. "Sam works at Lambert's," Chris finished up his introduction.

"Is that short for Samantha?" Charlie asked while still cupping her hand.

"Just Sam," Joe said as he thought, "every time. No wonder she was short with me when I asked." Then he added, "Sam also works for us at our strip club."

Charlie let her hand go and now looked her body up and down.

Sam said as calmly as possible to Joe, "devi essere uno stronzo ogni volta?" (must you be an asshole every time) Then said her goodbyes to Chris and Charlie. She walked off, fit to be tied.

Chris rode with Joe down to their uncle's.

"What was that?" Chris asked when they got into the car.

"What was what?" Joe replied.

"Joe, that was a lousy thing to do. I think Charlie was interested in Sam or was that the problem?"

"First of all, if Charlie's interested in her, he's going to find out where she works eventually. Secondly, if it's an embarrassment for her, she shouldn't be working there."

"That's probably why she's looking for another job," Chris pointed out.

"Do you know that for sure?"

"Yes, she asked me if we had any openings at Christos."

"When did Sam ask you that?"

"About a month ago," Chris replied.

"Did you tell Dominic or was this just between you and Sam?"

"Come on Joe; you're blowing this out of proportion."

"Chris, if they are looking for another job, they no longer have a loyalty to us. They are more prone to theft. You know this. I'm not saying anything new."

"So now you're going to fire her? Chris asked.

"I'm going to talk to Dominic. That whole accident thing puts a different light on things."

They got to their uncle's house and went into the downstairs office. Frank and Dominic were already there.

"You boys hungry?" Frank asked.

"No thanks, we ate at Mena's with Charlie," Chris replied.

"Why didn't you call me?" Dominic asked.

"I did. I left a message on your machine," Chris answered.

Frank laughed to himself. These three well-respected businessmen were still kids around each other.

Dominic started, "we have a problem. The rep was in yesterday about the glass washers. The machine in Azure did have a mechanical problem. It would sporadically speed up. They replaced it."

"Problem solved," Joe said.

"Not exactly. Tanya was there and said the same thing happened to her a few weeks before Sam got hurt," Dominic continued.

"Did she get hurt?" Joe asked.

"No."

"Did you ask her why she didn't report it to one of you?" Frank asked.

"Yes, she said she told me. The rep was there when she said that. I honestly do not remember her telling me."

Joe was furious, "was your dick in her mouth when she told you?" Dominic jumped up.

"Sit down Dominic," Frank said. "Does Sam know what happened to Tanya?"

"I'm guessing no, but I don't know for sure," Dominic replied.

"Shit!!" Joe said.

"I don't understand what's going on," Chris asked.

"Sam can sue us. Do you understand that?" Joe snapped at Chris.

"Okay, I have a question, and I don't want you to jump on me," Chris said to Joe, "I thought you couldn't sue workmen's comp?"

Joe waved his hand over to Dominic to answer Chris.

"If we had knowledge of faulty equipment, that shows negligence on our part. So if Sam decided to sue the company that made the machine, they could involve us because we were aware of the potential danger. She could also just sue us. We would be hard-pressed to get insurance after that," Dominic explained.

"Sam asked Chris about a job at Christos. We could move her over there," Joe said. "She'll be away from Tanya, and I doubt seriously they talk outside of work."

"When did she ask you about moving to Christos?" Dominic asked Chris.

"You three have to work on your communication skills," Frank intervened. "One hand doesn't know what the other one is doing."

They sat quietly for a moment. Joe broke the ice, "we'll move Sam over to Christos' next week." He looked at Chris, "tell Sandy to put her on the schedule."

"It doesn't work that way, Joe," Chris said. "Sandy does the hiring."

"We still own the place, right? You want me to tell Sandy?" Joe asked. "I'll explain why we're doing this."

"I can talk to Sandy," Chris replied.

"Don't talk, tell," Joe said. "And Dominic, you need to have a talk with Tanya."

"You know Joe, Chris and I don't need your help running the bars. We're here seven days a week, and you show up when you get bored with your garden district debutants. Now we have to step on Sandy's toes because you're hot for this girl," Dominic was practically screaming.

"You got a better idea? I'm all ears. Unlike you, when someone is reporting faulty equipment," Joe snapped back.

Frank's hand came down hard on the desk. It startled all three. "There is plenty of blame to go around," Frank said and pointed his finger at Joe, "remember, you're the one that put us in this position with Sandy. I'm going to go to Christos' tonight and talk to Sandy myself. This little girl that everyone is so hot over, she'll get the same schedule she had at Azure. No more, no less. And Joe, fuck her, don't fuck her, I don't give a damn, but don't even think about going to Chris or Sandy wanting her gone when you're done with her. Do you understand me?" Joe nodded. "I mean it, Joe. Why can't you two be more like your cousin Chris? You don't see him playing around with every girl that wiggles her ass in front of him."

"Saint Christos," Dominic said laughing, and Joe joined in.

Frank shook his head and said, "does everyone have the dinner on your calendars? I want all of you there. Is your mother coming?" he asked Joe.

"I'm not sure. I'll give her a call," Joe answered.

"Good, let your Aunt Carmela know. Are you bringing someone?" Frank asked.

"Yes," Joe answered.

"Okay we're done," Frank said. "You three have exhausted me."

Heckle & Jeckle

The thought of going into Azure that night was giving Sam a headache. She couldn't take much more of the roller coaster named Joe. It turned out to be an easy night. Tanya carried her weight, which was a first. Plus they made better money than usual, and it wasn't that busy.

When she pointed that out to Claude on the way home, he admitted to talking to Dominic about the split the other night. Claude said Dominic had Tanya in the office for a while before her shift started. "I figured Dominic was getting a blowjob," Claude laughed, "but she was unusually quiet for a while after she left the office. I think he straightened her out."

"Thank you, but I would have preferred not to get Dominic involved," Sam said.

"Oh, you prefer to have that cunt take advantage of you every Saturday."

"No, I'm not saying that. I appreciate you having my back, but Tanya knows how to handle Dominic," Sam said.

"Well you're wrong about that, plus you're one of the best bartenders they ever had. You're ringing a hell of a lot more than Tanya. Plus your Joe trumps her Dominic."

Sam laughed, "that asshole. He's tap dancing on my last nerve. Let me tell you his latest." She told Claude in great detail, about their last interaction. "I don't get him; I truly don't. He's like a Heckle and Jeckle," Sam ranted.

"The birds?" Claude chuckled.

"No, you know what I mean," she laughed.

"Jekyll and Hyde. He's just doing the equivalent of pulling your pigtails. You may have to fuck him to get rid of him," Claude joked.

"And please take notes. I want all the details."

Sam gave Claude a shove, and they both laughed. For years to come, Sam would have fond memories of her 3 A.M. walks home down Bourbon Street with Claude.

Sunday, October 24, 1993

Sam hated that she couldn't run. She was sure she would be totally out of shape by next week. Thinking a swim couldn't hurt anything, she'd have breakfast and walk up to the athletic club and do laps. Before she finished breakfast, it had started to storm. So she went about prepping her dinner. Felice was coming over. The caponata was time-consuming with all the vegetables to clean and dice. She'd serve that first with crostini, (little toast) then the fennel and orange salad, followed by rosemary and lemon roasted chicken with potato wedges. Sam loved to cook.

By the time the rain stopped, she had everything ready to go. She took the caponata off the stove, the chicken out of the oven and headed to the gym. This was a beautiful structure. Sam was so happy it was now open to women. Sam did yoga, weights, and swam there. Plus they had a jogging track if the weather was too unbearable. It also had a lounge and restaurant. They had a boxing area which she wandered into one day. She got the no place for a little lady speech. She wanted to tell them she forgot more about boxing than they would ever know. She loved the gym so thought better of spouting off and walked out silently. One day the room was empty. She walked in and began working the speed bag. When Sam realized she had drawn an audience on the other side of the glass wall, she stopped and left. No one ever said a word to her when she walked into the boxing area again. All the guys at the gym referred to her as flyweight. Occasionally she would sit in the corner of the room with her sketch pad, just as she had in her uncle's gym.

Felice was on cloud nine. Daniel had called her Saturday night, and they talked for close to an hour. He also called her Sunday from the airport. Sam was delighted for her friend but was concerned this might blow up in her face. She had never seen Felice so happy over a man before. If this didn't work out, Sam would never forgive herself.

"Don't you have any eye drops?" Felice asked.

"It will go away. My eyes always get bloodshot when I swim in a pool. It's the chlorine," Sam replied.

"It's not just the chlorine. It's the combination of pee with chlorine," Felice laughed.

"Oh, bullshit. My eyes would get bloodshot when I swam in my uncle's pool."

"You don't think your cousins peed in the pool?" Felice joked.

"Thanks, you just ruined swimming for me," Sam laughed. "Do you want to take any of this home?"

"I'll take some chicken," Felice said.

"And?" Sam asked.

"A little salad and caponata. But just a little," Felice replied. "Sam, would you take me to your gym as a guest?"

"Sure, just let me know when," Sam said with no inflection in her voice.

Felice was laughed at, preached to, and ridiculed about her weight her whole life. Her best friend never did or condoned any of that behavior. Sam was her safe zone. Even her family would occasionally bring her weight up. Sam knew this was a step Felice could only take when she was ready. Fingers crossed, maybe Felice was ready.

Sam packed up the salad, caponata, and fresh bread for Claude and was off to work. She walked in and handed Claude the bag.

"Thank you, Sha, what is it?" Claude asked.

"It's caponata and fennel and orange salad," Sam replied.

"What's caponata?" Claude asked.

"Eggplant, tomatoes, onions—"

Claude was holding his hand up to stop her. "I don't eat eggplant. What's the other thing?" Claude asked.

"Fennel and orange salad," Sam replied.

"What's fennel?"

"You know, it's like a fat celery but licorice-flavored."

Claude started to shake his head no, "but thank you," Claude said.

"You don't know what you're missing," Sam joked as she walked away.

"By the way, your boyfriend's upstairs," Claude called after her.

"Shit!" Sam said as she went upstairs to get her bank bag.

Dominic was sitting behind his desk, and Joe was sitting in one of the two chairs in front of the desk. Dominic handed her the bank while she simultaneously put down the bag.

"What's this?" Dominic asked.

"Hand me down leftovers," Sam smiled. "Claude doesn't eat eggplant."

"Parmigiana?" Dominic asked.

"No, caponata. I always make too much. Oh and fennel, orange salad. If you want it," Sam said, almost shyly. "I put some French bread in there too."

Dominic reached across the desk and brought the bag closer to him, "thank you."

"Sam, look at me," Joe said in an authoritative voice. "Why are your eyes bloodshot?"

"I was swimming," Sam replied.

"Swimming?" Joe questioned.

"At the athletic club. Chlorine," Sam said, waving her hand towards her eye."

"Sam, I belong to the athletic club," Joe's tone was deliberate, "it's a men's club."

"No," Dominic interjected, "they let women in now."

"Since when?"

"It's been a couple of years," Dominic answered.

"Really, I guess it's been a while since I've been there."

"You should go," Sam said, walking out the door, "it wouldn't take you much to get back in shape."

Dominic was howling, "I love that fucking broad."

"I guess she's not afraid to bite the hand that feeds her," Joe snickered.

"Easy boy," Dominic said, still laughing. "You can't fire her. Remember? Get some plates from that cabinet." Dominic called down for a couple of beers, then opened the bag.

"Do you really think she made this?" Joe asked as he put down the paper plates and plastic forks.

"Yes, the girl can cook. She brought meatballs in last week. As good as grandmas. I'm not kidding."

They ate and reminisced. "I think grandma used to put olives in hers," Joe said, scooping caponata on a piece of bread.

"Yes, she did. She didn't put raisins in hers, but I like the raisins," Dominic said.

"When you're right, you're right. The girl can cook," Joe said.

"You like this girl," Dominic said as more of an observation than a question.

"And you don't?" Joe replied.

"I don't mean fuck her, like her. I mean like her, like her," Dominic chuckled.

"You know she's been around," Joe said.

"So have you Cuz," Dominic laughed. "You think those uptown and garden district bitches you're so fond of haven't sucked a dick or two?"

"She's too young," Joe replied.

"Oh, I see; she's too young to go out with but not too young to screw," Dominic laughed. "Okay, you stick to what you know best. You've been successful so far."

"Fuck you, Dom," Joe said as he got up. "Let's go to Christos for one."

"I'd give Sandy a little time to cool off if I were you," Dominic suggested.

"So you threw me under the bus with Sandy?"

"No, of course not, Chris did," Dominic chuckled. He got up and slapped Joe on the back. "Come on; we'll go downstairs and have a drink with your girlfriend."

The bar was almost full. There was a large bachelor party and the usual single men in a wide range of ages. Three dancers latched on to the bachelor party.

Joe went to the bar and got two more beers. "Your caponata was good," Joe said as he picked up the beers.

"Thanks," she replied and walked away.

Joe joined Dominic standing near the front door.

"Sam, we need more cherries," one of the guys from the bachelor party hollered.

Sam brought them a rock glass full of cherries. "Slow down guys; I'm running out of cherries."

"Sam we really don't need the cherries, just need the stems."

"Do I want to know why?" Sam laughed.

"These girls are showing us how they tie a knot in a cherry stem with their tongues. Can you do it?" The young man asked, smiling.

"Honey, I got a better shot at tying your dick in a knot," Sam said and walked away.

Everyone in earshot howled. Joe could not believe what he just heard. Dominic backhanded Joe's arm and laughed.

Joe handed Dominic his beer bottle, "I gotta go."

On Joe's drive home, he gave himself a pep talk. He was going to get back into his normal routine. This little girl was sucking him back into his old life. He loved his family, but he had a different life uptown, and he intended to get back to it. The little bitch might be right about the exercise, he thought. He started to laugh remembering her cherry stem remark. She's unbelievable.

Claude waited outside of the club while Sam talked to Dominic. They walked out of the bar smiling, so it wasn't bad news. She joined Claude, and they said goodnight to Dominic.

"Let's hear it," Claude said.

"Hear what?" Sam giggled. "They are moving me over to Christos." She jumped up and down. "Can you believe it? I start next week."

"I don't get it," Claude said. "Out of the blue, they just decided to put you in Christos. Did you talk to Sandy?"

"No, I didn't talk to anyone about Christos since that conversation I had with Chris," Sam said. "You don't seem very happy for me. Is there something I'm missing?"

"No, Sha, I'm happy for you. I know you wanted out of Azure. I'll miss you," Claude hugged Sam's shoulder.

"Anything I should know about Sandy?" Sam asked.

"Professional. All business. I heard Sandy gets a percentage over a certain amount. So no games. The complete opposite of Azure. And there's no love lost between Sandy and Joe," Claude added.

"Why?"

"I don't know. They go back a long way. They all grew up together."

"You know we can still walk home together," Sam smiled.

"Of course," Claude grinned. "You didn't have a chance to say goodbye to any of the girls."

"Screw those whores," Sam snickered. "Hey Claude, do you think Joe had anything to do with this?"

"Sha, I think Joe had everything to do with this."

Eames Chair

Wednesday, October 27, 1993

Christos was located on the corner of Bourbon and Conti. There were three double-door entrances. One on Conti near the corner. The other two on Bourbon. One near the corner, the other parallel with the service end of the bar. The bar ran the length of the narrow room with 15 backless bar stools. A long bench with four small round cafe tables ran opposite the bar between the two Bourbon Street doors. Each had two bentwood chairs at them. The walls were covered with money, memorabilia, and knickknacks. There was an ornate oval clock above the bar register that was right twice a day.

Through the large archway going into the next room, you could see the stage. That room housed 19 cafe tables that matched the ones in the bar. The same bentwood chairs surrounded them. There were three doors to the right of the stage. The first went to the liquor room and upstairs office. The next two were men's and ladies restrooms.

The Conti end of the bar had a pull handle silver cigarette machine on a short wall between the door and bar. The service area for the waitresses was at the other end. There was a pass-through from the back bar to the music room. Next to the service bar was a door that led to the storage room that housed supplies, beer, and a drop safe. You had to go through that room to access the back bar.

"Hi, I'm Sam."

"Sandy. Come around and get behind the bar. You can leave your bag in the back room."

Sam did, and Sandy handed her a bank bag.

"This is always $200. Count it every time it's handed to you. You don't go into my register, and I don't go into yours. We run our charges the same as Azure. Why don't you put your money in the register and we'll go from there."

"Thank you for this opportunity," Sam said.

"Not necessary. I was told to put you on the schedule," Sandy replied, then walked away.

"Welcome fucking aboard," Sam said under her breath.

Sandy explained everything precisely. No room for question. "I always work service," Sandy said, "I'll take care of the first couple of barstools. You will need to be able to handle the rest. The bar gets two, sometimes three deep. Aren't you the one who had the accident?"

"Yes."

"Are you going to have a problem washing glasses?"

"No."

"Which hand?"

Sam held up her left hand and Sandy took her wrist to pull her hand up and closer for a better look. Sandy's thumb gently rubbed the inside of Sam's wrist, triggering an unwanted sensation.

"Can you move it okay?" Sandy asked snapping Sam back into the moment.

She wiggled her thumb. "Charity did a good job stitching me up."

That was the end of their chitchat. It was back to business. Sandy was slightly taller than average with the most incredible Caribbean blue eyes. They were almond-shaped with heavy brows and long lashes accenting them. A head of thick light brown hair that could easily sun bleach blonde. With shorts and a T-shirt as a uniform, it was evident Sandy was in good shape.

Sandy kept a watchful eye over Sam. It didn't take long to realize she was a winner. She was comfortable behind a bar. As the night went on and the crowd ebbed and flowed, they got a rhythm. It was like a choreographed ballet. Sam liked everything about Christos. The music, the pace, the clientele. Even the unsettled feeling she had about Sandy was subsiding. The time flew, and before Sam knew it, the band hit their last note. Then Sandy turned the lights up.

"What the fuck!" Sam spat out. The customers laughed. Sandy didn't. The lights were bright enough for a night game in Yankee Stadium. There was even an audible gasp from some customers. Sam ducked into the back room to her purse. She came back behind the bar sporting sunglasses. Sandy smirked, and customers were laughing. After the night's receipts were counted, Sam handed Sandy the tip cup.

"You count it," Sandy said. "Do you want a drink?"

"No, thank you," Sam replied. As she was counting and dividing the tips, there was a knock at the door.

Sandy waved an okay to Aaron, the doorman.

She heard Claude's voice directed to Sandy, "how do you like my girl?"

"She's good," Sandy said. "Want a drink?"

"No thanks. I'm going to walk Sam home and see what's shaking at the other end of the quarter."

"Sandy likes you," Claude said as they headed down Bourbon.

"What's not to like?" Sam joked. "What a body on that Sandy."

"No shit. And those eyes. Every drag queen in town would kill for those eyes," Claude laughed.

"I swear they're turquoise. I've never seen eyes that color. Do you really think Sandy likes me? The Sandy, Sam thing was annoying him. People were making jokes all night."

"Oh my god, you sound so needy. As long as you make him money, he won't give a fuck what your name is."

"He's very stoic," Sam remarked.

"That he is. I've never been able to figure him out. He plays his cards close to the vest," Claude noted.

"Girlfriend, boyfriend?" Sam asked.

"Girls," Claude laughed to himself. "Did I ever tell you about the time he kicked Joe's ass over a girl?"

"Joe DiLeo?"

Claude shook his head, "right on Bourbon Street. It was years ago. I never really knew the details, but I'm sure Joe had it coming."

"I thought you liked Joe?"

"I do, but that doesn't make him less of a prick," Claude chuckled. "I'm surprised you and Sandy hadn't crossed paths before now."

"Andrew didn't like jazz. After he left, I was hoping to get in the door, so I stayed out of there. Not too many people get hired off of a bar stool."

"You know, you're a smart girl for being so young."

"I'm an old soul," they both laughed.

Thursday, October 28, 1993

Sam's Eames chair and ottoman were being delivered today. She was so excited. She had wanted that chair since the first time she sat in one in Larry's apartment.

One morning shortly after she moved back, she met Felice for coffee and beignets (deep-fried fritter covered with powdered sugar) on her way to work.

"You want an Eames chair?" Felice asked. "I'm guessing you have no idea how expensive they are?"

Sam smiled, shook her head, and took a sip of her coffee.

"$2700 plus tax and delivery."

Sam choked on her coffee.

A couple of days later she met Felice at Mencher's. Felice was still with a customer, so Sam wandered around all the beautiful furniture.

"May I help you?" a young man asked Sam.

"I'm waiting for Felice Sax, but thank you."

"Your welcome."

"Oh, let me ask you. Do you have an Eames chair?"

"Sure, I'll show you."

"That's not necessary. If you could just tell me where it is, that would be great," Sam said as sweetly as she could.

"Sure, just take the elevator to four. It will be on your left when you get off," he said, pointing to the elevator on the back wall.

"Thank you so much. If you see Felice, would you let her know where I am? I'm Sam."

"Will do Samantha."

She didn't bother correcting him. Felice found Sam sitting in the Eames chair.

"I have to have this," Sam said, smiling. "How do you make it recline?"

"You don't. The chair doesn't recline."

"I saw one that did."

"It was a fake. Eames chairs don't recline. Never have. Never will."

"Asshole Larry," Sam said under her breath. "I don't want black."

"That's not a problem. We have a lot of colors to work with. The money part is the problem. I could get you a little discount for cash and throw in the delivery, but you're still looking at close to 27."

"I figured it out. I'm setting my checks aside from Azure for the chair."

"How much are your checks?"

"Somewhere between $85 and $100 a week."

"You're insane. You realize that, don't you?"

"Yeah, I know."

Sam ordered her chair five and a half months later. Felice said it would take as long as eight weeks to get the chair, so when she had $2000, she ordered it, agreeing to pay the balance on delivery. A beautiful warm tan leather with a medium finish on the wood. It complimented the sofa perfectly. She would never have bought the chair had she known Andrew would be going to Vegas. That money would have been in the bank. He didn't get the offer until a couple of weeks after she ordered it.

It was almost 4:30 when the delivery men got there. Sam made herself a drink and sat in the middle of the living room on the floor with her legs crossed. Drink in hand, staring at her chair; she made a toast, "here's to you, Larry Bateman, you piece of shit."

When Sam turned 22 she was working at a bar in Fort Lauderdale that was on the Intracoastal. There was plenty of dock space for large boats. The clientele was well-heeled. She worked days behind the patio bar. Monday through Friday, 11:00 to 7:00. Rainy days could kill the business but the sunny days more than made up for them. All the people that came by boat bellied up to the patio bar. Those were the customers that didn't care how much a check was and tended to tip above average. This was a terrific job, and Sam planned on being there for years.

One afternoon between lunch and cocktail hour, a 42' Hatteras sport fisherman docked. Five guys in T-shirts and shorts got off the boat and headed to the bar.

"Hey darling, how's your day going?" one of them asked.

"Good," Sam smiled. "You catch anything?

"We sure did. Five nice size dolphins and my friend Billy here got himself a huge black grouper," he said, slapping his friend on the back. "I think we're all going to have a beer and five shots of Crown."

"You each want five shots of Crown?" Sam joked. They all laughed. Sam went about making drinks. "What kind of beer?"

"Bud's good darling. What's your name?"

"Sam."

"Samantha?"

"No, just Sam."

"Well just Sam, I'm Larry," then he introduced his four friends. They ate and had a couple more beers. Laughing, joking, and reliving their perfect day on the water.

"Sam, you like dolphin?" Larry asked.

"Love it," she gave a big grin.

While Larry paid the check, one of the guys got Sam a large bag of fresh dolphin. Larry paid with a corporate credit card. Bateman - Tassino Construction. He left a 30% tip.

A week later, Larry walked into the bar. "Hey, just Sam. Do you remember me?" Larry smiled.

"Sure I do," Sam grinned. "What can I get for you, Larry?"

"Crown and ginger, darling. I'm impressed."

"Why?"

"You remembered my name."

"You don't forget customers that tip 30%," Sam thought.

Larry asked a few getting to know you questions. Then offered her a job working a party at his home the following weekend. As per Larry's request, Sam stopped by one morning before work to see if anything might be needed.

Larry lived in a well-secured high-rise overlooking Port Everglades. Sam's name had been left with the doorman for access. The apartment was huge. The housekeeper took Sam to the bar and offered her coffee.

"I'd love a cup. Black, thank you." The housekeeper returned with the coffee. "I don't see any wine. Is it kept elsewhere or should I put it on the list."

The housekeeper opened what appeared to be a closet door next to the bar. It had been converted into a temperature-controlled wine room.

"Wow, this bar is stocked better than the one I work at. The only thing I can see is gin. Larry could get a bottle or two. Otherwise, it's all good."

The housekeeper thanked Sam, and as she walked Sam to the door, she pointed out some of the apartments features. It was originally two apartments which accounted for the size. The balcony wrapped completely around the building, and so every room in the condo had balcony access. She didn't see or hear from Larry until that night.

A different woman answered the door and introduced herself as the caterer. Sam got behind the bar and set up what she needed. Soon Larry appeared. "Hey darling, got everything you need?"

"Yeah, fine."

Larry pulled out six bottles of wine, three white and three red, then locked the door. "If you need more wine, let me know. And Sam, I don't want you to take any tips from my guests."

The bar was located in the end room, which served as a den. The large space had a poker table opposite the bar by the sliding glass doors which led to the balcony. A television was built into the wall with a long sofa and chairs at either side facing it. The chairs were sleek with matching ottomans. Very contemporary and from the conversations Sam could overhear, extremely comfortable. As soon as someone got up, another eager person would replace them.

Larry stopped in to check on Sam from time to time but didn't stay. He was working the room. Sam pieced this scenario together. Larry owned a large construction company. The guests were former and current clients. Larry did interior construction. Large commercial spaces, office buildings, shopping malls.

It was almost midnight when everything was cleaned up. Sam was sitting in one of the much talked about chairs when Larry walked in. Sam started to get up.

"Stay," Larry said, waving his hand down.

"Great chair," Sam remarked.

Larry smiled and leaned over the chair, his left hand gripping the arm of the chair he moved in closer to Sam. His right hand slid down the side, then the chair reclined. Sam mistook his intention. She thought he was coming in for a kiss.

"Oh, I have to get one of these," Sam said in an almost sultry voice.

"I think an Eames chair might be a little out of your budget, darling."

Sam sat up. It took everything she had not to tell him off.

"What do you drink, just Sam?" Larry asked from behind the bar, oblivious to the fact she felt insulted.

"I'm good, Larry. I've got to get going."

The caterer stepped into the room. "Everything is done, Mr. Bateman."

Sam got up and stood alongside the caterer and her helper. Larry paid the three and walked them to the door. The two women stepped out before Sam. As Sam walked through the doorway, Larry leaned towards her. "I'd like you to stay," he said almost at a whisper.

Sam looked up at him and gave her head a slight shake, then joined the two women at the elevator.

Four days later, between lunch and happy hour, the Hatteras docked. Larry walked up to the bar with three of the four friends that were with him the first time.

"Hey darling, how's your day going?"

"Much better now that you guys are here," Sam said, smiling.

They had a few beers, they ate, and Larry asked for the check. "I need your help darling," Larry said as he was signing the credit card slip.

"Just make it an even $100," Sam joked. "It makes the math easier."

Larry laughed, "how am I going to get you to have dinner with me?"

"Ask," Sam smiled.

"Tomorrow night? Bring a change of clothes. I'll pick you up here on the boat."

Sam picked up the credit card slip as Larry walked to his boat. He left her a $100 tip.

Larry took Sam to a cute little place you could only access by boat. It was built in the twenties by a bootlegger. They had a few drinks in the bar once frequented by mobsters. Then had dinner in the restaurant once frequented by presidents.

Larry loved the stories of her uncle and her time spent in his gym after school. "Did your uncle teach you how to box?"

Sam chuckled, "no, but he taught me how to work a speed bag. I can't begin to count the hours I've spent on the speed bag," she laughed. "I'm actually quite good."

Larry told Sam all about his company, and it's meager beginnings. His ex-father-in-law was prominent in the construction business in New Jersey and helped him and his ex-wife get started in Florida. She was the Tassino in Bateman-Tassino Construction. His ex was still his partner. Larry said they had a good working relationship and only wanted the best for each other. No kids to complicate matters. Larry was 34. Sam didn't mind the age difference, in fact she preferred it.

Larry had never met a girl so comfortable in her skin. So unaffected by her looks. Most women couldn't pass a mirror without trying to get a glimpse. Larry witnessed Sam on two occasions, breeze right by mirrors and never turned her head. Once in his apartment and the other in the restaurant they just left. He liked that.

Larry docked the boat back at the marina. He took Sam below and slowly undressed her. She was breathtaking.

"Do you have a condom?" she asked.

Larry stood there with a stupid look on his face.

"That's okay; I have one," she said, reaching for her bag.

"She's a pro," Larry thought. When Sam handed him the condom, and he took a step back saying, "I'm not using one of those darling. I'm a grown-ass man."

"Then you're not getting laid, darling," Sam said sarcastically. Sam reached for her clothes.

"How the hell did this go sideways," Larry thought. She already had her bra and panties on. Larry cupped her shoulders to hold her still, "let's slow down darling. Please tell me why you think this is necessary."

"AIDS for one. Not to mention a laundry list of other diseases."

"You think I'm gay?" Larry's voice elevated.

"Please don't be naive. We're not just sleeping with each other. We're sleeping with all of our past partners and their partners. Are you 100% sure about them?" she asked.

Larry resigned himself to the fact that the only way he was going to have her was with a condom. "This'll be a first," Larry said as he took the condom out of Sam's hand.

"You've never used a condom?" she asked surprised.

"No darling, I haven't."

Sam took the condom back, "let me do this." She smiled, stood on her toes, and leaned in to kiss him.

He grabbed her hair with one hand and her ass with the other and pulled her in. His kiss was rough, and then he eased into it. Sam started to unbutton his shirt slowly. Her mouth followed, licking and kissing all the way down. By the time she got to his pants, his cock was so hard it sprang out ready to attack. She stroked it up and down a few times then held it up while she ran her tongue over his balls. She sat back on her heels and opened the condom. He watched as she placed the center of the condom on the tip of her tongue and then into her mouth. Her hand tightly gripped the base of his cock, her lips touching the head and in one quick motion, her mouth slid down his shaft and the condom with it.

Her mouth slid up and down a few more times when Larry grabbed her hair and pulled her up. He had to be in her. He propped her up on the edge of the bed. Her right leg was dangling, toes barely brushing the floor. He hiked her left leg over his shoulder and moved her panties to the side then slid two fingers in her and she moaned. She was wet. A guttural noise came out of her as he entered her with punishing force. He kept that pace holding her ass in one hand and her calf in the other until he came. It was so powerful his vision blurred.

"Are you okay?" Larry asked after he recovered.

"Of course," Sam smiled. "Why wouldn't I be?"

"I was a little rough."

"I like it rough," she said with a schoolgirl grin.

"You are so fucking hot," Larry said before kissing her again.

They heard a knock on the side of the boat. "Company?" Sam laughed.

"Mr. Bateman, are you onboard?" then the man knocked again.

Larry quickly put his pants on, gave Sam a peck on the forehead, "I'll be right back, darling." He was back in two minutes with a big grin on his face.

"Who was it?"

"The dock master. We're going to have to get you a muzzle," he joked.

As they drove back to Sam's car, Larry explained his schedule. He had a few big jobs going on throughout the state. He asked Sam to go down to Key West on his boat the following weekend. He was at the dock when she got off work. They had a great time, and so after only their first day in Key West, Larry was planning their next trip. It went on like that for months. He would plan short trips on the boat. Sometimes just for dinner, sometimes for a weekend. He took her to Atlantic City for a heavyweight fight. She would cook him dinner at her place and on one rare occasion, she spent the night at his.

Halloween fell on a Saturday that year. Larry was taking Sam to New Orleans for the weekend. She was going to have one of the night bartenders come in early so she could catch a 6:00 flight out of Miami on Friday. She made arrangements to see Felice. It was going to be a great weekend. So before leaving on Thursday night, she reminded the night bartender again that he was coming in early on Friday. A woman stopped her as she got out from behind the bar.

"Are you Sam?" she asked.

"Yes, can I help you?"

"I'm Angie, can we go somewhere to talk?" Sam had a confused look on her face. "Angie Tassino," the woman said.

"Larry's ex-wife?"

"Wife!" the woman sneered.

The color ran out of Sam's face. They went to a small 24-hour diner a few blocks away. Angie was older than Larry. She was well maintained but stuck in the style of her youth.

"So how long have you been screwing my husband?" Sam started to get up. "No, sit back down. Honey, how could you not know he was married?"

She was right. How could she not see it? All the questions she never asked herself came rushing to mind.

"How old are you?"

"22."

"Jesus Christ," Angie chuckled. "Sam, you're not the first. You're the youngest, but not the first. Unfortunately, you will probably not be the last. We're not getting a divorce. I don't want one, and he won't walk away from the money."

"Why would you want to stay married to him?" Sam meekly asked.

Angie grinned, "neither one of my parents are in good health. I've been back and forth to New Jersey more times than I can count this year. They made sacrifices, personal sacrifices to help get us going. And to keep us afloat. At one point they mortgaged their home. They love Larry. Sometimes I think more than they love me," Angie joked. "I'm not going to put my problems on their plate. I've done nineteen years. I can do a few more."

"19 years?"

"Yes, we'll be married 19 years in December."

"How is that possible?" Sam asked, genuinely surprised.

"We were young. Larry was 20, and I was 23." Sam looked stunned. "How old did he tell you he was?"

"34." Sam felt foolish. She apologized for what she had done and assured Angie she was out of Larry's life forever.

She was able to leave the restaurant before the tears started. Larry tried in vain to get Sam to talk to him. It was done. Sam was shell shocked for a couple of weeks and was hoping an evening out with her high school friends would bring her back to life. It was a bachelorette party being held at a male strip club.

Armed with $50 in singles, Sam met her friends there. Watching the women was a better show then the guys on stage. If a guy acted that way in a strip joint, he'd find himself in a dumpster. Sam was having a great time. She felt a tap on her shoulder. She turned to see a familiar dick in her face. A couple of the girls squealed, "Andrew."

"I feel like such an asshole," Sam said her head laying on Andrew's chest.

"Stop beating yourself up. Did you love him?"

"No, not really. So you heard my sad story, what's yours?" Sam joked.

"We were together for almost a year. I thought we should spice things up, so I talked her into a ménage à trois." Andrew paused, "she left me for her."

Sam tried in vain to suppress a burst of laughter. "I'm sorry Andrew."

"You're so empathetic."

"No please, don't be pissed. I am sorry."

"I'm not pissed. I'm sure I'll be laughing about it myself someday."

"Did you love her?"

"Yes."

"How long have you been dancing?"

"Close to a year now. The money is good. Are you still working at Jordon Marsh?"

"No, just bartending."

"Does your uncle still have the gym?"

"Yeah."

"How's your mother doing, or should I ask?" Andrew joked.

"Still crazier than a sprayed roach," Sam replied.

"You haven't changed," Andrew laughed. "Why did we break up?"

"I don't think we did. We just drifted in separate directions after high school."

And so they licked each other's wounds.

"Sam, are you sure you want to leave now? Why don't you stick around until after the season?" her manager asked.

"I know the timing doesn't make much sense, but Mardi Gras is in a few weeks. I'll miss you guys," Sam smiled.

"If it doesn't work out, you come see me. I can't promise your same job back, but I'll find a spot for you if you come back home."

Sam thanked him and thought to herself as she left. "I'm not leaving home; I'm going home. New Orleans."

Two Johns

Saturday, October 30, 1993

Bourbon Street was jumping earlier than usual, some people donning quite elaborate costumes.

The bar was already busy. Sandy handed Sam the bank bag on the run. She put her money in the drawer as quickly as possible.

"Count it, Sam," Sandy yelled while making a drink. Within 20 minutes, the bar was all caught up.

"Should I wear a costume tomorrow?"

"No. What's the first thing I said to you Wednesday?" Sam stared at Sandy wordless. "Count your bank every time," Sandy said in a sharp tone.

"It was busy, and I wanted to help."

"You wanna help? Do what I tell you to do. That's all the help I need from you."

"Holy shit," Sam thought, "this guy is gonna make my life miserable."

Sam and Sandy were hustling all night. A few hours into the night, Sandy said, "I guess I should have had you come in a little earlier, my mistake."

Sam took that as an apology.

Dominic and Chris walked in towards the end of the evening. Dominic left after a quick drink, most likely to Azure. The band hit their last note for the evening. Sam had her sunglasses ready. The lights came up and she saw Sandy wearing sunglasses too. They smiled at each other.

"How do you like it so far?" Chris asked.

"It's good. I like it a lot," Sam replied.

"Sam, we let the staff have a shift drink. Go ahead and fix yourself one, " Chris offered.

"No thanks," Sam said as she went about cleaning up.

Sam didn't seem herself to Chris. He'd hoped it wasn't a mistake moving her here. Christos was a much faster pace. Sandy handed Chris the reading from both registers. Chris studied them, then looked at Sam.

"Is something wrong?" Sam asked Chris.

"Just the opposite Sam. You've done well. Thank you."

"You're welcome, Chris."

Sam was ready to go as soon as Claude got there.

"I feel like I'm walking on eggshells around him," Sam said as they walked down Bourbon.

"Sandy's got a control thing going on. You were shoved on him. He'll come around. Just keep ringing that register."

Sunday, October 31, 1993

It was almost 11:00 when she woke up. She quickly made her bed, brushed her teeth, and got into her running clothes. She'd run through the Faubourg Marigny to Bywater and back. That would be three miles. It was cold; high 40's. Great running weather, once she got started.

As she was crossing Esplanade, she looked to the left. She noticed balloons halfway down the block on a sign she couldn't quite make out. Curiosity rerouted her to the beautiful two-story home. A couple was walking out with lamps in hand. A well dressed man approached Sam as she walked in.

"Hi, everything should be marked. It's cash only. If you have any questions, just ask me or my partner, John, over there," he pointed to an equally well-dressed man. "Feel free to look upstairs. I'm John."

Sam gave a look he was used to.

"Yes honey, we're both named John. Don't ask," he chuckled.

"I'm Sam."

"How cute," John said as he walked away to greet newcomers.

Sam wandered through the house. Some rooms were empty, others were picked over. She had her eye on a rug in one of the upstairs bedrooms. Sam made her way back down to the kitchen and spotted beautiful patio furniture in the courtyard through the window. All teak. A rectangular table with two armchairs and four side chairs.

"John, sorry to interrupt, but is the patio set for sale?" Sam asked.

"Honey if it's not nailed down, it's for sale," he said, leading her to the courtyard. "Grill too."

"I have a grill," Sam said. She was able to buy it from Andrew for $100. He realized he didn't have the grilling gene most men possess.

"Will $200 work for you?" John asked.

"$175 would work better," Sam jokes checking the flip side of the cushions.

John hesitated, "okay, $175. I noticed you admiring a rug upstairs. You want to throw that in?"

"I can't swing it. Sorry, I do love it though. So I'm going to run home and get the money. 15 minutes. I live on Chartres. I'll make arrangements to pick it up tomorrow morning if that's okay with you?"

"Sorry, Sam. Everything has to be out by 6:00 tonight."

Sam had no intention of losing this deal. "Okay, I'll figure something out."

Sam called Felice as soon as she walked into her apartment. She was relieved when Felice answered the phone. Sam explained her dilemma, hoping her friend had a solution.

"If it was any day but Sunday I could get a couple of the delivery guys. I don't know how I can help."

"We can carry it," Sam blurted out.

"Oh my God. Where do you come up with these insane ideas?"

"They're chairs. We can carry a few chairs a couple of blocks."

"And a dining table. Not to mention, getting it up the stairs." Felice sounded exasperated.

"We'll go over the balcony. I have rope. PLEEEASE. I really want this set. I'll owe you."

"I've lost track of all the ones you owe me. I'm on my way."

"Thank you, thank you, thank you. Let yourself in. I'm going back to pay the guy. I'll meet you here."

Sam ran back and paid one of the John's. She told him her plan, took one of the armchairs and walked out. When she got to the sidewalk, she hoisted the chair up, balancing the seat on her head and started to walk to Chartres.

"Sam, hey, Sam." It was Sandy in a white pickup truck on the opposite side of Esplanade.

"Hi Sandy," she yelled back and kept walking.

"What a piece of work," Sandy said to himself as he made a u-turn around the neutral ground. (median dividing the street) "You need help?" Sandy asked as she kept walking.

"No thanks, I'm good."

Sandy got out of the truck and took the chair off of Sam's head. "Get in the truck, Sam," Sandy said while putting the chair in the back.

"There's five more chairs," Sam said in a small voice.

"You were going to carry six chairs, one at a time balanced on your head to your place?"

"And a table."

"Of course. Come on, let's get the stuff."

"You know you really don't have to do this," Sam said, leading the way back into the house.

"Was that a thank you? I couldn't tell."

"Thank you. I really do appreciate this."

"Much better," Sandy said with a smile.

The two John's made a beeline for Sandy the minute they saw him. Sam did the introductions. They got a kick out of that Sam was the girl, and Sandy was the boy thing. They both helped Sandy put the chairs in the truck. The table was going to take a second trip.

Felice was already there when Sam walked in.

"Where have you been? I've been here for a half-hour."

"I got help," Sam said grinning. Sandy walked in holding a chair. "Felice, Sandy. Sandy, Felice."

"Hi. Where do you want this?" Sandy asked.

Sam went to the floor to ceiling windows and started to raise one, "outside, on the balcony."

"Sam, why don't you leave it inside until you get a dining room set?" Felice suggested.

"It'll look stupid," Sam said.

"You're right. The card table and folding chairs are a much better look."

"Ladies!" Sandy said still holding the chair.

"Inside," Sam conceded. The girls offered to help, but Sandy insisted on carrying the chairs up himself. "Do you want a beer or something?" Sam asked when he got the last chair up.

"I don't drink light beer."

"Neither do I. I have Heineken."

"Yes, thanks. That table might be a problem. I don't know if it's going to fit in the staircase," Sandy pointed out.

"Sam thought going over the balcony railing might be a better idea," Felice said.

"That's how they got the sofa in. I have rope," Sam added.

"Let's go get it and we can figure it out when we get back." Sam and Sandy headed back while Felice cleaned the chairs and heated up lunch.

"You have a great apartment."

"I love it. I hope to have it finished in a few more months. Thanks a lot. I really appreciate this."

"You're welcome. Maybe you can do me a good turn," Sandy asked with a boyish grin. "Can you come in an hour early?"

"Sure."

"You're doing good so far."

"Does that mean you're glad to have me there?"

"Baby steps Sam," Sandy laughed.

The two John's dropped what they were doing when Sandy walked in.

They got to the courtyard. Sam and Sandy looked at each other.

"Is this the same table?" Sam asked.

"Oh, we took the leaf out," John said, "easier to transport."

"Cool, I didn't realize that."

"We still have the rug."

"Sorry John, you got all my cash," Sam smiled.

"How much is it?" Sandy asked.

"$250, it's a Karastan," John said.

"Do you want it?" Sandy asked Sam.

"Yes, but—"

"John, what's the absolute best you can do for me?" Sandy interrupted Sam as he went into his pocket.

"$225," John replied.

Sandy counted his money. He looked at Sam, "do you have any money on you." She shook her head. "Here's where we are. I have $167 on me. I in no way want to insult you but given the timeline we have to work with, it's the best I can do. You guys talk it over."

As they were putting the rug into the truck, one of the John's came running out calling Sandy's name. He was carrying a carpet beater, "here Sandy, lagniappe. (something extra) It's an antique."

"Thank you," Sandy said. "What is it?"

"It's a beater," John replied with a smile.

"Turn around Sam," Sandy joked.

Sam took it from John and put it in the back of the truck, shaking her head. Sam was so happy she seemed childlike. Sandy couldn't help but smile. She was infectious.

"Alexander," Sandy said on the ride back to Sam's. Sam just looked at him, confused. "Sandy is short for Alexander."

"Oh, mines just Sam."

"I know. Dominic gave me a copy of your file."

"It was supposed to be Samangela. I don't know where the fuck my mother came up with that," Sam rolled her eyes. "At any rate, the hospital misunderstood and put Sam Angela Mancuso on the birth certificate. For reasons I will never understand, my mother didn't catch the mistake for months. She thought it was clever and here we are. Sam."

"That's a funny story. Sam suits you. Plus your initials spell Sam. Your mother was right. It is clever," Sandy smiled.

The two of them carried the rug up.

"Something smells good," Sandy said.

"Thanks. It's my homemade chicken soup. Stay for lunch. You'll love it. Big chunks of chicken and vegetables over pasta. It's more like a stew."

"We'll see. I should really get going after we get everything in."

"You have to eat. Please have a quick bite. Plus I'm a good cook," Sam smiled.

"And humble," Sandy laughed. "Alright, soup."

Felice was impressed with the rug. It was a tight squeeze, but they got the table up the stairs.

Sandy gravitated to the Eames chair. Felice cleaned and set the table. Sam was finishing up in the kitchen.

"I live on Toulouse," Felice was telling Sandy.

"I live in the Marigny. I bought a fixer-upper, I'm turning into a fourplex. Two of the apartments are completed. I'm doing a lot of the work myself." Sandy seemed relaxed, sipping his beer and chatting with Felice. He noted Sam moving in the kitchen with the same ease and confidence she had behind the bar.

"Get it while it's hot," Sam said as she put the bowls of soup on the table.

Everything looked delicious. Along with the soup was a large bowl of tossed salad and a basket of garlic bread. Appropriate plate and flatware at each setting.

"Sandy, would you like another beer?" Sam asked.

"No, thank you, water is fine," he said, holding the glass already on the table.

"I think I have about $60 in cash. I can give you a check for the rest."

"Just give me the money tonight."

"Nobody takes a fucking check anymore," Sam joked.

"You've got quite a mouth on you," Sandy snickered.

"Don't try to correct it, Sandy. It's been going on since she was a kid," Felice laughed.

"How long have you two known each other?"

The girls looked at each other and smiled.

"We've known each other since birth," Felice said.

"We were born at Charity on the same day," Sam said. "Our mother's shared a room."

"And you stayed friends your whole life? Sam, I thought you were from Florida?" Sandy asked.

"We lived in Florida most of my life. But Felice and I never lost touch of each other. Letters, phone calls. Her parents would come to Florida, and vice versa. Well, how's the soup?"

"The best I ever had. I'm not kidding."

Sam smiled.

The night got busy early, and Sandy was glad he had Sam come in ahead of schedule. He was business as usual.

"I love Halloween," Sam said to Sandy at 10:30.

"What's not to love. Drunk assholes in masks," Sandy sniped.

Sam knew Sandy wanted to distance himself from her. She didn't take it to heart. That's just who he was. Sam heard the faint sound of a siren. She looked down the bar. Sandy had stopped what he was doing. The noise got louder, and it was more than one. Outside the cops were scrambling to get people out of the street. The blaring sound of slow-moving fire engines down Bourbon was piercing. Customers were leaving the bar. Some were walking down to see what was going on. Others to flee the quarter.

Dominic stuck his head in, "it looks like they're stopping on St. Louis."

Sandy left the bar and walked down with Dominic. They were back in 20 minutes.

"Garbage can fire in the girl's room," Dominic said.

"Killed everybody's night because some stupid bitch put a cigarette in a garbage can," Sandy said pissed.

"They sent three fire trucks for a garbage can fire?" Sam laughed.

"Six. Three more came in from the other side of the quarter," Dominic said.

"That's crazy," Sam chuckled.

"No, it's not Sam," Sandy admonished her. "The french quarter burnt down twice. If someone says the word fire too loud, you're going to get a lot of fire trucks showing up."

Dominic went back to Azure. Sandy got back behind the bar. Some customers stayed. Few new customers came in. The night was shot. At 1:00 there were only two people at the bar. They were making out and didn't need attention. The band was playing for five tables. Sam and Sandy were standing side by side, staring out at Bourbon Street.

"Will you take a check now?" Sam laughed.

Sandy smiled, "you can pay me Wednesday."

"Will we close early?"

"No, we never close early," Sandy replied. "I like Felice. You're lucky to have her for a friend."

"I know," Sam smiled.

"You're a good cook."

"Thank you."

"You're a good bartender too. Welcome fucking aboard," Sandy snickered.

Woodstock

Tuesday, November 2, 1993

"I didn't eat lunch, so I'm starving," Sam said to Felice.

"Why did you skip lunch?"

"I had a customer, oh my god, what a pain in the ass. She got here at 10:30 and just left a few minutes ago. Five and a half hours."

"Did she buy out the store?" Felice laughed.

"One dress, one fucking dress for a dinner party with her boyfriend's family. Somebody needs to give this guy a heads up. I swear, if I see her coming in again, I'll run out the back door," Sam laughed. "So, where do you want to eat?" Felice hesitated. "Let me guess. Mr. B's."

"I love the place. And I'm calling in one of the I'll owe you one's."

"You know you're becoming very manipulative in your old age," Sam joked.

"I had a good teacher," Felice laughed. "I gotta go. I'll see you there, 6:15, 6:30."

"I have a good name for the place," Chris said.

"You don't get a vote. We lost our ass on your last good idea," Dominic joked.

"Go ahead, Chris," Joe chuckled.

"The Juke Joint," Chris said. "You know, like neighborhood blues bars."

"But we're putting jazz in here," Dominic reminded.

"Why, we have a jazz club a block away. We'd be competing against ourselves," Chris pointed out.

"See, he's not just a pretty face," Joe said to Dominic.

Charlie sat down with them after surveying the room. "Okay, if we get started on the 15th, we can get you up and running before New Year's Eve, providing there are no plumbing issues. If you leave the old bar, we won't have that to deal with. I'll get my plumber in here next week. That will give us a better idea of what we're working with."

"Good. Now, how many employees do we have here?" Joe asked Chris.

"Four. Two guys, two girls."

"Only four?"

"We're lucky we have that. They're not making money. Charlie agreed to use the guys as day laborers, and Dom and I will work the girls into the other clubs schedule. Now I'll have to deal with Sandy again."

"He can get off his high horse," Joe's voice elevated. "This is a temporary situation."

"Don't get yourself all worked up. I'll handle this," Chris said. "Are we done here? I have lamb shanks and orzo waiting for me. You're welcome to join us, Joe."

"No thanks, Chris. Give Lena my love."

"What am I, the redheaded stepchild?" Dominic bulked.

"You are coming to dinner at our house. Lena talked to Sarah this morning."

"Okay, I'm done," Joe laughed, as he picked up his briefcase and left heading up Bourbon.

Joe checked his watch. It was 6:10 and already dark. The time change. He got to Iberville, opened his car door, and noticed Sam crossing the street at the end of the block on Royal. "I'll bet she's going to Mr. B's," he thought. He stood there for a few seconds; car door still open. "Fuck it," he said out loud. He locked the car, threw his briefcase in the trunk, and walked down to Mr. B's. She was sitting at the bar by herself. The seats on either side were open. The bartender was placing her drink down just as Joe walked up.

"I'll have the same," he said and he pulled the barstool away from the bar.

"I'm waiting for Felice," Sam snapped.

"Whoa!" Joe said with his hands up.

"I'm sorry. I've had a trying day, and I haven't eaten a thing since 8:00."

Felice walked in the side door. "Hi Joe." She didn't seem surprised to see him next to Sam. "I have to beg off. I'm with a customer. They are renovating an entire house. I don't know when I'll be done."

"Go, make your money. I'm fine."

"I'll call you later," Felice said, walking. She turned back, "Joe make sure she eats. She gets mean when she's hungry."

"I already found that out Felice," Joe laughed, "the hard way." Then he turned to Sam. "Do you want to get something to eat? We can get a table," Joe asked.

"No," she snapped.

"Knock it off, Sam," Joe got the bartender's attention. "Can we get her a cup of gumbo and some bread?"

"Of course. Are you having anything?"

"Not just yet, but we'll take a couple of menus," Joe said.

Sam finished her gumbo.

"Better?" Joe asked.

"Yes, thank you."

"How are you making out at Christos?"

"Good," she smiled. "I really like it there, and I have a feeling, I have you to thank for that."

"You didn't seem very happy at Azure. So what do you like to eat?" Joe asked as they perused the menu.

"Pretty much everything. I'm not a fussy eater."

"You're a good cook."

"Is that a question?"

"No," Joe laughed. "Dominic said your meatballs and sauce were as good as our grandma's. That's quite a high bar in our family."

"Well, I learned from my grandmother. Maybe they came from the same village," she joked.

"Is that where you learned Italian?"

"Yeah, she didn't speak English."

They ordered dinner. Joe was looking at the wine list when the salads came, "Any preference?"

"The drier, the better," Sam said.

Joe looked up at Sam and smiled. Then he stood up and pushed his barstool back. He was looking all over the floor.

Sam looked down, "did you drop something?"

"No, I'm looking for your salad."

Sam giggled, "I've always eaten fast."

"Slow down. You're such a health nut. You should know that's not good for you."

"Health nut? I cook fresh. That's not nuts. That's as it should be."

"And how much do you work out?"

"I run three miles daily. Three of the days, I run to the gym and do a circuit on the machines and run home. Sometimes I throw in laps in the pool."

"You're so disciplined. Where does that come from?"

"My uncle. That whole body, temple thing," she chuckled.

"Your Uncle Jack?"

"Yeah, Uncle Giacomo."

"What is he doing now?"

"He has a gym in Fort Lauderdale," she smiled. "I've spent many hours there. When I was little, if my mom was working, I'd go to the gym after school. It was only three blocks from my school. I'd do my homework or draw. That's how the whole art thing got started. My little stick men became men."

"What art thing?"

"Oh, I thought you knew. I'm an artist."

"Portraits, landscapes?"

"No, just boxers. And boxing gyms."

"Do you sell your work?"

"Yeah, I've done some art shows in Florida. I tried to get into galleries here with no luck."

"I know a few gallery owners."

"Thanks, but I've already tried the ones in Orleans Parish."

"You've tried Buckingham Gallery?"

"They said my work was interesting, but the subject matter had too narrow of an audience." Joe gave her a look just shy of pity. "It's okay. One day you'll be telling people, she used to work for me," Sam smiled.

"I'd like to see your work."

"Well, next time you take me home from Charity, I'll show you my studio. It's in the loft of my apartment," Sam joked as she finished her second glass of wine.

"Do you want more wine? I can order another bottle," Joe grinned.

"No, Mr. DiLeo. I have to keep my wits around you."

"Tell me, Ms. Mancuso, how long did you live here before your parents moved to Florida?"

"Oh, that's too long of a story for this late in the evening," Sam smiled as the bartender cleared their plates.

Joe put his arm in front of Sam, showing his watch, "it's only 7:45. We have time for the Reader's Digest version."

Sam took his wrist and pulled it closer. She was surprised his watch was an old Bulova with a fraying brown leather band. She thought he would be sporting a Rolex or some equivalent. She ran her finger along the side of the band, just brushing his skin. Her eyes slowly rose to meet his. He could feel his dick getting hard. The bartender cleared his throat. Joe's eyes came up, looking at the bartender. Sam's eyes lowered demurely. They both grinned as people do when caught in a private moment.

"Can I get you coffee or dessert?" the bartender asked.

"Bread pudding," Sam blurted out.

"Okay, one bread pudding and two coffees," Joe looked at Sam, and she nodded her head in agreement. "And two Remy's also please."

The bartender put brandy snifters in front of them and poured the Remy Martin. "I'll be back shortly with your coffee and bread pudding," he said.

"Alright, let's hear it," Joe smiled.

"Fasten your seatbelt," she smiled as she picked up her brandy snifter. "So, you know, Woodstock?" Joe gave her a blank look. "The music festival in 1969."

"Yes, of course, I know what it is."

"Well, my mother and a couple of her friends went to Woodstock. She was 19. While at Woodstock, they heard about the New Orleans Pop Festival and decided to go. A lot of the same acts were appearing."

"One minute. The New Orleans Pop Festival?"

"Yeah, it was a couple of weeks after Woodstock. Well, it was held in Prairieville."

"That's near Gonzales," Joe interrupted.

"Okay, can you reserve all your questions and comments to the end of the story?"

"My apologies," Joe smirked. "I have just never heard—"

"You're still talking!" Sam scolded.

"The floor is all yours," Joe grinned.

The bartender returned with their coffee and bread pudding. Sam dug into the pudding, taking a quick bite and proceeded with her story.

"After the festival, they decided to spend a few days in New Orleans before going back to Florida. It was there that my mother realized she was pregnant by some guy she met at Woodstock."

"You're kidding; you were conceived at Woodstock?"

"So, I was told. Now sta zitto!" (shut up) Sam went on with her story. "Well, going home was out of the question. She was afraid and ashamed. She was able to find a job babysitting and light housekeeping in exchange for room and board. She told her family she was attending school here. After a couple of weeks, she told her employers about her situation. They talked to their priest, who came up with a solution. She would stay in her current position. A financially well to do couple who were unable to have children would adopt her baby. They would take care of all of her medical and personal needs in-kind. She could then return to Florida no one the wiser and her child would have a good home."

Joe was mesmerized by the story.

"Then, my mother went into labor at seven months. I was three pounds, ten ounces when I was born. My mother was put into a room with another woman who gave birth to a girl that day. The couple who intended to adopt me came to the hospital. He went to the office to let them know he was not going to be financially responsible for the medical bills. The hospital stood firm and made him pay as per their agreement for the birth and my mother's room. He didn't have to pay the future prenatal bills. The wife went to my mother's room to let her know they were not interested in adopting a baby with potential health issues. So there she was, not sure if she had a place to go, with a baby nobody wanted. She didn't know if I was going to live or die."

Joe cupped one of her hands in both of his.

"Her roommate was appalled by the way this good catholic couple treated my mother," Sam did air quotes when saying good catholic.

"She was heartbroken when hearing my mother's story. In the next days, when they brought her baby in for feeding, my mom would go down to the nursery to see me. The morning both women were to check out of the hospital, my mother was invited to stay with her roommate. She and her husband lived above their music store."

"Phyllis and Manny Sax," Joe said. He could see her eyes getting glassy.

"Yes. I was in the hospital for seven more weeks. After that, the doctors wanted me to stay in New Orleans for at least a month for follow up. You know, to make sure I maintained my weight. So during that time with Aunt Phyllis and Uncle Manny's help, my mother wrote my uncle, her brother, and told him the whole story. He came and got us. My Uncle Giacomo and Uncle Manny are good friends to this day."

"That's an incredible story," Joe said.

"Oh, wait. There's a addendum to the story," Sam said.

"Addendum?" Joe smiled.

"Yeah, wait. The fucking priest—"

"The fucking priest," Joe interrupted. "Really, Sam?"

"Aspetta," (wait) Sam held up her hand in a stop motion. "The priest," Sam smiled at Joe, "shows up at the Sax's shortly before we left for Florida. Told my mother, now that I was healthy, he had another good catholic couple that was interested in adopting me."

"Fucking priest," Joe said.

"I know. When my uncle heard that, he wanted to go to the church and kick the priest's ass," Sam laughed.

"So why, Sam?" Joe asked.

She told him the story. She told him about growing up in Fort Lauderdale, her cousins, her aunt, all prompted by him. Joe wanted to know everything about her. There were so many Sam's in those stories. She was cute. She was beautiful. She was funny. She was vulnerable. She was wise beyond her years yet childlike. Not wanting the evening to end, Joe ordered two more Remy's.

"Did you go to college?"

"No, I wanted to. Art, I wanted to get a fine art degree. I figured I'd work for a year and save for school. What can I say? Life got in the way."

"So, you tended bar?"

"Yeah, and worked retail. Jordon Marsh. It's like Holmes. I hate it when I do that."

"Do what?" Joe asked.

"Saying yeah. I've got to stop saying that word."

Joe laughed, "that's the word you say that upsets you?"

"Yes!"

"No other word?"

"Fuck no," Sam giggled.

Joe just shook his head. "And what brought you home?"

"Andrew and I were dating again, and he got the job at Blush. He asked me if I wanted to tag along. Here I am."

"Dating again?" Joe asked.

"Yeah," she took a deep breath. "Yes, we dated in high school. We started dating again just before he got the job here. Then he told Dominic about me, and I got the job at Azure. That's the end of the story."

"Andrew?" Joe asked.

"He's in Vegas now. All male revue."

"And now?"

"Now, I'm just breathing. Not dating for a while."

"Not dating? What do you call this?" Joe smirked.

"Oh Joe, you know what you call this," Sam gave Joe a devilish grin.

Svengali

There was a short discussion on who's place to go to. Joe won home-field advantage.

The conversation that flowed so smoothly over dinner ended, replaced by small talk about the weather and geographical points of interest. "Avere ripensamenti?" (have second thoughts) Joe asked.

"No sono sicure," (no I'm sure) Sam softly said.

They spoke Italian for the rest of the trip to Joe's house. The conversation was back to a natural flow.

It had been three weeks, and two women since Joe first laid eyes on Sam. She had been his every waking thought. That would end tonight. He would finally put her where she belonged. The past.

He pulled up to the side entrance of his house. They walked into the kitchen, and Joe turned the lights on. Sam's eyes widened.

"What I wouldn't give for a kitchen like this," Sam said.

"It was a kitchen and formal dining room. I wanted a more livable feeling, so I combined the two rooms," Joe explained.

The great room had a living and dining area. The appliances would bring out envy in any chef. Joe flipped on more lights, and through the windows above the sink, Sam could see the courtyard and a two-story slave quarter.

Joe had mentioned that his law office was in his home. "Is that your office?" Sam asked looking out of the window.

Joe walked up behind her and draped his arms over her shoulders, shedding her of her pashmina. He laid it over the back of one of the chairs. Sam watched the arch of his shoulders as he slowly took his jacket off. Almost catlike, she thought. He took his tie off, folding it in half and laid it over his jacket. Unbuttoning the first two buttons of his shirt Joe finally replied, "no, my offices are in the house. The slave quarter is pretty much a catch-all."

"Could I get a glass of water, please?"

Joe got a glass and filled it with ice. He walked over to Sam, still standing by the sink. She took the glass from him and turned to fill it from the faucet, took a sip, and placed the glass on the counter. He hadn't moved. Joe could hear her sharp intake of breath as he splayed his right hand across her stomach. He deftly opened the three buttons of her suit jacket with his left hand. She could feel his end of day stubble against her temple. His right hand started to gather her skirt up, smiling when he realized she had stockings on, held up by a garter belt. His left hand eased her right breast from the cup of the lace bra, then gently brushed the tip of her nipple with his index finger. His nose moved her hair aside. He nibbled down her neck.

There were so many sensations going through her; she couldn't think. He slid his hand inside her panties, working his fingers in a circular motion. This was a seasoned lover. He started to pull and pinch her nipple, the nibbling on her neck became small bites. He added more pressure on her clit until she hit her peak, letting out a loud moan. He pressed her close. His right hand cupping her mons, his left on her chest until she was back.

He turned her around, gently kissed her and with a broad smile across his face joked, "did you come?"

"Asshole," she laughed.

Joe pinched her cheek, "what are we going to do with that mouth of yours."

"I'm sure we'll come up with something," Sam chuckled.

Joe took her wrist and led her upstairs. While in the foyer he pointed out his office in the double parlor.

"This is beautiful Joe," Sam said when they entered his bedroom suite.

"Thank you. Can I get you a drink?" Joe asked, walking to the bar.

"No, thanks. Bathroom?"

"There," Joe pointed with his chin as he filled a glass with ice.

"Oh my god!" Sam squealed from the bathroom. She stepped back out. "I'm moving in here," then back into the bathroom.

"She's adorable," Joe thought. "Soda, juice?" Joe asked, raising his voice.

"Orange juice if you have it," she replied, sticking her head back out of the door.

"I do," Joe's grin widened.

"Cool."

"Cool," Joe repeated under his breath chuckling. Sam came out of the bathroom, put back together. Her jacket was buttoned. Her skirt lying straight and hair semi neat. "Going somewhere?" Joe asked.

"My purse, I left it downstairs. It might be in your car."

Joe handed her the juice, "I'll get it. You make yourself comfortable."

"It's a black clutch," Sam said as he was walking out of the room.

"I'm sure I'll be able to figure out which one is yours," he laughed.

Sam giggled.

Sam's purse was in his car. On the way back, he stopped in the kitchen to listen to his messages. He turned the volume down. There were three; the first was 11:30 that morning from Dominic, wanting to know where he was. "Jesus Christ Dom, you're like a fucking wife," Joe said out loud. The second call was a real estate broker he had done business with before. He had a few properties to show Joe for the family's new venture. Check-cashing stores. The third was Jennifer. He had gone out with her once before she left for Europe. He didn't intend to see her again; then the family dinner came up. Why he always felt it necessary to bring a date to these things escaped him, but he wasn't comfortable being the only man at the table without a woman at his side. So he called and asked her out. She managed to wrangle a dinner out of him. He managed to wrangle a piece of ass out of her. She was equally as bad as the first time he slept with her.

Joe made his way back upstairs, clutching Sam's clutch. He found Sam nude sprawled out in the center of his bed. Her hair fanned out on the pillow like a halo. He was looking at what could easily be the centerfold of any men's magazine.

"Jesus Christ, you're gorgeous," Joe whispered. Her smile broadened. He took off his shirt while simultaneously toeing his shoes off. She watched as he removed his watch, laying it on the nightstand, followed by his money clip from his pocket. He opened the nightstand drawer and took out a condom. Sitting next to her on the bed, Joe leaned down and kissed her slowly. With his hand cupping the side of her head, he brushed her eyebrow with his thumb and asked, "Cat got your tongue, little girl?"

"Fuck me," she mouthed.

Joe got up and continued to undress. Her eyes followed him. She flipped over onto her stomach. Joe thought her Venus dimples even sexier without the black bikini bottoms she wore at Azure. She crawled down to the foot of the bed dragging a pillow. She rested her chin on her crossed arms on top of the pillow and watched Joe finish undressing. She could tell he was holding his stomach in but wisely decided not to call him on it. He was in pretty good shape. He just needed a few sit-ups. His underwear came off, and he was fully erect. Her eyes widened as she said, "glad to see you have career options if the law thing doesn't work out for you."

Joe laughed. He gave her a small bite on her ass then worked his way down to the back of her knee. He licked and kissed her there until he got a response and then moved to the other. He rolled her over and turned her so her head was back at the top of the bed, then opened her legs wide and knelt between them. He kissed and bit her stomach working his way up. "Now," she pleaded while his mouth was on hers.

"Not yet baby," Joe whispered and started slowly making his way down again. He continued his treatment on the inside of her thighs. Then slid his tongue between her folds.

"No," she said sharply. Joe looked up, surprised. "I'm not comfortable with that."

"Okay baby," then slid a finger in her, took it out and circled her clit with his moist finger. He sat back on his heels with his legs spread. Put the condom on and pulled her wide-opened legs over his thighs slowly entering her. Joe had been with more than his share of women, but this little foul mouth beauty was the most responsive. He could feel her milking his cock just before she came. He watched her closed eyes squeeze tight as a long moan escaped. With his hands gripping her rib cage, he gained momentum again. Harder and faster.

"I can't," she whimpered.

He couldn't stop. He was there. A shrieking noise came out of her as he came. When his breathing returned to normal, he opened his eyes to see tears running down her face.

"Baby no. It's okay." He quickly rid himself of the condom, grabbing a box of tissues and her juice on his way back. He climbed into bed next to her and pulled the covers up over them. She clung to him. "I know. It was a lot. Do you want some juice?" She silently nodded. Sam dozed off with her head on his chest, half lying across his body. He followed shortly after.

She woke when she felt him stir, "am I squashing you?"

Joe laughed, "you're a little peanut. You can't squash anyone."

Sam's head came up, "I'm not a peanut," then came back down on his chest.

"Are you okay?" he asked.

Sam's head came up again and smiled, "Svengali," she said before her head fell back down on his chest.

Joe chuckled, "you can call me Sven."

"What time is it?"

Joe turned on the nightstand lamp and looked at his watch, "1:30."

She took the watch out of his hand and looked at it, "you need a new band."

"It was my fathers."

"Is that why you haven't replaced it?"

"No, just something I haven't gotten around too." Sam climbed over Joe to get up. "Where are you off to little girl?"

"Bathroom."

"Would you like a robe?"

Sam put her arm straight out and twirled in a circle, "I've got nothing to hide."

"No baby, you sure don't."

She came out a few minutes later, brushing her teeth with her finger, she gathered up her underwear with the other hand.

"What are you doing?" Joe asked.

She took her finger out of her mouth, "I should get going."

"Have you lost your fucking mind?"

"You don't have to take me. I'll get a cab."

"You're not going anywhere. Get your ass back in bed," then his tone softened, "I'll take you to my favorite breakfast spot in the morning."

"Show and tell?" Sam sarcastically asked.

"I guess you would prefer to go to a restaurant I haven't taken someone to before."

"That would be nice."

"We'll have to get up early. We'll be having breakfast in Baton Rouge," Joe said sarcastically. "Now stop acting like a child and get in bed."

Joe woke up at 6:45. Sam was gone.

Soap Opera

Wednesday, November 3, 1993

"How was your night?" Felice asked in her cute voice.

"I'm out the door in 30 seconds."

"Lunch, Palace Cafe 12:30?"

"Good, love you," Sam hung up and rushed to make her streetcar.

"I'll have a cup of gumbo please," Sam said. "And we're going to split a Cobb Salad."

"I'll have a cup of the turtle soup," Felice said. "Thank you."

"Well?" Felice asked the second the server turned to walk away.

"Memorable," Sam's face flushed.

"I have to ask you something. Don't judge me. Rumor has it Joe is well endowed."

"Yeah, he could do porn," Sam laughed.

"Was he romantic?"

"What do you want? A blow by blow."

"Nooo! I'm just curious as to where this is going."

"Nowhere, Felice this was sex, raw animal sex. And now we move on. He's probably high fiving his cousin Dominic as we speak. I banged her Cuz." Sam mimicked a man's voice. Sam put her hand over Felice's, "honey, what did you think this was going to be?"

The server appeared with their lunch. Perfect timing.

"I have good news," Felice smiled. "Daniel is coming back today.

In fact, he should be landing about now. We have our first date tonight."

"I don't have to ask if you're excited. Your grinning like the Cheshire Cat," Sam laughed.

They went on with their lunch discussing what Felice should wear. They talked about work.

They were finishing their coffee when Felice asked, "how did you leave it?" Sam just looked at her. "With Joe," Felice said.

"I know what you meant. Why are we back on this again?"

"It's a question, Sam. Don't get your Sicilian up. I was just wondering what was said."

"Nothing was said."

"Nothing?" Felice gave Sam one of her stop bullshitting me looks.

"I left at 5:30. I didn't see the point in waking him."

"You took a cab at 5:30 in the morning?"

"No, he lives on Prytania. I just walked over to St. Charles and caught the streetcar."

"At 5:30 in the morning?"

"Yeah. What's wrong with that?"

"So much, I don't know where to start. Let's go before my head explodes," Felice laughed.

"For fuck's sake Chris. It's the third. You should have had this shit done on the first," Joe snapped.

"You've been short with everybody today. Stop! Just stop. Please," Chris said.

Dominic remained silent.

Joe looked at his watch. It was 8:10. Sam started at 8:30. He didn't want to run into her. He didn't know how to react towards her. He'd always had to get rid of the girls in the morning. He never had one disappear in the middle of the night. He put the rest of the paperwork in his briefcase and got up slowly rubbing his thighs. "I started working out. A little sore."

"You have to start slow. You haven't worked out in a while," Dominic said.

"And stretch. Stretching is important," Chris added.

Joe headed for the door.

"Hold on Joe. I'll walk out with you. I gotta go to Blush. I wanna get in there before the dicks come out," Dominic laughed.

Joe stepped out into the bar just as Sam walked out of the lady's room.

"Sam," Dominic said, "how are you doing. We miss you at Azure."

"Thanks, Dom. I'm doing great," Sam smiled. Then her lips thinned, "Joe."

"Sam," Joe said, feigning an equal lack of interest.

Sam walked away. Both men watched her.

"You finally did it," Dominic said when they got outside.

"Did what?"

"Sam."

"You don't know what the fuck you're talking about," Joe snapped.

"Really? You're walking like a 90-year-old man. She's walking like she has a stick up her ass. And just so you know, neither one of you have a poker face," Dominic was laughing, "I'll bet she's a fun little toy."

"Knock it off, Dom," Joe snapped. "I'm serious."

"Okay, no disrespect," Dominic said with his hands held up.

Sam couldn't stop thinking about Joe's reaction when seeing her. Was her job in jeopardy? There wasn't much she could do about it now. She made her bed.

Friday, November 5, 1993

"Those are beautiful," Ruth said as she bent down to smell the flowers.

"Your nephew is a nice guy. Read the card?" Sam said, smiling.

Ruth read it out loud, "to the second-best blind date I ever had." Ruth smiled. "My nephew is so thoughtful. He likes Felice."

"It's mutual. Felice is on cloud nine."

"She's back," Ruth said in a low voice.

Sam looked up to see her nightmare customer.

"Is my dress ready? You said it would be ready this morning," she said arrogantly.

"Let me go to alterations and check," Sam replied.

Sam went in the back and took deep breaths. She returned with the dress and proceeded to put it into a garment bag.

"What are you doing?"

"Would you prefer a box?" Sam asked.

"I would prefer to try it on so I can make sure the alterations were done correctly."

"Of course. Follow me please," Sam said.

Sam came out of the dressing room, and sat down at the writing desk. She put her finger to her skull and mimicked shooting herself. Ruth laughed and walked away. Sam began writing a thank you note to a customer. The one in the dressing room would not be receiving one, Sam thought and grinned.

"Which one?" he asked.

Sam looked up to see Joe standing there with a tie in each hand. She tapped the one in his right hand with the end of her pen, "the Armani."

Joe looked at the yellow roses on the desk and saw the card addressed to Sam. He wasn't going to let that throw him off his game.

"You missed a good breakfast," Joe smiled. "Sam, I thought we had an incredible time."

"We did," Sam grinned.

"Joooe," a grating voice belted out. "What are you doing here?" Before Joe had time to answer, she started to talk again. "This is the dress I bought for tonight. What do you think? Of course, it will look better with the right shoes and makeup. Were you picking out a tie for tonight? Let me change, and I'll help you with that. I don't like either one of those." Never coming up for air, she looked at Sam and said, "make sure this is pressed before you bag it. Tonight will be the first time I'm meeting my boyfriends family, and I have to look flawless."

"Jennifer, we've only gone out a couple of times," Joe said firmly, but it fell on deaf ears. She scampered back to the dressing room.

"WOW!" Sam said, looking up at Joe.

He ran his fingers through his hair, "this is awkward."

"Joe, we had one night."

"Sam, I came here," he paused, "I was hoping to see you again."

"Joe, I'm not going to be a place you park your dick, while you sashay through the garden district searching for Miss Right."

Jennifer reappeared locking arms with Joe, "What are the two of you talking about?" Jennifer asked possessively.

"The garden district," Sam replied.

Jennifer pulled at his arm, "come Joe. We'll find you a tie while she's taking care of my dress."

"I already found what I want," Joe said, looking at Sam. "I'll take the Armani."

Sam returned with their packages. Joe thanked Sam as she handed him his bag. Jennifer said nothing when she handed her the dress. Joe thanked Sam again as she walked away.

"Jennifer, you thank people when they do something for you," Joe said, annoyed.

"She works here, Joe. That's her job," Jennifer said dismissively. "Are you sure you don't have time for coffee?"

"I'm already running late for an appointment. I'll see you this evening."

Jennifer attempted to kiss Joe, but he turned his face. She caught him on the cheek. Sam was watching.

"What are you doing?" Joe asked.

"I just got out of the shower," Dominic replied.

"Can you meet me at Azure? I need your ear."

"Why don't you just come to the house?"

"I would rather Azure."

Dominic huffed, "okay, where are you?"

"On Tchoupitoulas and Poydras, outside of Mother's. I'm going to pick us up a po' boy. We can split it."

"I want my own. Ham. Dressed." (lettuce, tomato, and mayonnaise)

"Dominic, we're going to have a big dinner tonight."

"You want a favor, and I only get half a po' boy?"

"Ham po' boy dressed. I got it," Joe snickered.

When Dominic got to Azure, Joe was behind the bar. Dominic

took the po' boys out of the bag.

"Give me a soft drink," Dominic said.

"You should get off those sodas. They're all sugar."

"You got me here to give me dietary advice?" Dominic laughed.

"Sam—"

"And we're off," Dominic interrupted.

Joe started waving his hand and head in unison, "I know. I sound like a girl. I'm sorry. Forget it."

"Listen, you dragged my ass over here. Let's hear it."

"I don't know what it is about her," then Joe told Dominic about his experience at Lambert's. He paraphrased what Sam had said to him.

Dominic laughed, "I love that fucking broad."

Joe went on ending with Jennifer trying to kiss him as Sam watched.

"First of all, I owe my wife an apology. I could never figure out her fascination with soap operas. Now I know. We can call this one, Joe's Many Loves."

"Fuck you, Dom."

"Joe, I'm jerking your chain. Don't be so sensitive," Dominic gave Joe a few seconds to calm down. "This isn't Sam's first rodeo. She knows you're dating other women. I'm sure she's not sitting home alone."

"Thanks, Dom."

"I've never seen you like this before. If you like the girl, go for it. You're both single. What the fuck. Enjoy," Dominic said. "Now what you're doing with this other broad I don't get."

"Her brother Jeromy fixed us up."

"Jeromy Kincaid?" Dominic's voice elevated. "Our banker?"

"Yes."

"Nice move, Joe."

"So you can see why I have to handle her with kid gloves. I don't want to strain the relationship with Jeromy."

They finished their po' boys and exited the bar.

"You were right about one thing," Dominic said as he put the key in the lock, "you do sound like a girl."

Joe punched him in the arm.

The waiters were setting the entree's down.

"Excuse me," Jennifer addressed one of the waiters. "My boyfriend needs more water."

"Jennifer, let them serve the dinners. They know their jobs. They're quite efficient here," Joe said.

"If they were efficient you would have water in your glass," she replied.

After dinner before the coffee and dessert came to the table, the men stepped outside. Frank lit a cigar.

"We're past the point of being able to tip enough," Chris said.

"I'm sorry Uncle Frank," Joe was obviously embarrassed.

"Well let's go back in there and finish up. I don't think the ladies are having a very good time," Frank said.

Jennifer sat in Joe's car crying while Joe gave her the it's not you, it's me speech. He didn't attempt to console her. He just wanted her out of his car and life.

Warholesque

Saturday, November 6, 1993

When you're on a roll, you're on a roll. Sam was on a roll. She didn't stop all day. She had by all measures a fantastic day at Lambert's, and that carried over to the night. Christos was rocking. There was a big convention in town, and they knew how to tip. Felice and Daniel stopped in for one set. Sandy bought them a round. Sam and Sandy had their moves down behind the bar. He already thought of her as the best partner he had at Christos. He was still all business, but she felt that she could be more herself.

"Felice's boyfriend seems like a good guy," Sandy said.

That sounded so nice to hear. Felice's boyfriend. That's the first time Sam had heard those words together. "Yeah, he's a sweetheart," Sam said and told Sandy about the beautiful flowers and card he sent. "That was nice of you."

"What was? I don't remember being nice," Sandy joked.

"Buying them a drink."

Sandy flashed a big smile, "you can go if you like."

"Just waiting for Claude."

"Sam, you know if you ever need a lift home, you're on my way."

"Thanks, I'll hold you to that when it's raining," Sam laughed. "I like walking home in this weather. It's perfect. Claude is an added plus. Always interesting."

"That he is," Sandy smirked.

"You and Sandy seem to be getting along better," Claude noted.

"We are, he's not as scary as I thought."

"I told you, you had nothing to worry about. By the way, I won't be here next weekend."

"Anything exciting?"

"Deer hunting with my father."

"There's not a snowball's chance in hell I would have ever guessed that," Sam laughed.

"Give a coonass (person of Cajun ethnicity some consider an ethnic slur) a gun and a swamp, HEAVEN!" Claude swayed side to side mimicking dancing and humming Cheek To Cheek. "Do you like venison."

"Absolutely, I can make venison chili. Or I can make stew."

"Well, you're going to have more venison than you know what to do with, Sha." They made the turn onto Chartres a half block from her apartment when Claude asked, "something you forgot to tell me?"

Joe was in front of her apartment, leaning against his car, talking to a cop.

"Is he having you arrested?" Claude joked in a whisper.

Sam didn't answer. As they got closer Joe and the cop said their goodbyes.

"Hi Joe," Claude said casually.

"Claude," Joe replied as he put his hand on her back, "thank you for walking Sam home."

Claude wanted to make light of the situation, but the look on Sam's face stopped him.

"You're welcome."

Joe followed as Sam walked over and put her key in the lock.

The first thing Sam did when she walked into her apartment was poured herself a scotch. She didn't bother with ice. She didn't offer Joe one. Joe was adjusting to the new furnishings. Then he spotted the chair. He walked over to it.

"You got an Eames chair? It's a knock off, right?"

Sam stepped out of the kitchen with her drink in hand, and calmly said, "I don't know how you get your pants on, your balls are so fucking big."

Joe tried to suppress his laughter. "It's a real one? I apologize."

116

"Yes, it's real, and I'm not referring to the chair. What are you doing here, Joe?"

"I thought we should talk. I came to Lambert's, and that turned out to be—"

"A dumpster fire," Sam snidely interrupted.

"It didn't go as planned," Joe took a deep breath.

"I guess your girlfriend being there put a dent in your plans," she snapped at Joe.

"First of all, she's not my girlfriend. Second, you need to ease up," He walked into the kitchen and got himself a drink.

"Perhaps if you were a little more assertive with—"

"Knock it off Sam. Now!" Joe interrupted. "I don't owe you an explanation. I'm going to give you one, but I don't owe you one. Are you jealous of Jennifer?"

"Seriously? No, of course not."

"Did you want a scene in Lambert's?" Sam shook her head. "Because if I handled that differently, it could have been one," They were both silent for a long count. "Take a shower," Joe walked up to Sam and kissed her on the top of her head, "and wash your hair. It smells like smoke."

Sam was in the shower. Joe stuck his head in. "Would you mind if I went up to your studio?"

"Knock yourself out. Don't touch anything."

She found him upstairs.

"These are good."

"Thanks."

"Sam, I mean it. I'm impressed. Why aren't you doing this full time?"

"Because this," she waved her hand palm up from left to right, "doesn't pay the bills. There is nothing I would rather do, but my success has been," she paused to think of the right word, "sporadic."

"Where was this one taken?"

"The triptych?"

"Is that what it's called?"

"Yeah, one image divided in three."

"You mean yes," Joe smiled.

"I meant yes," Sam smiled back. "It was my uncle's first gym. I took that picture with my little Fuji camera when I was 12," Sam grinned.

"It almost looks like a painting."

"It's a combination of photography and screen printing. Kinda Warholesque. I started as a painter just using the photographs as reference. Now I combined the two. I did a painting of that. It's in my uncle's gym."

"What would your price be on a piece like this?"

"$700, $750."

"What would a gallery get for it?"

"Probably $1,200. I'd have to bend on my end so they could make their mark, but I wouldn't have the cost of a show so I could take a little hit."

Joe took the towel off her head and draped it over her shoulders. He ran his fingers through her damp hair. Then gently kissed her lips, "You look tired. Let's get you to bed."

"I thought you wanted to talk?"

"Bed," Joe said as he led her downstairs.

He stood leaning on the doorjamb to the bathroom, watching her blow dry her hair.

"You know your little drop in was bullshit."

"It worked. I'm in," Joe grinned.

"I'm guessing someone with your active social life wouldn't like it happening to them."

"What are you implying, turnabout is fair game?"

"Joe, I don't chase men," she smiled. "Now Claude knows."

"Don't worry about it."

"He could tell Dominic."

"Dominic knows."

"What!" she almost shouted. "You're a fucking attorney. Can't you keep a secret? I told Felice you couldn't wait to tell Dominic."

"Felice knows?"

"Of course she knows. She left us together at Mr. B's."

"And you filled in the details."

"No," she dropped her head forward shaking it and then looked up. "Christ, it's probably going to be in the Times-Picayune next." They both laughed.

Joe hadn't seen Sam's bedroom. As was the other room, it was a work in progress. The bed had all-white linens. It had an unusual wrought iron headboard that curved around the sides of the mattress. It was anchored by a small burl wood bombe chest on one side, and a round skirted table on the other. The yellow roses were on the bombe chest, candlestick styled lamp on the other. The two folding chairs had made their way into the bedroom, opposite the bed, a large plant in the corner.

Joe took off his shoes and socks, placing them next to the folding chairs. He put the contents of his pockets, which included a condom on the bombe chest, then he picked up the vase of flowers and took them out to the living room. When he got back, Sam was grinning ear to ear.

"Did you want to say something?" Joe asked, raising an eyebrow.

Still smiling, she shook her head. She walked over to him and took his left hand and unbuttoned the cuff of his shirt. She pulled his hand closer and put her mouth on his thumb, slowly circling his thumb with her tongue and sucked gently, then repeated the process on his right hand. She unbuttoned his shirt, kissing his chest after each button, then took a little nip at his left nipple. He flinched. She walked behind him and slid his shirt off his back. Kissing and licking from his neck to his waist. She wrapped her arms around his waist and undid his pants. They slipped to the floor, followed by his briefs. She licked and kissed to the base of his tail bone. She walked around to face him, grabbing the condom off the chest on the way. She untied her robe and let it drop to the floor, then fell to her knees and put the condom in her mouth. Sam gripped the base of his cock in one hand and cupped his balls in the other. She looked up at Joe, almost serenely, and slid the condom on with her mouth.

"Jesus," Joe groaned.

She pulled back and looked up, "fuck my mouth," she whispered provocatively, then opened her mouth wide and placed the head of his cock on her tongue. He grabbed her hair with both hands and plunged forward. The visual of her watering eyes looking up at him drove him insane. With each stroke, he was able to go a little deeper. He stopped when her hands gave a slight shove on his thighs. He helped her up. Sat on the edge of the bed and moved her on top. Her legs spread wide easing herself slowly onto his cock. He leaned back on his elbows intently watching her gain momentum. Her up and down motions switched to grinding moves.

"Oh no, you don't," Joe said, smiling as she got close. He grabbed her ass, stood up, and laid her back on the bed. She whimpered. Grabbing her ankles he pulled her, so her ass was at the end of the bed. Joe then propped her ass up with two pillows. He slapped her clit with the head of his cock a couple of times, then slid into her. She gasped. With his hands on her calves, he pushed her legs towards her chest. His thrust was fast and hard. The pain and pleasure were so intermingled they were indistinguishable. Euphoria swept over her, not unlike a runners high. She was overwhelmed.

Once again she fell asleep splayed out half over him. At daybreak, a loud thump against the window woke Joe with a start. "What the fuck was that?"

"Newspaper."

He laid back down and pulled her into his chest.

He woke up hours later to the smell of coffee. "Sam," he propped himself up on one arm. "Sam," he called out louder. "Every time I wake up she's gone," he said out loud. He got up and made his way to the kitchen. He found a mug after opening several cabinet doors. Poured himself coffee, got the newspaper off the balcony, and settled into the Eames chair.

The DiLeo clan took the same route up Chartres to St. Louis Cathedral every Sunday. This week Chris and his family accompanied his mother, Nina, Aunt Carmela, and Uncle Frank. Joe was always a question mark on Sundays. You never knew if he would show or not.

Dominic was running late. He called to let them know they would meet at the church.

As they walked up Chartres, Frank asked Chris, "is that your cousin's car?"

"Uncle Frank, I think they made more than one black Mercedes," Chris replied.

Dominic and his family were waiting outside of the church. As they filed in, Chris gave the back of Dominic's coat a tug. They let the rest of the family go in.

"Joe's car is parked on Chartres. Should we try to guess who lives on that block?"

"Chris, he likes this girl."

"He likes them all until he doesn't like them anymore," Chris said irritated.

"Did my dad see Joe's car?"

"Yes. I told him there were a lot of cars like Joe's. I don't think he bought it."

After mass Dominic's family walked back with the rest of the DiLeo's. Dominic made an excuse to break away. He went to Azure. Got Sam's employee file and picked up the phone.

"You're up," she said as she walked into the bedroom after her run. The yellow roses were back on the bombe chest. She snickered. She took her shoes, socks, and sweatshirt off. Made the bed and walked into the kitchen wearing a sports bra and sweat pants.

"I missed mass," Joe said paging through the newspaper.

Sam laughed. She poured herself a cup of coffee.

He lowered the paper and arched an eyebrow as Sam came into the living room.

"Oh, you're not kidding," Sam said, trying to control her laughter.

She sat down on the floor, about three feet away from him. Legs crossed, drinking her coffee, and waiting to be acknowledged.

He was getting a kick, making her wait. He finally looked up from the paper giving her the attention she so patiently waited for.

"If I don't word this correctly, please don't be upset. This is not what I envisioned," Sam said. "I thought we'd get it out of our system and move on."

"You know you're like the thief who wants to study the possible consequences after he robbed the bank," Joe coldly said. "You were a willing participant."

"I'm not saying that. I just thought it was going to be one and done."

"You need to stop talking Sam," Then his tone softened. "A diplomat, you're not."

"I have other attributes," she said, with an impish grin on her face. "Do you want something to eat before you go?" She got up and walked into the kitchen.

"Are you throwing me out? Joe asked, following her into the

kitchen.

"No, you just seem like the hit and run type."

"Jesus, you're like dating a guy."

"We're not dating. In or out on the eggs?"

"I'll have mine over easy."

"If you want to order off the menu, we're surrounded by restaurants. Go to one of them." She turned her back to him and started cracking eggs into a bowl.

Joe walked up behind her. "You're so tough," he said as he slid his right hand down her pants and kissed her neck.

She could feel his hard-on. "Get that thing away from me," she laughed and she bumped him with her ass.

"That's what we're gonna call him, Thing?"

"We're not naming body parts. Now stop. I'm still sore from last night," she was laughing.

"I'll go nice and easy," he said as his fingers circled her clit. "Where are your condoms?" he whispered in her ear and then nipped at her ear lobe.

"I don't have any," she replied and let out a soft groan.

"Bullshit," Joe chuckled as he went about his seduction.

"My purse," she conceded in a breathy voice.

Joe took a quick shower while Sam finished preparing breakfast.

"Can I use your toothbrush?"

"NO!" She walked into the bathroom and took a toothbrush wrapped in cellophane from the cabinet under the sink.

"Guest toothbrushes?" Joe grinned.

"I get them from my dentist when I have my teeth cleaned," she turned to walk out. "Asshole."

Joe laughed.

She turned on the tv as he sat at the table.

"You like football?" Joe asked.

"Yeah." Joe rolled his eyes at her. "I mean yes," she smiled.

"Are the Saints playing today?"

"No, they're off this week. It looks like the Vikings and Chargers. Is that okay?" Sam asked.

"Fine. Scrambled eggs. How original." Sam gave Joe the finger. He laughed. "These are good," Joe said after he tasted them. "Why are these so good?"

"I added a little ricotta to them," she smiled. He ate every morsel.

"Would you like more?" she asked before picking up the plate.

"I'm good. Thank you."

"Today is it, Joe. I mean it."

"This song is getting old. What is it? Are you involved with someone? Daniel?"

"You read the card?" she asked, surprised.

"The card fell when I moved the vase. Sorry."

"Bullshit. Daniel is Felice's boyfriend."

Joe cupped her chin and tilted her head up. He gave her a quick kiss. "What are we going to do with this mouth of yours?" he smiled. "What is your apprehension? You're looking for problems that don't exist."

"Said the man with the winning hand," she sounded exasperated. "Joe, it's fine now. It's great. But I know how this ends. You want to stop seeing me; I'm fired. I want to stop seeing you; I'm fired. I'm the loser anyway this goes."

"I can't fire you," he paused. "I'm not bullshitting. Ask Dominic."

"I'm not gonna ask Dominic," she said dismissively. "Okay, I'll bite. Why can't you fire me?"

"It was my idea to move you to Christos. Chris didn't want to go around Sandy. So my uncle made the final decision. We could move you as long as I had no say in your employment. I think he figured this might happen."

"So Chris didn't want me there?"

"No baby, Chris likes you. He just didn't want to step on Sandy's toes."

"Why does Sandy carry so much weight?"

"It was a deal he cut with my uncle many years ago."

"Does Chris know about us?"

"No, just Dominic and of course Claude now."

The phone rang.

"Hello." ...... "Can your cousin fire me?"

Joe gave her an inquisitive look.

"It's Dominic," she handed Joe the phone shaking her head.

They talked for a few minutes. Joe hung up. "Chris knows."

"Jesus, Joe. I guess I owe Tanya an apology for what I thought of her. That's the club I belong to now."

"Trust me, baby, nobody will look at you that way. Unless you fuck Dominic," Joe laughed.

Joe spent the day at Sam's. They watched football. She worked in her studio. Not before she brought him a small plate of cheese and olives with a glass of Chianti. He eased into his new favorite chair with Sam's copy of John Grisham's, The Client. She cooked chicken scarpariello (braised chicken with Italian sausage and peppers) with a tossed salad for dinner. They had a quiet domestic day. Just like millions of couples do on Sunday afternoons. Joe dropped Sam off on Royal and Conti. A block from Christos.

Joe could not recall a day so relaxing. He made a mental note to keep a change of clothes in the trunk of his car.

Who Dat

"You sneaky little minx."

"Believe me. I was as surprised as you to see him standing there," Sam chuckled.

"Tell me everything," Claude was almost giddy.

"There's not a whole lot to tell. It seemed like a good idea after a bucket of booze. I thought it was a one-off. Evidently, Joe thought differently. He'll move on."

"That's it? All that sexual tension and this is what I get?" Claude laughed. "The man was waiting outside your apartment at 3:30 in the morning. Joe DiLeo doesn't do shit like that. You must have done something to get his attention."

"Or it was 3:30 in the morning, and he was running out of options," Sam joked.

"Okay, we'll play your game," Claude laughed.

"So I won't see you next week?"

"No, I'll see you on Wednesday. I'm just going on the weekend."

'Cool."

"When I get back, you're doing my painting."

"Promise."

Monday, November 8, 1993

Joe was in Baton Rouge most of the day. There were a lot of ducks to get in a row for their new endeavor. There were state, local and federal licenses and permits to obtain. There were decisions to be made on services offered. On locations. On hiring. On security. Joe's head was swimming. He stopped at Dominic's for dinner on the way home.

Dominic's wife Sarah knew all about Sam. It was Dominic's new total honesty policy to save his marriage. She was, of course, skeptical because Sam worked at Azure, but any woman was better than Jennifer.

"When are you going to bring Sam to dinner?" Sarah asked out of the clear blue.

Joe shot Dominic a what the fuck look. "Sarah, Sam and I have only seen each other a few times. Perhaps we should put that on the back burner for now."

"Okay, but the invitation is open," Sarah said as she finished clearing the table.

"Was that necessary?" Joe asked Dominic as soon as Sarah left the room.

"Sarah wanted to know where I disappeared to after mass. You know, when I went out of my way to give you a heads up."

"Is Chris going to give me shit about this?"

"Count on it," Dominic laughed.

Sarah kissed Joe on the cheek when he was leaving. "Thank you for coming."

"Thank you for having me on short notice. Everything was delicious. I'll see you on Sunday."

"Only if you show up for mass. My folks are in town Sunday afternoon, so we'll be spending the day with them," Sarah said. "Joe, would you like our Saints tickets. We're not going to use them."

"Are you sure?" Joe asked, looking at Dominic.

"Sure, let me get them," Dominic said.

"Thank you, Sam loves football," Joe caught himself too late.

Sarah and Dominic both grinned.

As usual, Joe checked his messages as soon as he walked in. He had five. None from Sam. One from Jennifer. She felt that they just needed to talk things over. She wanted their relationship to work. "We don't have a fucking relationship, you stupid bitch," Joe yelled out loud at the machine. It was 9:30. Too late to call her now. It would have to wait until tomorrow. He would straighten out this wack job tomorrow.

He called Sam.

"Hello."

"Sam, Joe."

No response.

"Joe DiLeo," Joe said.

She giggled, "I know who it is. What's up?"

"Did I catch you at a bad time?"

"No, not at all. I'm just a little surprised to hear from you so soon."

"I fucked up," Joe thought. "I know you book up early," he gave a little chuckle, "I have tickets to the Saints—"

"Yes!" she interrupted.

"Okay, I'll pick you up after church. They're good seats."

"I wouldn't expect anything less from you," she joked. "For a minute I thought you were going to cancel Thursday."

"Absolutely not. You sure you wouldn't rather go out to dinner?"

"No, I don't like to dress up on my days off. I'm going to make sugo (spaghetti sauce) and if you're a good boy, I'll make braciola," (stuffed rolled beef) she teased.

"Well, I am going to be a very good boy," Joe laughed. "What can I bring?"

"A nice Chianti and Thing," she snickered. "Oh, listen to this. I got a call today from an author who wants me to do the cover of her book. She's sending the manuscript, so that I can get a feel for the characters. It's a romantic novel. The heroine's love interest is a boxer."

"Have you done book covers before?"

"No, she saw the cover I did for Ring magazine last year and—"

"You did a cover for Ring magazine?"

"Yeah, so they gave her—"

"Which one? I mean, what boxer?"

"You're doing that thing I don't like."

"What thing?"

"That thing where you ask me questions in the middle of my story."

Joe laughed, "my apologies. It won't happen again."

"So Ring gave her my contact information, and that's it. It could be a foot in a door I hadn't thought about."

"May I ask my question now?"

"Riddick Bowe," she laughed. "How was your day? You went to Baton Rouge, didn't you?"

"Long, I hit rush hour traffic there and back. I did get a lot accomplished. Thank you for asking. I had dinner at Dominic's when I got back. That's where I got the Saints tickets. He has season tickets."

"Thank him for me."

"I will. Sleep well."

"I will. John and I are going to bed now."

"John?" Joe couldn't breathe.

"Grisham, the book. Remember?" she giggled.

"Don't stay up too late reading. Thing said goodnight," Joe joked.

"Give him a kiss for me," Sam laughed.

"If I could do that baby, I wouldn't be on the phone right now. Goodnight Peanut."

The phone rang less than a minute after he hung up.

"What did you forget?" Joe asked.

"Joe. It's Jennifer."

FUCK! "Jennifer, why are you calling?"

"I don't understand how you can just throw away what we have," she sounded on the brink of tears.

"Jennifer, I need you to listen to me. We went out a few times. That's it. We didn't have a relationship. Please, you need to put this into perspective."

"Is it another woman?"

"No, it just didn't work out. That happens."

"That's all you have to say? It was working out when you were screwing me."

"That's it. I don't want to see or hear from you again." She didn't answer. "Do you understand me?"

She slammed the phone down.

Tuesday, November 9, 1993

Sam and Felice met for dinner at Pastore's. Felice was flying high. Daniel was the evenings topic. Sam was concerned that this could be a big fall if something bad happened between them. Daniel and his aunt Ruth were having dinner at her parents Friday. Felice tried to get Sam to join, but the Bywater gym was having a fight night, and she would be there as the official photographer.

"Have you seen Joe?"

"Yeah."

"Let me reword that. Are you seeing Joe?"

"You know this has got disaster written all over it."

"Why don't you just give the guy a chance?"

"I am," Sam grimaced. "I know where this is headed."

"You know what? Stop seeing him. You're on pins and needles waiting for him to do something unthinkable. So just stop seeing him." Sam sat quietly for a moment. "Either give the guy a break and see where it goes or move on."

"I'm sorry. I didn't mean to upset you," Sam said.

"You didn't. You've had the gloves on since you met him," Felice took on a sweet tone. "You two do have the best meet-cute story ever."

Sam laughed, "that we do."

Wednesday, November 10, 1993

Sam told Ruth about her dinner with Felice. Ruth was excited about meeting Felice's parents on Friday.

"Ruth, be honest, do you think Felice and Daniel are moving too fast?"

"Sam, he's crazy about her. I've never seen him happier. I don't think a relationship has to go by a timeline."

"It's just that I feel a certain responsibility because I fixed them up. I can't imagine what would happen if Daniel hurt Felice."

"I don't think that's an issue. I think this time next year you'll be bitching about the ugly bridesmaid dress Felice made you buy," Ruth laughed.

"Your mouth to God's ear," Sam replied.

That night before she left, Sam told Sandy that she was going to take him up on his offer of a ride home since Claude was off this weekend. Sandy seemed fine with it.

"Yes, Joe and I are dating," Sam confessed after Claude badgered her into it. "Are you happy now?"

"I knew it! Now on a scale from one to ten." Sam slapped Claude's arm. "Please, throw me a bone," Claude laughed.

Sam looked at him and took a deep breath, "he is so fucking hot." She closed her eyes, "Jesus!"

"Just be careful. I don't want to see you get hurt."

"I'm getting the opposite advice from Felice. She's Joe's biggest cheerleader."

"She's a romantic. I'm a realist."

When they got to Sam's door, she gave Claude a hug and kissed him on the cheek. "Safe trip," Sam grinned.

"Make room in your freezer," Claude laughed as he walked down Chartres.

Thursday, November 11, 1993

Joe showed up at 3:30 much earlier than expected. He had his briefcase in one hand and a duffel bag in the other. "Brought a change of clothes," Joe said, lifting the bag slightly.

"Cool," Sam replied.

She was barefooted, wearing denim coverall shorts with a shear white wife-beater underneath. No bra. Her hair was piled on top of her head, wrapped around a paintbrush.

"You look nice," Sam said.

"Thank you," Joe replied with a big grin on his face. "And you my dear look absolutely fuckable."

Sam giggled, "get comfortable. You want a drink?"

"Yes, please."

Joe changed into jeans. He rolled up his sleeves and unbuttoned the first three buttons of his shirt. He padded into the kitchen, barefooted with a bottle of wine in hand.

Sam was standing in front of the sink, washing lettuce. Joe came up behind her. He put his arms around her and showed her the wine in his right hand. He slid his left hand between the bib of her overalls and her T-shirt and gave her nipple a pinch. She winced. Sam turned her head to her left. Joe kissed her temple, "it smells good, Peanut."

"I'm not a Peanut," Sam said under her breath.

Joe laughed. There was a long loaf of bread on the counter in a white paper bag. Joe ripped off a piece and dipped into the large pot of sauce on the stove.

"OH MY GOD!" Joe said.

"You like?"

"Me love," Joe smiled. "Where's the braciole?"

"In the sauce. What time do you want to eat?"

"Right now," Joe laughed.

"We'll figure it out after I take a shower," she went to the oven and took out a small baking tray.

"What do we have here?" Joe asked.

"Stuffed mushrooms," she split the six on two plates and handed one of them to Joe. "Here, now go sit down."

"You mean get out of your hair," Joe chuckled. He walked out with his drink in one hand and plate in the other. "Do you have today's paper?"

"No, I just get Sunday's."

He went into the bedroom and got the Grisham book he had seen on the table next to her bed. He sat in his favorite chair and opened the book. He was pleased to see his makeshift bookmark fashioned from a piece of newspaper was where he left it. Sam finished the salad, made dressing and set the table, then headed for the bathroom. Joe followed.

"You need the bathroom?" Sam asked.

Joe shook his head and smiled.

"Don't get any ideas, Sven."

Joe chuckled, unhooking the straps to her coveralls. They slid to the floor. He nuzzled against her cheek and kissed the corner of her mouth. He nibbled on her lower lip while stretching her shirt below her breast, then licked and bit at her nipples. He took the paintbrush out of her hair, watching it cascade down.

"Turn around," Joe ordered.

She was facing the mirror. He slid her panties off, then nudged her stance wider with his feet. She heard his zipper. He tossed the wrapper from the condom in the sink. Tilting her forward he entered her then pulled her back to his chest. His fingers started to circle her clit. She pressed her head against his shoulder and moaned.

"Open your eyes," Joe whispered into her ear as he methodically continued stimulating her. "Keep them open," he ordered as he patted her clit a few times. "I want you to see how beautiful you are when you come for me."

She came out of the bedroom in jeans and a white tailored shirt with the sleeves rolled up.

"We look like twins," Joe joked.

Sam went into the kitchen and made herself a drink. "Do you want anything?"

"I'm good, thanks. Ellis Marsalis is playing at Snug Harbor tonight. You want to walk down after dinner?" Joe asked.

"Cool."

Joe laughed, "cool that he's there or cool you want to go?"

"Both," Sam said, sitting at the end of the sofa. She opened a package pulling out a thick stack of papers.

"The book?" Joe asked.

"Yeah."

"Sam!"

"I mean yes," she looked up and smiled. "I Can't Fight My Desire," Sam rolled her eyes and laughed.

"That's the title?"

Still laughing, Sam shook her head. They both sat quietly reading. About a half-hour later, Sam started to giggle.

"What?"

"Her burning loins. It actually says her burning loins," Sam turned the page toward Joe to show him.

Joe smiled. "She's adorable," he thought.

Joe was in heaven. The braciole with rigatoni, the salad with homemade vinaigrette and garlic bread.

"Do you want coffee? Dessert?" Sam asked.

"I'm stuffed," Joe said. "Maybe a little coffee."

"Okay."

"Did you make the dessert?"

"Yes, lemon ricotta cheesecake."

"You're killing me," Joe grinned.

"Is that a yes?"

"Yes."

"Thank you," Joe said as they walked down to the Marigny hand in hand. "Everything was fantastic."

Sam gave a coy grin.

"And those mushrooms. What were they stuffed with?"

"It was sole and crab, but I can't take credit for them," she chuckled. "Pastore's, Felice and I ate there on Tuesday. I had crab stuffed sole. I took my leftovers, added a little sautéed onion and celery. Voila, I can't wait to tell Felice. She made fun of me for asking the waiter to wrap that little piece."

Friday, November 12, 1993

He had one more cup of coffee while jotting down notes on a legal pad. Sam was putting the dishes into the dishwasher.

"You've been with your share of women?" Sam asked.

Joe almost choked on his coffee. "Where are you going with this Sam?"

"You know, size-wise."

"What the fuck are you talking about?" Joe laughed.

"I mean some women are tighter than others. Right?"

"Are you getting this shit from that book you're reading?" Joe couldn't stop laughing.

"The heroine is very tight. So size wise, how am I?"

"Average."

"Is average okay, or would you prefer tighter?"

"Baby if I want tighter I'll flip you over," Joe chuckled.

Sam's face flushed.

"Do you want a lift to work?" Joe asked.

"Cool. That gives me a little more time." She ran up to her studio and came back down with a leather bag and a very impressive camera.

"What are you doing with all that?" Joe asked.

"I'm getting my stuff ready for tonight. The Bywater Gym is having a fight night. I'm doing the photography."

"Why didn't you tell me what you were doing? I would have changed my meeting."

"If you want to come, come. I'll be busy shooting the fight so I won't be much company, but there's a couple of good welterweights on the card."

"No baby, next time."

"Okay, have a productive meeting. I'm excited about Sunday. Who Dat!"

Breathe

It was a lovefest at the Sax's Shabbat dinner. Phyllis and Manny could not have been more gracious. You could easily see why Felice was such a sweet girl. Manny offered to give Ruth a lift home so the kids, as he called them could go out. Daniel had never seen the Neville Brothers, and they were playing that night at Tipitina's. Before they took off, Phyllis extended a Thanksgiving invitation to both Ruth and Daniel. They happily accepted.

Once they got inside the club, Felice asked Daniel to order her a drink while she ran to the ladies room. The line in the ladies room was so long her quick trip turned into 12 minutes. "Daniel's going to think I died," Felice thought. As she was walking back to the bar, she hesitated. Her heart sank. Joe DiLeo was standing at the bar with his arm around a woman's waist, not Sam.

Joe spotted Felice a few seconds later. His hand dropped off of the girl's waist. Before long, the four were standing together. Felice, Daniel, Joe, and his date.

"Joe, this is my friend Daniel Sullivan. Daniel, Joe DiLeo," they shook hands as the woman next to Joe laughed.

"I'm sorry," she said with a big smile on her face. "My name is Sullivan too. Bridget Sullivan." She was oblivious to how awkward the other three were acting.

Felice tried to put this behind her for the evening. She didn't want to ruin Daniel's night. He knew she was affected.

"I don't think you should say anything," Daniel said on the ride home.

"It's not an option. She's my best friend," Felice said. "You know she was apprehensive about him and I squashed that. I'm such a jerk."

"You're not. You wanted to see your friend happy, and it didn't work out." Daniel reached over and squeezed her hand.

Saturday, November 13, 1993

Felice called Sam first thing in the morning. She tried to arrange a time to meet, but Sam's schedule wouldn't permit it. Felice felt this news had to be delivered in person. Sam promised to stop by her place after her run Sunday morning.

The DiLeo's were in Frank's office in the afternoon. All their business was updated, so they were on the same page. Joe got Dominic off to the side before leaving.

"I think I fucked up," Joe said to Dominic.

"It's been my experience that if you think you did, you did. I'm going to take a wild guess. Sam?"

"I went to see the Neville Brothers last night with a date and—"

"Sam was there?" Dominic interrupted.

"No, her best friend."

"Are you trying to get Sam to dump you?" Dominic laughed.

"It's not a joke Dom," Joe ran his fingers through his hair.

"Well Cuz, the hurricane's gonna hit. You just have to wait to see how much damage it causes."

"You're a big help," Joe said.

Sunday, November 14, 1993

As per arranged Sam stopped at Felice's. Sam could see the pain on Felice's face as she told her about the encounter with Joe.

Sam cupped her hand as a sign of support. "Felice I know about Jennifer. Joe was dating her before me. I foolishly assumed he had stopped seeing her."

"Her name wasn't Jennifer. It was Bridget. Bridget Sullivan."

Sam walked the few blocks to her house, despondent. She couldn't believe how affected she was. The thought of more women. A demeaning feeling washed over her. "I'll never be enough for him," ran over and over in her head.

Joe decided to test the waters with a phone call first. Sam was polite. No witty repartee. She told him she would be outside waiting for him.

After they rode a few blocks in silence, Joe decided to pull the bandaid off, "can we talk about—"

"Joe," Sam stopped him, "let's just enjoy the game today."

Things got more comfortable as the day went on. Unfortunately, the Saints lost. Joe insisted on coming up to Sam's apartment after the game.

"I know how you feel," Joe said in the most empathetic voice he could muster.

"Joe," Sam replied in a sultry voice, "I want you to visualize me lying naked on this rug. My legs opened wide and one of those hard body dancers from Blush over me. Imagine me wrapping my legs around him—"

"Stop it, Sam!" Joe snapped.

"As he slides his stiff cock inside me—"

Joe grabbed her shoulders and shook her, "I said, stop it."

Sam looked down at one of his hands still gripping her, then looked up at him. "Now, you know how I feel."

Joe took his hands off Sam and backed up.

"I think we need time to breathe," Sam said.

"My thoughts exactly," Joe replied and walked out.

Sunday night was busy, and so Sam had little time to think. Sandy gave her a lift home.

"Are you okay?" Sandy asked.

"Sorry, just thinking about the fight pictures I took," she lied. "There was a really good welterweight match. Some of those club fights are better than title matches."

"I never get to go to those. They're always on a Friday."

"Durán is fighting in Bay St. Louis next month on a Tuesday. My uncle is coming up with a super middleweight."

"Tuesday, are you sure?"

"Yeah, Tuesday, December 14. If you wanna go, I can get you tickets."

"Thanks, I might just take you up on that. I'll let you know."

Monday, November 15, 1993

"We're just going to take a breather."

"I don't know what that means," Felice said.

"I don't either. This whole thing was moving too fast. We just need to slow it down."

"So you're still going to see Joe?"

"I honestly don't know. I'm so busy right now; I don't need the distraction. The author that wants me to do the cover is bugging me for a preliminary sketch. The gym wanted pictures yesterday. That's on top of my normal day to day."

"Okay, I got it. You're not ready to talk about Joe."

"No, you don't get it. I have a lot of balls in the air right now. Can you just give it a rest with this Joe shit?"

SILENCE

"Felice," no answer. "Felice, please, I'm sorry."

"Mom wants to know if you're coming for Thanksgiving."

"Yes, I'll give her a call today," Sam said.

"Okay, talk later," Felice replied.

"Felice please."

"Sam, let me go. I have things to do also. Bye," Felice hung up.

Sam felt terrible. Sam would never intentionally hurt Felice. She wanted to call back and try to make it right but didn't. She figured everyone needs breathing room.

Wednesday, November 17, 1993

Felice called in the morning as she was getting ready for work. "Do you think you can fit lunch in today?" Felice asked.

"Absolutely."

"Palace Cafe, okay?"

"Sure, 12:30."

"12:30," Felice repeated and hung up.

Lunch was good as usual. They talked all the way through like the close friends they have always been.

"You know I can tell you are losing weight," Sam said with a smile.

"Let's not jinx it," Felice laughed.

"Alright, we won't talk about it."

"I do like the gym. Daniel is thinking about joining."

"That would be great," then Sam's tone shifted. "Felice, I'm so sorry I snapped at you on the phone. This whole thing has got me off balance."

Felice afraid of pissing Sam off again just gave a tight-lipped head nod.

"It just felt right. You know, familiar. I guess I thought it was the same for him. Claude warned me," Sam chuckled.

"Has he called?"

Sam shook her head, "no."

"What if he does."

"I don't know."

Chris came down from the office as the band was setting up. He walked into the storage room that led to the back bar. Sam could see him talking to Sandy. Sandy called Sam over.

"Chris wants to talk to you," Sandy said.

"Shit, I'm getting fired," raced through her head.

"Sam, have you heard from Claude?" Chris asked.

"No. Why?"

"He hasn't shown up to work."

"Maybe he overslept."

"Sam he didn't show last night either," Chris sounded concerned. "Dominic called his father. Maurice said he left Houma Monday."

The night was busy enough to put thoughts of Claude on the back burner. Her concern for her friend returned as they slowed down toward the end of the evening. Sandy took Sam home.

"What do you think?" Sam asked.

"About what?"

"Claude."

"Sam, don't worry. He's probably tied to a bed somewhere," Sandy grinned.

"It's not funny, Sandy."

"I wasn't trying to be. You know he leads an unusual lifestyle. I'm sure he'll show up with a great story."

Thursday, November 18, 1993

Sandy had to get to the bar. He was running late for the liquor deliveries. He would drive up Dauphine to Conti and one block down to Bourbon. Conti was closed to traffic. "Another fucking movie," Sandy thought. A cop stood in the middle of the street waving cars off to St. Louis. Then he had to go one block down Burgundy to Toulouse. Toulouse to Royal. Royal up to Bienville. Bienville to Bourbon and Bourbon to Conti.

"Jesus fucking Christ!" Sandy blurted out loud when he got out of his truck. He looked up Conti to see roadblocks near Dauphine. He noticed Dominic walking down Conti towards Bourbon. As Dominic was nearing the corner, he stopped, bent over and threw up. Sandy stood there, not knowing how to respond. Dominic straightened up and continued walking toward Sandy. Sandy unlocked the bar and held the door open until Dominic walked through. Dominic got behind the bar and splashed water on his face. He grabbed the first bottle of brown liquor he saw and poured a healthy shot into a rock glass. He drank it down and repeated the process. Then his face contorted as he fought back tears and said one word.

"Claude!"

Sandy was sitting at the table. Sam's mind was racing. What on earth brought Sandy here. "You sure I can't get you anything?"

"No, thank you. Sam, please sit down," he swallowed his breath. "It's Claude," Sandy paused, "he's gone."

It took Sam a moment to process what she just heard, "How?"

"Probably suicide. You need to prepare yourself. It's going to be in the newspapers and on TV."

"Tell me."

"I'm sure you are aware that Claude's private life was unconventional," Sandy said. "Dominic went to his apartment this morning. There was no answer, but the smell near the door alarmed him. He got the manager to let him in. They found a man tied to the bed with a belt around his neck. Claude was next to him with a plastic bag over his head. They had been dead for a couple of days."

Sam got up, went to the bathroom, and came out with tissues. She wiped her eyes and sat back down.

"He probably went too far," Sandy continued. "Realizing his partner was dead, he took his own life."

Sandy stayed with Sam until she was cried out, "call me if you need anything."

Sam shook her head.

"Even if you just want to talk."

"Okay. Thank you."

When she felt she could talk about it without breaking down, she called Felice. Felice was horrified.

Sam couldn't eat. She sat at the table with her sketch pad, drawing Claude from memory. It was shortly after 8:00 when the phone rang. She thought about ignoring it, but if it was Felice, she would walk down to see if she was alright.

"Hello," she sniffled.

"It's Joe, baby," his tone empathetic. "I know about Claude. I'm sorry. How are you doing?"

"I'm okay," she could barely get the words out.

"Do you want me to come over, or you could come over here."

"No, I'll be okay."

"If you need anything. Anything at all—"

"I'm fine," Sam interrupted. "I need to hang up now. Thank you."

"You're wel—"

Sam hung up before he could finish.

She took a container of chicken soup out of the freezer. Filled the sink halfway with warm water and put the container in. She walked into the bedroom and got out of her clothes, slipping on sweatpants, and a T-shirt then laid on top of the comforter and closed her eyes. When she opened them, it was 4:15 in the morning. The lights and tv were still on in the living room. It took her a few seconds to piece things together. Her friend was gone.

She thought of Sandy. The way he connected to her pain. She saw yet another facet to Sandy. He was laser focus to her needs.

She slid her right hand under her shirt and cupped her breast, rubbing her thumb back and forth over her nipple. The piercing blue-green of Sandy's eyes came to mind. Her hand slid over to her other breast gripping and pulling the nipple. She could feel her panties sticking. Leaning back on her shoulders, she lifted her ass enough to slide her pants down. She released one leg from them then widened her spread. She was wet. She found her relief quickly as her left hand grasped at the comforter, her right hand gliding across her engorged clit.

She laid there recovering. Her mind drifted back to her friend. How addicting was that high? Was it worth two lives?

Ashes

Thursday, November 25, 1993, Thanksgiving

"Are you sure you two don't need a hand?" Daniel asked, then gave Felice a quick kiss.

"No, thank you. We have this down to a science," Felice replied as she wrapped leftovers.

Sam was at the sink washing dishes. "You got a winner," Sam said to Felice after Daniel left.

"Thanks to you," Felice smiled. "How are you doing?"

"Could you be more specific?"

"No, you'll yell at me," Felice joked.

"Joe called to see how I was doing the day Claude's body was discovered."

"What did he say?"

"How are you? If you need anything. The usual. Blah, blah, blah. This whole thing has thrown me. You know Claude's family refuses to claim the body."

"How do you know that?"

"Chris and Dominic were talking about it at the bar last night. What do you think happens if nobody claims the body?"

"I don't know Sam."

Friday, November 26, 1993

Friday after Thanksgiving is always hectic in a retail store. Sam didn't get her lunch break until 1:45. She stepped out onto Canal and flagged a taxi. She went to the Orleans Parish Coroner's Office.

"You did what?" Felice asked, shocked. "Your ability to surprise me is never-ending."

"Well, his family is just abandoning him. You'd think the city would be pleased that someone wanted to retrieve the remains."

"Sam, listen to yourself. You're asking the Parish Coroner to give you a body. Then what?"

"I'll have him cremated. How much do you think that will cost?"

"I don't think it makes a difference, seeing as they aren't going to give you the body."

"I spoke to an assistant. Maybe if I spoke directly to the Parish Coroner, you know, it would be making their job easier."

"Move on, Sam. I know how upset this whole thing has made you, but you have to put it to rest, so to speak."

"That's what I'm trying to do. He was discarded, Felice. By his own family that he loved and he thought loved him."

"I'm sure however the coroner's office handles it, it will be with respect," Felice said in a comforting voice as she and Daniel got up from the bar. "Come on, join us for dinner? You know you're always welcome at Shabbat."

"No thanks, I'm going to get a bite here. You two have fun." Sam asked the bartender for a menu.

On her way home, she cut over to Bourbon Street and stopped into Azure. The new doorman didn't know Sam.

"Hi, is Dominic in yet?" Sam asked.

He thought her out of place in her well-tailored coat and expensive boots. "He's in his office upstairs. Is he expecting you?"

"I'm Sam. Would you ask Dominic if I could come up please."

"Sammm!" an unforgettable high pitched voice called from behind the bar.

Sam walked to the bar while the doorman called Dominic. Tanya went on about her grief over Claude. Claude couldn't stand Tanya, and Sam was quite sure the feelings were mutual. The doorman gave Sam the go-ahead. Sam said her goodbyes to Tanya and headed up to Dominic's office.

Dominic figured this was going to be a conversation about Joe. Normally, Dominic wouldn't have entertained a one on one about anyone's love life, but he was invested in this story. Plus he always got a kick out of Sam.

Sam walked into Dominic's office and took off her coat. She had on a long-sleeved, black turtleneck knit dress that clung to her tight body. Her mahogany hair fell over one eye.

"My cousin is an asshole for fucking this up." Dominic thought. "What can I do for you, Sam?"

"I need help getting Claude's body."

"Sam, I wouldn't begin to know how you're going to get the body without the family's permission. Maurice wouldn't even discuss it with my father, and they go back forty years. Claude's family is devastated, the circumstances being what they were."

"I thought you might know someone in the coroner's office or some official that could pull a few strings."

"Honey you need to talk to Joe if that's the route you want to take. He's the one with all the connections."

Sam thanked Dominic and went home. She got Joe's answering machine when she called.

"Joe, Sam. Could you give me a call when—"

"Hi. Let me turn this off," he said, speaking over the message. "How are you?"

"I'm good. Joe, I need your help with something," she then pled her case.

"Baby are you sure about this? The Parish will take care of the remains if no one claims the body."

"I want to do this. Can you help me?"

"There's nothing I can do until Monday. I'll make a few calls."

"Thank you."

"Have dinner with me." .... "Sam this isn't tit for tat. I'm going to make the calls for you. I think this is something we should be able to straighten out. If not, it could have a better ending. It'll give you a chance to have a nice meal." Joe chuckled.

That got a small laugh out of Sam.

"Monday night?" Joe asked, hopefully.

"Tuesday," Sam replied.

"I'll pick you up at Lambert's."

"Cool."

"Goodnight Peanut."

Joe's confidence was back. He was going to play his hand right this time. He wanted to stop at Sam's Sunday after church but restrained himself. Joe was at the coroner's office when they opened Monday. It was an easy fix. He called Sam in the afternoon to update her on his progress.

"Everything is taken care of," Joe said.

"What do I have to do?"

"Nothing baby. Claude's body will be picked up by the crematorium. It will take a week or two before we get the remains. I assume you want the ashes?"

"Yes, I do. When do I pay them? I don't even know how much."

"Sam, the DiLeo's are paying for everything."

"Joe, I didn't call you so you would do that."

"I know that. I talked to Uncle Frank, and he felt the family should take care of it."

"Thank you."

"I'll see you tomorrow?"

"Yes, thank you so much, Joe."

"You're more than welcome baby."

Tuesday, November 30, 1993

Joe opened the car door for her.

"How does Delmonico's sound?" Joe asked.

"Perfect."

The first thing out of Joe's mouth when he got into the car was an apology. Sam stopped him.

"Joe, you have nothing to apologize for. We haven't been dating that long." Sam could see the relief on his face. "That said, I want you to understand how I felt."

"Sam, I—"

"You're doing that thing again."

"What thing?"

"That thing where you start talking in the middle of me trying to make my point."

"Oh the thing," Joe grinned. He mimicked, locking his mouth shut and throwing away the key.

Sam smiled. "I was embarrassed that my best friend saw you. I was embarrassed that her boyfriend's first impression of you was with another woman."

"Sam—"

"Not done yet," Sam warned. "I have never had a more intense sexual experience then I have had with you. I incorrectly assumed it was a unique experience for you also, and I was fulfilling your needs. That said, I feel my little speech I gave you at Lambert's turned out to be prophetic. I'm the waiting in the wings gal."

Joe pulled the car over. "Are you done?" Joe's inflection was forceful. Sam didn't answer. "Because if this is going to be your tone for the evening, I don't think a restaurant is where we should be heading." Joe took a deep breath. "What do you want Sam?"

"I don't know?" she replied in a small voice.

"That's helpful. Sam, I want to straighten this out, but I don't know how. On one hand, you say I have nothing to apologize for. On the other, you're upset with me. What do you expect? I'm clueless."

"I'm sorry," she mouthed.

"I asked you out multiple times, and you gave me cryptic answers. Why wouldn't I think you were seeing someone else."

"You knew I had dinner with Felice on that Tuesday."

"I only found that out when we had a fucking conversation about stuffed mushrooms. I found out by accident that you had a gig that Friday."

"Okay, if I'm understanding you, your plans were based on perceptions of what I might be doing. You could have canceled your date when you realized I wasn't going out with another man."

"I could have. In retrospect, I should have, but I didn't. Ball's in your court, Sam. Where do you want to go from here?"

She paused for a moment then said, "dinner."

Joe pulled her close and gave her a deep kiss. He grabbed her chin and said, "you're giving me acido." (heartburn) Then gave her a quick peck.

"Good," Sam smiled.

They were able to get back into their groove by dinners end. Joe held up the last piece of shared dessert on his fork, offering it to Sam.

Sam shook her head and giggled, "I'm stuffed. I can't put another thing in my mouth."

"Questo mi delude," (this disappoints me) Joe laughed.

It was only 9:15 when they got to Sam's apartment.

"Are you coming up?" Sam asked.

"Baby, you'd need a gun to stop me," Joe joked.

Joe grabbed his briefcase and duffel bag out of the trunk. Sam took a shower while Joe changed into jeans. He stuck his head into the bathroom. "Where's the book?" Joe asked.

"What book?"

"The Grisham book."

"On the bookcase below the tv."

Joe sat in his favorite chair and opened the book. He smiled when he saw his bookmark was still there. Sam came out of the bathroom in her oversized white robe and headed for the kitchen.

"Would you like hot chocolate?"

"With marshmallows?"

"Yes. You look hot."

"Do I?" Joe laughed.

"Yes, you do. Very fuckable."

"Hot chocolate first. Let me finish this last chapter baby, and I'll fuck you senseless," Joe chuckled.

"A true romantic," Sam laughed.

Sam sat at the end of the sofa, curled up with her sketch pad.

Joe finished the book and got up. He took the sketch pad out of Sam's hands and put it on the table, then led her to one of the dining chairs. Joe had his hands on the arms of the chair, caging Sam in, bending down he softly kissed her. Next, he untied her robe and opened it, getting down on his knees he opened her legs wide. He kissed her breast and bit her nipples. She moaned as he worked his way down to her stomach. His bites left faint imprints. He kissed the inside of her thighs and sucked hard until marks were left. He slid his hands under her ass and raised it, bringing her toward him while simultaneously bringing his mouth down to her clit.

Sam gripped the arms of the chair and pulled back, "no."

Joe stopped, moved up, and kissed her. She could taste herself. "Tell me what's wrong baby," Joe whispered.

"I'm just not comfortable with it."

"You're going to get comfortable with it," Joe said with confidence. "You're going to get comfortable with a lot of things you haven't explored." With each of his index fingers, he flipped the ends of the belt of her robe over the chairs arms and her wrist simultaneously. He deftly tied down her right wrist.

"What do you think you're doing?"

Joe smiled.

Sam's eyes doubled in size, "Joe."

"Shush, behave."

Her breathing quickened as she watched him do the same to her left wrist. His smile broadened as he spread her legs and knelt. His hands back under her ass, he moved her forward. She closed her eyes as she felt his tongue skillfully take her to la petite mort.

Wednesday, December 1, 1993

He was showered, shaved, and partially dressed just minus his shoes and socks. His jacket hung over the back of the chair and his tie over his shoulders. "This looks good. Thank you," Joe said as he dug into the hash and eggs Sam made from her previous night's doggie bag. "Will you please sit down."

"Do you want more coffee?"

"Sam," Joe waved his open hand to Sam's chair. "We have plenty of time. Relax, enjoy your breakfast. I've been meaning to ask you, now that Claude is no longer with us, how are you getting home from work?"

"Sandy. He lives in the Marigny."

"I know where he lives."

"Is that a problem?"

"You tell me. Has he ever hit on you?"

"Of course not," Sam said defensively. "You know green is not an attractive color on you."

"I'm a man. I know how this shit works."

"You're being ridiculous. You don't have to trust him. You just have to trust me." Sam reached over and put her hand on his cheek, "Okie Dokie?"

"Okie Dokie," Joe laughed. "We might be having dinner with Dominic and his wife on Friday. They want to have you over. I'll let you know tomorrow."

"Should I make a dessert?"

"Hold off on that. I'm going to try to talk them into going out. I'll share this with you, but if you repeat it, I'll call you a liar. Dominic's wife can't cook."

Sam giggled, "what about Chris's wife?"

"Lena, she's a good cook. She's Greek. You're the best cook in the group."

Sam grinned. "Can I ask you a question about last night?"

"Sure," Joe answered raising an eyebrow.

She hesitated.

"Baby, ask me."

"What did you mean by I'm going to get comfortable with things I haven't explored?"

Joe grinned, "don't panic. No circus acts will be involved."

"And no other people."

"You won't have to worry about that."

"Then what did you mean?"

"Enough questions. Eat your breakfast."

She picked up her fork and started to eat. That was one of the many things Joe liked about her. She knew when he was done with a conversation.

Sweet and Sour

Wednesday, December 1, 1993

Sandy and Sam were both leaning against the bar on their forearms, staring out onto Bourbon Street.

"It's going to be hit or miss until after Christmas," Sandy said as he played with the bandaid coming off his finger. "Do you have a bandaid in your purse?"

"I might, I'll check." Sam was back in a minute after looking in her purse. "No luck. I can run over to the mini-mart and get some."

"No thanks, I'll go," Sandy said as he pushed himself away from the bar. "I'll be back in a few."

Sam was at the service bar when a voice from across the bar asked.

"Where's Sandy?"

Sam turned to see familiar blue-green eyes. He was slightly taller than Sandy. 30 to 40 pounds lighter. His eyes were sunk in. His face sallow. Had he approached Sam on the street, she would have been nervous.

"Where's Sandy?" he repeated more aggressively this time.

At that moment, Sandy was standing at the door on Bourbon, "Ryan, get out here."

When the man got closer to the door, Sandy grabbed his arm and yanked him out of the building. Sam couldn't hear them, but it was obvious they were arguing. The man with Sandy's eyes walked down Bourbon. Sandy got back behind the bar and barely spoke the rest of the night. He was visibly annoyed.

"You need a lift?" Sandy abruptly asked.

"If you don't mind," Sam replied.

"Why would I mind?" Sandy's tone softened.

They road a few blocks in silence.

"I know you caught the brunt of my aggravation tonight. I apologize."

Sam didn't reply.

"He's killing himself, and he's taking me and my parents with him."

"I'm sorry," was the only response Sam could think of.

They didn't speak the rest of the ride.

Thursday, December 2, 1993

It was 2:30 in the afternoon. "What are you doing here this early?" Sam asked as she took a baking dish out of the refrigerator.

"I was on my way to Uncle Frank's and saw the perfect parking place right below your apartment. I thought I better grab it," Joe said as he watched Sam over her shoulder. "What do we have here?" He kissed her cheek.

"Coniglio alla stimpirata." (sweet and sour rabbit.)

"I can't fucking wait to tell Dominic," Joe snickered like a little boy. "Remember we're having dinner tomorrow with Dom, Chris and their wife's."

"Chris too?"

"He's warming up to the idea of us. You're gonna love Lena."

"What about Sarah?"

"She's a sweetheart. The dinner was her idea but don't take offense if she's a little standoffish at first since you worked at Azure."

"Does she think everyone that worked at Azure slept with her husband?" Sam asked.

"She knows he was screwing around. She just doesn't know with who," Joe walked into the bedroom to change but still carried on the conversation. "How was last night."

"Slow," Sam replied. "This was strange. A guy named Ryan came in looking for Sandy."

"Sandy's brother. How was he?"

"He was in rough shape. Scary looking."

"I'm surprised the fucking guy's still alive. At one time he was in better shape than Sandy."

152

"Those days are long gone. He almost looked like someone with AIDS."

"Could be. He's been living on the street a long time," Joe replied, walking out of the bedroom. "He's been fucked up on crack for years."

"Has anyone tried to help him."

"I'd like to have the money Sandy and his parents have spent on rehab and doctors. Let alone attorneys fees keeping him out of jail. What a waste. Ryan was a sharp guy at one time."

"Why couldn't you help and save them attorney fees?"

"Baby I have on more than one occasion. Pro bono. So has Dominic when he still had his license."

"I felt sorry for Sandy. He was embarrassed. What time do you want to eat?"

"6:30, 7:00 if that works for you," Joe said as he grabbed his briefcase. "I'll be back in a couple of hours."

"Cool. I'll have plenty of time for an uninterrupted shower," Sam laughed.

"I'll interrupt you later. Joe smiled and gave Sam a quick kiss. He picked up her keys off the counter and put them in his jeans pocket.

"Whoa, big boy. Where do you think you're going with those?"

"What if you're in the shower?"

"Okay, you got me on that one. Next time ask."

"You don't make it easy," Joe smirked.

Sam laughed, putting her arms around his waist and grabbing his ass. He gave her a kiss. "Go," she grinned.

She took her shower and put on a casual jersey dress. Fixed her hair and applied a touch of makeup. Something she rarely did on her days off.

Dinner was set, and the entire apartment smelled inviting.

"Peanut?" Joe called out.

"In the kitchen Sven."

Dominic nudged Chris, "they have nicknames."

Sam was surprised to hear Dominic's voice then Chris's.

"It smells like our childhood," Chris said.

"This is a nice surprise," Sam replied.

"You mean our cousin didn't call to let you know we were coming?" Chris asked.

"No, but that's not necessary." Sam tried to ease Chris's

discomfort.

Dominic gave Joe a shove, "asshole."

Joe laughed, "can I get you something to drink?"

"Yes, please. What would you like? Chris, I just opened a nice dry white wine. Gavi," Sam offered.

"That would be nice. Thank you, Sam," Chris replied.

"Dominic, what can I get you?" Sam asked.

"Beer if you have it."

"I do."

Chris and Dominic were studying the fight posters above the sofa. Sam poked her finger into Joe's chest and mouthed, "I'm gonna fucking kill you."

Joe grinned, took her hand and bit her finger. She giggled. Joe got two beers, while Sam poured the wine. Dominic was standing at the window.

"May I?" Dominic asked, pointing to the balcony."

"Sure," Sam replied.

Dominic raised the large window and walked out onto the balcony. Chris followed. Joe and Sam with drinks in hand behind them.

"Nice size. You could do a lot with this space," Dominic said.

"The table and chairs inside were bought for the balcony. My apartment is a work in progress. My friend Felice is on the lookout for a dining room set for me," Sam replied.

"Felice Sax," Joe clarified. "She works at Mencher's."

"Really?" Chris said. "Lena wants a new sofa. I'll let her know."

They went back inside, and Joe took his cousins up to Sam's studio while she checked on her dinner. After which she joined them.

They were looking at the triptych of Sam's uncle's first gym.

"Sam, these are wonderful," Chris said, staring at the picture.

"Thank you."

"Jesus, it looks just like him," Dominic said, his eye wandering to a sketch of Claude.

Sam gave him a faint smile.

"He was lucky to have you as a friend," Dominic finished.

"So?" Joe asked, looking for a response from his cousins.

"I'm good with it," Dominic said.

"Absolutely, he'll love it," Chris added.

"We'll take it," Joe said to Sam.

"WHAT!"

Joe laughed, "baby, we jointly get Uncle Frank a Christmas gift every year. This is perfect for his office."

They went back downstairs, and Sam placed two small plates of coniglio alla stimpirata on the table with a basket of warm crusty Italian bread. "Dominic, Chris, mangiare," (eat) Sam said.

"No, Sam, that's your dinner," Chris said.

"There's plenty. Your cousin won't go hungry," Sam laughed. "Un piccolo antipasto," (a small appetizer) she waved her open hand towards the table.

Dominic was already breaking off a piece of bread when Chris thanked Sam and sat down.

"You didn't have to do that," Sam said as they ate dinner.

"Do what?" Joe asked.

"A couple of things. Bring your cousins without giving me a heads up, for one thing. What if I greeted you nude. And talk them into buying one of my paintings."

"Sorry about the first thing. You are right. But the painting is probably going to be one of the best gifts we ever got Uncle Frank. Sam, stop selling yourself short. The minute I saw that piece, I pictured it in my uncle's office."

"Thank you."

"Surely you can think of a better way to show your gratitude," Joe smiled and gave her a wink.

Friday, December 3, 1993

"I've always wanted to eat here," Sam said to Joe as he held the car door open.

"You'll love it. Upperline is one of my favorite restaurants."

Chris and Lena were standing near the front door.

"God, they're beautiful," Sam said under her breath as they got closer.

"We're sexier," Joe whispered in Sam's ear.

Joe did the introduction, "are we waiting for Dom and Sarah, or should we go in?"

"They're already inside checking on our reservation," Chris answered.

With Joe's hand on Sam's back, he led her in. The walls were covered in art. Sam's smile widened as they walked through a series of rooms to get to their table. Just as they had begun to sit down, a familiar voice hit them like a bucket of cold water.

"Joe, can I talk to you?" Jennifer said.

All of them were frozen in their spots.

"As you can see Jennifer, we are about to sit down to dinner," Joe replied.

"I'm afraid I'm going to have to insist," Jennifer's voice started to rise.

"Vai avanti," (go ahead) Sam said softly.

"Mi dispiace," (I'm sorry) Joe replied.

Before Joe walked off with Jennifer, Sam stopped him saying, "Lascia la pistola, prendi i cannoli." (leave the gun, take the cannoli.)

Joe smiled and walked out with Jennifer.

Chris and Dominic were trying to muffle their laughter.

Their night was ruined. When Jennifer wasn't crying she was screaming. Joe tried to reason with her to no avail. Jennifer was threatening Sam's job at Lambert's as Joe walked away.

"I don't understand. Did she follow us? How did she know we were there?" Sam asked.

"She was there on a date and saw us walk in."

"Where was her date?"

"He walked out in the middle of it. Jennifer pretty much told him to go fuck himself, so he left."

"What are you going to do? What are we going to do?" Sam asked.

"Trust me; this shit ends Monday morning. That cunt will be dealt with."

Joe was almost scary, Sam thought. They didn't have sex that night. Joe held her tight until she fell asleep.

Joe drove Sam to work Saturday morning.

"I mean it, Sam, if you see her, call me. Okay?"

Sam gave a faint smile, "I'll be fine."

"I'm not fucking around. Call me. Do you understand?"

"Yes."

Joe picked Sam up from Lambert's. He drove her to Christos that evening. As far as Sam was concerned, this was becoming absurd. When Joe showed up at Christos just before closing that night, she had enough.

"What the fuck are you doing here?" Sam asked.

"Picking you up."

"This is bullshit," Sam snapped at Joe. "I don't want everyone here to know about us."

"For fuck sake, Sam. You're on Bourbon Street. What they don't know, they'll make up," Joe barked back. He took a deep breath and regained his composure, "I'm sorry I got you into this. I'll fix it."

He made love to her gently that night. "How do you feel?" Joe asked afterward.

"Cared for."

He dropped her off and picked her up Sunday at Christos'.

Monday he left her apartment suited up in attorney mode. He had two appointments before he saw Jeromy Kincaid.

Jeromy went first, "I find myself in a precarious position. Though you have been a valued client of this bank for years, your treatment of my sister has to be addressed. She's completely devastated. She's taken to her bed since she realized you've started up with the store clerk who blatantly made advances toward you. I feel a certain amount of responsibility as I was the one who facilitated this courtship. I must confess, you are a bit of an enigma. When I extended that more than generous credit line for your family's new venture, I assumed I was dealing with a gentleman."

Joe unruffled asked, "Is that your home run swing, Jeromy? You're going to dangle our business relationship? The courtship with your sister consisted of three dates in two months. Her reaction after I told her I didn't intend to see her again was so disproportionate I question, as should you, her stability. The store clerk as you call her has been nothing but gracious in spite of the abhorrent treatment your sister has doled out. In fact, your sister tends to talk down to most people in any service business. As far as your generous credit line goes, I have two banks that would be more than happy to match it for the opportunity to have the DiLeo business. I'm giving you two options, number one, control your sister, and keep her away from my girlfriend. Number two, I close all the DiLeo accounts. That's how you hit a curveball, Jeromy."

Because of Jennifer's total dependence on family money, Jeromy only had to pull a few purse strings to convince his sister to move on. Neither Joe or Sam ever heard from Jennifer again.

The Sicilians have a saying that roughly translates; cold fish has sweeter meat. Within a year, all of the DiLeo's accounts had been moved to another bank.

Duràn

Friday, December 10, 1993

Sam and Joe were standing in front of Upperline, waiting for Chris, Dominic, and their wives.

Dominic and Sarah arrived a minute later. "We're going to try this again?" Dominic chuckled.

"Sam has never eaten here, so yes," Joe said hugging Sam's shoulder.

"As long as you're paying, I'm good," Dominic ribbed.

"Joe, that's not necessary," Sarah said.

"Yes, it is," Dominic rebutted.

"Sarah, I insist. After all, I'm the reason we didn't get to eat here last week."

"Oh, your cousin had a very nice meal when we got home," Sarah smiled.

Dominic rolled his eyes behind her back.

"Joe said you're quite a good cook," Sarah said to Sam. "We'll have to trade recipes."

"That sounds like a good idea," Dominic grinned.

It was all Sam could do to keep from laughing, remembering Joe's remark about Sarah's cooking.

They were seated as soon as Chris and Lena got there. The ladies bombarded Sam with questions. Joe found things out that he didn't even know.

"I'm doing the book cover with a contract for the next two," Sam was explaining to the table.

"How does that work?" Chris asked. "Who holds the copyrights to the image?"

"I'm not 100% clear on it. I'm going to have an attorney look at it."

Joe leaned his face in front of Sam. "Hello!"

"I know, but I should show it to someone who's better versed at copyrights," Sam said.

"Are you kidding me?" Joe asked while the rest of the table laughed.

"That's an expertise, you know like criminal law or tax law," Sam tried to clarify.

Joe picked up her fork with a shrimp on it, "here baby, have another bite."

They all laughed.

"You were a hit," Joe said on the ride home.

"I like them," Sam replied. "I feel sorry for Sarah."

"Why would you say that?"

"You can see the desperation in her eyes when she looks at Dominic."

"They're working things out, Sam. Dominic would fall apart without her."

"Then why does he fuck around?"

"He's cleaned his act up," Joe said. Sam laughed. "Knock it off, Sam," Joe's voice was stern.

They walked into Sam's apartment, Joe carrying the usual duffel and briefcase. They both went into the bedroom to get out of their suits. Joe took his jacket off and hung it in the closet. He was undoing his tie when he stepped behind Sam and kissed her neck. With his tie, he covered her eyes. Her hands came up to the sides of her head as her breathing quickened. Joe tied it around her head. His mouth close to her ear softly saying, "you're safe," over and over until her breathing slowed down. "I'm going to take care of you."

Joe undressed her, then gently laid her on the bed. With the tips of his fingers, he lightly brushed the inside of her right thigh, opening her leg. Her breathing picked up again. "Keep your leg like that." He did the same with her left leg. "You're doing good baby." He took her left hand by the wrist and moved her arm above her head, wrapping her fingers around the wrought iron headboard, "hold on." He let his fingers lightly graze the length of her arm.

Joe bit her nipple hard then sucked gently on it. She gasped. "Don't move." He walked around to the other side of the bed, removing his shirt along the way. He took her right hand and brought it up to the headboard, "you're doing good baby." His fingers slowly moved down her arm. "Are you mine?" Joe asked.

"Yes," her reply was barely audible. The next thing she felt unnerved her. She felt the leather of his belt brush over her stomach. Her breath hitched. "Joe!"

"Quiet Baby," his voice was more authoritative now -- quick light slap across her mons, then the inside of her thighs. The motion steady working his way down to her feet. She felt off-balance, wanting him to stop yet wanting more. He worked his way back up. It was rhythmic. It was when his belt lightly slapped her nipple that she came. Joe rolled her over onto her stomach. He had her place her hands through the wrought iron headboard, so they dangled on the other side. He fastened them together, using her panties. Joe laid the belt down next to her face to prop her hips higher with pillows. He picked the belt back up and dragged the end down her spine slowly. He added intensity with each strike until her ass was bright fuchsia and warm to his touch. Joe climbed between her thighs and entered her.

Afterward, she quietly laid in his arms, twirling the hair on his chest around her finger.

"Peanut, are you okay?"

She looked up at him and smiled. "Yes."

He kissed her forehead. "You know I love you."

"I know you think you do."

Joe chuckled, "and I know you love me."

"Unfortunately," she joked, smiling up at him.

Tuesday, December 14, 1993

They hadn't spoken of that night. Sam thought they should but didn't know how to approach it. Today would not be the day for that conversation. Today she was going to see her uncle. Monday night Sam put all the Christmas presents for the family in Joe's trunk. They would leave right from Lambert's to the Casino Magic in Bay St. Louis. Her uncle's boxer was fighting just before Durán so although they wouldn't have time for dinner, they didn't have to rush.

"Tell me again, why you gave the tickets to Sandy," Joe asked.

"Really? We're doing this again?" Sam replied.

"I'm sure Dominic and Chris would have liked to have gone," Joe said, keeping his eyes on the road. "What is it with you and Sandy?"

"I was about to ask you the same thing," Sam sighed. "Joe, Sandy's nice enough to give me a ride home. My other option would be to walk home at 3:00 in the morning alone, or you could get up in the middle of the night and come get me."

"Did United Cab go out of business?" Joe sneered.

They were quiet for a few minutes, then Sam said, "Joe, please don't ruin this night for me. I haven't seen my uncle for almost a year, and I have been looking forward to this for months."

Joe felt foolish, "I'm sorry."

Sam pulled a brown paper bag out of her purse. "I have tea sandwiches," she smiled.

"God she's precious," Joe thought. "Who else would bring tea sandwiches to a boxing match."

They ate the sandwiches and talked about their day while Joe drove. Even the best of conversations have an occasional lull. It was at that point Joe told Sam his story.

"I went through a real asshole stage when I was a kid. Ryan and I got into all kinds of shit."

"Sandy's brother?" Sam interrupted.

"Yes. Our thing was ripping off street dealers. What are they gonna do? Call a cop? There was a guy we were eyeing. Lived on St. Ann in a double shotgun. He loved the strippers. When he got a few bucks in his pocket, he would head to the nearest jiggle joint. That's when we would break in. Which meant we needed Sandy."

"Hold it. Sandy?"

"There's not a lock that Sandy can't get past."

"I'm sorry for interrupting again. You have to fill in some blanks."

"Remember this next time I have a question in the middle of one of your stories," Joe laughed. "You know Sandy's parents have that hardware store in Algiers."

"Yeah, Gillespie's Hardware."

"Yes," Joe corrected. "Well, it was originally Gillespie's Lock and Key. His grandfather, as well as his father, were locksmiths by trade. When most kids were learning to tie their shoes, Sandy was learning how to pick a lock. He excelled at it. Ryan, on the other hand, had no interest in learning the family trade. So Sandy got us into the house and we were ransacking it looking for drugs and money. We were on the wrong side of the shotgun. A couple walked in. They got Sandy. Ryan and I managed to get away. Ryan and I were both nineteen. Sandy was seventeen. Sandy never talked. He took the rap and was sent to a juvenile correctional facility. That was my scared straight moment. I cleaned up my act and focused on school and my future. My uncle assured Sandy's parents that he would be taken care of when he got out. Back then my Uncle Frank was very hands on with all the bars. He took Sandy under his wings and taught him every end of the business. Sandy started as a doorman at Christos and worked his way up."

"When Uncle Frank and Dominic got indicted he put Sandy in charge of Christos and ordering the liquor for all the clubs. That was to take some of the pressure off Chris. Sandy gets a small percentage of profit plus a nice salary and tips. In retrospect, getting busted might have been the best thing to happen to Sandy," Joe chuckled.

"Wow! Do you hear yourself?"

Silence.

Joe parked the car. He reached over and turned her to face him. "Sandy blamed me. He blamed me for having the wrong side of the house, which I did. But he also blames me for Ryan. Ryan started his downward slide when Sandy went away. I distanced myself from him. I was done with that shit. There was animosity when Sandy got out. At any rate, Sandy and I have built a tolerance for each other through the years."

Sam kissed Joe, "I love you. You piss me off, but I love you."

"Back at you, Peanut," Joe laughed.

The casino was a riverboat. The fight was held in a circus size tent on land close to the casino. It was the middle of a round when Sam and Joe walked in.

"Not exactly Vegas," Joe said as they looked for their seats.

"Stop it," Sam snapped back.

They found their seats. Sam sat next to Sandy and Joe next to her. Sandy's father who he introduced at the end of the round sat on the other side of him. Ian Gillespie was a good looking man. Same eyes as his sons but the color was more of a blue-gray. You could see the love Sandy had for his father. That hard exterior of Sandy's thinned a little around him. Sam couldn't recall seeing Sandy smile so much.

"Thank you for the tickets," Ian leaned over and said to Sam.

"Sandy tells me you know more about boxing than most men."

"You're welcome," Sam smiled. "I grew up at my uncle's gym. It rubbed off on me."

Joe noticed Sam's hand on Sandy's thigh when she leaned forward to talk to Ian. Joe whispered in her ear, "Togliti la mano dalla gamba di Sandy." (take your hand off Sandy's leg.)

She removed her hand and sat up straight. When the fight ended, Sam went to the ladies room. Joe was sitting next to Sandy when she got back. She didn't say a word, she just sat in the empty seat next to Joe.

Sam stood up when they were entering the ring. Her uncle got a glimpse of her and waved. She sat back down, smiling, "that's Fred Davis with him. He's one of the best cut men in the business."

A few guys looked over at her. Joe smiled. Name one other girlfriend that would know what a cut man was. The fight went five-rounds but should have ended in three. Her uncle's boxer far outmatched his opponent. Durán won his match in eight. A TKO.

After the fights, they all went to a locals bar for drinks and a bite to eat. On the ride from the casino to the bar, Joe came unglued.

"What the fuck was that?" Joe said so low and deliberate that she didn't recognize the voice.

"What are you talking about?"

"Don't fuck with me. Your hand, Sandy's leg."

"Joe, you're joking, right?"

"Joking! I'm as serious as a fucking coronary. It was so natural for you. Like something commonplace. He didn't flinch."

"Joe, you're acting so erratic. Why are you doing this? Please! I don't know what I can do to appease you."

"Appease me? So I'm crazy?"

"Joe you've doubled down on crazy."

They walked into the bar. Joe, as any good attorney was unreadable. Sam might as well have worn a T-shirt that said I'm miserable.

Her uncle concerned asked, "Cosa c'e' che non va?" (what's wrong?)

"Just a little tired Uncle Giacomo," Sam replied with a forced smile.

Her uncle realized Joe spoke Italian when she answered in English.

"Would you prefer Jack or Giacomo?" Sandy asked.

"Jack's good. My wife and niece are the only two that call me Giacomo."

Because Sam was the common thread, the conversation revolved around her. Her uncle regaled them with humorous anecdotes. It was easy to see she had her uncle's heart. He lifted her spirits.

As the night wound down, Joe excused himself to go to the restroom. Sam knew he was probably picking up the check on the sly. Her uncle held her hand, "Vedo che sei ben curato." (I see you are well taken care of)

"Lui mi ama," (he loves me) Sam replied.

"Entrambi ti amano." (they both love you)

Sam looked up at Sandy. What did her uncle see that she didn't? What did Joe see?

They exchanged boxes of gifts in the parking lot. Her uncle scolded her for spending so much money. She reassured him they were all token gifts, which they weren't. The ride back to New Orleans was quiet. She thought of Sandy, playing over all their interactions in her mind. Joe thought of his ungodly behavior. It was so uncharacteristic of him. He didn't recognize or like this Joe.

He placed the cardboard box full of gifts on the patio/dining table. She turned her back to him in bed. He spooned her kissing her neck. "I love you," Joe whispered. He got no response.

Wednesday, December 15, 1993

She wasn't in bed when he woke up. Probably on her morning run, he thought. He picked up his watch to check the time. 9:30. He couldn't believe he slept that late. Sam had already left for work. I have to make this right was racing through his mind when he walked to the kitchen to make coffee. The presents were stacked up at the end of the table. There was a small gift-wrapped box in front of his usual seat with a note placed under it.

The note read: The coffee is ready to go. Just press the button. The gift is from my family. Lock the door when you leave.

He stared at the box through two cups of coffee. He wasn't the kind to open presents early, but he clearly wasn't himself of late. It was a tasteful silver frame with a picture of a pigtailed little Sam with pink boxing gloves on. A small envelope accompanied it. The card inside read: Thank you for taking good care of our little girl.

Cannoli

Wednesday, December 15, 1993

"Sam, the vase is Baccarat," Ruth said, looking at the beautiful pale salmon-colored roses.

"No, you think so?" Sam asked.

"I know my crystal. What's the occasion?"

"He fucked up."

"Well, he apologizes in style," Ruth chuckled.

That put a smile on Sam's face. She read the card: No excuses. I was wrong. Forgive me, Sven.

Joe walked in just before closing. "I thought you might like a lift home," he said, looking at the flowers a few feet away.

"Thank you," she replied.

"Do you like the flowers?" he asked much like a little boy looking for his mother's approval.

"They're beautiful. My favorite color."

He smiled, "I know." He didn't. "And the vase?"

"Joe, it's stunning."

Ruth, who was in earshot, spoke up, "it's Baccarat, right?"

"Yes, " Joe chuckled.

"I know my crystal," Ruth gloated.

He stood in the kitchen, watching her as she prepared dinner. "Would you prefer I take a cab home from now on?" she asked.

"No, I was being—"

"A petulant child," Sam interjected.

"Asshole is a more appropriate description," Joe grinned. "I have a question I've been meaning to ask."

"Shoot."

"Is there a point when I can stop using condoms?"

"Sure, we can go to the AIDS clinic and be tested. Once the test comes back, we're good to go."

"You're going too?"

"Of course. You have a right to know my test results as well."

"Can we go tomorrow?" Joe asked.

"If you like."

"How long does it take for results?"

"Around three or four days."

"That can be my Christmas present," Joe laughed.

"Good, I'll save a few bucks," she grinned. "Speaking of presents, where is yours?"

"I opened it," he said with a boyish grin.

Sam laughed, "so what did you get?"

Joe went to his briefcase and took out the picture. He didn't show her the note.

Sam smiled, "those were my first boxing gloves. I loved them. The minute I walked into the gym, I'd have one of the guys help me put them on."

Joe smiled at Sam, "I don't think it's possible to get a better gift this year."

"Hey, I'm giving you condom-free sex."

Joe kissed her and thought, I can't fuck this up.

That night was the slowest she had worked at Christos. True to his word, Sandy kept the bar open til 3:00 A.M.

They talked a lot that night. Sam didn't know if it was lack of business or just knowing each other better that turned Sandy into a regular Chatty Kathy.

"My father and I had a good time last night."

"Good, I'm glad you enjoyed it."

"My dad needed it. Ryan showed up at my parent's house last weekend with some bullshit story that got him in the door. He showered, had dinner, and rifled my mother's jewelry box while they were sleeping."

"Sandy, I'm so sorry."

"It never ends with him. My parents promise me they won't let him in if he shows and then they see him and buy whatever garbage he comes up with."

"You can't blame them," Sam said.

"I don't, it just drains me."

Sam didn't reply. There are no right words of comfort for this situation.

"I got Claude," Sam said to redirect the conversation.

"In an urn?"

"Yeah, for now."

"What's that supposed to mean?"

"Claude talked about a bayou outside of Houma that he loved. Some day I'll sprinkle his ashes out there."

A smile came to Sandy, "Claude took my brother and me there fishing a couple of years back. Ryan had just gotten out of rehab. It was a good day." Sandy had a forlorn look on his face. "Claude would like that."

Thursday, December 16, 1993

The next morning when Sam got back from her run, Joe was standing at her door.

"Did I forget something?" Sam asked after giving Joe a kiss.

"Test, you said we could go get our test today."

"Oh yeah,"

"Yes," Joe corrected.

"Yes," she smiled. "Did you have breakfast yet?"

"No, we can go out if you want."

"I'll make something light. We can have lunch after the test."

"Good. You know, you should give me a key," Joe said casually.

"I don't think so, but nice try," Sam laughed.

"Sam, I'm serious."

"I'm sorry. I didn't mean to make light, but it's still no."

"Don't sugar coat it."

"Speaking of sugar, I'd like to make a dessert to take to your uncle's on Christmas Eve. Cannoli or a rum cake."

"You make homemade cannoli?"

"Yes, I do," Sam smiled. "Every holiday season."

"Cannoli, make cannoli."

Joe was ambivalent about Christmas most years, but not this year. This year was different.

The days up to Christmas flew by. Felice and Daniel were visiting his family in New York over the holidays. The girls put together a couples dinner before they left. You could tell Joe wasn't Daniel's brand of scotch and vice versa. It was the first meeting that stuck in Daniel's craw. Not what Joe did to Sam but how it upset Felice.

Sam made enough cannoli for select coworkers and friends, plus the DiLeo dinner. Cannoli shells covered every surface in the apartment. Joe hung around Sam's apartment on cannoli making day. He gave Dominic a heads up and so Dominic just happened to stop by because he saw Joe's car.

"You two stronzo (assholes) are tap dancing on my last nerve," Sam laughed.

She gave them each a cannoli. "When you're finished go play outside." They laughed. "I mean it. Get out when you're done."

"I love this fucking broad," Dominic laughed.

"Come on Dom; we'll get out of Sam's hair. We can go to Uncle Frank's."

Dominic kidded Joe on the walk to his father's house. "I knew she was the one, the first time she called you an asshole."

"She just might be," Joe smiled.

Thursday, December 23, 1993

"I don't know what to do with myself. Five days off in a row," Sam said.

"I'm sure we can come up with a few ideas. Maybe we could spice things up."

"Joe we've been together two months. How are we at the spice up phase of our relationship already? I thought that applies to bored housewives."

"I'm talking about taking it to the next level," Joe smiled as he wrapped his arms around her and gave her a little peck.

"What are we talking about here? Fucking on Bourbon Street?" Sam joked.

"We're talking about things we have done before, just a little more intense."

"Like?"

"Tying you to your bed."

"And?"

"Belting you."

"Why?"

Joe looked surprised. "Sam we've done this before. You enjoyed it."

"I don't know how I felt about it. We've never talked about it."

"We're talking about it now," Joe sounded frustrated. "What is your apprehension?"

"It seems like a Pandora's box."

"It's open, Sam. Let me teach you how to appreciate it."

"Why?"

"Again with the why," Joe said, running his fingers through his hair. "It's a part of my life I want to share with you."

"Isn't this the same thing Claude was involved in?"

"No! Claude was involved with edge play."

"Knives?"

"It can be, but that's not what I'm referring to. He was into riskier behavior. Erotic asphyxiation for one thing. There are many kinds and intensities of dominant/submissive relationships. It's not one size fits all. Sam, I pull your hair and you like it. I bite you, and you like it. And I know you liked it when I used a belt on you. Whether you want to admit it or not. I was there. Remember? I saw how you reacted. We'll go at your pace until you are comfortable with it."

Sam was quiet for a long time. "Can you live without this?"

"Yes, but I don't want to."

He took her by the hand and led her into the bedroom. She stood quietly while Joe undressed her. He bit her breast and her stomach. He kissed her and bit her lip. "Give me your hands," he ordered, then bound her hands with his tie. "Kneel at the top of the bed facing the wall."

She did. He knelt next to her and fastened her hands to the top of the headboard. He then went into the closet and returned with the belt from her robe, wrapping it around her waist and then attaching it to the headboard. He removed his shirt. His efforts at the gym were starting to pay off. He was in much better shape. He had an air of authority; his moves were deliberate. Her breathing picked up as he removed his belt. With the first slap of the belt across her ass, her breathing got out of control. He climbed in bed next to her. One hand rubbing her back in a circular motion, the other gliding up and down her arm.

"It's okay baby. It's okay. Did it hurt?"

"No."

He kept massaging her until her breathing was normal.

"I'm going to blindfold you, baby."

She didn't answer him.

"Is that all right?"

She nodded her head.

"Peanut, talk to me."

"It's okay," she said softly.

Joe opened the bottom drawer of the chest next to the bed. He took out a long scarf and covered her eyes. He picked up the belt and started again. Lightly at first keeping a steady rhythm, moving from one side of the bed to the other for a different angle. He was counting to himself in the beginning but lost track. He noticed her face was flushed almost matching the color her ass had become. He stopped when her body gave way, the restraints holding her up were digging into her skin as she sunk down. Joe took off his pants and climbed into the bed between her legs, releasing her waist restraints and pulling her towards him by gripping her hips. He slid into her fast and hard, hitting her red ass with every stroke. She was past the point of delirium with all the sensations flowing through her. It was the first time without a condom.

He left her tied and blindfolded, only to return a minute later with a warm damp cloth and lotion. He untied her and ever so gently took care of her needs. He climbed into bed and embraced her. She drifted off to sleep in his arms.

Friday, December 24, 1993

The feast of seven fishes is a Christmas Eve tradition in a Sicilian home. The DiLeo's did it bigger and better than anyone else in Orleans Parish. It was an open house. All the family and some of the who's who in the city would stop in to wish Frank DiLeo well.

Joe's mother came with her husband. They stayed for less than an hour. She was reserved. Almost standoffish. Leigh was still an attractive woman. Her interaction with her son was a puzzle to Sam. They were polite to one another, as you are to an acquaintance. Not so much as a kiss on the cheek. He was more at ease after she left.

Joe coerced Sam into going to midnight mass with the family. They were back in her apartment at 1:45 A.M. They opened the gifts they got each other.

Joe got Sam an exquisite pair of antique Art Deco hair combs. They were two-prong tortoiseshell with a pavé diamond rope design at the top.

She sprung into his arms, "Joe, they're beautiful. Thank you."

He kissed her. "You're welcome. Now don't let me see pencils, paintbrushes or chopsticks in your hair."

"You won't. Now open yours."

He smiled the second he opened the box. It was a black alligator band for his fathers watch. "It's perfect."

"Really?"

"Really, I love it. Thank you, baby."

He tenderly made love to her that night. How is this the same man that had her tied to the bed the day before, she thought.

Christmas Day was almost like being at home. All the family milling around the kitchen, slipping in and out of Italian.

"Joey, your Italian is getting better," Carmela said.

"We speak Italian at home a lot," Joe replied.

All eyes at the table were on Joe when he said that. They were happy for him.

After dinner, the women went to the kitchen while the men went downstairs to Frank's office. Joe and Chris had gotten in there earlier and hung the triptych. Frank just stood there, staring at it hanging behind his desk.

"Boys, you've outdone yourselves," Frank said, staring at the painting. "Do you know what gym this is?"

"It's Sam's uncle's first gym," Joe answered. "She painted it."

Frank turned, "your little girl did this?"

"Uncle Frank, I told you she was an artist."

"She really is an artist. What is she doing wasting her time on Bourbon Street?"

"You're going to have to ask her that. She shuts me down when I bring it up."

"Boy, you better take the bull by the balls. You let her stay on that street, you'll lose her."

"Well, you took that out of my hands, Uncle Frank," Joe chuckled.

Frank looked Joe straight in the eyes, "marry her."

Blankie

Sunday, December 26, 1993

Joe had commandeered the table; his paperwork sprawled out from one end to the other. They got away from the idea of free-standing buildings for the check-cashing stores. Now they were looking at high traffic outdoor malls that had a grocery or hardware store as an anchor. Sam was in her studio. Most women Joe had known were always a distraction when he was trying to get work done, not Sam. She had her own thing, her own life. She didn't need to piggyback off a man's. She would appear at the appropriate time with food or drink. Not interrupting, she would set down her offering to his side and go back to whatever she was up to.

The phone rang. Sam leaned over the railing, "can you get that please."

Joe picked up the phone, "hello."

"Joe, Sandy. Can I speak to Sam, please?"

Joe didn't respond to Sandy. "Sam, it's Sandy for you."

"What does he want?" Joe asked as he handed her the receiver.

She shrugged her shoulders. "Hi Sandy. How was your holiday?"

Joe stood there, watching her.

"I'm sorry to hear that." ...... "No, it's not a problem. I'll see you tonight."...... "Okay, bye." She hung up the phone and said, "I have to work tonight."

"That's bullshit!"

"Please don't start. Debbie, the girl that was supposed to work for me has a family emergency. Her father had a stroke."

Before Joe could reply, the phone rang again.

"Andrew! Oh my god. How are you?"

"This just keeps getting better," Joe said under his breath.

"Yeah, I'm at Christos now."

Joe didn't budge.

"She's great. She has a boyfriend."

Again under his breath, Joe said, "so do you."

Sam waved her hand at Joe, and mouthed stop it.

"What was that?" Joe asked when she hung up the phone.

"What? He just called to wish me a happy holiday."

"Right!" Joe snapped.

"I don't know Joe. Maybe he was lonely. Maybe he dialed the wrong number," Sam said, opening the refrigerator. "We're having pork chops."

"Don't try to pull off naive. You can't sell it," Joe snarled.

"Are you kidding?" Sam grinned.

"I'm not laughing Sam."

"You're upset because a guy I used to date—"

"Lived with," Joe interrupted.

"Joe, if I wanted to be with Andrew, I'd be in Vegas right now."

"Felice has a boyfriend? You're one of those fucking broads that always leaves a door open."

"This door is starting to close," she said, continuing her dinner preparation. A few seconds later, she heard the door slam.

He walked, she cooked. Both were trying to make sense of what just happened. She buzzed him back a half-hour later.

"I'm—", he started.

"Don't! Just see if you can get the salmon color roses," she laughed.

He put his arms around her and pulled her in, "I love you. I truly do," then kissed her.

They went back to their prior task. As she put the finishing touches on her dinner, she said, "get the table cleared off. Dinner is ready."

Once he was done, she set the table. He sat watching her, grabbing her ass at one point.

The last thing she put on the table was a key in front of him.

"What's this?" Joe grinned.

"Your blankie," Sam laughed.

Truer words could not be said. That key gave him back the confidence that had slipped slightly.

"I'll get you a key to my house."

"Not necessary. I wouldn't go there if you weren't home," she smiled. "If you can't get the salmon-colored roses, get yellow."

"You got it," Joe laughed.

The following day the most beautiful yellow roses fringed in a deep coral graced her table in the Baccarat vase.

"I appreciate this, Sam. I wouldn't have called had I another option," Sandy said.

"Sandy, I get it. Don't worry," Sam replied. "So, what happened?"

"Debbie was pretty upset when I spoke to her. From what I could make out, her father had the stroke last night. Some Christmas present."

"Didn't she go up there?"

"Yes, she had planned to fly back today. I didn't think to get her number when we spoke. I'll have to wait to hear from her. I might need you to work tomorrow night?"

"I can't. I'm sorry."

"Joe?"

"Lambert's, it's a busy week there. You don't like Joe, do you?"

Sandy didn't answer. He just walked to the other end of the bar.

On the way home that night, Sam told Sandy she was aware of his and Joe's youthful indiscretions.

"How forthcoming of Joe," Sandy said sarcastically.

Sam dropped it. Sam told Sandy she would help out if she could while Debbie was away. She also explained that she wouldn't jeopardize one job for the other.

Driving off, Sandy noticed Joe's car. He had resigned himself to the real possibility that Sam wouldn't be at Christos much longer.

Joe was sound asleep when Sam walked in. She took a quick shower and climbed in bed curling up with her back to him. His arm flopped over her waist and pulled her close.

"How was your night?" Joe asked and then kissed the back of her head.

"It was okay," Sam replied. "I see you're using you're blankie already."

"Thing likes waking up next to you," Joe chuckled.

She rolled over and kissed him. Thing didn't wait till morning.

Tuesday, December 28, 1993

The Juke Joint had a soft opening. The place looked good. The new bar had 22 barstools. There were 28 small tables which surrounded the half-round raised stage. The blues trio was wailing. The place filled up close to 10:00 and stayed that way most of the night. Chris spent the entire night smiling, which was uncharacteristic for him. This was his baby and this night the vindication he had hoped for after the Blue Room fiasco.

Of course, there's a flip side to every coin. The successful first night shined a light on the staff and how woefully unprepared they were. They were three days away from two of the busiest nights of the year.

More bad news came in the way of a phone call to Sandy. Debbie's father passed away, and she wouldn't be back until the 5th of January. Much to Joe's chagrin, Sam worked New Year's Eve. Much to Joe's surprise, he ended up tending bar also that night.

Friday, December 31, 1993

Joe had just dropped Sam off. He walked down to The Juke Joint to have a drink with his cousins. Chris was standing outside, talking to the doorman.

"Where's Dominic?" Joe asked.

"He's inside getting us a drink," Chris replied.

Dominic walked out and handed Chris his drink, "did you know one of your bartenders is fucked up?"

The three walked into the bar and watched for a few minutes.

"I've seen enough," Chris said. "Joe, get behind the bar."

"Why me?"

"Because Dominic and I each have two bars to run," Chris answered.

"These are Zegna!" Joe said while looking down and pointing to his slacks.

"You'll be the best-dressed bartender on Bourbon Street," Dominic laughed. "I know I've never acknowledged it, but you're a better bartender than us."

"Go fuck yourself, Dominic," Joe laughed as he got behind the bar.

With Joe settled in, Chris felt comfortable enough to leave and check in on Christos. He told Sam that Joe would be behind the bar for the rest of the evening. Sandy gave Sam the go-ahead to run down to The Juke Joint to see Joe.

Sam walked in with a huge grin on her face. Joe lit up when he saw her. He kissed her and asked, "what are you doing here, little girl?"

"I brought you a present," she handed him a small book — Mr. Boston's Bartender's Guide.

"Very cute. It's like riding a bike baby. Now get back to work," Joe gave her a swat on the ass.

She leaned in and kissed him, "Happy New Year."

"Happy New Year Peanut. Love you."

"Love you too," Sam replied and went back to Christos.

The night went incredibly fast. Just before midnight, Sam asked Sandy the time.

"About 5 minutes to go," Sandy answered.

"I've gotta go to the bathroom."

"Okay, go."

"No, I'll wait till midnight. No line."

As the band started it's count down, Sam made her way to the end of the bar. When they yelled Happy New Year, Sam gave Sandy a kiss. He grabbed her arm tightly, pulling her back. He looked at her with such fury; she froze.

"Go to the bathroom, Sam," Sandy said sternly then let go of her arm.

They barely spoke the rest of the evening. Joe got there a few minutes before 3:00. He looked exhausted.

"How did it go?" Sam asked.

"Not bad. In fact, it was fun," Joe replied.

"How much did you make?" Sam joked.

"I gave my tips to the staff to wack up."

"Ah, that was sweet," Sam reached over the bar and squeezed his hand. "You want a drink?"

"Yeah."

Sam laughed, "You mean yes."

"You're ruining me."

"I'm trying," Sam put the drink in front of Joe. "Let me finish up here. I want to go home."

As they were leaving Sandy thanked Sam for working that night. The earlier contempt in his voice had subsided.

Joe was complaining as they walked into Sam's apartment, "these slacks are ruined."

"They're not ruined," Sam laughed. "The dry cleaners can take care of it, so stop whining."

"I'm not whining. Do you have any idea how much they cost."

"Yes, I do. I work in the store where you bought them," Sam smiled. "You want anything before I jump into the shower?"

"I'm taking a shower with you,"

"That'll be a tight squeeze."

"Even better," Joe grinned, unzipping Sam's pants.

She took her shirt off while Joe was sliding her pants down her legs. He unfastened her bra next.

"What's this?" Joe asked, looking at her left arm.

She looked. It was unmistakably made by a hand, "That must have happened when Sandy grabbed me."

"What do you mean, he grabbed you?" Joe's voice elevated.

"I tripped, and he grabbed me to stop my fall."

"He had to grab you that hard?"

"It's better than my face hitting the bar." She surprised herself on how effortlessly she lied. "Don't go starting shit with him. I'm sure he would feel horrible if he knew he did this."

Saturday, January 1, 1994

The fourth quarter of the Sugar Bowl had just started when she left her apartment. She went into Christos two hours earlier than the norm. She got behind the bar, and Sandy handed her the bank bag.

"It's all going to hit at once, about 15 minutes after the game ends," Sandy said.

Sam stood there, not saying a word.

"Did you have a question?" Sandy asked.

"No, I have to tell you something," Sam said. "I have bruises on my arm from last night when you grabbed me." She took a deep breath, "Joe wanted to know how I got them. I told him I tripped, and you caught me and stopped my fall." She waited for a response, but he didn't give one, "I thought I should tell you." He still didn't respond.

"Sandy?"

"Let's get going Sam. It's going to be a busy night."

Busy it was. They were piling in donning their school colors. The party was on. She saw Joe and Dominic just outside talking to Aaron, the doorman. They couldn't get near the bar. Chris just walked behind the bar with three bottles of Jack Daniel's. A crash pierced through the room.

Sandy hit the lights. "Sam get the glass off of the bar," he yelled.

Chris herded the waitresses into the storage room behind the bar. Joe, Dominic, and the doorman pushed through the crowd.

Within minutes it was over. The bar was cleared out and doors closed. One table and three broken chairs were the only fatalities. The police had two large men handcuffed. Chris was checking with the staff to make sure everyone was alright.

Joe, Dominic, and Sandy were bellied up to the bar regaling their one-round fight.

"Sam, pour us all a shot of Herradura please," Sandy asked.

Sam lined up three glasses and the bottle of tequila.

"Everyone, Sam," Sandy motioned to the other room. He whistled, "Can I have your attention for a minute, please?" They gathered around the three men. "Are we all okay?" They all confirmed they were. "Can you be up and running in ten?" Sandy directed the question to the band. They were good to go. The shots were passed back until every person had one. Sandy raised his glass. "Okay guys, we had a little stumble. Let's not let those assholes ruin our night. Open in ten." They drank their shots and went back to work.

Joe was trying to enlist sympathy from Sam, showing off his swollen right hand. There were fate markings of teeth on his knuckles. The skin was not broken.

"You hit him in the mouth," Sam said, shaking her head in disgust.

Dominic roared, "I love this fucking broad."

"You have nothing to laugh about Dom. The only one of you that can throw a punch is Chris," Sam joked.

"He should. He lettered in boxing," Joe chimed in.

"Chris, I'm impressed." Sam said. Chris' acknowledgement was a bashful smile. "You never told me that," Sam admonished Joe.

"Careful Joe, you might lose her to pretty boy here," Dominic ribbed.

"Not likely," Joe said with a grin to Dominic. "I'm heading home baby. I'll see you in the morning." He gave her a kiss and left as the doors opened.

The night was equally as busy as New Year's Eve. As the night wound down, Sam told Sandy she would take a cab home.

"Don't be silly, Sam. I'll take you home."

"I just thought after last night—"

"I said I'll take you home," Sandy interrupted.

While in Sandy's car, Sam tried to explain her actions, "people kiss people they don't even know on New Year's Eve."

"I was just taken aback, Sam. You caught me off guard. I should never have touched you without your permission. For that, I apologize," Sandy sincerely said. "Why did you concoct that story."

"Joe would have misconstrued it. He has a jealous streak.

"Joe, jealous?" he chuckled. "I have a piece of advice, take it, or leave it. Don't do anything you have to lie about."

"I'm sorry, Sandy. Can we put this behind us?"

"Forgotten." Sandy didn't want to start this year out on a sour note. "See you tonight."

She got out of his truck, feeling a weight lifted.

S.A.M.

Tuesday, February 8, 1994

"Do you want to split something?" Felice asked.

"Sorry, not today. I only had a croissant for breakfast," Sam replied. "So, tell me this news that couldn't be told over the phone. It's nothing bad, is it?"

"No, it's good news. Well, I think it is. Let's order first."

Lunch was ordered, and Felice was ready to talk. "Daniel and I are moving in together," she blurted out as soon as the waitress stepped away from the table.

Sam just sat there. The right words didn't come to mind.

"Say something," Felice said. "Say anything."

"I don't know what to say. You've caught me flat-footed. Tell me everything."

Felice was let down by Sam's lukewarm response, "I know what you're thinking. But this is right. I'm sure of it."

"Honey, I only want the best for you, and if this is it, go for it. Now tell me every mushy detail."

Felice was beaming. They were almost done with their lunch when Felice finished her story. "There is one thing that has come up. The rental agency is giving Daniel a hard time about breaking the lease. Do you think Joe might be able to help?"

"I can ask."

"Great, thank you. What are you two doing Valentine's Day?"

"Valentines falls on Lundi Gras this year. I'm working. Can hardly wait," Sam said sarcastically.

"Are you working Mardi Gras too?"

"Of course, I'm either at work or with Joe," she said as if talking

183

to herself.

"Sam, what's going on?"

"I don't know. I'm just"... "I don't know if overwhelmed is the word. I have no time to myself. I haven't walked up to my studio in over a week. I'm sorry. I don't mean to dump this on you," Sam shook her head. "Joe's going to Florida next week for a few days. I'll be able to refocus then."

"Florida, I'm surprised you aren't going along."

"He's going to Tallahassee. They want to open check cashing stores in the panhandle. They haven't even gotten one opened yet, and they're expanding," Sam laughed. "Joe's obsessed with these stores."

"And you," Felice added.

"He wants me to move in," she paused, "and quit Christos."

Felice waited in silence for Sam to finish her thought.

"I said no to both. This is going insanely fast." Then she caught herself, "I'm not referring to your situation."

"Stop walking on eggshells. I get it. And I agree. But for the first time in my life, I'm not going to play it safe. I'm taking a page out of your playbook," Felice grinned. "Now what's the deal with you and Joe?"

"I can't do it. I can't live in that house."

"Sam, Joe has a beautiful home."

"Without a doubt. But I would be tripping over ghosts."

"You have a few skeletons rattling around your apartment," Felice laughed.

"Fond memories," Sam smiled. "It's his home. It will always be his home, and I will always be a guest. Just like the women before me and the ones after."

"Why are you so sure there's an expiration date on this. From what I can see, the man is in love with you. A little rocky start but he seems to be past that."

"Is he paying you?" Sam joked. "You know I love my apartment. I'm not ready to give it up."

"Which do you love more? Joe or your apartment?" Felice asked. "if you're not ready yet, that's okay. When you are, you won't worry about ghosts."

Thursday, February 10, 1994

"Peanut?" Joe called out.

"I'm up here. Come on up. I want to show you something."

"Is that your uncle?" Joe asked, leaning over Sam's shoulder.

"Yes. What do you think?"

"Baby it's terrific."

"Let me show you the rest."

"The rest?"

"I mean the pictures I'm going to be working from. I'm doing a series of four called The Corner," Sam smiled.

"You're in a cheery mood today."

"I am."

"Okay, I'll leave you to it." Joe kissed her on the forehead, "I've got some calls to make."

Sam came down an hour later. She fixed a small plate of salami, cheese, and olives for Joe. He was sitting in the Eames chair going through what looked to be a contract. He took her hand and kissed it after she put the plate down.

"Thank you, baby," Joe said, then looked back down and continued reading.

"Felice wanted me to ask you," Sam stopped until he looked up. "Daniel wants to get out of his lease, but they're giving him a hard time. Can you make a call or something? I'm guessing that he has a sizable deposit he doesn't want to lose."

"Sure, they usually back off if they get a letter from an attorney. What's the problem?" Sam gave Joe a blank look. "With the apartment. Why does he want to move?"

"Oh, he's moving in with Felice."

"Really?" Joe's lips thinned.

"Yeah."

"Sam," Joe warned.

"Yes. I bought a dining room set," Sam said as she walked back into the kitchen.

"More furniture?" Joe asked, then he laid the paperwork down on the floor and followed her into the kitchen.

"I can finally move the table out to the balcony. It'll be nice. We can eat outside. I won't get it for a couple of weeks. It's beautiful. Birdseye maple. Art Deco. One of Felice's customers is selling it to make way for a new set. Felice said an antique dealer would have probably given them twice what I paid for it. Are you good with eggplant parmigiana?"

Joe walked up behind her. He put his arms around her waist, then unbuttoned her jeans. She turned her head slightly to look back at him.

"Eyes forward," Joe ordered in a voice that made her breath hitch. He unzipped her jeans and brought them and her panties down together. He put his foot between her legs on the jeans and panties, "step out."

Not without a little effort, she wiggled her feet one at a time out of the jeans and panties.

He placed his hand with fingers splayed in the center of her back, giving her a slight push, "bend forward, hands on the counter." He kept his hand on her back as she complied. "Step back a little baby."

Her head hung down between her stretched arms. She looked up when she heard a drawer open. She saw him take out a plastic slotted spatula.

"Head down Sam," he sounded irritated. He paddled lightly on her ass, alternating sides, then sped up the pace along with the force. With her eyes closed, she tried to center herself. She was hoping to find that high that understood the pain. It didn't come. She was unsure of how much more she could take. Her legs were shaking. He stopped when her left leg buckled. He tossed the spatula into the sink.

"Don't move," he ordered. The inevitable sound of his zipper came next. He fucked her with a frenzy of jackhammer moves. He slowed when she came, reveling in the control he held over her. He grabbed her by the hair and pulled her back to his chest and put his other hand across her stomach.

"You freaky fucking bitch," he amusedly whispered in her ear before he went back to his previous intense pace. His pelvis was now hitting her sore ass. She was incoherent when he finished. He walked her into the bathroom and cleaned her, then to the bedroom, and he laid her under the covers and climbed in next to her. She clung to him as he repeatedly said, "good girl."

She started to stir about a half-hour later. Joe pulled her back to his chest. "Where are you going, little girl?"

"Start dinner," Sam replied.

"Dinner can wait. Lay here for a little while longer. We need to talk."

"Are you mad at me?"

"Not anymore," Joe chuckled.

"I'm sorry I can't give you what you want. I'm not ready."

"How long were you with Andrew before you—"

"Please don't start this again!" Sam interrupted. "It's two different situations. You're asking me to move into your life."

"You say that like it's a bad thing."

"It's an exciting thing that I'm looking forward to in the future. Let's enjoy this phase of our relationship. Slow down," Sam kissed his chest. "Don't make me be the grown-up here."

"I have a counteroffer, and I don't want an answer for a few days. I want you to give this serious consideration. I want you to quit Christos. I'll cover all your household expenses. Rent, electric, phone."

Sam started to say something.

"I said a couple of days," Joe laughed. "You are such a S.A.M."

"I don't understand what you mean when you say that."

"I mean I don't want an off the cuff answer."

"No. I mean when you say, you're a Sam. You've said that before. I don't know if I'm supposed to laugh at that or not."

"It's not Sam. It's S period, A period, M period.," Joe grinned. "It stands for smart ass masochist."

"You're fucking with me?"

"No baby, I'm not. It's a kink term."

"I'm not a masochist."

"Baby, you're the poster child," Joe laughed. "Take pride. You're a natural."

"Natural what?" Sam said in a sharp tone.

"Pull in your reins little girl, unless your ass is ready for round two," Joe chuckled.

She silently buried her head into his chest.

Friday, February 11, 1994

"How was your day, baby?" Joe asked as Sam got into the car.

"Good, and yours?"

"Productive," Joe smiled. "And how are you feeling?"

"You mean my ass?" Sam grinned. "It's fine. Do you think I should change?"

"You're good. We're going straight over to Uncle Frank's."

"Can I ask you?"

"What Sam?"

"Have you had this kind of relationship with other women you've dated?"

"No. Haven't we been through this before?"

"Not really," Sam paused. "So why me?"

Joe smiled at her. He didn't answer.

"How did you get involved with it."

"The same way you did. I was seeing someone that was into it."

"Care to expound on that?"

"You're not gonna let up, are you?"

"Not this time," Sam laughed.

"I guess I was predisposed to it with my father taking me to work with him."

"He took you to strip joints when you were a kid?" Sam asked, shocked.

"And the whore houses," Joe laughed.

"Oh my god!"

"One of the houses catered to a more adventurous clientele," Joe amusingly added. "Some years later, when I was 19, I was seeing this woman. Girl, she was your age, married. Her husband worked on oil rigs so he'd be gone a couple of weeks at a time. After the first time, her husband had been home and gone; she had bruises. When I questioned it, she told me her husband beat her because of me."

"Jesus Christ."

"Wait, this gets better," Joe smirked. "She told her husband about me so he would beat the shit out of her. That was their thing. When he was gone, she'd fuck around and report back. After a while she wanted me to hit her. She was a true pain slut. When it ended between us, I found I missed that part of our relationship. I'd occasionally hire a professional submissive. I had a few relationships that included occasional spankings with my hand. You're the only woman I've had a full-blown dominant/submissive relationship with. You're perfect," Joe brushed her cheek with the palm of his hand.

"Is that why you love me?"

"It's one of many reasons. And baby, it's one of the reasons you love me."

As they walked up the stairs to the DiLeo home, Sam asked, "whatever happened to her?"

"She's with some guy who's pimping her out of the Iberville projects. I see her on Bourbon Street every once in a while."

Letters

Saturday, February 12, 1994

Sandy looked at his watch when Sam walked into the bar at 6:45. She turned heads. She had on a black tank dress with an off white two button faille jacket. Black sheer hose three-inch heels. A black pocket scarf with a gold fleur de lis design accented the outfit. She was carrying a large leather satchel with her coat folded over it.

"Thanks for coming in early," Sandy said.

"No problem," Sam replied.

"Did you get a chance to eat?"

"Yeah, Popeye's."

"Debbie's working the end. You're in the middle. Get changed."

The bar was busy, and there was a line coming out of the ladies room. "I'll change in the backroom," Sam said.

"Whatever works for you. Let's get going."

She stepped into the back storage room behind the bar and proceeded to change. Sandy caught a glimpse of her when she was down to her panties and bra. He noticed bruises on her back left upper thigh. He handed her the bank bag when she got behind the bar. She gave him a curious look.

"How are we doing this? Are Debbie and I working out of the same register?"

"We brought another one in for Carnival," Sandy replied, pointing to the end of the bar. "Count your bank."

The night was insanely busy, and the tips were unbelievably shitty. Carnival is about volume. You can make big bucks, but it's blood money.

"I can't wait to get out of these clothes," Sam said to Sandy on the short ride to her apartment.

Sandy laughed, "you looked nice tonight."

Sam chuckled.

"I don't mean now. I meant when you came in tonight."

"Thank you I think," Sam snickered.

"I mean you clean up good."

"Oh my god Sandy, I can't take any more flattery," Sam was almost hysterical now.

"Sam, you looked stunning."

Sam was taken by surprise, his remark being uncharacteristic. She didn't answer.

"Thank you for today," Sandy went on, "I'll see you at 3:00 tomorrow."

That conversation repeated in her mind while she showered. Joe wasn't there. She thought about Joe's jacuzzi tub and wished she was sitting in it. Sam fell asleep the minute her head hit the pillow. She woke to Joe sitting next to her in bed, lightly brushing her hair away from her face.

"Good morning, Peanut," Joe smiled. "How was your night?"

"I hate Carnival," Sam giggled. "I could have used your jacuzzi last night."

"Why didn't you come over?"

"I didn't want to bother you." The smell of freshly brewed coffee permeated the air. "You made coffee?"

"I did," Joe smiled.

Joe watched her padding into the bathroom. He got a kick out of her morning waddle. When she got to the table, Joe had her coffee waiting for her. She sat down and yawned.

"You're exhausted," Joe said.

"No, I'm not," she was quick to reply.

"What time are you going in today?

"3:00."

"Oh, that's total bullshit. You're going to work a 12-hour shift?"

"Joe, please."

"No, Sam. No, Joe, please. You were only supposed to work from 8:30 to 3:00, three nights a week."

"It's Carnival."

"I don't give a fuck if it's the second coming of Christ," Joe realized he was upsetting her. "Baby I'm just concerned. Rightfully so. You've lost weight."

Sam wordlessly sat there like a child being scolded by their parent.

Joe reached over and lifted her chin, "let's go to brunch. You can get ready while I'm at church."

Sam went on her run and then got ready.

After mass Joe got Chris off to the side, "this shit ends now Chris. You handle it or I will. That fucking Gillespie is taking advantage."

"I'll take care of it," Chris reassured Joe. "Just let me get through Mardi Gras."

"And the young lady is having Eggs Sardou." As soon as the waiter walked away, Joe took Sam's hand and kissed it. "Have you given my proposal any thought?"

"I have," Sam replied. "I want to wait until after Jazzfest."

"And then you'll move in?"

"We're back on moving in?" Sam grinned. "We'll discuss all the options after Jazzfest."

Joe didn't like it but wisely recognized this was the best he was going to get. "I have one request. Please stop buying furniture."

"All I need is a chest of drawers."

"I have my grandparents furniture in the slave quarter. When I get back, you can take whatever you want."

"You'll be back on Tuesday?" Sam asked.

"Yes. I have an evening flight."

"Sandy is giving me off Wednesday, and I'm taking a personal day at Lambert's. So I'll have two whole days off."

"Well Ms. Mancuso, we'll have to come up with something special to do."

For a brief second, Joe thought of telling Chris not to say anything to Sandy, but he felt that drawing the line when it came to Sam was the way to go.

Monday, February 14, 1994

The doorbell rang at 12:45. Sam looked over the balcony to see who it was. She saw a floral truck. Joe sent two dozen of the most beautiful peach colored roses. Times like this helped quell her apprehensions. She would move in with Joe as soon as she met her goal of $10,000. That was the number. She wanted $10,000 in her savings account before she moved in with Joe. That way if something happened, she wouldn't be out on the street.

She had $4,200 when she moved to New Orleans, most of which came from the sale of her car. She managed to save another $3,600 since she was back. Since she had been at Christos her savings were on steroids. The $2,200 she needed to meet her goal would come easy with Mardi Gras, French Quarter Fest, and Jazzfest in the next couple of months.

Tuesday, February 15, 1994, MARDI GRAS

Felice and Daniel stopped in for a drink covered in beads. "Oh my god!" Sam burst out laughing. "Did you kids have fun at Rex?"

"And Zulu," Daniel replied, holding up a coveted coconut.

"Happy Mardi Gras," Sandy said, holding out his hand to Daniel. "How are you doing my friend?"

"He's doing great," Sam interjected. "Dan got a Zulu coconut."

"I know people that have tried for years to get one of those," Sandy laughed. He gave Sam the sign to buy them a drink.

Before they left Daniel asked Sam to extend his gratitude to Joe for his help retrieving his deposit. She was glad that Daniel and Joe were getting along better. Not quite drinking buddies, but they seemed to be comfortable in each other's company.

Just when you think you've seen it all.

"That's $19," Sam said to the young man who just ordered a round of drinks.

"I have free drinks coming," he replied.

"Honey, I don't know what you're talking about," Sam said puzzled.

At that same time, Debbie came up to Sam and asked, "do you know anything about free drinks?"

She waved Aaron the doorman over. "Are we charging a cover? Those three," Debbie pointed to the end of the bar, "said the cover includes their first drink."

Before Aaron could answer Sandy was there. "What's going on?"

Debbie filled Sandy in. He got out from behind the bar and walked out of the building, reappearing holding some guy by the throat. The cops took him away in handcuffs.

"This is a beauty," Sandy said with a grin. "That asshole was standing flush against the building, collecting a cover charge from people walking in. Some balls." Sandy shook his head, laughing.

"What about the people that thought they were getting a free drink?" Sam asked.

"Give it to them. Write it down," Sandy replied, still laughing.

The three of them never stopped until they heard the sirens of the midnight sweep. All the employees and the band donned their sunglasses. It had become a Christos thing. Sandy hit the lights. The parade of police proceeded down Bourbon Street.

"1994 Mardi Gras is officially over. Please clear the streets," repeatedly came over the megaphone as the police on horseback, marching and in squad cars followed by street cleaning machines slowly made their way through the crowd.

"My favorite parade," Sandy said, picking up the Chivas bottle. "Sam, you want a drink?"

"Yes please, neat."

As Aaron opened the door to let the last of the customers out, Joe and Chris walked in. Joe leaned over the bar and kissed Sam.

"When did you get back?" Sam asked.

"A couple of hours ago. We're staying at my place tonight. I stopped at your place and got you a change of clothes for tomorrow."

"Did you bring my running shoes?"

"Yes and sweats. You look like you're ready to drop."

"I'll never work another Mardi Gras."

"I'll hold you to that," Joe laughed.

They talked the whole way to Joe's house. He filled her in on his meetings in Florida. She told him about the guy collecting the cover at the door. Joe laughed hysterically. She also extended Daniel's thanks.

"Glad to help. When is he moving in?"

"Well they're practically living together now, but I think March 1 is the official day."

"What is he going to do with all his furniture. He paid a small fortune to ship it here."

"Ruth's house has a slave quarter. She said he could store everything there."

A light went off in Joe's head.

Wednesday, February 16, 1994

Joe was in the kitchen, having his coffee and reading the Times-Picayune when Sam got back from her run. She poured herself a cup of coffee, and before she could sit down, Joe was standing up.

"Come on. Bring your coffee," Joe said as he took a key out of a drawer and headed outside to the slave quarter.

He opened a few of the shutters and then the door. It had the stale smell a closed-off room has after a long period. Sam's eyes widened. It was packed with furniture. There was a narrow walkway the length of the room.

"This is everything that was in the house when I got it. Pick out what you want. There's more upstairs."

Sam was like a little kid Christmas morning. "I don't know where to start," she said, opening a bureau drawer. "Joe there's clothes in here."

"I never got a chance to go through anything," he nonchalantly answered.

"You're joking, right? Aren't you the least bit interested in what could be in here?"

"No, I'm not. Now could you please focus for one minute."

"Okay. What?"

"I have some plans I want to go over with you. I know part of your apprehension is what you would do with your furniture and studio. I could clear all this stuff out, and you could put your furniture in here. You could have your studio upstairs or vice versa. I'll get Charlie over here and fix the place up. Paint, refinish the floors. I'll update the appliances. It'll be your little haven."

"Joe, I thought we were going to wait—"

"I'm not saying move in tomorrow," Joe cut her off. "I want to make this a comfortable transition for you. Why are you fighting me on this?" Joe closed his eyes and took a deep breath. "Sam, are you going to move in with me or not? I know you don't want to do anything until after Jazzfest, but you can give me an up or down on moving in."

"I'll move in, but after Jazzfest," Sam emphasized.

Joe pulled Sam into his arms and kissed her deeply. "Now was that so hard?"

"Yes," Sam grinned.

Joe took her hand and gave it a little pull, "Breakfast."

"You go ahead. I'm going to look around."

"You're cooking," Joe laughed.

Sam giggled and followed Joe back into the house. Over breakfast, they agreed on donating his grandparent's furniture to the AIDS clinic for their upcoming yard sale. Joe went into his office after breakfast, and so she spent the better part of the day in the slave quarter.

Although most of what was in there was not her taste, everything from the furniture to the clothing in drawers was beautifully made. Sam appreciated good craftsmanship. Odd people, Sam thought. How could they live 20 minutes from their only grandchild and never see him? Then leave most of what they own to him. You couldn't write this stuff.

She found the perfect chest of drawers on the second floor. She was done. Next to the chest was a semainier, a narrow seven drawer lingerie chest. It was very feminine with hand-painted roses on every drawer. I'll bet it was in Leigh's room, Sam thought. She opened the top drawer and took out two full-length slips, one in black, the other white. Below them was a hosiery box. Sam opened it to find letters and pictures. The three letters had Leigh DiLeo as the sender. There were four pictures, one of a baby in a bassinet. Must be Joe, Sam thought. Two images were of Joe in cap and gown. One was his college graduation, the other from law school. The last picture was of Joe's wedding. She was a beautiful bride. Joe told Sam the marriage was annulled after four months with the help of a $25,000 settlement. She couldn't wait to show Joe her find.

Joe was on the phone when she bursts into his office. He held up a finger, her cue to stop talking. She stood there fidgeting until he got off the phone.

"Wait til you see what I found."

"Money?" Joe joked.

"No," Sam replied. "Come in the kitchen."

"Okay baby, just give me a few minutes. I have one quick call to make and then I'm all yours.

Sam made her way to the kitchen, got a glass of water, and sat down at the table. She placed the four pictures side by side in chronological order by age and put the envelopes in order by postmark dates. She opened the first letter.

Dear Mother and Father,

I write to you in hopes you can find it in your hearts to forgive me. Of course, you were right about the type of man Vincent DiLeo is. My foolish emotions blinded me to it. With that fog lifted, I find myself mourning my past life. I am not sure how much longer I can stand the humiliation I must endure with this man. Please allow me back into your lives and home.

Your loving daughter,
Leigh

Sam sat there, stunned. She quickly opened the next letter.

Dear Mother and Father,

Enclosed is a picture of your grandson. Joseph Anthony DiLeo. He is the chain that will ever tie me to a man I loathe. I pushed him out of my body along with every hope and dream I had for my life. Sleep well knowing the consequences of your punishment.

Your daughter,
Leigh

Sam was putting the note back into its envelope when she heard Joe in the foyer. She was able to hide the letters in a drawer before Joe walked in. He gazed at the pictures on the table. It was almost a look of amazement on his face.

"I found those in a dresser. Baby Joe was very cute." Sam kissed him on the cheek. "What do you want for lunch?

Joe didn't answer.

"Earth to Joe."

Joe looked up at Sam. He was holding his law school graduation picture. "Whatever you fix is fine. This new thing of yours, asking my opinion on the meals."

Sam grinned.

"I don't like it," Joe chuckled.

"I promise it will not happen again. Your wife was pretty."

"Not my wife. It was annulled."

"The woman you exchanged vows with at St. Louis Cathedral in front of friends and family was pretty."

"Cagna." (bitch)

Sam laughed.

After lunch, Joe went back to his office. Sam couldn't wait to read the last letter.

Dear Mother and Father,

I am sure you are aware from the newspaper and television coverage, that my husband was murdered. My son, your grandson, and I remain living with the DiLeo's as we have been left penniless.

I am confident you would like to see your grandson raised in a better environment. I'm now able to break away from the DiLeo's to do just that. Unfortunately, I need money to start anew. I know you will find this letter beneath dignity, but that's something I lost years ago.

I've done my penance. Let me come home, please.

Your only child,
Leigh

Sam found the letters heartrending and was unsure as to what to do with them. She tucked them away.

The weeks ahead flew past Sam. She was settled into the idea of moving in with Joe. Everything was out of the slave quarter, and Charlie's crew had started work on it. The DiLeo's opened two check-cashing stores in that time with immediate success. DiLeo Financial Services opened first in Metairie and the second in the upper quarter, a few blocks from the casino.

Wednesday, March 16, 1994

The lights were up and customers gone. Aaron the doorman and a couple of waitresses were sitting at the bar having their shift drink. Sandy handed Sam a drink, and she handed him his share of the tips for the night.

"St. Patrick's tomorrow," Sam said with a grin.

"Oh God, don't remind me," Sandy laughed.

Sam raised her glass to Sandy. "Erin go Bragh."

"Is that your last name?" One of the waitresses asked Aaron. Laughter filled the room.

The ride to Sam's took a more serious note.

"Rumor has it, you're leaving Christos," Sandy said eyes never leaving the road.

"I'm not sure yet. Are you going to fire me?"

"I'm going to miss you," Sandy said under his breath. He quickly regained his composure. "You'll give me two weeks."

"I promise."

Sunday, April 3, 1994

Easter and Sam's birthday fell on the same day that year. Sam went to mass with the DiLeo's after which they had brunch at Frank and Carmela's home. Leigh made a brief appearance with her husband. The kitchen had a flurry of activity when Leigh came in to say goodbye.

"Leigh, can I speak to you for a minute?" Sam asked as she motioned to the courtyard.

Leigh a bit surprised but curious followed Sam outside. Chris was watching through the kitchen window when Dominic walked up.

"What do you think is going on out there?" Dominic asked.

Chris just shrugged his shoulders.

"I got Sam for $50 in the fight." Dominic laughed and walked away.

Sam handed Leigh the letters. Leigh's eyes slowly rose from the letters to Sam's face.

"I found them in a box with four pictures of Joe," Sam explained.

"Did you read them?" Leigh asked.

"Yes."

"Did Joe read them?"

"No, I didn't show them to him. Just the pictures."

"I only sent them one picture of him as a baby."

"They had one each of his college and law school graduation and one of his wedding."

"Odd," Leigh replied. "Joe's like his father in many ways."

Sam thanked her for sharing insight about Joe.

"That wasn't a compliment, Sam. That's a warning." Leigh walked away letters in hand leaving Sam in the courtyard, stunned.

Chris came out to join Sam. "I see you and Leigh had a nice little talk."

"Nice! You're throwing that word around loosely," Sam chuckled. "Why does she bother coming to family events?"

"She gets a monthly check from the family."

"Well, that explains it. Has she always—"

"Yes," Chris answered before she finished her sentence. "I don't know that she ever fit in. I can only remember her as distant."

"Do you remember Joe's father."

"Yes," Chris grinned. "He was one of those vampire kind of guys. Slept all day, out all night. He was a lot of fun. Not for Leigh or any other woman who fell for him. From what I have heard through the years, Leigh earned every check she gets."

Sam remembered Claude's advice.

Daniel and Joe took Felice and Sam to Commander's Palace that evening. Daniel bought Felice diamond stud earrings. Joe got Sam matinee length Mikimoto pearls. The girls had a wonderful time. Joe couldn't wait to share the news about Sam moving in. He told them about his plans for the slave quarter. Joe was confident that all her furniture and studio would fit comfortably. Perhaps with the exception of the Eames chair which he would be happy to make room for in his office. They all laughed. As the men spoke business, Joe caught a snippet of the girl's conversation.

"You have the $10,000?" Felice asked, surprised.

"Not quite. I will by the end of Jazzfest," Sam replied.

On the way home, Joe asked, "what were you and Felice talking about?"

"I don't know, clothes," she answered.

"$10,000, does that ring a bell?"

Sam didn't answer.

"Sam what's going on. Are you in some sort of trouble."

"No." She decided to come clean before he dragged it to another level. "I want to have $10,000 saved before I move in. You know, in case something happened."

"No, I don't know. What do you think is going to happen?"

"If we broke up and I had to move."

"That's who you think I am? Some asshole who would kick you out penniless."

"Joe, that's who I think everyone can be. You're an attorney. You've seen things spin out of control at the end of relationships."

"How much more do you need?"

Sam didn't answer.

"Sam, how much more do you need?"

"It has to be my money."

"It will be when I give it to you."

"No, thank you."

"You are hands down the most stubborn woman I have ever met."

"I love you too," Sam laughed.

Joe fell asleep quickly after they made love. Sam laid on her side, staring out the window thinking of Claude. "Joe's a fun ride, but that's all he is."

Safety Pins

Every woman has that dress. The dress you never forget. The one time you knew for sure all eyes were on you. It's not just wearing an outfit; it's wearing confidence. Some times a special occasion is attached to it. A night you'll never forget or a perfect day. Sometimes it's life-changing. Like the safety pin dress that famously launched a starlet's career. That dress changed her life.

Parisian's on Canal had the spring collection that dress was part of in their windows. All the dresses and suits were very revealing with mere safety pins holding the fabric together and keeping your private parts private. Parisian's windows were more cutting edge than Lambert's and so were often a topic of conversation. One of those conversations happened at Houlihan's after work on a Friday in early March. Occasionally the sales staff stopped for a drink together.

"I wish we carried that designer. Even the men's suits are a sharper look," One of the guys said.

"Our clientele wouldn't buy it. They're too conservative. Plus a European cut is a tough fit," Ruth rebutted. "What do you think of the safety pin dresses?"

"I love them. My birthday is April 3rd if you guys are thinking of chipping in, I'll take the suit," Sam joked.

"Oh, that would look cute on you. You should have Joe buy that for you," Ruth said.

"Joe doesn't buy my clothes. He also does not pay my bills, in case that was in the back of anyone's mind," Sam laughed.

"Well, girl, you're doing something wrong," one of the guys joked.

The next time Sam walked past Parisian's windows, they had changed. A spur of the moment decision had her in the store trying on the little dark blue safety pin suit. The jacket was fitted with an off-center closure held together by three large safety pins. It was short, just coming down to where her legs started. There were two-inch slits throughout the body, back and sleeves of the jacket that skin showed through. The skirt came down just five inches longer than the jacket with a two-inch gap showing her right thigh from waist to hem held together with three safety pins. The suit hugged her tight body as if she were the fit model. Sam walked out of the dressing room and caught the attention of everyone near.

Much to the salesgirl's surprise, Sam talked herself out of the suit while changing back into her clothes. After all, she couldn't wear it to work. She would be lucky to get two or three occasions to wear it before it became dated. Even though it was marked down, it was still an extravagance.

Tuesday, April 5, 1994

Sam was at Lambert's getting ready for her day. She checked with the receptionist to see if she had any messages. Sam had two. The first was a regular customer who wanted a blouse she had purchased in another color. The second was from the salesgirl from Parisian's. The safety pin suit took another markdown. Sam went to The Shoppes on Canal on her lunch hour and bought the suit. Friday she and Joe were having dinner with his law school buddies and their wives. The same three he was having dinner with the night she met him. She would debut her new suit that night.

Friday, April 8, 1994

Joe and Sam had a lot in common. They liked the same music, books, movies. They had the same taste. They disliked tardiness to the point of annoyance. And so Joe running late for their dinner was a source of agitation for both of them.

Sam was in her new suit backing out of the bathroom to get a better look at the whole package. Times like this she wished she owned a full-length mirror. The phone rang. Sam looked at the clock on the kitchen wall as she answered. It was 7:40. Their dinner was at 8:00.

"Hello."

"I'm leaving Uncle Frank's right now. Meet me downstairs," not waiting for a response; Joe hung up.

She stepped out onto the balcony to gauge the weather; she needed a coat. Joe pulled up seconds after she locked the door. He had that look on his face that made Sam anxious.

"Sven, breathe," Sam said, putting her hand on his thigh.

Joe smiled back, "it's just been a hectic day. I fucking hate being late."

"We're not going to be late. We're five minutes away." That seemed to calm him. "Tell me about your friends."

"You met the guys."

"Not really," Sam interjected. "I met Trey. The other two were down the bar. Remember?"

"Well, Bob doesn't need much explanation. You've seen his ads on tv. He's making a fortune. His wife is his perfect counterpart. She can be a bit brash after a drink or two. A little overly made up. But a good egg at heart. They met in college."

"What does she do?"

"Bob," Joe laughed. "She's one of those broads that went to college to find a husband."

"Palmer?" Sam prompted.

"Brilliant guy. You don't ever want to go up against him in a court of law. Total nerd," Joe chuckled.

"And his wife?"

"Also brilliant. She went to law school with us on a full scholarship. She came from nothing. She grew up in the Desire Projects. I can't think of a woman I admire more. After you, of course, baby," Joe pinched Sam's cheek. "She's a judge. Youngest ever in Orleans Parish."

"What about Trey's wife?"

"That was grist for the gossip mill," Joe smiled. "Trey went to work in his then fiancée's father's law office right out of school. He hadn't even taken the bar yet. They fixed him up with a corner office and his own secretary. He was there about a year and still engaged when his secretary left on maternity leave. They hired a temp, Melissa, and that was it. Trey walked away from everything for Melissa. Best fucking move he ever made. We all thought he had lost his mind at the time. They didn't have it easy. He burned a lot of bridges when he did that, but they stuck it out, and now he has a much-envied law practice, and they have, I think four kids."

They walked into the restaurant at 8:05. Everyone else was at the bar.

"First fucking time Trey is on time in his life," Joe whispered into Sam's ear.

"You're late," Trey laughed.

"Ignore him," Melissa smiled and introduced herself.

The hostess walked up. "Your table is ready, but if you care to wait another ten minutes, we have a window table opening up." Everyone looked around at each other. "It's up to you."

"That would be great," Trey spoke up.

Joe continued the introductions while helping Sam off with her coat.

"Oh my God," Bob's wife Kim squealed. "Is that the suit that was in Parisian's window?"

"Yes, it is," Sam answered with a big smile.

"Che cazzo stai indossando?"(what the fuck are you wearing) Joe said under his breath.

"Non ti piace?" (you don't like it?) Sam was surprised by Joe's reaction.

"Sembri una puttana," (you look like a whore) Joe replied with no inflection in his voice.

Sam's heart stopped. She knew she was in for a long evening. When their table was ready, Joe took note of every man ogling her as they walked through the dining room. The conversation centered around Sam; everyone was eager to know more about Joe's young girlfriend. Joe abruptly steered the conversation in another direction when the question of school came up. It never occurred to Sam that her not having a college degree bothered Joe. Kim was a little colorful. She brought up the suit and how well Sam wore it, which didn't help Sam's case. As the waiter cleared the table, everyone was discussing coffee and dessert. There was no way Sam could put off the ladies room if they were going to be there another half hour. She excused herself and got up. She could feel Joe's eyes following her through the room. Coming back was worse. Joe was laser-focused on her. She could see the tension in his jaw when she sat down.

"Sam, it's all up to you," Trey said.

"What is?" Sam asked.

"We're trying to get Joe to buy us a round at The Juke Joint. Joe said it's your call."

Sam reached over and turned Joe's wrist to look at his watch. It was almost 10:00. By the time they finished dessert, coffee and paid the check it would be around 10:30. She agreed to go for one set, delaying the inevitable fight a little longer.

Joe called from the restaurant to make sure a table would be available for them near the stage. The set had just started when they walked in. Cassandra, Palmer's wife, knew two of the musicians. They grew up in the same neighborhood. She waved, and they greeted her back over the microphone in the middle of a song. When the set was over, the musicians that knew Cassandra pulled up chairs joining the table. Joe left the table to talk to Chris who had just walked in. When Joe came back, he took Sam by the upper arm to help her out of the chair while saying their goodbyes.

"Sorry to have to cut it short but Sam has to work tomorrow. The check is taken care of. Please stay and enjoy. You three stiffs can throw in a little extra for the waitress," Joe joked.

The group stayed for another set. On the way home, Melissa asked Trey, "what do you think?"

"About Sam?" Trey asked.

"About Sam with Joe."

"He was all in the minute he laid eyes on her," Trey laughed.

"Do you think she's too young for Joe. There's got to be ten maybe twelve years age difference."

"Joe said she just turned 24. I think Joe turns 36 this year. She's no naive kid. Don't let her quiet demeanor tonight fool you."

"He told her she looked like a whore. That might have had something to do with her demeanor," Melissa replied.

"Are you sure?" Trey asked, surprised.

"Yes, my Latin finally came in handy. Plus the way he grabbed her when they were leaving."

"He was helping her up."

"He had a vice grip on her arm. Joe's obsessed with her."

"Sweetheart, do me a favor and stop reading those smutty paperbacks," Trey joked.

Melissa leaned over and gave him a kiss on the cheek. "Where do you think I get all my naughty ideas?"

The only words spoken on the way to Sam's apartment were out of necessity. She walked straight into the kitchen and poured herself a glass of water. At the sink facing the wall, she could hear him behind her.

"Whatever bug you have up your ass is going to have to stay there. I have to get some sleep," Sam said, then turned. She looked at the clock. It was 12:20."

Joe tucked his hands between her lapels and skin, gripped tightly and yanked in the opposite direction ripping the jacket open. She was frozen in fear. His hands then moved to the slit in the skirt. He tore it open. One of the safety pins unsnapped grazing her right thigh, drawing blood.

"Joe, please," Sam repeated as tears rolled down her flushed face. "I'm sorry. Please." As he continued to tear at her clothing.

He held her by the back of the neck and walked her over to the table. He tossed the end chair and the one next to it aside with one hand while still gripping the back of her neck. He pushed her forward. "Bend over," Joe demanded. Sam was slow to comply. "I said, bend the fuck over!" Joe shouted this time.

She did it knowing this was not going to be like one of their scenes. This was not meant to be enjoyed. Joe lifted up what was left of her skirt and pulled her panties off. With her head laying flush on the dining room table, she was eye level to him removing his belt. His first strike was with such force her breath was knocked out of her. The blows came fast and hard. Even her tears didn't soften the impact.

Joe abruptly stopped when he saw specks of blood. The sight of what he had done sickened him. He walked into the kitchen and took a drink of water from the same glass Sam left on the counter. Joe couldn't bring himself to comfort her. Why would she want him to touch her after what he had just done? Grabbing his coat, he walked out, leaving her laying on the table hysterical. Joe got in his car and drove, ending up on Airline Highway when the reality of the evening washed over him. The first payphone he could find was outside of a familiar bar. He called Sam's but the line was busy. Who was she talking to? Felice? Her uncle? Was she telling someone what he had done to her? Disheartened, he walked inside the bar to get a drink.

Sam laid on the table, crying herself out. She got up and began to clean up the remnants of a nightmare. She called Joe but got the tape. The tears had started again. She couldn't speak. The message left was inaudible sobbing. She was ravaged. She needed a shower and sleep. While she was in the shower, she heard Joe come in. She finished quickly and walked out of the bathroom. He grabbed her by the neck with one hand and her crotch with the other, picking her up and throwing her into the living room. It wasn't Joe.

Aftermath

The lights had just come up at Christos when they heard the sirens. Chris was standing close to the bar across from Sandy. They both stopped to see if they could detect the direction they were moving in. Chris saw Mike one of the Vieux Carré (another name for the French Quarter, it means Old Square) cops at the door talking to Aaron.

"Mike, how's it going?" Chris asked, holding out his hand.

"Good Chris," Mike replied.

"What's going on?" Chris asked.

"I don't know. It sounds like it's coming from the lower quarter. I was just headed over to the station to find out myself."

"If you get a chance, let us know."

"Will do, Chris."

Chris walked back over to the bar.

"So, what's up?" Sandy asked.

"He didn't know," Chris replied. "Would you mind giving me a lift home?"

"Sure."

Twenty minutes later, Chris was locking the bar doors when Mike walked up.

"Hey Chris, no fire. It was a break in down on Chartres. I don't know why they sent fire trucks."

"Thanks, Mike. Stop by one night. Let us get you a drink."

Sandy's truck was parked on Conti just past Royal. They made a left on Decatur. When they were passing Jackson Square, Chris ask Sandy to cut back over to Chartres. As soon as they made the turn onto Chartres, they saw a flurry of activity on the next block down.

"It's Sam's," Sandy said.

Chris jumped out of the truck and ran down the block while

Sandy looked for a parking space. A fire truck was pulling away. A squad car and an ambulance were blocking the street, plus a mounted policeman who was controlling a few onlookers. A handcuffed man was being put into the back seat of the squad car. There were two men in suits on the balcony.

Chris was trying to talk his way into Sam's apartment when Sandy got there. "My cousin is up there," Chris was explaining to the unsympathetic cop. Out of desperation, Chris used his uncle's name.

"Detective Biosseau," the cop yelled up to the balcony. "This boy here is a DiLeo. He said his cousin is up there."

The detective looked down and then gave the go-ahead for them to come up. When they got up to the apartment, Chris stood there stunned. Some of the dining chairs were knocked over; the dining table was askew. The sofa cushions were scattered on the floor. The rug was flipped up. There was blood on the arm of the sofa and the coffee table was broken. The detective walked over and introduced himself.

"Is my cousin Joe here?" Chris asked.

"No, just Miss Mancuso. And of course, the intruder."

Sandy heard the paramedics and walked into the bedroom. The sight horrified him. Sam was sitting on the bed with a comforter wrapped around her. She looked so small. The entire left side of her face was beaten purple. Her eye was swollen shut. Her jaw bruised. There was dry blood under her nose and the corner of her mouth. Her lips were triple in size. One of the paramedics was trying to communicate with Sam. She wouldn't let him touch her. The other one addressed Sandy as soon as he walked in.

"Sir, you can't be in here."

"Shut up!" Sandy said as he sat next to Sam on the bed. "Sam." Sandy tilted her chin up so she would look at him.

"Sandy," Sam mouthed and scooted closer to him as if looking for protection.

"They're just going to check you out. Make sure you're okay."

"I'm okay," Sam whispered.

"No honey, you're not," Sandy spoke in a tone you would use on a child.

The paramedics proceeded with their protocol. "We're going to have to get her over to Charity."

"No!" Sam protested.

"Sam put your arms around my neck," Sandy said as he picked her up.

While that was going on in the bedroom, the detective was filling Chris in on what they knew so far.

"He got in through the balcony window. The latch doesn't appear to be tampered with. It was most likely unlocked. She fought him the best she could. He didn't get off unscathed. We don't know if she was sexually assaulted. She won't talk to anyone. She's in shock. What she did was remarkably level headed. She yelled fire over and over again. That's what got her the quick response. Most of the time, people will ignore a scream in the quarter. We had four calls. We were already here when he tried to escape. The motherfucker got out of Angola less than a month ago. I guess he couldn't wait to get back."

Sandy walked out of the bedroom, carrying Sam. Chris gasped. "I'm going to Charity with Sam," Sandy said.

Chris shook his head in acknowledgment.

When Joe walked into his house, it was close to 4:00. He listened to his messages. The last one was Sam. It came in about the time he had tried to call her. It was just sobbing. Joe felt sick. "What the fuck have I done?" he said out loud, then picked up the phone and called her.

"Hello."

"Chris?" Joe asked, surprised.

"Yes."

"I'm sorry. I meant to call Sam."

"You did. I'm at Sam's." Then Chris explained what had happened.

Joe's mind was racing. He couldn't figure out what was going on. Did Sam call the police on him? Did she make up some bullshit story to cover up what he had done to her?

"They got the guy," Chris said.

"What guy?" Joe asked.

"The guy that attacked her," Chris replied. "Joe, do you

understand what I'm saying?"

"Put Sam on the phone."

"Joe, she's in an ambulance on her way to Charity right now. Sandy's with her."

"Charity, What the fuck, Chris."

"Joe, she's in bad shape," Chris cautioned.

Joe hung up.

Chris called Dominic and filled him in. Dominic went to the hospital to be with Joe. Chris finished up with the police, afterward making his way to Charity.

Joe ran into the emergency room, where he spotted Sandy.

"Where is she?"

"The doctors looking at her now," Sandy replied.

Joe walked up to the counter, "Sam Mancuso. Where is she?"

"Are you a relative?" the nurse asked.

"Yes, now where is she?"

"The doctor will be out as soon as he finishes examining her."

Joe felt a hand on his shoulder. "Come on, Joe. Let them do their job," Dominic said.

Having Dominic there calmed Joe slightly. Chris showed up and related the story as told to him by the police detective.

"I guess once he sees a judge, they'll ship him back to Angola," Chris finished.

"I want a fucking welcoming committee waiting for that cocksucker," Joe said to Dominic. "Do you understand me, Dom?"

"Joe, it's done. I'll take care of it," Dominic replied.

"Hello, I'm Doctor Gardot. I believe we've met before," he said to Joe.

"Yes, we have," Joe replied. "How is she?"

"Remarkably, nothing broken. Bruised ribs. Some of her teeth are loose. She should see an orthodontist also an ophthalmologist. One eye is completely shut. We've given her something for pain and to calm her. We'll be moving her upstairs in a few minutes."

"Doctor, may I speak to you privately?" Joe asked.

"She was not sexually assaulted," the doctor said anticipating the question. "That does not mean she was any less traumatized," he sternly warned. "I'll take you back. She's been asking for you."

Joe never thought himself a man capable of murder until he saw Sam. It was a rage beyond reason. He wanted to pull her to his chest and hold her tightly but was afraid of hurting her.

"Joe, I didn't," she said, drawing in a quick breath. "I didn't; I didn't let him —"

"Shhh, baby, don't. I know," Joe said softly and placed his hand on the right side of her face.

"Can we go now?"

"No baby. You're going to stay here a little longer. But I'll be here with you. Okay?"

"Okay."

The world seemed to swirl around Sam for the next couple of days. Joe took her to his place. Felice came every day. Sam made her promise not to tell either one of their families. Lena, Chris's wife, brought avgolemono soup. (Greek lemon chicken soup) Joe's Aunt Carmela brought pasta fagioli. (Italian bean and pasta soup) Joe made sure someone would be there if he had to leave.

To the disbelief of all, Sam seemed unfazed by the bruises. Growing up in her uncle's gym, she understood swelling goes down, bruises fade, and teeth tighten back up. The rest, the emotional part, she shut out. She wouldn't speak of that night — any part of it, including what happened before the break-in.

Joe went to her apartment to get a few things. Art supplies and clothes. It hadn't occurred to him that the remnants of that night had not been cleaned up. He couldn't let Sam see this. He called Dominic.

"Remember that cop that has a side hustle cleaning up crime scenes," Joe asked.

"Yes, you need him?"

"Dominic, you can't believe what this place looks like. The fucking cops don't even clean their shit up. That fingerprint powder is all over the place."

"You want me to have him call you?"

"Just set it up, please. I'll make sure someone is here." He hung up and made another call. "Felice, Joe."

"Is Sam alright."

"She's coming along. I'm hoping you could help me with something."

"If I can."

"Sam's cocktail table is damaged. I don't think it can be repaired. Do you have one similar to replace it."

"I'm sure I can come up with something close."

"Thank you, Felice. And please don't say anything to Sam."

Joe had everything ready to go. He opened the refrigerator and got a coke. Sam always had those little glass bottles. They just taste better Joe thought as he guzzled it down. He opened the garbage to throw the bottle away, and there it was, the blue suit in shreds. He picked a piece of it out of the garbage. It was the first time since his father's death that Joe cried.

Friday, April 15, 1994

"Can we go to my place today?" Sam asked while clearing the breakfast dishes off the table.

"Are you sure?"

"Joe, I want to do this. I want to get back to my life."

"Of course, I'll take you. I've got to go to Uncle Frank's this afternoon. Is that good with you?"

"Yes," Sam kissed Joe on the cheek.

They walked into Sam's apartment. Joe stood back and watched Sam slowly walk through the apartment. She studied each piece of furniture as if she were in an art gallery, then moved on to the next. When she got to the cocktail table, she looked back at Joe.

"I replaced it," he said.

"Thank you," Sam replied and then looked back at the table. "I like it."

She raised the window and walked out onto the balcony. Joe followed.

"It's beautiful today," Sam said. "Let's eat out here tonight."

"I thought we were having dinner with the family tonight. Aunt Carmela is making a prime rib."

"Give her my apologies," Sam said matter-of-factly.

"Won't you need groceries?"

"They deliver," she cut him off.

"Are you going to be okay by yourself."

Sam wasn't going to know the answer to that until he left but assured him she was fine. She made herself busy cleaning out the refrigerator. Figuring out dinner and calling the grocers. Then she called Sandy. She hadn't seen or heard from him since that night.

"I'm at that yellow with light purple highlights stage," she giggled. "I'll be ready for Jazzfest if I still have a job."

"Sam, whenever you're ready. Don't rush yourself. We got you covered."

"Trust me, I'm ready," Sam joked. "Sandy, thank you for what you did."

"Sam, you don't have to—"

"I do Sandy," she interrupted. "It's important to me that you know how much I appreciate how you handled everything."

"I'll see you next Saturday," Sandy replied. Sandy wasn't the kind of guy that took bows.

Joe called twice to check up on her. He had been so patient and thoughtful throughout everything. She knew he was riddled with guilt over what had happened. That wasn't his fault. He can't be blamed for someone else's actions. He can, however, be blamed for what he had done to her. Neither one of them had addressed it. They had a nice dinner. It was the first time since that night that they made love. It was the first time since they had been together that she didn't come.

Saturday, April 23, 1994

"Back to normal? I guess," Joe said. "I don't know. She's different. You know I remodeled my slave quarter for her. New everything. Floor to ceiling. New kitchen, bathroom. Hell, I wouldn't mind living there."

"And?" Dominic prompted.

"Lackluster. That was her response. It's like nothing is registering," Joe said, sounding exhausted. "She starts back at work tonight. I can't believe I'm saying this, but maybe that will help. I gotta go. I'll stop in after I drop Sam off."

"Hang in there Cuz," Dominic said before he hung up.

Sam got behind the bar smiling. It was busy. Sandy handed her the bank bag.

"I've never seen anyone so happy to come to work. Welcome back," Sandy grinned. "Now, let's get going and count your money."

Joe walked into Azure after dropping Sam off. He stopped at the bar to get a drink to take upstairs with him.

"Hi Tanya. Can I get a scotch please?"

"Joe. How have you been? And Sam. How horrible," Tanya went on.

"She's good. Back to work tonight."

"Joe," a tall thin blonde called and waved from the stage.

Joe's heart sped up. "Tanya, what's that girl's name?" Joe nodded his head toward the stage.

"Bunny." Tanya looked back at the stage to be sure. "Yeah, Bunny."

Dominic was on the phone when Joe walked in. Joe sat down and finished his drink. "What's she doing here?" Joe asked when Dominic got off the phone.

"What's who doing where?" Dominic chuckled.

"Bunny, when did she start?"

"She started last week. Bunny! Where do these broads come up with their names." Dominic shook his head. "She said you sent her."

"When have I ever sent—" Joe stopped mid-sentence, leaning forward he cupped his head in both hands as his elbows rested on the desk. "Dominic, I fucked up. I fucked up so very bad."

"Bunny?" Dominic laughed. "Don't beat yourself up over it."

"Dom you don't understand," Joe replied and proceeded to tell Dominic a slightly altered version of that night. "The night Sam was attacked, we had an argument, and I walked out. I got in my car and drove. Just drove. I ended up on Airline Highway by the time I calmed down. I tried calling her, but the line was busy. Come to find out she was trying to call me at the same time. The phone was outside of John Tory's strip club, so I went in for a drink. John was there. We talked, and had a couple of drinks together. Bunny came around after her dance for tips. She said it was her birthday, so I threw her a half a yard. ($50) I couldn't get rid of her after that."

"Jesus Christ, Joe."

"So, while my girlfriend was getting the shit beat out of her by some fucking animal," Joe paused, "I was getting a blowjob."

"Fuck," Dominic said. "Listen to me. Go home. I'll take care of this."

"Dominic if Sam finds out—"

"She's not going to find out anything," Dominic interrupted. "Go, let me handle this."

As Joe made his way out of the bar, he heard, "Joe, Joe." Then he felt her hand grabbing his arm from behind. "Are you leaving already?"

"Yes," he said brusquely.

"I have something for you," she sounded almost desperate.

"Sorry, Bunny. I'm running late for a meeting, but I'll be back later," he lied. Joe took note that Tanya was watching the whole thing play out.

Dominic wasted no time. He called John Tory. John had no problem hiring Bunny back. She was a money maker. After her last set on stage, Dominic called her into the office. He explained it wasn't working out. Nothing to do with her performance. He told her she had her old job back if she wanted it and gave her $500 in cash as a severance. She wanted to see Joe. Dominic was crystal clear that it wasn't going to happen.

Joe went to Sam's apartment. He planned on calling Dominic later. He tried to get some work done, but couldn't concentrate. He turned on the tv, laid on the sofa and closed his eyes.

Sam had a good night. She made money, had fun, and never once thought of that night. She was dividing the tips when there was a knock on the door. Sandy gave Aaron the go-ahead to open it. Tanya walked in and made a beeline to Sam.

In that voice that grated on Sam's nerves, Tanya went on about how traumatized she was, hearing of Sam's attack. She asked Sam to have a drink with her, but Sam begged off.

"Sam, one drink. Somebody wants to meet you," Tanya badgered. "A friend of Joe's."

"What are you trying to pull Tanya?" Sam questioned.

"Did Joe tell you where he was the night you were attacked?"

Sam agreed to meet Tanya. Sandy tried to talk Sam out of it, but the hook was set.

Tanya had that cat that ate the canary look on her face when she saw Sam walk into the bar. Tanya did the introductions and eased into her barstool to watch the show. Sam wasn't going to have an audience. She politely thanked Tanya in a dismissive tone. The conversation didn't take long. Sam asked no questions. Before Bunny left, she handed Sam a plastic bag and asked Sam to return it to Joe. Inside was the Armani tie she sold him. He was wearing it that night.

Joe woke up and looked at his watch. It was almost 4:30. He couldn't believe Sam just left him on the sofa. He walked into the bedroom. No Sam. Panicked he called Sandy.

When Joe walked in, Sam was the only one sitting at the bar. There were two men shooting pool. The bartender put a napkin on the bar in front of Joe.

"Can I buy you a drink?" Sam asked, trying to control her slurred speech.

"Let me get her check," Joe said to the bartender.

"No!" Sam snapped. "I don't need your fucking money."

The two men shooting pool stopped. The bartender gave them an all good signal, and they went back to their game.

She dug through her purse and pulled out money. "Thank you. Keep the rest," she said, then took the plastic bag out of her purse handing it to Joe. "I have good news and bad news. The good news is I got your tie back. You're a bright guy. I'm sure you can figure out the bad news."

Goodbye

Tuesday, August 16, 1994

"You wanna get a quick drink?" Felice asked.

"Sure, why not," Sam replied.

"Ernst's?"

"Cool." Sam smiled.

The busy bar went dead silent when they walked in. They bellied up to the bar.

"Two shots of Jager, please," Sam said then turned to Felice. "You wanna split a beer?"

"Sam, I don't have any money."

"Don't panic. I always have a twenty in my bra."

"You don't have a bra on." They both started to laugh hysterically.

"Hold on," Sam said to the bartender. "We didn't come prepared."

"Baby, you're good," the bartender said as he poured the shots.

"No, thank you," Felice said. "We can't let you do that."

"Sha, four different people have offered to pay for your drinks," he smiled.

"See, I told you, you looked good in white," Sam laughed. "Please thank whoever bought this for us."

"You can thank him yourself," the familiar voice said.

"Shit," Sam mouthed to Felice then turned around. "Of all the gin joints," Sam said to Joe.

"Felice, you're absolutely breathtaking," Joe said. "So, what are you two up to?" They all laughed.

They exchanged pleasantries for a few minutes until Sam broke it up. "We should be getting back. Someone is sure to have missed the bride by now. Thank you for the drink, Joe."

"You're welcome, Peanut," Joe said, then quickly kissed her cheek. "Felice, congratulations. Daniel is a lucky man."

"He still cares about you," Felice said as they walked back to Windsor Court. "You still feel something too. I can tell."

"Felice, don't even. You can't possibly understand."

"You're right; I can't, because you refuse to talk about it." Sam didn't respond. "You had to run into him sooner or later. How long has it been?"

"Almost four months," Sam said solemnly.

Felice could tell it was time to back off. "Thank you for introducing me to Daniel." She took Sam's hand and gave a little squeeze.

"Thanks for not picking out a shitty looking bridesmaid dress."

They were laughing as they walked back into the reception hand in hand.

"I saw Sam today," Joe said.

"Oh Jesus," Dominic rolled his eyes.

"No, it was good. She was with Felice. I ran into them at Ernst's," Joe grinned. "Felice got married. So here they are, Felice in her wedding gown and Sam in her bridesmaid dress having a shot of Jager. You should have seen it. You would have laughed your ass off. The wedding was at Windsor Court."

"On Tuesday? Who gets married on a Tuesday?"

"Jews, you illiterate fuck. It's considered good luck. At least that's what Felice told me," Joe laughed. "Felice has to have lost 40, 50 pounds. She looked terrific. Sam was beautiful as always."

"Cuz, do yourself a favor and leave it alone. She's moved on."

"She's seeing someone?"

"A few more than one," Dominic chuckled.

"You're not fucking around with her Dom?"

"Of course not. Do you honestly think I would do that to you?"

"Tanya!"

"Two different things. You didn't give a shit about Tanya,"

Dominic said. "In fact, you were glad to get rid of her if I remember correctly. Which reminds me, you'll be happy to hear Tanya's leaving at the end of the month — moving to Vegas. She met a guy. He's in management with—"

Joe raised his hand to stop Dominic, "I could care less.

"Joe, I know you don't believe it, but that whole night was a series of bad coincidences."

"Sam asked Tanya to have a drink, and Bunny showed up. Bullshit!"

"Did you ever ask Sam?"

"It's hard to ask someone something when they're hurling a cocktail table at you. She does have a Sicilian temper," Joe smirked.

"I would've given everything in my pocket to have seen her toss the table over her balcony," Dominic laughed. "What did that cost you?"

"For the table or the hood of my car?" Joe laughed. "I miss her, Dom."

Wednesday, August 17, 1994

"Oh my god, it was fabulous." Sam started talking the minute she walked into the bar. "I got a few good pictures, but Felice took my camera away." She walked around and got behind the bar.

"Sam, Joe's upstairs," Sandy said.

"Here we go," she rolled her eyes. Her mood took a 180.

It wasn't long before Chris, Dominic and Joe came downstairs and huddled around the cigarette machine. Joe asked Sam to get them a round of drinks.

"You remember what I drink?" Joe shined his pearly whites.

"Sure," Sam said and yelled to the other end of the bar, "Sandy, where did you put the hemlock?"

Joe chuckled, "see Dominic, I told you she wasn't bitter."

Sam laughed. She busied herself with the customers sitting at the bar, but she could feel his eyes on her. Thankfully he only stayed for one drink. Sam couldn't shake it off. She knew what he was up to. She also remembered how tenacious he could be.

Sandy, as usual, gave Sam a lift home with a slight difference that night. He pulled into a space, turned off the ignition, and followed her to the door.

"What are you doing?" Sam asked, already knowing the answer.

"Something I should have done the day I met you."

She was ready, having fantasized about this moment many times. "Get yourself a drink. I'm going to take a quick shower." She came out in a robe. Sandy was sitting in the Eames chair, holding a beer by the neck of the bottle. The new cocktail table was pulled away from the sofa.

"Lay down," Sandy said. She did. He got up and walked over to her. "Open your legs," Sandy ordered, staring into her eyes. She did as wide as she could without her robe opening too far, revealing everything. Still holding the beer bottle by the neck, he ever so slowly dragged the edge of the heel of the bottle from just below her ear, down her neck and between her breast. Her breath hitched. He opened her robe further with the heel of the bottle exposing her right breast and circled her nipple. "Put your left leg on top of the sofa." She hesitated. "Were my directions unclear?" Sandy smiled, his eyes never leaving hers. She finally did as he requested. He ran the heel of the bottle from her upper inner thigh down to her ankle. She could barely control herself. "Now, show me how you come." She was sure she had stopped breathing. "You can do it," he said as he took her right hand and placed it between her legs.

"I can't," Sam whispered.

"You can. Just relax." She closed her eyes and took a deep breath. He ran the heel of the bottle down her other thigh lightly grazing her. "Keep your eyes open," he walked back over to the chair, sat down and took a swig of beer, "take your time."

She didn't understand why she did as he asked, but she did, hypnotized by his melodic instructions, perhaps. It didn't take long before her back arched, and a long low moan escaped. When she was done, Sandy walked back to her. He stood there watching her for a few moments.

"Good girl," he said then he walked into the kitchen to rid himself of the empty bottle.

Sam laid there just as he posed her. Her eyes closed, her breathing back to normal, waiting for him. She couldn't believe she went along with this. This was an insane thing to do, but she left sanity a long time ago. She heard the door.

WHAT THE FUCK! Was screaming in her head. He left.

The next three days, her mind went wild. Bizarre theories explaining that night. She even thought Sandy did that because he had a hard-on for Joe. Thoughts of moving back to Fort Lauderdale crossed her mind. How did she fuck up her life so bad? Now she really had jeopardized her job.

Saturday, August 20, 1994

Sam's plan was to mirror Sandy's reactions. If he didn't say anything, she wouldn't. Whatever happened, she had to remain professional. And he didn't say a thing. This guy missed his calling, Sam thought. He's the best actor she's ever seen. But the act was going to stop soon. It was 1:30, and she was going to address Wednesday night on the ride home. Best laid plans. What a joke. Joe walked in. NOOOOO! He was freshly shaven, and his hair was slightly damp. She could smell his body wash as he got closer to the bar. She always liked that scent. She picked up the Chivas bottle and iced a glass. Joe gave a slight head shake no.

"Want a beer?"

"No, just a club soda. Is Chris around?"

"I haven't seen him," she answered as she put the drink down.

"Thank you, Peanut."

"Perhaps we should go back to Sam and Joe."

Joe gave Sam a faint smile. He stood at the end of the bar nursing his club soda and making small talk when Sam was in close enough range.

"Can I give you a ride home?"

"I already have one. Thank you," she replied, looking down the bar toward Sandy.

"Maybe lunch next week? It will give you a chance to have a nice meal," Joe smiled.

Sam walked out from behind the bar. "I'll be back in a minute," she said to Sandy as she walked by him. She walked the length of the room past Joe and outside. Joe followed. "Joe, I didn't think I could be in the same room as you again," Joe huffed. "Un minuto," (one minute) Sam said. "But I'm glad I ran into you, and the awkwardness is behind us. That said, please don't misconstrue this as a door opening."

"I was hoping we could talk."

"We can't," she paused, "I don't want to Joe. I have to get back in there."

Sam walked back into the bar. Joe didn't. Sam had little to say the remainder of the evening. Sam and Sandy got into his truck.

"You've been uncharacteristically quiet. Are you okay?" Sandy asked.

"Yes."

"Was there a problem with you and Joe?"

"He mistook kindness for weakness," Sam replied. They were silent for a few blocks. "What's your deal with Joe?"

"He told you," Sandy replied.

"He did. Now I would like to hear your version."

Sandy took a deep breath. "Joe told you I took the wrap for that cluster fuck he set up. I was only 17. The part I'm sure he left out," Sandy paused, "I was seeing a married woman at the time. Her husband worked oil rigs and would be gone weeks at a time. I had it bad for her and Joe knew it. He took up with her as soon as I went away. When I got out, she wanted nothing to do with me. I went to jail for that prick, and that's how he repays me. Joe dumped her shortly after that."

Sandy was talking about the woman that got Joe involved in kink. Does this mean Sandy is too? It would make sense. His demeanor was that same controlled air that Joe had. She wished she could bottle it. Sam could feel her face flushing. She missed it. She wanted to ask, but if he wasn't into the same thing, he might get turned off by the question.

Without asking, Sandy came up to Sam's apartment, and they danced the dance couples do leading to sex. Sandy undressed her then himself. Sam was awestruck by the beauty of his body. She had been around fit men her whole life, but this is what Greek statues were modeled after. She wanted to paint him.

Try as he might he couldn't generate the same response he got from her the other night. Their timing was off from the first kiss. In mere seconds after he entered her, she started to scream.

"Leg cramp, leg cramp, oh fuck, get up, get up, get up."

He jumped up, and as he did, her knee came up and hit him dead center in his balls. He rolled on his back and let out a loud groan. Sam was rubbing her calf, begging his forgiveness. He felt like throwing up. In an attempt to get up, he slid off the bed onto the floor. Sam hobbled into the kitchen and came back with ice wrapped in a towel.

"Sam, give me a few minutes alone, please."

She went into the kitchen and poured herself a shot. She didn't know if she was going to laugh or cry. Sandy walked out fully dressed a few minutes later.

"I'm gonna get going," Sandy said, standing hands off distance from her.

"You okay?"

"Yeah. I'll see you tomorrow," he said, walking out slowly.

Sunday, August 21, 1994

Sam ran to the athletic club. She swam 50 laps and ran home. She thought that would help with some of the anxiety she was feeling. It didn't. That night the bar was empty when she walked in. She was hoping for customers to buffer the awkwardness. Sandy handed her the bank. She thanked him, not looking up.

"When you get settled, I'm going across the street to get a piece of pizza."

"Okay," Sam replied, still avoiding his eyes.

"You want anything?"

"No, thank you."

Sandy stood outside the restaurant, his back leaning against the brick building eating his pizza, staring across Bourbon into the bar at Sam.

It was about an hour into the shift when Sam was ringing up a drink. She looked down the bar. Sandy was at his register, looking back at her. The vision of Sandy holding his balls falling off her bed flashed in her mind. Sam tried to suppress a laugh. Sandy smiled. Sam let go and started to laugh out loud. Sandy joined in. When their laughter subsided, Sandy walked over to Sam, and in her ear, he whispered.

"I can honestly say, my first night with you; I saw stars."

"You want to try this again?"

"I can do better."

"Let's hope so."

The rest of the night was an exchange of smiles and giggles.

"I'm parked on Dauphine," Sandy said as he locked the bar door.

Sam leaned against a light pole waiting for Sandy to unlocked the truck. He stood in front of her and grinned. He tilted her chin up, bent down and nibbled on her lower lip. She placed her hands flat on his chest and leaned in. His right leg slid between hers, and she started to ride his leg. He took her wrists and brought her arms back around the light pole. He opened his mouth wide, consuming her. She rubbed back and forth on his thigh, picking up speed as she came closer to her peak.

He abruptly pulled his leg back, still holding on to her wrist. "Not yet," Sandy whispered.

"Please," she whimpered.

"No," he smiled down at her. "Let's go."

She got out of the shower to find a shirtless Sandy turning down her bed.

"Take off your robe and lie down on your back, please," Sandy requested. "Do you have baby oil?"

"Under the bathroom sink."

He poured baby oil into his palm, then rubbed his hands together. "Close your eyes," Sandy said as he picked up her foot and started to rub. She let out a groan as he kneaded her soreness away. He worked his way up her leg, paying special attention to her calf, not wanting a repeat of the leg cramp incident. He picked up her other foot and duplicated his moves. Sam's arms were next, starting with her fingers up to her shoulders. Sandy wiped off her legs, and arms with a hand towel and then rolled her over onto her stomach. He massaged her thighs and then skipped up to her shoulders and worked his way down. He got to the small of her back and stopped to add more oil to his hands, then returned to her lower back. Sandy proceeded down sliding the length of his index finger between her cheeks and eased his finger in. She squeezed tightly and said no at the same time.

"Alright baby," he said as he wiped her down. "Relax, I'll be back in a few."

She felt so pampered. She opened her eyes when she heard the shower turn off. He walked back in with a towel wrapped low on his waist.

"You're magnificent," Sam whispered.

"Am I?" Sandy smiled, dropped the towel, and climbed into bed.

She came twice.

He played with her hair as her head rested on his chest. "Are you doing this because of Joe?" she asked.

"Doing what?"

"Me."

Sandy could feel her lips draw up to a smile against his chest. "No, and in the future, let's not mention his name in bed."

Sam giggled, "okey-dokey."

Sandy laughed.

Sandy's eyes opened in the morning to see Sam tying the laces of her running shoes. "Coffee's made. If you wanna stick around for breakfast, I'll be back in a half-hour."

"What if I want to stick around after breakfast?" Sam looked up. "What are you doing today?"

"I was going to stay home. Cleaning, maybe spend some time in my studio. Did you have something in mind?"

"Take a ride with me?" Sandy asked.

"Where?"

"It's a surprise."

"I like surprises." Sam was excited. She rarely left the quarter since she broke up with Joe.

The surprises started when she got back from her run. Her bed was made, and Sandy was in the kitchen, freshly showered, cooking breakfast. She walked up behind him, put her arms around his waist, and kissed his shoulder.

"You can cook?"

"Not as well as you, but I can throw a meal together." He looked over his shoulder and smiled. Sam's hand slid down to his crotch. "No, you don't. I don't have another condom."

"I do."

"Sit down," Sandy was firm. "We'll lose the day if we go back to bed."

After breakfast, Sam showered, and Sandy cleaned up. "Grab Claude," Sandy said before they walked out.

"Claude's coming?" Sam grinned.

"Claude's coming," Sandy smiled back.

They stopped at Sandy's, where he changed and hooked up his bass boat to the truck.

On the way to Houma, they exchanged stories about Claude. It was a perfect day to be on the bayou. She released Claude into the still waters watching his ashes disappear. She then let the urn follow to the bottom of the water. With a tear rolling down her cheek, she faintly said, thank you. Sandy didn't respond, not knowing if that was meant for him or Claude. God, she's beautiful, he thought.

Afterward, they stopped at a little hole in the wall restaurant sitting on the bayou.

"Those were the best chargrilled oysters I ever had," Sam said getting into the truck.

"Stick with me babe, I know all the hot spots in Houma," Sandy smiled.

"Why didn't you call or come see me after the break-in?"

"Wow! Right to it," Sandy sounded uneasy. "Chris was updating me on your progress. Besides, it wouldn't have been appropriate."

"Appropriate?"

"Sam, I know you and Joe were involved in kink. You must have figured out that Joe and I had the same teacher. I don't mess around with other dominants subs. That's hands-off for me."

"You automatically assume if I'm with Joe, I'm into S & M."

"I saw the belt marks on you." Sam thought he was referring to the night she was attacked. "During Carnival, you changed in the back room. I remember how off guard that caught me. I thought Joe was just into professional subs."

"So, that's when you found me appealing?"

"Sam, I've always found you appealing."

"You're just not into the breaking in part."

"That mouth of yours could get you in trouble," Sandy smirked. "Sam, I have no interest in bringing someone into our lifestyle."

"Why?"

"We lead a closeted life. Why would I introduce someone into that." There was a lull. "Did you do it to appease Joe or because you were curious?"

"I've always liked it rough so as he got more aggressive I didn't say anything."

"You mean to tell me he didn't discuss it with you?"

Sam shook her head.

"DiLeo's such a fucking asshole. He should have had your permission."

"I liked it, and I miss it," she said, looking out of the passenger side window.

"I'd like to have a scene with you. Do you think that's something we can discuss?"

"Discuss?"

"Yes, we have to discuss your limits. What you find acceptable, what you don't."

"It's fine. Whatever you want to do."

"Sam, honey, you don't know what you're talking about. Has Joe ever taken a cane to you or a crop?" She was silent. "What about a bullwhip or a tawse?" She didn't answer. "Sam, I play at a different level then Joe. I live in this world. I'm not an occasional visitor."

"What exactly would you expect of me?"

"Eventually, a total power exchange, but we would work up to that."

"Which means what?"

"I use you the way I like. You'll be well trained at that point."

"Trained?"

"Yes, honey, you will learn in an emotionally safe environment what pleases me. It's all stuff we will discuss in detail."

They pulled up to Sam's apartment. "Are you coming in?"

"No, honey. It's been a long day. An amazing day," he grabbed her chin and pulled her to his lips. "I want you to take a couple of days and weigh everything we talked about. Thank you for allowing me to be part of yours and Claude's goodbye."

Pink Tutu

Tuesday, August 23, 1994

"This is Sam, how can I help you?"

"Sam, Alfonso. Sorry, I have to reschedule you. I won't be in on Thursday. If you want, I can do you tonight."

"I don't get out til 6:00. Is 6:30 okay?"

"See you at 6:30."

Sam walked into the shop at 6:40 and sat down in the shampoo chair. "Sorry running late."

"You're good." Alfonso went on about his friends coming in town on Thursday while washing Sam's hair. "How much are we taking off?"

"How would I look in that haircut?" She pointed to a picture on the wall.

"Cute. You have an oval face. You can wear any style."

"Let's do it."

"Are you sure? I don't want to hear you whining, it's too short," he mimicked Sam's voice.

"I don't whine, I bitch." They both laughed.

Alfonso proceeded to cut Sam's hair into a shoulder-length bob with long layers.

"What do you think?" Alfonso asked.

"I like it," Sam said and shook her head to see how it moved. "What do you think?"

"I think it's sassy," Alfonso smiled. "Oh, before I forget, are you coming to the drag race at Lafitte's. I'm in it this year. It's on the ninth."

"As much as I would love to see you break your ass running in high heels, I can't. I work on Saturdays."

"The ninth is a Friday."

"Well then, I wouldn't miss it for all the hurricanes in Pat O's," Sam laughed. "In fact, I'll bring my camera. We're going to want to document this disaster."

Wednesday, August 24, 1994

"Adorable," Sandy said as he handed Sam her bank bag.

"Really? It's not too short?"

"Really, it looks cute." Sandy smiled.

It was slow that night. At one point there was no one sitting at the bar.

"Are you coming over tonight?" Sam asked.

"Sam, that's not a conversation I want to have in this building," Sandy replied.

Later in the evening, Sam asked if he'd like to have lunch with her, on Thursday.

"That's two," Sandy said in a cautionary tone.

"Do you want a drink?" Sam asked when they walked into her apartment.

"A beer, please," Sandy replied as he walked to the center of the living room.

Sam walked up to him with a beer in hand. "Stand right here," Sandy said, pointing to a design in the rug. He went to a dining table and turned a chair to face Sam. "Take your clothes off."

It took her a few seconds to respond before she slowly started to lift her shirt.

"I'm not looking for a striptease. Just do as you're told."

She became self-conscious, standing there while he sat drinking his beer. "Stand up straight," he snapped. "Hands behind your back." After a few more minutes, he called her over. He gave a quick pull on her pubic hair, "this has to go." Sam let out a small gasp. He took her wrist, gave a tug pulling her across his legs. "We never discuss our private life in Christos." His hand came down hard on her ass. Her legs were flailing as he continued. He captured them between his making it impossible to avoid his blows. He stopped when the begging ended, and the crying began. She clung to him as he cradled her in his arms.

Joe had never spanked her with his hand or over his knees. There was an intimacy difficult to put into words. It was cathartic. As though the affliction called Joe had been purged.

Thursday, August 25, 1994

"Do you like blueberry pancakes?" Sam asked.

"I do. You ran already? I didn't hear you leave," he said as he bent over to kiss her. "Your mattress is so comfortable. I was out cold."

Towards the end of breakfast, he got into the conversation she was hoping to avoid. She was reluctant to discuss her relationship with Joe.

"Believe me, I would prefer not having those images in my head, but it's important I know your experience and limitations," Sandy said in his understanding way.

When he laid out all of the potential scenarios, it became apparent; she was quite inexperienced in the ways of a dominant/submissive relationship. In Sandy, she would have a master and a mentor. He went down a laundry list of pain and pleasure. She was getting wet as he explained the marks each instrument could leave. The humiliations he would inflict for disobedience. She wanted it all.

Wrapping up the conversation with, "I'd like us to get tested. I should be done with my liquor deliveries by 2:00. We can go after that."

This caught Sam off guard. It seemed to be moving fast. "Already?" Sam questioned.

"Sam, it's not to avoid condoms. Although that will be a big plus, at our level of play, there could be an exchange of fluids," he explained. "Always better to be safe. Right?"

She shook her head in acknowledgment.

Sam didn't hear from Sandy after they went to be tested.

Saturday, August 27, 1994

"This is Sam. How can I help you?"

"Can you talk?" Sandy asked.

"To some extent," Sam replied.

"I just need yes's, or no's. Do you have a sexy black bra and panty set?"

"Yes."

"Do you have a black garter belt?"

"Yes."

"Wear them under your uniform tonight with black hose. You can carry black high heels in your bag." He hung up, not interested in a reply.

She had to wear pants instead of shorts to cover the garter and hose. It was sweltering. The hose were sticking to her skin. The night dragged with a few spurts of activity.

As he turned the lock on the door, he said, 'we're going to a dungeon." She started down Bourbon. "Where are you going?"

"The Dungeon," (a famous French Quarter bar) she replied.

Sandy grinned, "Sam, we're going to a dungeon, not The Dungeon. Come on, I'm parked on Bienville."

They pulled into the driveway of a magnificent garden district mansion on Coliseum. The courtyard in the back of the house was used for parking. Sam's heart was racing as they got out of the truck. Sandy took a large duffel from behind the driver's side and placed it on the hood of the truck. He unzipped a side pocket and pulled out a collar.

"This is a training collar. No one will bother you while you have this on. Also, they will be more understanding of mistakes," Sandy said as he placed it around her neck. "This doesn't mean I've collared you. Do you understand the difference?"

She nodded even though she didn't fully understand what he was talking about. They walked into the house, holding hands. There was a robust girl sitting behind an ornate rosewood desk to greet them. She had blue/black hair with heavy arched brows to match. A nose ring accented her turned-up nose. Her lips were as red as the garnet walls. She was wearing a black patented leather vest that zipped down the middle. Sam couldn't see the bottom half of the outfit.

Her smile broadened when she saw Sandy. "How have you been?" she asked touching his arm.

Am I invisible? Sam thought.

"Good, and you?" Sandy replied. After a few more pleasantries, he made the introductions. "Sam, this is Ramona. Ramona has some paperwork for you to fill out. Give her your I.D."

Ramona took a quick look and handed it back, after which she gave a clipboard and pen to Sam. "The first and second pages are the rules. Please check the box after reading each one and sign the bottom of the last page. The third is a release of liability. We need your legal name on that one. And finally, a layout of the house. You can keep that."

Sandy went over everything with Sam. She handed the paperwork back and thanked Ramona. "If you have any questions don't hesitate to ask one of the dungeon monitors. Your dominant is one of the best. You'll be fine." Ramona smiled.

They then went into the coed changing room. Two of the walls were lined with lockers. Full length on one side and half lockers opposite, Sandy had paid for a full-size locker. One wall was mirrored floor to ceiling. Sandy slipped out of his clothes and into leather jeans and boots. No shirt. He looked hot. Sam was down to her black underwear.

"Ramona seems nice," Sam said with a sarcastic undertone.

"Yes, she is. Put your heels on." She did. "Stand up straight." She squared her shoulders. "Good, no pink showing."

Sam gave an inquisitive look.

"No private parts showing on the first floor." Sandy smiled. "House rules."

"Have you and Ramona ever—"

"Had a scene together?" Sandy interrupted. "Yes."

"Are you still," she stopped.

Sandy smiled and put a finger between her neck and collar, pulling her closer. "I guess that will depend on you." Then he kissed the tip of her nose. "You talk to no one without my permission," he reminded her.

They walked into the kitchen/great room, which was a gathering place with nonalcoholic beverages and snacks. This tops Mardi Gras, Sam thought. Every shape, size, age, and sexual preference was represented in that room. There was a woman probably in her 50's, not much more than 5 feet tall and just as wide, sporting a pink leather ballerina outfit.

"A lot of pink showing there," Sam said under her breath and giggled.

The look on Sandy's face put Sam on alert. He grabbed her arm and walked her out of the room to a corner in the foyer. "This is a safe place. It may be the only safe place for many of these people to express themselves. How would you like to have someone laugh at you in your most vulnerable moment? Let's go."

Sam was taken aback. "I'm sorry." He didn't look at her. "I truly am. It was more of a nervous release. Please. It won't happen again."

"If it does, I'm going to have a nervous release across your ass." Sam suppressed her laugh. "Don't think you're off the hook. We'll address this at home."

They went back in, and Sam soon realized how right Sandy was. These were nice people. Especially the pink ballerina. She was ashamed of her behavior and hoped no one overheard her remark.

They left the room of pink ballerinas, adults in diapers, and human puppies, to name a few more unusual guests. They crossed the foyer that had a Gone With the Wind staircase with a red velvet theater rope at the base that was opened and closed by a dungeon monitor. Sandy proudly led Sam into a ballroom size double parlor.

The room was a visual feast. The artist surfaced in Sam, snapshots clicking in her mind. In the center of the room, on an 18 inch high, 6 foot round pedestal, surrounded by Saint Andrew's crosses, spanking benches, and bondage chairs, stood Paige. She was spectacular. A full head of long silver hair crowned her statuesque body. She had a hand-tooled leather corset on with 4 inch high heeled boots that cuffed above the knee. She had work done but by a good doctor. The only age giveaway was the inside of her upper arms. She was holding a riding crop in one hand while the other was gripping the hair of her submissive. The submissive was attached to a chain hanging from the ceiling by her wrist cuffs. Just 27 hours earlier, this same submissive was tied to a bed in Joe DiLeo's guest room. After checking on her, Paige stood back and proceeded to whip her. Tap, tap, tap, and then a strike. All the other pieces of furniture were occupied, but Paige garnered most of the attention.

Sandy sat in one of the chairs scattered around the room for people waiting a turn on their favorite equipment. His eyes pointed to the floor next to him. Sam didn't move. He mouthed floor, as his brows drew together. She quickly sat between his feet. She wrapped her arms around one of his legs and rested her head on his knee. He played with her hair while watching Paige. When Paige finished, she unhooked the girl from the ceiling. Another girl helped her into a long terrycloth robe and walked her out of the room. Paige hung back to talk to Sandy.

"Your little girl is precious," Paige said, looking down at Sam.

"Thank you," Sandy replied.

"Center stage is available," Paige waved her hand to the center of the room. "You two would look good up there."

"Not tonight," Sandy smiled, "but thank you."

"I have you on my list to call on Monday. I'm glad you stopped in."

"What's up?"

"There's going to be a lot of people in town for Labor Day. I was thinking of doing some classes. I was hoping you could do a demonstration on the correct use of whips."

"We're not going to be ready for that," he rubbed Sam's head.

"I can provide a sub for you to use," Paige said.

"I'll give you a call," Sandy replied.

"Soon, please," she smiled. "Let me check on my girl. Talk later."

They stayed for another half hour with Sandy explaining the furniture and the differences between all the tools and toys. It was almost 6 A.M. when they walked into Sam's apartment. Sandy took off his shirt. He still had on his leather pants and boots.

"Take off your clothes. Leave on the garter belt, hose, and heels." She did as told. He took her by the back of the neck and walked her into the bathroom. "Look! You ended up on the right side of the gene pool." She didn't say anything. "Too bad, the inside doesn't match."

"I'm sorry. I really am."

He picked up the wooden hairbrush and walked her to the dining set. He turned a chair around and sat down. He pulled her pubic hair. "You don't follow directions very well," he said and pulled her over his lap. "I'm not going to put up with a brat." Then the brush came down on her ass.

She was exhausted. She had been up for close to 24 hours. She just wanted to get into bed. Sandy walked her into the bathroom and turned on the shower. "I know you're tired, but you'll feel better after a quick shower." He checked the water temperature and held her hand as she stepped up to get into the shower. He handed her a razor. "Do you need help?" Still crying, she shook her head. Sandy closed the shower curtain. Sandy opened the curtain when the water went off. He wiped her off, taking extra time on her newly shaven mons and led her to the already turned down bed, covered her, and kissed her forehead. "I'm going to take a quick shower. Are you okay?" She started to cry again. He held her until she stopped. "All better?" She shook her head while blowing her nose. "I'll be five minutes." She was fast asleep when he got back.

Sunday, August 28, 1994

Sunday would not be Sunday without the parade of DiLeo's walking up Chartres to Saint Louis Cathedral. Dominic and Chris were at the back of the pack. They spotted it at the same time. Chris's eyes grew large. Dominic looked at Chris and said, "fuck" drawing the word out. They slowed their pace to distance themselves a little from the family.

"What are we going to do?" Chris asked.

"Nothing," Dominic replied.

"We can't just do nothing."

"Chris, use your head. Sandy's truck outside of Sam's apartment could mean a lot of different things. It doesn't put him in her bed. But that's the first thing that's gonna go through Joe's mind if we say anything. And if he is up there in her bed, it could just be a one-nighter. Just leave it alone. Please!"

"I'll talk to Sandy tonight."

"Jesus Christ, Chris. Stay out of this."

"Joe will eventually find out."

"Not from us," Dominic ended the conversation as they walked into the church.

He woke shortly after 2:00. Sam's hair was tickling his face. She was sprawled out on top of him, holding his cock and rubbing up and down. He grabbed her hair to lift her head.

"What are you doing, baby girl?"

"Good morning," she smiled and kept rubbing up and down.

"Not now," Sandy said grabbing her wrist.

When Sandy let go of her wrist she continued with a grin on her face.

He rolled her back, opened her legs, and brushed her folds back and forth with the pad of his thumb.

"I want you to shave every day," he said just before his mouth sucked out her hard tip from it's hiding place. It didn't take long before her legs stiffened. She was there. Just a few seconds more. He stopped.

WHAT THE FUCK! Was screaming in her head. "Get up. I wanna eat."

"You were eating," Sam snapped.

"Cute," Sandy smiled. "You're very cute."

As he was turning around to walk out, Sam stood on the bed and jumped on Sandy's back, throwing her legs and arms around him. "Pleeeeease!" she whined.

"Sam, get down," he said, prying her arms lose.

"Fuck you then," she stomped off to the bathroom and slammed the door.

Sandy, right behind her, opened the door and leaned on the frame arms crossed. "What do you think you're going to gain with this behavior?"

"I'm peeing. Get out."

"Go ahead, pee."

"I'm not going to pee with you here."

"Well, I'm not moving, so how long do you think you can hold it?"

She let go. "You know my first impression of you was right," she said while wiping herself. "You're a prick."

"I'm a prick?" Sandy laughed.

"Yes, you're a controlling, manipulative prick."

"You just described a dominant," he laughed.

She walked into her bedroom and put her running clothes on.

"Make coffee before you go."

She walked straight to the door. Sandy caught her before she got out.

"As amusing as I find your little tantrum, it's over. So turn around and make the coffee."

He stood next to her as she made the coffee. In a small voice, she asked, "why are you doing this?"

"Doing what exactly?" Sandy smirked.

"Being mean."

"Honey, I explained what I was looking for in a submissive. When I say no, it's no. With training, you will get there."

"I'm not a puppy."

"No, you're not. Although you would look adorable with a little tail sticking out of your ass," he laughed. "Surrender. Just let go, and I will make you happy."

"Was that you making me happy when you stopped just before I came?"

"I control your climaxes. I decide when and if we have sex. It would behoove you to keep that in mind. Now go run."

Her mind was running as fast as she was. What had she gotten herself into? Talk about not being able to judge a book by its cover. She was in way over her head. Sandy was the major league of BDSM. When she got back Sandy was in the kitchen.

"I found lamb chops in your freezer. I thought we could grill them with potato wedges and a salad."

"That sounds good." She gave a faint smile.

"Take your shower."

She noted the bed was made as she undressed. When she came back into the bedroom after her shower, the bed was turned down. He came up behind her.

"Take off your robe and lay on your stomach."

He massaged her. He slid his finger between her cheeks, the same as before. This time he slid a finger inside of her.

"Relax that ass," Sandy ordered.

She did her best to comply as he brought his finger in and out.

"Good girl," Sandy said as he continued.

He rolled her over and tied her wrist to the headboard with a silk scarf. He rubbed her breast then attached a clothespin to each one of her hardened nipples. She gasped from the pain.

"You're doing good. Deep breaths."

He continued rubbing down to her toes. Then he spread her legs wide, and his tongue picked up where it left off earlier. He stopped just as her legs started to twitch. He climbed up next to her and kissed her. He wiggled the clothes pins awakening the pain.

"Please," she pleaded.

"Shhh!" he kissed her again. "Breathe."

He worked his way back down, kissing and biting her breast and stomach. He ran his tongue from the bottom of her folds to the top and latched onto her clitoris. He brought one hand under her and reinserted his finger, with the other hand, he released the clothespins. He sucked hard, and she flew apart. With little time to recover, he entered her. She came again. She cried afterward.

"I'm sorry," Sam said almost in a whisper.

"For what?"

"Crying, I'm always crying with you."

"It's your hormones surging. That happens with intense play," he smiled. "You're fine."

She fell asleep in his arms. She woke to the smell of lamb chops. She stepped out onto the balcony through the bedroom window. Sandy was at the grill.

"You're up," he broadly smiled. "How do you feel?"

"Good. Calm," she said. "What can I do?"

"Relax, I've got this."

And he did. He cooked, cleaned up, and waited on her. He coddled her. She thought of the sea. Sandy's like a huge wave rushing to shore. After the waves break, the sea is peaceful.

Chop, Chop

Wednesday, August 31, 1994

Joe walked into Christos just shy of midnight. His two cousins were at the end of the bar. Dominic laughed, "we were just getting the ransom money together. Where the hell have you been?"

"I've been spending some time in Baton Rouge," Joe grinned that grin that was easily decoded to mean a woman.

"Can I get you something?" Sam asked while placing a cocktail napkin down.

"Scotch, please. You got your hair cut."

Sam smiled, "Yeah."

He didn't correct her. "Looks nice."

"Chris, Sandy needs you," Sam said when she returned with Joe's drink.

"Thanks, Sam," Joe said and returned to his conversation with Dominic.

"I'm glad to see you're moving on," Dominic said when Sam and Chris were out of range.

Joe gave him an inquisitive look.

"You know, putting this Sam thing behind you."

"She just needs more time Dom. I'm giving her space."

Dominic took Joe's upper arm. "Let's go outside for a minute."

They walked out, drinks in hand.

"Make it quick," Joe said. "It's like a fucking sauna out here."

"Look at the plus side." Dominic waved his hand towards the people in the street. "The girls are wearing fewer clothes." Joe shook his head, laughing. "Joe, you gotta put this Sam thing behind you. It's been months. It's over, man."

"I know you're just looking out for me, but I'm fine."

"I just think it's not healthy—"

"I'm fine, really," Joe interrupted. He lightly slapped Dominic on the cheek. "Let's get back inside. My balls are sweating."

"So, how was Joe?" Sandy asked as they walked to his truck.

"What do you mean?"

"Still giving you a hard time?"

"No. Actually, he was normal."

"Joe DiLeo, normal. I doubt that," Sandy laughed. "I told Paige I'd do the demonstration on Monday night."

"Oh."

"I'm using Ramona." There was silence for the next few minutes. "Ramona's a pain slut, and I know her limitations." More silence. "I don't want you to be upset."

"I would have liked to have had the option. You could have asked."

"First of all, you're mine. I don't ask, I tell. Plus, there is no way you are ready for what I'm going to do to that girl." Sam didn't respond. "I will give you one option. I'd like you to be there. But if you're uncomfortable with the idea, and don't want to come, I will respect that."

"I don't know."

"Paige will watch you while I'm doing my demonstration. You'll be safe."

"I wasn't worried about that. I know you'll take care of me."

Sandy enjoyed taking care of her. He enjoyed it differently than when he struck her. It was new to him. Caring about someone else was a foreign experience, an awakening of sorts. Sandy picked up the mail that had been dropped through the slot. There was a thick manila envelope that he held up.

"That's the manuscript of a book I'm doing the cover art for," she smiled and bumped him with her shoulder. "It's erotic."

"Really?" Sandy's brows raised.

He drew her a bath. Helped her into the tub and got her a drink. He took off his shirt and sat on the toilet seat. He opened the manuscript and began to read to Sam.

After 20 minutes, he stopped. "People really read this stuff?"

"Yes," she laughed. "Thank you for taking your shirt off."

Sandy chuckled. "Sam, you haven't had a lot of luck with your past experiences. I'm not them. I know how to hurt women. I don't know how to be cruel. I'm doing the demonstration as a favor to Paige. Please come."

Sam's heart melted. "I will," she smiled. "Now read."

Thursday, September 1, 1994

His mind was fuzzy, her waking him out of a deep sleep. "Sandy, I need you please."

He picked up his watch. 9:30. "This better be good," he thought.

"Just for a few minutes, then you can go back to bed."

Sandy slipped into his jeans, not bothering with the top button and walked into the kitchen and poured himself a cup of coffee. He stood at the counter sipping his coffee watching her. "What ..... on earth are you doing?" he finally asked.

There was a camera and a variety of different lenses on the dining table. Sam was setting up a tripod. "You look hot," she said and picked up the camera. She shot a rapid-fire series of pictures. "I have an idea for the cover."

"What cover?"

"You know. The book."

"Oh yes. The epic novel," he grinned. "You want to use me on the cover?"

"Us. Just our bodies. I need you over here." She kept moving while she was talking. "Chop chop. I'm not going to have this light for long."

"Chop, chop?" Sandy laughed as he took his place.

"Okay, lose the jeans."

"No, no, no. You're not taking pictures of my dick."

"Calm down. I'm going to be in front of you."

Sandy was impressed with her direction and confidence. She quickly went from one pose to another. Sandy's hands and arms covering her pink parts. She really did know what she was doing. His cock was getting hard. He couldn't hang on much longer, and she knew it.

"We're done," Sandy said, picking her up and carrying her into the bedroom.

He was still inside of her, propped up on his elbows, brushing her hair off her face. "I have a surprise for you."

"Really?"

Sandy shook his head, smiling. "I'm taking off tonight. We can go to dinner, a movie or bowling. Whatever you want to do."

"How are you going to pull this off?"

"Ed's working for me. Chris is going to close."

"Ed?"

"Ed O'Cleary. He worked for you those couple of weeks you were out," Sandy said as he rolled off Sam and got up.

"Was he the one that was in the motorcycle accident?" She followed him into the bathroom.

"It's taken him a year and a half and two surgeries to get back on his feet. He was managing Blush when he had the accident." Sandy turned on the shower. "Our test results are in today. Let's get that out of the way. I'll get my liquor deliveries, and the rest of the day is ours."

"Cool."

Friday, September 2, 1994

"Next time someone asks if you can bowl, the answer is no," Sandy said, sitting up in bed.

"Haha. I wasn't that bad."

"Sweetheart, you do many things well. You can take the hit on bowling," Sandy joked. "You look nice."

Sam was dressed ready to go to Lambert's. "Thank you. I had fun last night."

"Me too," Sandy stretched. "Your mattress is so comfortable. I could lay here all day."

"Stay, just lock the door when you leave," she smiled.

What are your plans tonight?"

"I have to work on that cover. I'm having lunch with Felice. She got back yesterday."

"Behave," Sandy said, repositioning the pillows.

"I'll give it my best shot," Sam replied and gave Sandy a quick kiss goodbye.

"You know how I felt when Daniel picked Israel for a honeymoon. I was wrong. It was a fabulous trip."

Felice talked through the entire lunch. Sam let her go on. After all, most of the time, the conversation centered around her. She owed Felice a few.

"What's going on with you? Any more Joe sightings?" Felice laughed.

"I've been seeing Sandy."

"What!" Felice was genuinely shocked. "You do like drama."

"Felice, Sandy's a great guy."

"Oh, I agree wholeheartedly. I like Sandy. I'm just thinking of Joe. That couldn't have gone well."

"He doesn't know. And what if he does?"

Felice let it go. Conversations about Joe haven't gone well since they broke up.

Monday, September 5, 1994, Labor Day

"Let me see what you're wearing tonight. Put it on."

Sam returned wearing the skimpiest of teddies. It was purple lace with a plunging neck and a g-string back.

Sandy smiled, "turn around." She did. "It looks good."

"It feels like I'm wearing dental floss," Sam replied. "I might as well be naked."

"If that were an option, you would be."

He slapped his thigh, which signaled her to lay over his lap. Sandy wanted full access to her body, and so with the aid of a phallic shaped toy he opened her a little more each time they were together. With saliva as a makeshift lube, Sandy worked the toy in and out of her, going deeper with each stroke. With his other hand, he brushed her hair off her face.

"You're my good little girl," he repeated over and over until he was finished with her.

The early afternoon they were across the river at his parents for a cookout. Sandy's aunt, his mother's sister, and her family were in from California. Sam felt as if it were a rarity for Sandy to bring a girl to his parents. They fawned over her. Sandy's mother and aunt both had green eyes. Beautiful, but not as intense as Sandy's and his brothers turquoise. Sam spent time with his father Ian, talking about her uncle. Sandy's father was quite fond of him and vice versa. Sam overheard Sandy's mother asking if he had seen his brother. The look on her face was heart-wrenching. Drugs don't just affect the addict. Sam would have been content to stay there, but at 6:00 sharp, Sandy said their goodbyes.

There was a man sitting behind the rosewood desk when they walked in.

"You're cutting it close Sandy," he said, eyeing Sam the way men did at Azure. "I need your submissive's I.D."

"Ramona already got her information."

"Ramona's not here. She's in there," he pointed, "waiting for you. May I see your submissive's I.D., please?"

"Give him your I.D. Sam," Sandy ordered with a forced smile.

He looked at it and looked up at Sam, handing it back. "Thank you, Sam." He didn't release his hold on it when she took it back. She had to give a little tug. He grinned, never taking his eyes off hers.

Sam noted that no money changed hands as it did the last time they were there. There were a few people leaving the changing room as they walked in. "I feel violated," Sam said.

"Oh, Nolan would love to violate you," Sandy laughed. He put the training collar on Sam, this time with a leash.

"Do I have to—"

"Yes," Sandy replied, anticipating her question. "Now you behave and do whatever Paige tells you. Okay?"

As he led her into the double parlor, she felt as if she were on display. The large round platform was gone. The back half of the room had folding chairs lined up, most of which were already occupied. Some people were milling around, looking at the different equipment. There were a lot of unfamiliar faces. Probably out of towners. Ramona was talking to Paige. Ramona had a black leather bikini on her pear-shaped body. She didn't seem to be phased by the stretch marks on her hips. Sam marveled at her confidence. Ramona seemed genuinely pleased to see Sam again. Sandy handed over the leash to Paige and took Ramona by the hand, holding it high and led her to the center of the room. He attached her arms above her head to the hanging chain by her wrist bracelets. Paige sat in the front row of folding chairs. She motioned to the floor. Sam obediently sat in the position Sandy had taught her.

Sandy started talking as he circled Ramona holding what looked to Sam to be the type of whip a lion tamer would carry. There was a man towards the back of the room, sharing his thoughts on Sandy's narrative. It was distracting. Sandy let the whip uncoil, reared back, and let the whip fly. There can't possibly be another sound that will get your attention quicker.

"As I was saying," Sandy calmly picked up where he left off. The man stopped talking.

He was incredible. He talked continuously for 40 minutes about safety, techniques, and positions, for both subs and doms. Constantly circling Ramona, he displayed the effects of each whip on her body as she squirmed and moaned. Sam could feel herself getting wet, wishing it were her up there. Sam looked over toward the large archway that lead from the foyer to the parlor. Nolan was standing there looking back at her. Sandy closed out with the bullwhip. With each strike, the whip wrapped around Ramona's body. Sam thought it a sensual image.

"How was my little girl?" Sandy asked Paige as he took her leash.

"She was perfect," Paige replied with a big grin. "I've never pictured you as a Daddy."

"I'm not," Sandy rebuffed.

"You are with her."

For the next hour, Sandy fielded questions from Dominates and Dominatrix, holding tight to Sam's leash.

It was almost 10:00 when they got to Sam's apartment. Along with his gym bag, he carried a long narrow box that Paige gave him.

"Get undressed," Sandy said as he turned down the bed.

She was completely naked and waiting for direction.

"On your back," Sandy ordered. He took her left ankle and bent her leg lying flat on the mattress. He rubbed her inner thigh. "Good girl. Now don't move." Sandy laid the long box next to Sam on the bed and opened it. "I worked a little trade out with Paige. We have a nice start to your toy box," Sandy grinned as he took out a leather riding crop. "This is nice," he said, inspecting it. He tapped on her inner thigh lightly with the tip. "Very nice." It took only one quick flick of his wrist to land the blow and then searing pain. For a brief period, she couldn't breathe or speak. She clutched the sheets.

"That's what Ramona felt. That's why I couldn't use you. You're not ready for a scene that intense. It's something we will work up too." Sandy tapped on her nipples with the end of the crop. "There are many sensations to get from each instrument. Do you like that?" Sam shook her head. His next strike made her wince. The box also held a rattan cane with a leather grip and wrist cuffs that buckle closed with a D-ring sewn into the leather. They were fleece lined.

"Roll over onto your stomach," Sandy said as he moved the box to the floor. He hiked her hips up, so she was in a kneeling position with her head and shoulders on the bed. With the crop, he gave a few quick taps on her ass, followed by two fast and sharp strikes. The crop marked her instantly. Sandy climbed in bed behind her, ordering her to place her hands on her ass and offer herself to him. He entered her slowly, allowing her time to adjust to this new sensation. Something she had once thought of as a humiliating intrusion, she was now pleased to make available to her dominant.

Drag Race

Thursday, September 8, 1994

"Well, forget the baby back ribs," Sam said as she hung up the phone.

"They're not coming Monday?" Sandy asked.

"They're coming, but Felice and Daniel are reconnecting with their religion. So no pork."

"Beef short ribs. They're delicious on the grill," Sandy smiled. "I'll pick them up tomorrow."

"Great idea." Sam hiked herself up to the balls of her feet and kissed Sandy. "Thank you."

"Okay, I have to get going. Dinner was great." He cupped the side of her face with his hand. "I'll see you Saturday."

Friday, September 9, 1994

The humidity of the day followed through to the evening. She had laid out cargo pants and a long-sleeved cotton shirt to change into. She put them away and opted for khaki cargo shorts and a sheer white tank top. You could see the faint shadow of the lace on her bra through the shirt. She stopped in the kitchen to grab a cold drink before going up to her studio. There was a package wrapped in butcher paper on the top shelf. It was the short ribs. She called Sandy.

"Did you look at them? They're nice," Sandy said.

"Thank you, yes. How did you get in?"

"Child's play," Sandy laughed.

"You picked my lock?" her voice pitching up.

"Honey, calm down."

"Calm down. My locks are child's play. That gives me a real sense of security."

"Sam, I'm sorry. I didn't think—"

"Correct, you didn't think," she cut him off.

"I'm sorry. I never meant to upset you."

She was quiet for a few seconds. "I gotta go," she said in a measured voice.

"You okay?"

"I'm fine. See you tomorrow." She hung up.

With a camera around her neck and her lens case over her shoulder, she walked up Chartres making a right onto Dumaine. On the corner of Royal, she waited as three cars passed. The last being a black Mercedes. It was Joe.

"Where are you off to?" Joe smiled.

"Drag races at Lafitte's. Alfonso's in the race."

"Alfonso?"

"My hairdresser, Alfonso."

A car pulled up behind Joe. "You need a lift?"

"One block?" Sam laughed.

The car behind him honked. "See you later." Joe pulled off.

The bar was busy, and it took Sam a few minutes to find Alfonso. He was a pretty drag queen.

"How do I look?"

"I'm jealous," Sam joked. "I'll be right back. I wanna run upstairs and see what kind of pictures I can get from up there."

"No, have a drink first," Alfonso insisted. "Just a quick shot." Alfonso grabbed her arm and pulled her to the bar. "We need, one, two, three," he was pointing his finger at people while counting. "seven shots of Jager."

Sam drank her shot. "Okay, I'm going." She turned to go and was facing Joe. "What are you doing here, Joe?"

"What? I stop here all the time for a drink," he smiled.

"Asshole," she laughed.

He followed her upstairs. She was standing at the balcony rail looking down through her camera.

"All you're going to get up here are tops of heads."

"Yeah, this isn't going to work."

"You mean yes," Joe smirked.

"Don't start, Joe. What are you hoping to accomplish here?"

"Just wanted to have a drink with you for old times sake."

"Because the old times were so great?"

"There were great times, Sam. As horrific as it ended, there were some pretty great times."

The crowd around them seemed to disappear. There was a moment. "There you are. Come on. The race starts in a few," Alfonso said.

The few minutes turned out to be closer to 30. Rounding up drag queens is similar to herding cats. The mood had lightened between Sam and Joe. Another shot of Jager helped that along.

The girls were in their positions a block away, and the finish line was Lafitte's. Sam and Joe jockeyed for a good spot. "This is useless. How am I gonna get a decent shot?" Sam was getting frustrated.

"Get on my shoulders," Joe said.

"You're crazy," Sam laughed.

"Okay, grow a foot taller," Joe grinned. "If you want a good shot, those are your options."

Joe stooped down, and Sam climbed onto his shoulders. She got some great pictures, and her friend came in second in a seven drag queen field. They went back into the bar to celebrate. Joe bought a round of Jager.

"You want another drink or a beer?" Joe asked.

Sam put her hands around his arm and forehead on his shoulder then looked up. "I haven't eaten."

"Jesus Sam. Guys we're going to get going," he said to Alfonso and his friends.

A few hugs and kisses later, they walked across Bourbon to the Clover Grill. They sat at the counter.

"She'll have a cheeseburger," Joe said.

"Dressed," Sam chimed in.

"French fries." He turned to Sam, "you want a soft drink?" She bobbed her head up and down. "And a coke."

"And what are you gonna have gorgeous?" the waiter asked with a huge grin.

"Coffee please."

Sam gobbled down the burger.

"Slow down," Joe laughed. Every woman Joe had ever dated tried to be so dainty and picked at their food. He loved that Sam didn't put on pretenses. "You know you can see through that top."

"Are you going to rip it off of me?" she sarcastically asked between bites. Joe didn't reply.

He walked her home, and while she was putting the key in the door, Joe kissed her on the shoulder near her neck. "Joe, I'm seeing someone."

"So am I," he replied and continued up her neck. He pushed the door open and them into the hallway. He turned her around and wrapped his arm around her waist and the other hand in her hair. He nipped at her lip then kissed her deeply. He drew back and pulled her head to his chest. "I didn't think you would ever be in my arms again."

The floor of the apartment from the entrance to the bedroom was blanketed with their clothes. Joe entered her immediately. No foreplay. He had to be in her. She was ready for him. So wet. After a few minutes, he made his way down her body kissing and licking. He nipped at her stomach.

"No marks," Sam whispered.

"Why?" Joe looked up.

"I told you, I'm seeing someone."

"I'll get rid of mine, you get rid of yours," Joe joked and nipped at her stomach again.

"Joe, I'm serious. Don't!"

"What is this, Sam?"

"A better ending. Please, Joe. Don't complicate this."

He continued down and spread her legs wide.

"I see you got more than one haircut," Joe said, rubbing his hand back and forth on her mons.

Sam giggled.

"And what's this? he asks, rubbing just his thumb over the bruise on her inner thigh.

"It's from a riding crop."

"You've come a long way, baby."

"If you're done with the inspection, would you fuck me please."

"Oh, I fully intend to, but first things first," then his tongue started between her folds.

They laid there quietly for a long time afterward, her head resting on his chest while he played with her hair.

"You have to go," Sam said, twirling his chest hairs around her finger.

"You're throwing me out?"

"Once again, I'm seeing someone."

"And he's going to show up in the middle of the night?"

"Possibly. Now don't be a jerk off."

"You're still a romantic," they both laughed. "Have dinner with me?"

"No."

"Lunch?"

"NO! Can't you just accept what this is."

"I guess I don't have a choice," his voice couldn't disguise his disappointment.

"Thank you," she kissed him. "It was wonderful."

Joe's mind was at a gallop on his drive home. His routine was as usual when he walked into his house. He poured himself a glass of water and listened to his messages. It hit him. He called Sam.

"Hello."

"Is it Gillespie?" he asked. She didn't answer. "Sam, is it Sandy?

A barely audible, yes, came through the phone, followed by silence. She finally spoke. "I'm sorry," then hung up.

Saturday, September 10, 1994

Sam was distracted at Lambert's. The sales she made were dumb luck. She put no effort into them. Ruth made note that she was off as she put it. Sam attributing it to a headache she couldn't shake. Her manager took pity on her and let her go home at 2:30. Business was slow. This gave Sam time to take a nap.

The angst grew as she walked up Bourbon to Christos. She walked into the door across from Sandy's end. There were two couples sitting at the bar. Joe and Chris were at the opposite end. Her heart was pounding.

Sandy handed her the bank bag. "I'm gonna get a piece of pizza when you get settled."

"Okay."

"Sam, he's drunk."

She didn't reply. She counted her bank and let Sandy know she was good to go. After he left the bar, Sam checked on the two couples.

"Sam." she tried to ignore him. "Sam, come here please," Joe said a little louder this time. "I'll have another Chivas and my cousin will have another Tanqueray and tonic."

Chris was waving no behind Joe.

"Joe, maybe you should call it quits for tonight," Sam said as gently as possible.

"See Cuz, this is a prime example of familiarity breeding contempt," Joe said to Chris.

"Come on Joe, let's go. I'll give you a ride," Chris said.

"In a minute, Chris," Joe snapped. "So Sam, let me ask you, did you tell your boyfriend I fucked you last night?"

"Fucking asshole," Sam said as she walked away.

"I'm a fucking asshole? Said the fucking whore," Joe shouted.

"Said the son of a whoremonger," Sam shouted back.

Chris got Joe out of the bar. Sandy walked in a few minutes later and was updated by all three waitresses. It was the longest night Sam and Sandy had worked. Her anxiety built towards the end of the night. She rushed to get out of there. She handed Sandy his half of the tips.

"I'm giving you a lift," Sandy insisted.

Crickets, until they got into her apartment.

"Clothes off," Sandy ordered. "Stay there; don't move."

"Sandy, I'm—"

"Shut up," he said as he rifled through her cosmetic case. "Hands behind your back."

He opened the lipstick and wrote across her chest.

SLUT

"Don't move," Sandy said then went upstairs, reappearing with her camera. He snapped a picture of her, laid the camera on the table, and walked out.

She cried and cried and cried to the point of making herself sick. It was almost 10:00 A.M. before she went to sleep. She got up at 3:30. She didn't run; she didn't eat; she just cried. Sandy was alarmed when Sam walked in.

"Have you eaten?" Sandy asked with concern.

"I'm fine, thank you," she replied.

"I'm ordering you something. What do you want?"

"I don't want you to do that."

"And I don't want you to pass out behind the bar." Sandy picked up the phone.

A few minutes later, Chris walked in. "May I borrow Sam for a minute?" he addressed Sandy.

"Of course, Chris," Sandy replied.

They walked outside through the Conti door towards Royal. "Sam, I would like to apologize for what happened yesterday. I had no idea your relationship with Joe had deteriorated to that point. As you're aware, Joe has no say-so in your employment. I realize he triggered your response. Quite frankly, I've never seen that side of my cousin before. That said, he is one of the owners as well as family, and I cannot allow you or any other employee to speak to him in that tone. Whatever is between the two of you outside of this building is not my concern. I think you're one of the best we've had behind this bar and at one time, we had all hoped you would join the DiLeo family. That said, a repeat of this behavior will leave me no option. I'm confident we can put this behind us. Let's get back in."

By the end of the night, she was physically and mentally done. She almost lost her job. She lost a man she cared about for a man she was trying to get over. This must be what self-destruction looks like. She got in Sandy's truck, hoping to fight back the tears until she got home. To her surprise, Sandy parked.

"You're coming up?" Sam asked.

"I just want to make sure you're okay. I'm not staying," Sandy replied.

He drew a hot tub for her and helped her in. He sat on the toilet seat. "Why Sam?" was all he said, and the waterworks were back on. "Shhh, we can't talk when you're like this."

"I know," she gasped. "I'm sorry, I know I fucked up." She took a minute to gain control. "I got scared when I realized how easily you could get in here. And that night came flooding back. And it never really felt finished with Joe."

"Is it finished now?"

"Yes, it won't ever—" She started to cry again.

"Okay, come on, let's stop it," Sandy said. "Honey, I didn't think, but please know what's child's play for me would be difficult for the average thief. I'm a locksmith. A very good one I might add. I would never intentionally resurrect that memory."

"Are you going to give me another chance?"

"I don't know Sam. I need some time. What time are Felice and Daniel coming over tomorrow?"

"5:00, 5:30," she replied as he helped her out of the tub. "Are you going to come?"

"Yes, I'll be here."

"Will you stay tonight?"

"Baby steps Sam." He put her to bed and left.

Loss

Monday, September 12, 1994

Sam walked back out to the balcony. She started to gather the placemats off the table. He grabbed her wrist. "Sit down for a minute," he said, handing her a glass of wine. "It was a nice night. They are a terrific couple. You're quite the matchmaker."

"That's my only matchmaking endeavor," Sam laughed.

"That means you're batting a thousand," Sandy smiled.

Sam took a deep breath, "I love the smell of jasmine." She took a sip of wine. "Please give me another chance."

"I remember the night you started at Christo's; when you put your sunglasses on after the lights went up. I laughed about it the next day. And when I drove down Esplanade, seeing you carrying that chair on your head. Determined to get the set here one piece at a time." He tapped his hand on the table. "Little tough girl," he laughed. "I started to look forward to the nights we worked together and disappointed when I dropped you off. The reason I didn't come to see you after the break-in...., I wouldn't have been able to stop myself from taking you in my arms and holding you tight. You see Sam, I've been with you a lot longer than you've been with me. No more Joe."

"No more Joe,' she replied. Sandy squeezed her hand.

Tuesday, September 20, 1994

"You wanna check on a table or is the bar okay?" Sam asked.

"The bar is fine," Felice replied.

"What time does Daniel's flight get in?"

"9:30, we have time." The bartender got their order before Felice continued. "Daniel and I are going to start house hunting after the holidays."

"Really! That's fantastic. Any idea of the area you want to look?"

"Irish Channel. Where else would you expect the Sullivan's to live?" Felice chuckled.

"I'm so happy for you. I can't believe you want to leave the quarter. Shit," Sam said, looking into the back bar mirror.

"What?" Felice looked straight ahead and saw what Sam did. "I thought you two were good now?"

"Not exactly. I'll tell you later," Sam said as Joe approached the bar.

"Hello Felice," Joe said as he walked by, ignoring Sam. He was with an attractive brunette, dressed more for a late-night club than dinner in an upscale restaurant. There were two barstools between him and Sam. The two of them took turns glaring at each other through the back bar mirror. Joe was halfway through his drink when the hostess came and took them to their table.

"What was that?" Felice asked in a whisper.

"I'll explain when we get out of here."

Sam gave Felice a brief synopsis on their walk home.

"So, Sandy knows?"

"Yes."

"And he forgave you?"

"Yes."

"Don't you find this a bit ironic. Sandy can forgive you, but you couldn't forgive Joe when the shoe was on the other foot."

"It's not that easy, but no, I don't find it ironic," Sam's tone told Felice it was the end of the conversation. "I'm sorry I ruined your dinner."

"Are you kidding me. Your life amazes me. I love watching you squirm out of these messes you get yourself into."

"Thanks, I'm happy you find my problems so amusing."

"When did you become thin-skinned?" Felice laughed. "Don't be mad."

"I'm not. Love you. Love to Daniel."

Joe's date ended as they all do. A substitute, lying in his bed, thinking of Sam as he entered her.

Saturday, October 1, 1994

Mike, the Vieux Carré cop and Sandy, were in the small storage room behind the bar. Sam was making her way up and down the bar and servicing the waitress's drinks. Sandy reappeared, but his mind didn't.

"Are you alright?" Sam asked after a few minutes.

"Fucking Ryan is back in jail." On the way home, he filled her in. "Ryan got caught breaking into cars. They have him in the parish jail." He dropped Sam off. She wanted him to come up but didn't push.

Sunday, October 2, 1994

"Did you go see Ryan today?" Sam asked shortly after she got behind the bar.

"Yes," Sandy replied, then moved closer, "I want to have a scene tonight after work."

There was no need to reply. It wasn't a request, it was a statement of fact. Towards the end of the night, she was getting a combination of nervous and excited. Sandy said little on the way to Sam's.

"Where's the rope?" was the first thing out of Sandy's mouth when they walked into Sam's apartment.

"Rope?"

"You said you had rope. When we moved the patio table."

"Oh yeah. In the closet upstairs."

"Go take your shower," he ordered.

When she came out, Sandy was barefooted in jeans, no shirt. She felt herself getting wet just looking at him. The dining table and chairs were pushed forward. Her cuffs, a ball gag, a cane and the antique carpet beater were sitting on the table; rope dangled down from the loft's wrought iron railing on either side of the kitchen archway. Sandy deftly fastened her cuffs to her wrist, centering her facing the kitchen. He took her left arm and fastened the rope to the D-ring on the cuff. It pulled her arm up and towards the left. He repeated on the right side. His hand grazed the inside of her right arm coming down to her breast. He pulled at her nipple, then bent down and bit it.

"We are going to try something new. I'm going to start off soft and slow. I want you to take as much as you can but not more than you can handle. Do you understand?"

"Yes."

"If you need to stop, you say red. Not please, not stop or no. I will only stop if I hear the word red. Do you understand?"

"Yes."

"Move your two fingers like you're making air quotes." She did. "If you get too loud, I'll gag you. The air quote motion will be the signal for red. Do you understand?"

"Yes."

He started slowly, tap, tap, tap, and a slap with the carpet beater. He stayed in motion going from right to left and back again. After he warmed up and her ass was getting pink, he switched to the cane. His arm was tiring as her ass reddened. She was doing good. She was taking more than he thought she could handle. His cock was straining against the zipper of his jeans. Soon he would part those red cheeks and enter her. Just a few more hard whacks. She giggled.

"Sam, are you alright?" She didn't answer. He walked around and lifted her head. "Are you okay?" She smiled. "Alright little girl, we'll let you have some fun now that you fucked up my night," he laughed.

Sandy went back to caning her ass as she giggled. After a few minutes, he untied her and carried her to bed. It was almost a half-hour before she was coherent. She was laying on him while he rubbed his hand up and down her back. She looked up.

"Are you back from your little trip?" Sandy chuckled.

"That was incredible. Thank you." She kissed his chest. "Did you have a good time?"

"Let's just say it was cut short." He gave her a slap on the ass. She jumped.

"What happened? Did I do something wrong?"

"No honey. You just went into subspace. A little unexpected, you owe me one," he smiled.

"You didn't have to stop. I would have been fine."

"No, sweetie." He lifted her chin so she would look at him. "When you're in subspace, you can't consent. You were incoherent."

She started to kiss his chest and made her way down kissing his stomach.

"What are you doing little girl?"

"I'm not incoherent now," she snickered just before her mouth latched onto his cock.

Afterward, she thought of the incredible high Sandy called subspace. She wondered if that was the same high Claude was looking for.

Monday, October 10, 1994, Columbus Day

Sandy and Sam headed over to the West Bank for a bbq at his parent's place. "You think I should have made another dessert?" Sam asked.

"The cheesecake is enough," Sandy said parking the truck.

Sam and Sandy walked into the kitchen to drop off the cheesecake. His mother gave Sandy a kiss on the cheek and a hug for Sam.

"Is this the girlfriend they're all talking about?" A voice walking into the kitchen asked. He stuck out his hand. "Hi, I'm Ryan. Sandy's older brother."

Sam and Sandy both stood there at a loss for words. Ryan didn't remember Sam from the bar. He looked better than their first meeting. In fact, much better. He was a long way from being the man his brother was physically but not too many women would throw him out of bed. It was those eyes. Those blue-green eyes that he shared with his brother. Sandy hustled Ryan out of the kitchen while their mother occupied Sam with small talk.

Sandy filled Sam in on the way home. "The guy dropped the charges. Tourist didn't want to fuck with coming back for a trial."

"He looked good," Sam trying to put a positive spin on it.

"He got out two days ago. Give it a week and then tell me how he looks." He closed his eyes and took a deep breath. "Sam, he's my brother, and I love him, but it never ends well with him."

Thursday, October 20, 1994

"Sandy, can you get the phone, please?"

"It's Jamie Taylor," Sandy said.

Sam shrugged her shoulders. Her hands were in a large bowl of ground meat, eggs, and bread crumbs. "Tell him I'll call him back. Can you get a number?"

"It's a her," Sandy replied.

Then it hit Sam. "One minute." Sam washed her hands and took the call. "This is Sam."

"Sam, Doctor Taylor. I'm sorry for the confusion. I don't say doctor if I'm not sure who I'm speaking to. Saves undue concern."

"Oh sure. It's fine. It just took a second to click." Sandy stood there, listening to the conversation.

"Would it be possible for you to come into the office today or tomorrow? I'd like to run another test."

"Is there a problem with my blood work?"

"I would just like to double-check something."

"Late afternoon okay," Sam asked.

"3:00?"

"That's good."

Sam hung up and went back to her meatloaf.

"Something wrong?" Sandy asked.

"My doctor just wants to double-check something."

"Bloodwork?"

Both their minds went back to her night with Joe. Did he use a condom? Sandy wondered. Sam didn't have to wonder. Joe didn't use one. This was a day and age a doctor questioning blood work put fear in the hearts of the bravest of souls.

Sandy made a call, "Chris, I need a favor. Would it be possible for you to get the liquor deliveries today?"......... "Thank you.".…..... "No, everything's fine. See you later." He hung up the phone. "Call your doctor. See if you can get an earlier appointment."

At 1:15, they were sitting in the doctor's private office. "When did you get your last period?" the doctor asked, looking down, going through Sam's file.

"I'm not quite sure. My periods aren't always regular."

"Not unheard of with women that exercise as much as you do."

"Does that concern you?" Sam asked.

"No. What does concern me is the pain you're having during intercourse," the doctor replied. Sandy tried hard to control his surprise. How could Sam not discuss this with him? "I'd like to do a pelvic ultrasound. That should give us a better idea of what's going on. We can do it right here."

In less than an hour, they were sitting back in the doctor's office. "Sam, you are pregnant. Unfortunately, with complications. Are you familiar with the term ectopic pregnancy? Tubular pregnancy is another term used."

"Yes," Sam replied softly. Sandy squeezed her hand.

"Then you understand the fetus can not survive, and quite frankly to let the pregnancy go on much further could be life-threatening. You are already six weeks. I'd like you to check into Baptist now, and we can do the procedure in the morning."

After the surgery, Sam had a frank discussion with her doctor about her lifestyle choices. Both she and Sandy felt responsible for their loss. Doctor Taylor assured Sam that it was unlikely. More likely, it was the IUD. Though they have a very low percentage of pregnancy, there is a higher than average probability it would be an ectopic pregnancy. She also explained that having to take the tube because of the placement of the fetus, her chances of pregnancy were considerably lowered, and the chance for another ectopic pregnancy increased.

Sam insisted Sandy not take off work when she got home from the hospital. He asked Felice and Lena, Chris's wife to check in on her. Lena and Sam had become quite friendly and unbeknownst to Joe, carried the friendship on after their breakup.

Friday, November 4, 1994

"I gotta use the men's room," Chris said.

"I'll be outside," Joe replied. He stood on the corner as a motorcycle crossed over Chartres on Iberville.

The motorcycle pulled over, and the driver removed his sunglasses. "Where y'at?"

"Jesus Christ, Ed O'Cleary. I never thought I'd see you back on a bike," Joe grinned.

"Gotta face your fears, man," Ed laughed.

"How you been. I heard you're still filling in for us."

"Yeah, Chris And Dominic have been giving me some shifts. In fact, I got a check over at Christos from when I filled in for Sam. If you're heading over there, I'll swing by and pick it up."

"If the check is still sitting there, it's void. They're only payable for six months. Give me a few days. I'll have the bookkeeper reissue it."

"You're on the wrong page, Joe. I'm talking about a couple of weeks ago. When she had the miscarriage. Hey Chris," Ed acknowledged him as he stepped out of Mena's. "I was just asking Joe if I could swing by this morning to pick up my check."

"Sure, Ed. We're on our way over there," Chris replied. Joe turned his back to Chris once Ed pulled off. He tried to process what he had just heard. "We just felt it better for all involved if you didn't know," Chris said. Joe turned to face Chris as he continued. He explained what had happened to Sam.

"We as in you and Dominic?" Joe asked.

"Yes."

"So, the two of you figured it would be better for me to find out on a street corner from a bartender that I might have lost a child?"

Chris stood there, speechless. Joe turned and walked away.

The first one through the doors of Lambert's, when they opened, was Joe. Sam was straightening out sweaters on a display table.

"Hi," he said softly.

Sam gave a faint smile. Her heart was sinking.

"Do you think we could go somewhere and talk?"

"I don't think so," Sam replied.

"Have it your way. Was it my baby?"

"Please Joe," Sam pleaded, looking around to see if anyone was in earshot. "Give me a minute." She walked in the back. "I have ten minutes," she said when she reappeared.

She explained in detail, squelching any need for questions, as they walked around the block.

"Was it mine?" Joe asked.

"There really was no way of knowing that, Joe."

"Could it have been mine."

"Yes. I'm sorry." Sam took his hand and squeezed it as they continued to walk around the block.

They were approaching Canal when Joe stopped and hugged her, pressing her head to his chest. "How did we get here, Sam?" He kissed the top of her head and let go. She walked off back to the store. "Sam." She stopped and looked back. "Do you love Sandy?" She smiled and kept walking.

The first thing she did when she walked back into the store was to call Sandy. "Have I ever told you that I love you?"

"No, you haven't," Sandy replied, smiling to himself.
"Well, I do. Gotta go. See you tomorrow."
"Love you too, sweetheart," he laughed.

Holiday Drama

New Orleans is a town steeped in tradition. In many cases, jobs or trades have been passed down from generation to generation. From restaurant owners and staff to the locally made lanterns that grace the entryways of historic buildings. New Orleanians pride themselves in the traditions of their ancestors.

Tom LaLicata inherited his trade. Tom was the youngest of Angelo's seven children, six girls, and baby Tommy. Angelo took Tom under his wing at a young age. Angelo figured being so outnumbered by women in the house would hamper his son's growth as a man. Tom idealized his father and was eager to follow in his footsteps.

Angelo was the muscle for Tony Frazzano back in the day. He also took care of anything that needed a more permanent resolution. He was faithful to Tony and after Tony's illness, equally as loyal to Frank. There were a few in Tony's organization that tried to sway Angelo into a takeover once Tony was out of the picture. They considered Frank too young, but Angelo saw the same thing that Tony did in Frank. Many felt Angelo passed up the opportunity to force Frank out because he lacked the ambition to lead the family, though none said it to his face.

Tom, Angelo's son, was as ruthless as his father in administering his assignments. He was as faithful to the DiLeo family as was his father. The only difference between father and son was Tom was ambitious. Joe DiLeo saw that in Tom even as kids. When Frank and his son Dominic went to jail for racketeering, Joe seized the opportunity to move the family in a different direction. One that didn't include jail time or a loss of his law license. He handed over all the dock and drug business to Tom for a token of future revenue.

Tom didn't want the whore houses, having moral issues with that. He had no problem putting a bullet in someone's head, but running whores was out of the question. Must have been all that estrogen surrounding him when he grew up. Tom was smart. Joe always thought he was a wasted talent. Tom could have chosen many different directions for his life, but he loved the streets. He was filtered as much as any man could be from most of his crew. He trusted few. Anyone perceived to be a threat was taken care of swiftly. And so the DiLeo crime family was no more. The LaLicata's now reigned the streets.

Thursday, November 24, 1994, Thanksgiving Day

"What time do we have to be there? Sam asked her head laying on Sandy's chest.

"Well, dinner is at 3:00, so 2:30," he chuckled. Sam slapped his chest. "We'll go about 1:00, 1:30."

Sam and Sandy were the last to arrive at his parents. Italian rum cake in hand.

"Jesus Mom, open a window," Sandy said, walking into the kitchen. "It's gotta be 100 degrees in here."

"Happy Thanksgiving to you," Moira said and gave him a kiss on the cheek. "Sam, thank you, but you didn't have to do that."

"Mom, you can't stop her. She can't walk into a house empty-handed," Sandy said, reaching over the sink to open a window.

"He never could stand a warm house. When he was little, he used to strip down if the house was too hot. He'd run around the house naked holding his little pee-pee. He was so cute. I have pictures."

"Moooom!" Sandy snapped.

"He still does that Moira," Sam joked. Sandy gave her a swat across the ass. They all laughed.

"Sounds like the party is in here," Ryan said as he walked into the kitchen. He kissed Sam on the cheek. "Welcome back, Sam. Glad to see my brother hasn't run you off yet?" Ryan's attempt at humor fell flat. He opened the refrigerator. "You want a beer?" Ryan asked, looking at his brother.

"Sure, why not," Sandy replied.

"So Moira, What can I do to help?" Sam asked.

"Nothing sweetheart. You go in the living room and relax."

"Mom, you have someone here who knows her way around a kitchen."

"Please, I take direction well," Sam said then looked up at Sandy and smiled. Sandy smirked.

Sam stayed in the kitchen while the brothers joined the rest of the guest. After a little chitchat, they made their way outside.

Ryan lit a cigarette then offered Sandy one.

"I don't smoke," Sandy replied.

"Since when?"

"Since I was 23," Sandy said, shaking his head in disbelief. "You look good Ryan. Are you staying clean?"

"I wouldn't look good if I wasn't."

"Always a cocky answer."

"I'm working for Tom LaLicata now."

Sandy chuckled, "you're working for Tom LaLicata? That's a great way to turn your life around."

"Unfortunately I don't have a lot of career opportunities coming my way. Listen, six months will set me up real nice. I'm sitting on a stash house. I live there, so I have no out of pocket. I'm saving every penny so I can get out of this shithole."

"Ryan, you get busted, and you'll never get out of jail."

"This will set me straight. I'm willing to roll the dice. LaLicata is a sharp businessman. He knows what he's doing." There was a lull. "I heard a rumor about your girlfriend. Is it true she is Joe DiLeo's ex?" Sandy didn't answer. "Well, I guess you finally evened that score," Ryan snickered.

"You're an asshole, Ryan. Always have been, always will be." Sandy walked back into the house.

"Ryan seems to be doing okay," Sam said on the ride home. Sandy didn't answer. "I had a nice time."

"Good," Sandy smiled and squeezed her knee.

"Did you and Ryan argue?"

"Leave it alone, Sam." A few minutes went by. "Sorry sweetheart. I don't mean to release my frustrations on you. At least we'll be drama free for Christmas."

Sam laughed, "you only met my uncle. Wait."

"For what?" Sandy smiled.

"My mother. You're in for a treat. Let me know it she hits on you," Sandy laughed. "I'm serious," Sam said.

The month flew by. They didn't go back to Paige's dungeon. Sandy had his mate. It was the closest he had ever come to happiness. Sandy had tied Sam to almost every piece of furniture in her apartment and a few in his. She was pliable to all the forms of play he had introduced her to.

Sandy was finishing up the last unit in the house he had bought in the Marigny. He broke it up into apartments and renovated inside and out. He was toying with the idea of selling it. Hoping to open his own bar someday and if he got what he thought he could for the house, Sandy would be that much closer.

Friday, December 23, 1994

Sam's cousin Jimmy picked them up from the airport. They drove the beach route to her uncles so Sandy could see the ocean. She explained points of interest as well as any tour guide. They had planned one day on the beach. Sandy and Jimmy hit it off. Jimmy was the oldest of her two cousins. Single but with a long term girlfriend. Her other cousin, Paul, was married with three boys. They would be staying in the small guest house behind her uncle's house. The swimming pool separated the houses.

"This is nice," Sandy said when they walked in. "You lived here?"

"Yeah, a couple of different times. Felice's parents stay here when they come down."

"I'll let you guys get settled. Come over to the house when you're done," Jimmy said.

Sandy put their suitcase on the bed and opened it. "I can't wait to jump in that pool."

"After we go to the house and say hi to my aunt. Do you want to see my uncles gym?"

"Absolutely. Where's your swimsuit?" Sandy asked rifling through the suitcase.

"I didn't bring one. I have some questionable marks on my thighs," She gave a faint smile.

"Sweetheart, I should have kept our trip in mind. I would never intentionally screw up your vacation. You know that, don't you?"

"A dominant with a conscience, a true paradox," Sam laughed.

"Tread lightly little girl," he grinned. "You could find yourself over my knee."

Sandy had a great time in those few days. They spent an hour with Sam's aunt Rose, who fed them and insisted they use her car. Rose planned on spending the next two days in her kitchen getting ready for Christmas Eve's seven fish feast. Rose was expecting around 30 between family and friends.

"So they gave your aunt the car?"

"I think it's a lease. At any rate, she has it for two years, and if her numbers are the same or more, she gets another new car for two more years."

"And orchid is the only color it comes in?"

"Lilac, it's the company's signature color. Loraine Lilac Cosmetics." Sam started to laugh hysterically. "When Aunt Rose first got the car, my uncle was going to have it painted black. The body shop called with a quote. I thought she was going to kill him."

"She must do well with it if they are giving her a new Cadillac to drive."

"She started selling Loraine Lilac to help out with my cousin's college tuitions. Today she's one of their top salespeople in the country. She's an amazing woman."

They got a warm welcome at the gym. Sam knew a lot of the guys there. Sandy listened intently while her uncle showed Sandy around pointing out pictures and posters of boxers who had trained in his gym. Then Sam took Sandy to the bar she worked at on the Intracoastal.

"How could you ever leave here?" Sandy asked on the ride back to the house. "Everything is so clean and beautiful."

"This isn't utopia. Not all of Fort Lauderdale looks like this. Just like not all of New Orleans looks like the garden district."

"I guess."

"Besides, there's a different kind of beauty on Bourbon Street."

"And smell." Sandy laughed.

The next day Sandy went to the beach with Sam's cousins and Paul's three boys. Sam helped her aunt with the feast. The two women complimented each other in the kitchen. They had everything set and ready to go, giving them enough time to relax and have a drink.

"Honey, your uncle got your favorite scotch for you."

"Then I'll have one."

"I will too."

"Auntie Rose, since when do you drink scotch?"

"Since now." They both laughed. Rose took a sip. "Interesting. Maybe a little ginger ale."

"Aunt Rose, I say this with love. Never and I mean never put ginger ale in scotch." Sam laughed. "How about a little club soda."

"No, I'm going to power through." Rose giggled. "Sandy seems like a good man. You can tell he adores you."

"I have to pinch myself from time to time to make sure I'm not dreaming. He's as beautiful on the inside as he is outside."

"My God, the two of you will have beautiful children." The look on Sam's face changed. "Honey, what's wrong?"

Sam swore her aunt to secrecy and told her about her pregnancy, and the possibility children may not be in her future.

Last Christmas Sam spent $85 on the alligator watch band for Joe, which was an obscene amount of money to spend on a gift for a man she hadn't been dating that long. She had every intention of curving her spending this year. Then Mrs. Cohen walked in with a large box in hand. By the time she got done with Mr. Highsmith, Lambert's store manager, his blood pressure was considerably elevated. Mrs. Cohen's husband passed away 18 months ago. Surprised everyone, he was a strapping man. So as she explained to Mr. Highsmith, her husband never got the opportunity to wear the suit. In fact, it hadn't been altered. The tags were still attached. She understood that the length of time that had lapsed made it impossible to get the full amount back, but she wasn't budging until she got some compensation. After all, her good patronage counted for something. And it did. Mrs. Cohen was one of Lambert's premier customers. Mr. Highsmith and Mrs. Cohen finally settled on a $150.00 store credit. One-tenth of what she paid for the suit. She immediately spent it on Hanukkah gifts. For Mrs. Cohen, it wasn't about the money. It was about her status as a customer.

The Highsmith-Cohen stand-off was the topic of conversation in the employee lounge. "It's a beautiful suit." One of the guys from menswear was telling Sam. "Charcoal gray Zegna."

"They'll just put it on the sales rack in January. They'll probably make money on the deal." Sam chuckled.

"They won't chance upsetting Mrs. Cohen, so I doubt they'll mark it up much. It's a larger size and a European cut. Not an easy sell." The salesman rebutted. "If I were a 44 long, I'd be offering Highsmith the hundred and a half so he can get it off the books."

"44 long?" Sam double-checked what she just heard. "Do you think Mr. Highsmith would go for that?"

"The worst he can do is say no."

Sam got the suit. She also bought a shirt and tie. Sandy walked into Sam's apartment after work to find the dining table stacked with presents. One had Christmas wrap, another in birthday wrap and one had plain red paper for valentines.

"What's all this?" Sandy asked.

"It's your Christmas and birthday present. Oh yeah and Valentine's Day. But you have to open them now." She was like a little kid dancing around excited.

"Christmas is three weeks away." Sandy pointed out laughing.

"I know. Just open them. You'll see."

He opened the Christmas box first. The suit jacket was in that. Sandy was taken aback. "Sam this is too much."

"Don't you like it?"

"Honey I love it," he said taking it out of the box.

"Try it on."

Sandy put it on over his long-sleeved T-shirt. Perfect. Sandy rubbed his right hand up and down on his left arm feeling the material while Sam straightened out the collar. Sandy opened the other two boxes. He was overwhelmed. Sandy had always admired the way the DiLeo's dressed, especially Joe. This is something he never would have done for himself. A couple of days later Sandy brought his suit into Lambert's for alterations. He bought himself a pair of shoes and a belt to finish off the ensemble.

The house was bustling with activity when they walked in. Sam had on an ice blue form-fitting cocktail dress which complimented Sandy's charcoal suit. He could have been the December cover of GQ magazine. It was hard to take your eyes off them. Sam's mother, Connie was already there with her date. She was sultry and could easily pass for her mid 30's. She had dark hair and an olive-toned complexion. Her eyes were deep-set, such a dark brown they almost looked black. She, like all the Mancuso's, was in good shape.

There was a weariness in Sam's introduction. Sandy commented on the stark difference in their looks.

"She must resemble her father." Connie's date remarked.

"I guess so. Woodstock was a bit of a blur." Connie laughed.

"Sempre di classe ma." (always classy ma) Sam said.

"Oh calm down. Everyone knows the story." Connie laughed.

"Yeah, that big question mark hanging over my head is a real fun fact." Sam snapped. "I'm gonna go check on Aunt Rose to see if she needs a hand." Sam could hear her mother as she walked away.

"I guess I hit a nerve," Connie joked.

"She's such a fucking bitch," Sam said as she walked into the kitchen.

"Language young lady," Rose said.

"It's nothing you haven't said about her," Sam replied.

"Why do you let her get to you?"

"She has to prove she's a shitty mother like it's a badge of honor. And that creepy guy she's with. He made my skin crawl when he looked at me. Where the fuck did she find him?"

"La tua bocca." (your mouth)

"Sorry."

Sandy walked in with a drink in hand. "Here," he handed it to Sam. "Are you okay?"

"Yes, thank you," Sam replied then kissed his cheek.

"Sandy you look so handsome," Rose smiled.

"He's hot, isn't he Auntie Rose?" Sam chuckled.

"Stop it," Sandy said.

"He gets embarrassed," Sam laughed.

"Sandy, where in California did your parents go?"

"San Diego, my aunt lives there. My mother's sister."

"Next year you bring them here. We have two empty bedrooms in the house and a guest house."

"I'm sure I won't have to ask twice. They would love it."

The night was going wonderfully. The food was set up buffet style. Sam cleaned the kitchen with the help of Jimmy's girlfriend so her Aunt Rose could enjoy the party. On one of her trips back into the living room to pick up dishes, she noticed her mother standing behind the chair Sandy was sitting in. She was rubbing Sandy's shoulders.

"Togli la mano da lui." (take your hands off him) Sam snapped.

"Sei ridicolo." (you are ridiculous) Connie said calmly as she took her hand off Sandy's shoulders.

"Sono ridicolo? Vaffanculo! (I'm ridiculous? Fuck off) Sam's voice pitched higher and louder.

Sandy got up, excused himself and took Sam by the arm walking her outside.

"What was that?" Sandy asked.

"She always has to fuck things up."

"Right now, the only person fucking things up is you. Your aunt and uncle spent a lot of money on this evening, and your aunt has been cooking for days. You just made a good number of their guests uncomfortable. What are you upset about?"

"She had her hands all over you. You don't find something wrong with that?"

"Of course I do, but there was no need for a scene. She was trying to trigger a reaction out of you and it worked. Now you keep whatever issues you have with your mother out of your aunt and uncles house." Sam didn't talk. Sandy cupped her chin and raised her head. "Do you understand?"

"Yes," Sam replied in a small voice.

They walked directly into the kitchen. Her cousin Jimmy was opening and closing cabinets, obviously looking for something.

"What are you looking for?" Sam asked.

"The sugar bowl," Jimmy replied.

"It's already on the table. I'll make the coffee."

"Are you on drugs?" Jimmy asked. "Or have you just lost your god damned mind. Telling your mother to go fuck herself. Thank god my mother didn't hear you. I'd be rushing her to Broward General right now."

"I didn't tell her to go fuck herself." Sam rebutted.

"Sam I heard you." Jimmy snapped back.

"You need to work on your Italian. I said fuck off."

"Well, that's much better. Get your shit together Sam." Jimmy said and walked out of the kitchen.

Sandy just stood there taking it all in. "Are you okay?" Sandy asked

"I'm fine."

"Does your aunt have rice?"

"Rice? Just regular white rice?" Sandy nodded his head and smiled. "It's in the upper cabinet to the right."

He took the jar out of the cabinet. "Any bags?"

"Bags?"

"You know the plastic ones that zip shut."

Sam pulled a quart-size bag out of a drawer and handed it to Sandy. He poured rice into it and put the bag in his jacket pocket. Sam was dying to ask but didn't. An hour later they were opening presents.

"Did you two exchange gifts?" Rose asked Sam.

"Sandy got me the 3.0 photoshop upgrade." Sam excitedly blurred out. The room was filled with blank stares. "It will help me make adjustments on pictures." She got a collective Oh. This was going nowhere, Sam thought.

"Sam got me this suit." Sandy intervened. That got a lot of oohs and aahs. Outside of Sam's little outburst the night would be long remembered by Sam and Sandy.

"Take off all your clothes," Sandy said as soon as they walked into the guesthouse. She did as he said, his tone was one she knew not to question. He walked over to a corner and poured his bag of rice on the terrazzo floor. "Kneel on the rice facing the wall." She did. "Ten minutes," Sandy said and walked into the bedroom to undress.

The pain set in before the first minute had ended. It's funny how a measure of time can feel so different depending on the activity. Sam was trying to count the seconds to take her mind off the pain. It didn't work. Nothing distracted from the pain. This was a punishment she never wanted to repeat. Sandy helped her up and picked out a few grains of rice stuck to her knees. He ordered her to clean the floor which she did. Then came the tenderness. He cradled her in his arms sitting on the sofa. He explained how disappointed he was with her behavior. That hurt in a different way. Sam never wanted to disappoint Sandy.

Christmas was laid back during the day and South Beach that night. The following morning before they left, they had breakfast on the pier and watched the sunrise. A thought fluttered through Sandy's mind of a wedding ceremony on the beach.

Machiavelli

Saturday, December 31, 1994

In spite of the rain, it was as busy as any other New Years Eve. Joe got there a little after 11:00. He was with his latest fling and another couple who seemed to be her friends. Aaron, the doorman, offered a table in the other room near the band. Joe declined it much to his dates chagrin. Civility had finally set into Joe and Sam's relationship. That was a blessing to everyone around.

Ryan showed up with five people close to midnight. He pushed his way to the bar and ordered the drinks for his party from Sam. "Ask my brother if he's buying this round," Ryan joked. Sam looked down the bar at Sandy, and before she could ask, he said no.

Kiss Sandy at midnight and make her way to the ladies room. That was Sam's plan. At the stroke of midnight, Sam was in Sandy's arms, giving him a deep kiss. She dropped down off her toes; Sandy pulled her back with his hand around her neck and his thumb under her chin tilting her head up. Another quick kiss and a nip at her lower lip sent her on her way.

Ryan was enjoying the show; not the one on stage but the one at the bar. While his brother was kissing Sam, Joe who was at the other end of the bar was kissing his date, eyes open, staring down the bar at Sam. "Eat your heart out motherfucker," Ryan said out loud laughing.

"What?" One of his friends ask.

"Nothing, just talking to myself," Ryan replied.

The bar started to clear out within an hour. Joe and his group had left, and Ryan was paying his check. "Thanks for the drink, asshole," Ryan said to Sandy.

"You're welcome," Sandy chuckled.

"You and Sam wanna come over after you close. I'm taking the party to my house."

"You have lost your fucking mind."

"Don't worry, the house is empty," Ryan said under his breath. Sandy just shook his head and walked away. "Bye Sam," Ryan yelled down the bar and waved.

"Happy 1995!" She hollered back and waved.

Sam hadn't been working in her studio for weeks except for an occasional book cover. The most recent update to photoshop that Sandy got her for Christmas put her back on track. She was looking at her art with a different eye, planning a new series of Bourbon Street musicians. She would find a gallery uptown that would carry a few of her pieces. Sandy was making his plans also. He talked to a few different realtors about listing the house. They all thought he should do some landscaping before putting it on the market.

Tuesday, February 14, 1995, Valentine's Day

Sandy took Sam to a beautiful little gulf coast restaurant in Pass Christian, ending with a night in a nearby bed and breakfast. He tied her to the four-poster bed, then teased and taunted her until she could take no more. She begged and pleaded for him. She came seconds after he entered her. He laid curled up with his head on her stomach while she played with his hair. He wanted to tell her how much she meant to him but couldn't find the words. He settled for a simple I love you. She was his life. We replaced I in his vocabulary. How do you explain that, he thought?

Thursday, February 16, 1995

Sandy was signing for a liquor delivery when Dominic walked in. "They're upstairs," Sandy said.

Dominic hung around until the delivery guy left. "Got a minute?" he asked Sandy.

"Sure, what's up?"

"I'm hearing shit about your brother."

"Like?"

"Like Tom LaLicata is looking for him." Sandy didn't respond. Dominic got behind the bar. "You want a drink?" he asked Sandy.

"Am I gonna need one?" Sandy replied.

"I think there's a contract out on your brother," Dominic poured a healthy shot of Jameson's into a short glass and pushed it over towards Sandy.

"Can you talk to LaLicata? Find out what's going on," Sandy asked.

"Sandy, he's not gonna talk to me," Dominic said. "The best I can do is keep an ear open. If you know where to find your brother, get him the fuck out of town." Dominic got out from behind the bar. "Sorry Sandy," he said and went upstairs.

Sandy called his parents. They hadn't heard from Ryan. Sandy tried to keep the conversation casual so as not to alarm them. He thought of talking to Frank DiLeo. Sandy hung around until Dominic came downstairs. He was with his cousins. Sandy called him to the side and asked if he thought his father could intervene.

"Listen, Sandy; I don't want to get my father involved with this. Besides, my dad isn't in the Ryan Gillespie fan club. I know this is the last thing you want to hear but if you want help, my cousin Joe is the only one I know who can get to LaLicata." After a moment, Sandy gave Dominic the go-ahead to call Joe over. Joe agreed to talk to Tom LaLicata with no guarantees.

Saturday, February 18, 1995

Sandy was awakened by the phone. It was Ryan. He was in Kenner at an ex-girlfriends house. An hour later, Sandy was in Kenner. For the first time in Sandy's life, he saw his brother scared. Sandy didn't have to ask to know what happened. Ryan had a party at the house, but this time there was product there. Ryan said he thinks he was mickeyed. When he woke up, everyone was gone, and the house was tossed. $3,300 of his own money and jewelry were gone plus all the coke.

"How much coke?" Sandy asked.

"I don't know. A lot," Ryan replied. "Sandy, I'm fucked. I'm really fucked this time."

"Did you tell anyone else?"

"No"

"Mom, dad?"

"No"

Sandy went into action. He called his cousin in California and got him to agree to let Ryan stay a couple of weeks, and also made him promise to keep this away from either of their parents. He talked Ryan's ex-girlfriend into driving him to Baton Rouge to get a flight to San Diego. He would catch an evening flight to Dallas and a morning flight to San Diego. Sandy didn't want him flying out of New Orleans airport. Once Ryan was out of New Orleans Sandy could breathe. Now he had to wait for Joe. Ryan, being gone was only a temporary fix. They would find him eventually.

"What's going on?" Sam asked.

"What do you mean?" Sandy replied.

"You seem out of sorts."

"I didn't sleep well."

Sam let it go. They were busy that night. Sandy got back into his groove. It was after 1:00 when Joe walked in and headed straight to Sandy. They spoke for a minute; then Joe walked outside.

"Watch the bar. I'll be back in a few," Sandy said to Sam and walked out to join Joe standing in the middle of the street.

So unusual was this that Aaron asked Sam what was going on. "I have no earthly idea," Sam replied.

"He agreed to meet with you on Tuesday," Joe said. "In the interim, you might want to get your brother out of town."

"He's gone. You have any idea of what he's gonna want?"

"No, but I can tell you what I want for my end."

It shouldn't have caught Sandy off guard, but it did. After all, he wasn't Joe's friend. Their relationship had been polite tolerance for years. "Okay Joe, let's hear it."

"I want you gone."

"And what do you think your uncle is going to have to say about that?"

"Oh, I'm not firing you. You're quitting," Joe smirked. "Maybe you could go spend some quality time with that junkfuck brother of yours."

"I knew this was going to turn out to be bullshit."

"Cards on the table; you have no options. There is a contract out on your brother. I don't care where you've got him holed up, eventually, they will find him. Your brother turned Tom LaLicata's stash house into a party house and lost $180,000 in the process. That's not going away. That's the hand you're playing. Now let me show you mine. I gave Tom a business when he was making a living braking body parts. He went from a two-bedroom shotgun in Bywater to a mansion on the lake. You are looking at the only man he owes something to. If you think I'm giving away that goodwill, you are sadly mistaken. I want my pound of flesh. You leave. Take a little vacation, say for a year, and start fresh."

"You want me out of Orleans Parish?"

"I want you out of Louisiana. You, not Sam."

"Now it makes sense. What if she decides to follow me."

"Then our deal is off, and you can start making funeral arrangements for your brother."

Sandy walked back into the bar crestfallen. Few words were spoken between Sam and Sandy the rest of the evening.

"I'm going to my place tonight," Sandy said as they pulled up to Sam's apartment.

"What's going on?" Sam ask."

"Sam, don't."

"Why won't you talk to me?"

"It's Ryan, okay. Now can you stop asking questions? I obviously don't want to discuss it."

"I'm sorry," she whispered.

"Don't be. I'll see you tomorrow night."

Sam gave a slight nod. Sandy kissed her on the cheek and said goodnight, which was her cue to leave.

Tuesday, February 21, 1995

"It's Sandy. Where and when?"

"Where are you?"

"I'm leaving Sam's now."

"Stay there. We're coming to you. Did she leave for work?"

"Yes but I'd rather—"

"Just go with it, Sandy," Joe interrupted. "And we're good on our end, right."

"If my brother walks away from this, you'll get your year."

It was almost two hours before they showed up. This was a more mature Tom LaLicata than the one that Sandy ran the streets with as a kid. More polished. Porcelain crowns replaced the gap between his two front teeth and his wild curly hair now precision cut. Designer threads instead of the polyester jackets Tom once sported. The only thing that didn't change was the yat accent.

"Where y'at Sandy?" (New Orleans greeting) Tom said, extending his hand.

"Thanks for meeting with me, Tom." Sandy replied shaking Tom's hand.

"You want something to drink Tom?" Joe asked, opening the refrigerator.

"I'm good," Tom replied, sitting down at the dining table.

Sandy fought to keep his mouth shut. This prick is just making himself at home, Sandy thought.

They got the small talk out of the way and sat at the dining table.

"Sandy, Joe here has convinced me I might have other options when it comes to getting my property back that could benefit all. I feel a small amount of responsibility for what has happened. You see, I would not have hired your brother. One of my guys did, and when I found out, I was less than pleased with his choice. But somehow I let him persuade me that a leopard did change his spots," Tom chuckled. "Well, here we are. You realize I have to handle these situations with an iron hand or lose credibility. That said, I wouldn't be in my position today without Joe. Consider yourself lucky to have him as a friend."

Whatever bullshit Joe had laid on Tom was working.

"Joe tells me you possess a unique set of skills." Sandy gave him a blank look. "Supposedly there isn't a lock in Orleans Parish you can't get past."

"In most cases," Sandy answered.

"There's a couple of wannabe wise guys who got run out of Chicago that moved in. They got a place on Bourbon Street they're working out of."

"Bourbon Street?" Sandy said in disbelief.

"I thought that too but the more I think about it, it's kind of brilliant. They got my stuff and theirs in the house now. The two of them are working the house and they got a couple of guys working the streets. If my information is correct, this could not only be a nice score, I wanna hit them hard enough to put them out of business."

"So you need me to get in, grab the stuff and get out."

"Pretty much. You'll have two of my guys with you."

"Is that necessary?" Sandy asked.

"Yes, unless you think you can shoot someone if need be," Tom smiled. Tom told Sandy the plan. They would hit them Mardi Gras day. The more Tom talked, the more Sandy could see the noose loosening on Ryan's neck.

"If this works, Ryan walks, right?" Sandy ask.

"Plus he doesn't come back from California," Tom replied.

That sent chills through Sandy. He thought he did a masterful job hiding Ryan. As the meeting wound down, Sandy locked eyes with Tom.

"Joe give us a minute, please. I'll meet you outside." Sandy was relieved that Tom read him. "Is there something else, kid?"

"Yes, you mentioned their stuff."

"Yes."

"I'm guessing you are going to make a nice piece of change on this."

"I am. What are you getting at Sandy?"

"I just think there should be a little lagniappe (something extra) in there for me."

Tom laughed, "I like you kid. Your balls are almost as big as mine. What are you looking for?"

"A percentage of profits."

"How much?"

"40%."

"Don't get greedy kid."

"You tell me."

"10%."

"20%," Sandy smiled.

"You got it. I like you kid, but I got to be honest. There's a bullet out there for your brother. He avoided mine, thanks to you, but he'll find another one."

"I'm not going to watch my parents bury a son."

Sandy distanced himself a little more each day from Sam. He got his affairs in order. He put his place up for sale. The listing would come out the day after Mardi Gras. He would join his brother in California for a little while and figure out his future from there.

Tuesday, February 28, 1995, Mardi Gras day

"Fuuuuck!" Sam shouted, coming in from her run.

"I told you it was going to rain," Sandy laughed.

"I told you it was going to rain," Sam mimicked, pulling her soaked shirt off.

"I'm not working today," Sandy casually mentioned.

"It's Mardi Gras!"

"It's important, or I wouldn't do it."

"Who's working?"

"Ed's going to cover."

"Tell me, Sandy, what's so important that you're taking off the busiest day of the year."

"It's Ryan," they said in unison. "Can you give me a break here?" Sandy said.

"Give me one! You've been acting so strange the last couple of weeks, and you snap at me when I show concern. It's Ryan; it's Ryan, it's Ryan. What the fuck did he do? Is he in jail?"

"I'll explain the whole thing tomorrow," Sandy solemnly said. "For today, can you give it a rest?"

Sam walked into the bedroom. Sandy followed a few minutes later. He slowly and tenderly made love to her for the last time.

The whole job went smoothly. To even Tom's surprise, there was almost three times what he anticipated in coke and cash. After all the expenses were taken out, which included a nice piece of change for Joe, Sandy left town $55,000 richer.

Exhausted and reeking of booze, all Sam wanted was a shower. Walking directly into the bedroom she stripped, then headed to the bathroom. She spotted an envelope laying on the dining room table. Repeatedly she read it as if that would change the message. Trembling she dialed Sandy's number:

THE NUMBER YOU HAVE CALLED HAS BEEN
DISCONNECTED AT THE CUSTOMERS REQUEST.

She slumped to the floor wailing.

Friday, March 3, 1995

Felice had good news, and good news is meant to be shared. Sam was meeting her friend for lunch. Felice was immediately concerned when Sam walked in.

"What's wrong?" Felice asked as Sam sat down.

Sam reached into her purse and took out an envelope, wordlessly handing it to Felice.

"I don't understand," Felice said after reading the letter.

"I don't either," Sam replied, desperately trying to fight back the tears. She explained how out of character he was the last couple of weeks. He kept insisting it was Ryan.

"Maybe he'll come back," Felice tried to calm Sam.

"Felice, he quit his job. His phone is disconnected, and there's a for sale sign in front of his house."

"Have you tried calling his parents?"

"I don't have their home number, so I called the hardware store. His father was nice but said he couldn't help me. I don't understand this." She could no longer hold back the tears. Felice's good news would have to wait. It would be another week before she told Sam they found a home.

Thursday, March 9, 1995

When Joe walked into Christos, Chris was behind the bar, and Dominic was sitting on a stool.

"It's about time you got here," Dominic said.

Joe looked at his watch. "It's 12:10, I said I'd be here by 12:30.

Don't panic Dom; you won't miss a meal."

Chris laughed. "You want anything?"

"Water."

Ed walked in and greeted the cousins. He was given Sandy's job and was there for the liquor deliveries that would be arriving soon. After a little more small talk, the boys were ready to leave when Ed threw a curveball.

"I'm making a few changes on the schedule next week," Ed said. "I'm bringing in a new bartender. I'm going to start her out with one night. Saturday."

"Did Sam give up the shift?" Chris asked.

"No, but she works a day job. Someone who needs the money should have the better nights."

"Sam's the best bartender we have now that Sandy left," Chris pointed out. He saw the slow burn in his cousin's eyes. "Are you having a problem with her?"

"No, I'm just thinking a little fresh blood. You know, new broom."

Stop talking was all Chris was thinking.

"Ed, I think you misunderstood the position," Joe said. "Manager is more of a moniker than a job description. You are a key holder that can hire the people we tell you to hire and fire the people we tell you to fire. My uncle gave Sam Mancuso this job. You know what that makes her?" Ed didn't answer. "Bulletproof," Joe paused. "Ed, were you hired by my uncle?"

"No, I was hired by Dominic," Ed said all the wind having been taken out of his sails.

"Not bulletproof. So have this girl you're fucking or want to fuck, talk to one of my cousins, and if they find her acceptable, we'll give her the next spot that opens at one of our places.

"Oh my god, was that necessary?" Chris asked when they got outside.

"Cocksucker was begging to get back in the door, and now he rules the roost. Fuck him. Find a replacement."

"Joe, he didn't know."

"He's a cocky prick. Replace him."

Wednesday, March 15, 1995

Joe was at the bar closing time. "Sam, do you need a lift home?"

"No thanks, United Cab is still in business."

"Steel trap," Joe laughed. "You never miss a chance to take a jab."

"Stop leading with your chin," Sam scoffed.

"I just thought—"

"You just thought now that Sandy's out of the picture, you'll give it another shot," Sam interrupted. "Find somebody else's life to fuck up Joe."

He stood there chuckling, watching her walk down Bourbon. "I'm not done with yours baby," he said under his breath.

1 Year, 6 Months, 24 Days

Thursday, March 23, 1995

Sam had adjusted her running route to go past Sandy's house in the Marigny. Ian Gillespie was standing in front of the building that morning.

"Ian," Sam shouted, running up to him. "Ian, can I talk to you for a minute, please?

"Sam, I'm just waiting for the realtor."

"Ian, please, can you ask Sandy to call me? Just call me, please."

"Sam, I can't get involved in this. I'm sorry sweetheart. Just move on with your life. He's not coming back."

Sam could hear the pity he felt for her. She went home not finishing her run. She stood under the shower until the water ran cold. In a robe, she went to the balcony and sat there. Her mind floated from one scenario to another, trying to analyze what was happening to her. She only moved to answer the phone. She looked at the clock while picking up the receiver. It was almost three o'clock. She had been sitting outside for hours.

"Hello."

"Sam," she stopped breathing. "Sam, you have to stop this. I don't want you bothering my parents," Sandy said.

She begged, she groveled, she pleaded. She was crying so hard he could barely understand her.

"Sam, listen to me. I can't talk to you while you're like this. Get yourself together, breathe," he waited a minute while she calmed down. "I know I handled this poorly, but the outcome stands. I'm gone and not coming back. If I wanted you with me, I would have told you my plans. Put this behind you. Let it go, Sam. We're done."

There was a moment of silence. "Sam, are you still there?"

"You once told me you didn't know how to be cruel. You were wrong. You do it well." Her voice sounded weak. After another moment of silence, Sandy hung up.

She cried until she threw up. Suicide briefly crossed her mind. Then she cried herself to sleep. When she woke up, it was dark. Brush my teeth. That was the first thing that came to mind. Afterward, she walked into the kitchen. It was four o'clock in the morning. She made coffee. While it was brewing, she sat at the table and thought back to the way this all happened. Sandy's ruthlessness was stunning. What happened with Joe hurt deeply, but she knew what he was capable of. But what happened with Sandy blindsided her. She was finished. Finished mourning the life she had with him.

After work that day she stopped at a hotel bar. One that had a piano player during cocktail hour. She could feel her second drink, not having eaten much in the last couple of days. A salesman from Milwaukee was buying her drinks trying to explain the parts his company built for boat motors. After the third drink, she was in his room. Afterward, she gathered her clothes and dressed in the bathroom.

He knocked on the door. "Sandy, where would you like to go for dinner? I'll bet you know all the good spots," he said through closed doors."

"Sorry I have to go," Sam replied walking out fully dressed. She had moaned Sandy's name at one point, and he assumed that she was reminding him of her name, which he had forgotten. You know what they say about assume.

He went to kiss her and she turned, so it landed on her cheek. "Sandy write down your number. I'm in town a couple of times a year."

She wrote down Sandy's disconnected number. She noticed he was wearing a wedding ring that was not on his hand in the bar.

Monday, April 3, 1995

It was Sam and Felice's 25th birthday. Felice's parents insisted Sam join them with a few other well-wishers for dinner. Sam sat at her dining table, wrapping the gifts she got for Felice. A beautiful designer evening black clutch. Felice was always borrowing one from Sam. Plus a leather-bound book she had made, the title read:

EVERYTHING I KNOW ABOUT COOKING

BY

FELICE SAX SULLIVAN

The book was blank inside. Sam was laughing while she wrapped it. The doorbell rang. Sam looked over the balcony to see a delivery man. It was two dozen spectacular pale salmon-colored roses. For a brief moment, she thought Sandy. Down deep, she knew better. They were from Joe.

Sunday, April 9, 1995

It was the last day of a busy French Quarter Festival. The night flew by. Various musicians that played at the festival popped in, and a few got on stage and joined the band. Joe and Dominic wandered in towards the end of the evening.

"The flowers were beautiful. Thank you, Joe."

"You're welcome, Peanut."

Sam let it go and went on to waiting on customers. Two musicians walked in with horn cases. "I love horns. I find them arousing," Sam said to nobody in particular. Her delivery was seductive.

"Could you be any more obvious?" Joe remarked.

"I always wanted to fuck a horn player. There, was that more obvious?" Sam said leaning across the bar towards Joe.

"Your punishments are stacking up little lady," Joe chuckled.

"Punishments?"

"I'm keeping track of all your faux pas' that I intend to address when we're back together," Joe laughed.

"Being back with you would be punishment enough," she leaned in closer, "and given our history, do you think you should be joking about punishments?"

Joe leaned in towards Sam. "Given your history after me, I think you crave it," he smirked as Sam walked off. "I've got her on the ropes, Cuz," Joe said to Dominic.

"Is that how you saw that going?" Dominic rolled his eyes. "Joe, give it up. It's been a year. The two of you have been broken up longer than you were together."

"There's something about her Dom. Some kind of residual effect I can't shake." Joe slapped his cousin on the back. "Come on, let's go."

Sam gave some thought to what Joe had said to her over the next couple of days. Crave may be a strong word, but she did miss it. Not necessarily all of it but the serene feeling afterward was worth it. And the subspace, that she did crave.

Friday, April 14, 1995

She got out of the taxi and walked around to the back of the house. She knocked on the door. There was no answer. She looked for a buzzer but didn't find one and so tried the doorknob. It was open.

"Hello," Sam called out. No answer. She stepped in a little further. "Hello."

"Sam!" Ramona said as she walked into the foyer. "You're a little early. We open at eight tonight." It was just after seven.

"I'm sorry. I was hoping to speak with Paige," Sam said as they headed into the kitchen.

Ramona went about her job getting the refreshments ready for the night. She was half-dressed. She had on a black leather bustier with jeans and flip flops. "Sit down. I'll see what we can do." Ramona was back in a few minutes. "She's coming down. Is there anything I can get you, Sam?"

"I'm good. Thank you. Is there anything I can help with?"

"No, but sweet of you to ask."

It was 20 minutes before Paige appeared. She sat down next to Sam and took her hands, squeezing them. "What can I do for you, Sam?"

Sam explained the best she could that she was introduced to this lifestyle by one partner and her next partner schooled her in intense play. She wanted to stay involved but didn't know if it was okay or safe for her to be there by herself. Paige took a few minutes to explain the do's and don'ts of a submissive in search of a dominant. Paige encouraged her to enjoy scenes with different people and offered her services. Sam awkwardly explained her preference was men. Paige seemed to get a kick out of that. She offered Sam a collar of protection that evening, which would give her a stress-free night. The dominants wouldn't get too aggressive with that collar on her. Paige explained the upstairs had no limits except for edge play. If a dominant took her to one of the rooms upstairs, he most likely would be expecting sex. Sam felt comfortable enough to stay.

Sam changed into her black bra and panties she wore her first time there. She walked around for the next hour, watching the activity and talking to a few people. Paige checked in on her to make sure she was okay. Two different women had approached her. The first said she was a switch and was just as comfortable top or bottom. The other was a very butch dominatrix. A man asked if she was interested in doing a scene with him, but his timid demeanor didn't inspire much confidence. She turned down all three offers. There was a guy intently watching her. He made her a little uneasy. He didn't approach her, just stared. Soon she saw him over a spanking bench with a guy taking a tawse to his ass. She was sitting in the kitchen/lounge having a soft drink when he asked if he could join her.

"Hi Sam, I'm Nolan."

"I remember you, Nolan, you work here," Sam smiled.

"Used to, now I occasionally fill in," Nolan smiled back. "Is it alright if I join you?"

"Of course," Sam said scooting over on the loveseat to make room.

They talked for a while, and Sam felt at ease with him. Nolan suggested a room upstairs. Sam wasn't ready for that. Although she felt self-conscious about having a scene in front of people, she was more wary of being alone with a dominant she didn't know. They discussed her limits. Before they went back into the playroom, Nolan detoured into the dressing room and took a duffle bag out of his locker. He was very well equipped. It didn't take long before a Saint Andrew's cross became available. As he strapped her in, he repeated the directions he had given her in the lounge. She was sure Nolan could hear her heart pounding. With a flogger in his right hand Nolan ran his left hand down the side of her body, from her upper arm to her breast. He cupped her left breast and squeezed her nipple until he got a moan out of her. "Are you ready?" Nolan whispered in her ear."

"Yes," she replied looking back at him.

"Yes, Sir. Everything you say to me ends in a Sir."

"Yes, Sir."

Nolan stood back and struck. Before long, the rest of the room drifted away. It was just her and Nolan. She couldn't gauge the time she was on the cross. 15, 30, 45 minutes. Afterward, he walked her back into the lounge. They sat on the very same loveseat they were on earlier. Nolan got her a drink and talked to her until he was confident she would be fine. He expressed an interest in having more scenes with her. He never hugged or kissed her. She missed the intimacy she had with Sandy and even Joe after a scene.

Sam was home and in her bed by 11:00. By now, she was aware that kink had no real rule book. It was different things to different people. Tonight reinforced one thing. She wanted an emotional attachment to her dominant. Paige's dungeon had seen the last of her.

Saturday, April 22, 1995

Joe walked into Christos a little after 10:00 with his arm around the waist of a cute blonde. There were two seats at the service end of the bar. Joe opted for one seat at the other end, which meant he would have to stand. That would ensure Sam waiting on him.

"Sam, this is Eve," Joe smirked.

"Hi Eve," Sam replied, putting cocktail napkins in front of them. "What can I get for you?"

"We'll have two Remy's," Joe intervened.

"Of course you will," Sam snickered and walked away.

"This prick is a Jekyll and Hyde," Sam thought. "First he's hitting on me then he's parading girls in front of me." Claude came to mind. Sam remembered the time she tried to tell Claude that Joe was a Jekyll and Hyde but mistakenly said Heckle and Jeckle. She started to laugh. She was still laughing when she put the brandies in front of Joe and his date and continued every time she looked at him. This was not the response Joe was hoping to achieve.

After their second drink, Joe's date clawed at his arm. "Joe I need some air," Eve said with a panicked look.

Joe walked her outside. Aaron kept an eye on them. "Holy shit!" Aaron blurted out. "She just threw up on Joe."

"Nooo!" Sam ran to the end of the bar to look out the window.

Aaron was outside with his second bucket of water, rinsing off Joe, along with his date and the sidewalk. Joe had taken his shirt off and threw it into a garbage container on the street. They had drawn enough attention to be a sideshow for the tourists, several appalled, most amused. He walked back in the bar bare-chested and asked Sam for a T-shirt. She got the largest one they had out of the cabinet and tossed it to him.

"Sam!" Joe yelled. "What the fuck is this?" He was holding up a huge T-shirt.

"You put on a few pounds," she laughed.

"Not funny Sam," he threw the shirt back.

She exchanged it, trying but failing to suppress her laughter. He stormed out T-shirt in hand.

Sunday, May 7, 1995

Sam's friends had come in from Florida for Jazzfest. Sam was able to get them free tickets, and they wanted to take her to brunch to reciprocate. Sam was the first one to arrive at Mr. B's. She sat at the bar, waiting for her friends, harking back to all the happenings since her return to New Orleans. It had been one year and almost seven months since the first time she laid eyes on Joe. So much had changed. After brunch she strolled home down Royal, past the shops, restaurants and street musicians, chronicling that time. Felice was married, she was happy about that. It was the bright spot in her memory.

As she walked, she thought of Claude, as well as Sandy. She thought of the baby she had lost and of course, Joe. Just like the streets she walked through, the same exterior with internal modifications. She looked at her life through a different lens. There was a void, so to speak, in her life now. People stared at her when she passed by only to realize tears were rolling down her face.

Last night of Jazzfest was hopping. Debbie was working service. She ended up with Sandy's old schedule. Sam was happy about that. They worked well together. Aaron was now the key holder. He was grateful for the opportunity and didn't let it go to his head as Ed did.

Chris and Joe were at the end of the bar holding up the cigarette machine when the lights went up. "Joe, you or Chris want anything else?" Sam asked.

"No baby, we're good." Joe replied.

She poured herself a Chivas and proceeded to clean off the bar, "Joe, do me a favor, hand me the dirty glasses off the cigarette machine."

Joe placed the glasses at the end of the bar. Sam put her drink down then grabbed the dirty glasses and washed them. While Debbie was counting the tips, Sam went down to the end of the bar to retrieve her drink.

"Where's my drink?" Sam said out loud to herself. Then she noticed it. "Joe, you're drinking my drink."

"No, I'm not," Joe replied.

"Your's is on the cigarette machine," Sam chuckled and rolled her eyes.

"I guess old habits die hard," Joe laughed and handed her back her drink.

She walked down the bar, drink in hand laughing. She got her tips from Debbie, went into the back room, and grabbed her bag. When she came back out to the bar, she was surprised to see Joe had left.

Chris was standing at the door, keys in hand. Aaron had just checked the restrooms to make sure no drunks were left behind. As they filed out of the bar, Sam spotted Joe standing in the middle of Bourbon, giving directions to a couple of tourists.

Sam strolled up to Joe when the couple walked away. "Did I forget something?" Joe asked.

She splayed her right hand in the middle of his chest and leaned in, "yeah me."

"You mean yes," Joe corrected.

"Yes," Sam smiled.

Joe brushed her cheek with the back of his index finger, then tilted her chin up and asked, "what are you up to little girl?"

"Take me home," she was almost demure in her response.

Joe paused, weighing her request. "You know I'm gonna hurt you," he warned.

Barely audible, Sam replied, "I know."

About The Author

I've always wanted to write a book. I made half-hearted attempts in my 20's. Years pass and priorities get in the way of dreams. Then Stephen King wrote a book; On Writing: A Memoir Of The Craft. I gobbled it up. This book reignited my desire to write. That was in the year 2000. I would periodically write on a legal pad. Notes, chapters, and outlines. The legal pads stacked up and I would visit them for inspiration from time to time, but nothing came together.

In 2018, on my way back from the New Orleans Jazzfest, I for the first time verbalized my idea to my friend, on our hour and a half flight home. I stumbled through the plot, which would have New Orleans as one of its characters. All taking place in the time frame when I lived there.

So at the age of 68, I began my book. I went to my pages app on my iPhone to jot down notes, on my taxi ride home. Instead of notes, I came up with the first line of the book. I continued on my iPhone and wrote the entire book in chronological order. I finished the book at age 69. So what was once a fantasy of a young girl became an X on something completed on my bucket list.

Thank you for spending time with my characters. They have more to say and I am on my iPhone writing the rest of their journey.

Made in the USA
Columbia, SC
24 January 2022

54495832R00172